The Dead Man Said,

"He's not like you at all, Harry. A light in the darkness of death, that's what you are. But Dragosani—"

"Go on, Keenan," Harry said, feeling the dead man's shudder of absolute terror shaking his spirit.

"He just reaches in and takes, steals. You can't hide anything from him. He finds his answers in your blood, your guts, in the marrow of your bones. The dead can't feel pain, Harry — but when Boris Dragosani works, we feel it. I felt his knives, his hands, his tearing nails. After one minute I would have told him everything, but he preferred to rip it from my dead body!"

Harry, eyes closed, felt sick and dizzy. "He has to be stopped," he murmured. "I have to stop him. But I can't do it alone."

"You won't be alone, Harry," said the shade of Keenan Gormley. "All of the world's dead will be with you."

TOR BOOKS BY BRIAN LUMLEY

BRIAN LUMLEY'S VAMPIRE WORLD

Blood Brothers
The Last Aerie
Bloodwars

THE PSYCHOMECH TRILOGY

Psychomech
Psychosphere
Psychamok!

THE NECROSCOPE SERIES

Necroscope
Necroscope II: Vamphyri!
Necroscope III: The Source
Necroscope IV: Deadspeak
Necroscope V: Deadspawn
Necroscope: The Lost Years
Necroscope: Resurgence

OTHER NOVELS

The House of Doors
Demogorgon

SHORT STORY COLLECTION

Fruiting Bodies and Other Fungi

Brian Lumley
NECROSCOPE

TOR
HORROR

A TOM DOHERTY ASSOCIATES BOOK
NEW YORK

This is a work of fiction. All the characters and events portrayed in this book are fictitious, and any resemblance to real people or events is purely coincidental.

NECROSCOPE

Copyright © 1986 by Brian Lumley

Cover art by Bob Eggelton
Inside cover art by Dennis Nolan

A Tor Book
Published by Tom Doherty Associates, Inc.
175 Fifth Avenue
New York, N.Y. 10010

Tor ® is a registered trademark of Tom Doherty Associates, Inc.

ISBN: 0-812-52137-4
Library of Congress Catalog Card Number: 88-50342

First edition: September 1988

Printed in the United States of America

For 'Squidge'

Prologue

THE HOTEL WAS BIG AND RATHER FAMOUS, OSTENTATIOUS IF
not downright flamboyant, within easy walking distance
of Whitehall, and . . . not entirely what it seemed to be.
Its top floor was totally given over to a company of
international entrepreneurs, which was the sum total of the
hotel manager's knowledge about it. The occupants of that
unknown upper region had their own elevator at the rear of
the building, private stairs also at the rear and entirely
closed off from the hotel itself, even their own fire escape.
Indeed they—"they" being the only identification one
might reasonably apply in such circumstances—*owned* the
top floor, and so fell entirely outside the hotel's sphere of
control and operation. Except that from the outside looking
in, few would suspect that the building *in toto* was anything other than what it purported to be; which was exactly
the guise or aspect—or lack of such—which "they" wished
to convey.

As for the "international entrepreneurs"—whatever such

1

creatures might be—"they" were not. In fact they were a branch of Government, or more properly a subsidiary body. Government supported them in the way a tree supports a small creeper, but their roots were wholly separate. And similarly, because they were a very tiny parasite, the vast bulk of the tree was totally unaware of their presence. As is the case with so many experimental, unproven projects, their funding was of a low priority, came out of "petty cash." The upkeep of their offices was therefore far and away top of the list where costing was concerned, but that was unavoidable.

For unlike other projects, the nature of this one demanded a very low profile indeed. Its presence in the event of discovery would be an acute embarrassment; it would doubtless be viewed with suspicion and scorn, if not disbelief and downright hostility; it would be seen as a totally unnecessary expenditure, a needless burden on the taxpayer, a complete waste of public money. Nor would there be any justifying it; the benefits or fruits of its being remained as yet entirely conjectural and the mildest "frost" would certainly put paid to them. The same principles apply to any such organization or service: it must (a) be seen to be effective while paradoxically (b) maintaining its cloak of invisibility, its anonymity. Ergo: to expose such a body is to kill it . . .

Another way to dispose of this sort of hybrid would be, quite simply, to tear up its roots and deny it had ever existed. Or wait for them to be torn up by some outside agency and then fail to replant them.

Three days ago there had occurred just such an uprooting. A major tendril had been broken, whose principal function it had been to bind the vine to its host body, providing stability. In short, the head of the branch had suffered a heart attack and died on his way home. He had had a bad heart for years, so that wasn't strange in itself—

but then something else had happened to throw a different light on the matter, something Alec Kyle didn't want to dwell on right now.

For now, on this Monday morning of an especially chilly January, Kyle, the next in line, must assess the damage and feasibility of repairs; and if such repairs were at all possible, then he must make his first groping attempt to pull the thing back together. The project's foundations had always been a little shaky but now, lacking positive direction and leadership, the whole show might well fall apart in very short order. Like a sand-castle when the tide comes in.

These were the thoughts in Kyle's head as he stepped from the slushy pavement through swinging glass doors into a tiny foyer, shook damp snow from his overcoat and turned the collar down. It was not that he personally had any doubt as to the validity of the project—in fact the opposite applied: Kyle believed the branch to be *all*-important—but how to defend his position in the face of all that scepticism from above? Scepticism, yes. Old Gormley had been able to pull it off, with all his friends in high places, his ''old school tie'' image, his authority and enthusiasm and sheer get-up-and-go, but men such as Keenan Gormley were few and far between. Even fewer now.

And this afternoon at four o'clock Kyle *would* be called upon to defend his position, the validity of his branch's being, its very existence. Oh, they'd been quick off the mark, right enough, and Kyle believed he knew why. This was it, the crunch. With nothing to show for five years' work, the project was to be terminated. No matter what arguments he produced, he'd be shouted down. Old Gormley had been able to shout louder than all of them put together; he'd had the clout, the back-up; but Alec Kyle—who was he? In his mind's eye, he could picture the afternoon's inquisition right now:

3

"Yes, Minister, I'm Alec Kyle. My function in the Branch? Well, apart from being second in command to Sir Keenan, I was—I mean I am—er, that is to say, I prognosticate . . . I beg your pardon? Ah, it means I foresee the future, sir. Er, no, I have to admit that I probably couldn't give you the winner of the 3:30 at Goodwood tomorrow. My awareness generally isn't that specific. But—"

But it would be hopeless! A hundred years ago they wouldn't accept hypnotism. Only fifteen years ago they were still laughing at acupuncture. So how could Kyle hope to convince them in respect of the branch and its work? And yet, on the other hand, coming through all the despondency and sense of personal loss, there was this other thing. Kyle knew it for what it was: his "talent," telling him that all was not lost, that somehow he would convince them, that the branch would go on. Which was why he was here: to go through Keenan Gormley's things, prepare some sort of case for the branch, continue fighting its cause. And again Kyle found himself wondering about his strange talent, his ability to glimpse the future.

For the fact was that last night he had dreamed that the answer lay right here, in this building, amongst Gormley's papers. Or perhaps "dreamed" was the wrong word for it: Kyle's revelations—his glimpses of things which had not yet happened, future occurrences—invariably came in those misty moments between true sleep and coming awake, immediately prior to full conscious awareness. The clamour of his alarm-clock could do it, set the process in motion, or even the first crack of sunlight through his bedroom window. That's what it had been this morning: the grey light of another grey day invading his room, getting under his eyelids, impressing upon his idly drifting mind the fact that another day was about to be born.

And with it had been born a vision. But again, "glimpse" might be a better word for it, for that was all Kyle's talent

4

had ever permitted: the merest glimpse. Knowing this—
and knowing that it would only occur once and then be
gone forever—he had fastened upon it, absorbed it. He
dared not miss a thing. Everything he had ever "seen" in
this way had always proved to be vitally important.

And on this occasion:

He had seen himself seated at Keenan Gormley's desk,
going through his papers one by one. The top right-hand
desk drawer was open; the papers and files on the desk in
front of him had come from there. Gormley's massive
security filing cabinet stood as yet undisturbed against the
wall of his office; its three keys were lying on top of the
desk where Kyle had tossed them. Each key would open a
tiny drawer in the cabinet, and each drawer had its own
combination lock. Kyle knew the combinations and yet
had not bothered to open the cabinet. No, for that which
he sought was right here, in these documents from the
drawer.

As if realization of that fact had galvanized the image of
himself where it sat in Gormley's chair, Kyle had then
seen himself pause abruptly as he came to a certain file. It
was a yellow file, which meant that it concerned a pro-
spective member of the organization. Someone "on the
books," as it were. Someone Gormley had had his beady
eye on. Perhaps someone with a real talent.

As that thought dawned, so Kyle took a step towards
himself where he sat. Then, dramatically, as was always
the case, his alter-image at the desk had looked up, stared
at him, and held up the file so that he could read the name
on the cover. The name was "Harry Keogh."

That was all. That had been the point where Kyle had
started awake. As to what the thing had meant or was
supposed to signify—who could say? Kyle had long since
given up trying to predict the meaning of these glimpses,
other than the fact that they had meaning. But in any case,

if something could be said to have brought him here today, it would have to be that brief and as yet inexplicable "dream" before waking.

As yet it was still fairly early in the morning. Kyle had beaten the first rush of heavy traffic in London's streets by just a few minutes. For the next hour or more all would be chaos out there, but in here it was quiet as the proverbial tomb. The rest of the admin team (all three of them, including the typist!) had been given today and tomorrow off out of respect for the dead man, so the offices upstairs would be completely empty.

In the tiny foyer Kyle had pressed the button for the elevator, which now arrived and opened its doors. He entered and as the doors closed behind him he took out his pass-card, sliding it easily and smoothly through the sensor slot. The elevator jerked but made no upward movement. Its doors opened, waited for a long moment, closed again. Kyle frowned, glanced at his card and silently cursed. It had run out yesterday! Normally Gormley would have renewed its validity on the branch computer; now Kyle would have to do it himself. Fortunately he had Gormley's card with him, along with the rest of his office-related effects. Using the ex-Head of Branch's pass-card, he coerced the elevator into carrying him to the top floor, going through a similar procedure to let himself into the main suite of offices.

The silence inside was almost deafening. High up above the level of the street, with soundproofed floors to shut out hotel noises from below and double-glazed, tinted windows for additional privacy, the place seemed set in a sort of vacuum. The feeling crept in that if you listened to that silence long enough, it would become hard to breathe. It was especially so in Gormley's room, where someone had been thoughtful enough to draw the blinds at the windows. But the blinds had jammed only a little more than half-way shut, so that now, with bands of light coming in through the green-tinted windows, the entire office seemed decorated in a horizontal, sub-marine pinstripe. It made this once familiar room strangely alien, and it was suddenly very odd and unreal not to have the Old Man here . . .

Kyle stood in the doorway, staring into the office for long moments before entering. Then, closing the door behind him, he stepped to the center of the room. Several hidden scanners had already picked him up and identified him, in the outer offices as well as in here, but a monitor screen in the wall close to Gormley's desk wasn't satisfied. It beeped and printed up:

SIR KEENAN GORMLEY IS NOT AVAILABLE AT PRESENT. THIS IS A SECURE AREA. PLEASE IDENTIFY YOURSELF IN YOUR NORMAL SPEAKING VOICE, OR LEAVE IMMEDIATELY. IF YOU FAIL TO LEAVE OR IDENTIFY YOURSELF, A TEN SECOND WARNING WILL BE GIVEN, FOLLOWING WHICH THE DOOR AND WINDOWS WILL LOCK AUTOMATICALLY . . . REPEAT: THIS IS A SECURE AREA.

Feeling irrationally aggressive towards the cold, unthinking machine, and not a little perverse, Kyle said nothing but waited. After a count of three the screen wiped itself clean and printed up:

TEN SECOND WARNING COMMENCES NOW . . . TEN . . . NINE . . . EIGHT . . . SEVEN . . . SIX . . .

"Alec Kyle," said Kyle grudgingly, not wishing to be locked in.

The machine recognized his voice pattern, stopped counting, commenced a new routine:

GOOD MORNING, MR KYLE . . .
SIR KEENAN GORMLEY IS NOT—

"I know," said Kyle. "He's dead." He stepped to the desk keyboard and punched in the current security override; to which the machine replied:

DO NOT FORGET TO RE-SET BEFORE YOU LEAVE

—and switched itself off.

Kyle sat down at the desk. *Funny world*, he thought. And, *funny bloody outfit! Robots and romantics. Super science and the supernatural. Telemetry and telepathy. Computerized probability patterns and precognition. Gadgets and ghosts!*

He reached into a pocket for his cigarettes and lighter, came out with both items and also the keys to Gormley's security cabinet. Without thinking, he tossed the keys on to an empty corner of the desk. Then he paused and stared at them lying there, forming a pattern—the pattern from this morning's glimpse into the future. *Very well, let's go from there.*

He tried the drawers of the desk. Locked. He took out Gormley's notebook from the inside pocket of his overcoat, checked the code. It was OPEN SESAME.

Unable to suppress a chuckle, Kyle punched OPEN SESAME into the desk keyboard and tried again. The top right-hand drawer slid open at a touch. Inside, papers, documents, files . . .

And here comes the funny bit, he thought.

He took out the papers and placed them in front of him on the desk. Leaving the drawer open (his "glimpse" again), he began to check through the documents, placing each one back in the drawer in its turn. He knew that by now his talent shouldn't really surprise him any more, but it always did—and so he gave a small involuntary start as he arrived at the yellow file. The name on the cover was, of course, Harry Keogh.

Harry Keogh. Apart from Kyle's dream, that name had only ever come up once before: in an ESP game he had used to play with Keenan Gormley. As for this file: he had never seen it before in his life (his conscious life, anyway) and yet here he sat staring at it, exactly as in his dream. It was a very creepy feeling. And—

In the dream he had held the file up to himself. Now the thought set the act in motion. Feeling foolish—not understanding why he did it, but at the same time feeling his skin charged with alien energy—he held up the file to the empty room, as if to a ghost from his own recent past. And just as a thought had triggered the action, now the action triggered something else—something away and beyond all of Alec Kyle's previous experience or knowledge.

God almighty! Gadgets and ghosts!

The room had been comfortably warm just a moment ago. Centrally heated, the offices were never cold. Or should not be. But now, in a matter of seconds, the temperature had plunged. Kyle knew it, could feel it, but at the same time he retained enough of instinctive reasoning to wonder if perhaps his own body temperature had also taken a tumble. If so, it wouldn't be hard to explain. This must be what shock felt like. No wonder people shivered!

"Jesus Christ!" he whispered, his breath pluming in the suddenly frigid air. The file fell from his twitching fingers, slapped down on the desk. The sound of its falling—that and what he saw—galvanized Kyle into an almost spastic reaction of motion. He jerked back in his chair, causing its legs to ride through the pile of the carpet, tilting it back-

9

wards until it slammed against the window sill and rebounded.

The—apparition?—the thing, where it stood half-way between the door and the desk, hadn't moved. At first Kyle had thought (and had dreaded the thought) that it could only be himself he saw standing there, somehow projected forward from the dream. But now he saw that it was someone—some*thing*—else. Not once did it enter his mind to question the reality of what he was seeing, and not for a moment did he consider it to be anything other than supernatural. How could it be anything else? The scanners where they constantly swept the room, the entire suite of offices, had detected nothing. Entirely independent, if they had picked up anything at all intruder buzzers would be going off right now, and getting louder by the minute until someone sat up and took notice. But the alarms were silent. Ergo, there *was* nothing here to scan—and yet Kyle saw it.

It, he, was a man—a youth, anyway—naked as a baby, standing there facing Kyle, looking directly at him. But his feet weren't quite touching the carpeted floor and the bars of green light from the windows penetrated into his flesh as if it had no substance at all. Damn it—it *had* no substance at all! But the thing stared at him, and Kyle knew that it saw him. And in the back of his mind he asked himself: Is it friendly, or—?

Inching his chair forward again, his eyes spied something in the back of the open drawer. A Browning 9 mm automatic. He'd known Gormley carried a weapon but hadn't known about this one. But would the gun be loaded, and if it was would it be any good against this?

"No," said the naked apparition with a slow, almost imperceptible shake of its head. "No it wouldn't." Which was all the more surprising because its lips didn't move by the smallest fraction of an inch!

10

"Jesus Christ!" Kyle gasped again, out loud this time, as he once more gave an involuntary start away from the desk. And then, controlling himself, *to* himself, he said:

You . . . you read my mind!

The apparition smiled a thin smile. "We all have our talents, Alec. You have yours and I have mine."

Kyle's lower jaw, already agape, now fell open. He wondered which would be easier: to simply think at the thing or to talk to it.

"Just talk to me," said the other. "I think that will be easier for both of us."

Kyle gulped, tried to say something, gulped again and finally gasped out: "But who . . . what . . . what the hell are you?"

"Who I am doesn't matter. What I have been and will be does. Now listen, I've a lot to tell you and it's all rather important. It will take some time, hours maybe. Do you need anything before I begin?"

Kyle stared hard at the . . . whatever it was. He stared at it, jerked his eyes away from it, peered at it out of the corner of his eye. It was still there. He surrendered to instinct backed up by at least two of his five senses, those of sight and hearing. The thing seemed rational; it existed; it wanted to talk to him. Why him and why now? Doubtless he'd shortly be finding out. But—God damn!—he wanted to talk to it, too. He had a real live ghost here, or a real dead one!

"Need anything?" he shakily repeated the other's question.

"You were going to light a cigarette," the apparition pointed out. "You might also like to take your coat off, get yourself a coffee." It shrugged. "If you do these things first, then we can get on with it."

The central heating had come on, turning itself up a notch to compensate for the sudden fall in temperature.

11

Kyle carefully stood up, took off his overcoat and folded it over the back of his chair. "Coffee," he said. "Yes—er, I'll just be a moment."

He walked round the desk and past his visitor. It turned to watch him leave the room, a pale shadow of a thing floating there, skinny, insubstantial as a snowflake, a puff of smoke. And yet . . . oh, yes, there was a power in it, Kyle was thankful it didn't follow him . . .

He put two five-pence pieces in the coffee machine in the main office, fumbling the coins into the slot, and headed for the gents' toilet before the machine could deliver. He quickly relieved himself, picked up his steaming paper cup of coffee on the way back to Gormley's office. The thing was still there, waiting for him. He carefully walked round it, seated himself again at the desk.

And as he lit a cigarette he looked at his visitor more closely, in greater detail. This was something he had to get fixed in his mind.

Taking into account the fact that its feet weren't quite touching the floor, it must be about five-ten in height. If its flesh was real instead of milky mist, it—or he—would weigh maybe nine stone. Everything about him was vaguely luminous, as if shining with some faint inner light, so Kyle couldn't be sure about colouring. His hair, an untidy mop, seemed sandy. Faint and irregular marks on his high cheeks and forehead might be freckles. He would be, oh, maybe twenty-five years old; he had looked younger at first but that effect was wearing off now.

His eyes were interesting. They looked *at* Kyle and yet seemed to look right through him, as if he were the ghost and not the other way about. They were blue, those eyes— that startlingly colourless blue which always looks so unnatural, so that you think the owner must be wearing lenses. But more than that, there was that in those eyes which said they knew more than any twenty-five-year-old

12

had any right knowing. The wisdom of ages seemed locked in them, the knowledge of centuries lay just beneath the faintly blue film which covered them.

Apart from that, his features were fine, like porcelain and seemingly equally fragile; his hands were slim, tapering; his shoulders drooped a little; his skin in general, apart from the freckles of his face, was pale and unblemished. But for the eyes, you probably wouldn't look at him twice on the street. He was just . . . a young man. Or a young ghost. Or maybe a very old one.

"No," said the object of Kyle's scrutiny, his lips immobile, "I'm not *any* kind of ghost. Not in the classic sense of the word, anyway. But now, since you obviously accept me, can we begin?"

"Begin? Er, of course!" Kyle suddenly felt like laughing, hysterical as a schoolgirl. He controlled it with an effort.

"Are you sure you're ready?"

"Yes, yes. Go right ahead. But—er—can I record this? For posterity or whatever, you know? There's a tape recorder here, and I—"

"The machine won't hear me," said the other, shaking his head again. "Sorry, but I'm only speaking to you—*directly* to you. I thought you understood that? But . . . take notes if you wish."

"Notes, yes . . ." Kyle scrabbled in the desk drawers, found paper and a pencil. "Fine, I'm ready."

The other slowly nodded. "The story I have to tell is . . . strange. But working in an organization such as yours, you shouldn't find it too unbelievable. If you do . . . there'll be plenty for you to do afterwards; the truth of the things I'm going to tell you will come out then. As to any doubts you may have about the future of your branch—put them aside. Your work will go on, and it will go from strength to strength. Gormley was the head, but he's dead.

Now you will be head—for a little while. You'll be up to it, I assure you. Anyway, nothing that Gormley knew has been lost; indeed, much has been gained. As for the Opposition—they've suffered losses from which they may never recover. At least, they're about to.''

As the apparition spoke, so Kyle's eyes opened even wider and he sat up straighter and straighter. It (*he*, dammit!) knew about the branch. About Gormley. About "the Opposition,'' which was branch parlance for the Russian outfit. And what was this about them suffering heavy losses? Kyle knew nothing of that! Where did this—being—get its information? And just how much did it know anyway?

"I know more than you can possibly imagine,'' said the other, smiling wanly. "And what I don't know I can get to know—almost anything.''

"See,'' said Kyle defensively, "it's not that I doubt any of this—or even my sanity, for that matter—it's just that I'm trying to adjust, and—''

"I understand,'' the other cut him off. "But, please, do your adjusting as we go, if you can. In what I'm about to tell you, time-zones may overlap a little, so you'll need to adjust to that, too. But I'll keep it as chronologically sound as I can. The important thing is the information itself. And its implications.''

"I'm not sure I quite under—''

"I know, I know. So just sit there and listen, and then maybe you will understand.''

Chapter One

Moscow, May 1971.

CENTRAL IN A DENSELY WOODED TRACT OF LAND NOT FAR out of the city—where the Serpukhov road passed through a saddle between low hills and gazed for a moment across the tops of close-grown pines towards Podolsk, which showed as a hazy smudge on the southern horizon, brightly pricked here and there with the first lights of evening— stood a house or mansion of debased heritage and mixed architectural antecedents. Several of its wings were of modern brick upon old stone foundations, while others were of cheap breeze blocks roughly painted over in green and grey, almost as if to camouflage their ill-matching construction. Bedded at their bases in steeply gabled end walls, twin towers or minarets decayed as rotten fangs and gaunt as watchtowers—whose sagging buttresses and parapets and flaking spiral decorations detracted nothing from a sense of dereliction—raised broken bulbous domes high over the tallest trees, their boarded windows glooming like hooded eyes.

The layout of the outbuildings, many of which had been recently re-roofed with modern red brick tiles, might well suggest a farm or farming community, though no crops, farm animals or machines were anywhere in evidence. The high all-encompassing perimeter wall—which from its massy structure, reinforced abutments and broad breast walls might likewise be a relic of feudal times—showed similar signs of recent repair work, where heavy grey concrete blocks had replaced crumbling stone and ancient brick. To east and west where streams ran deep and gurgling over black boulders, flowing between steep banks which formed them into natural moats, old stone bridges supporting lead roofs green with moss and age tunnelled into and through the walls, their dark mouths muzzled with steel-latticed gates.

All in all grim and foreboding. As if the merest glimpse of the place from the highway would not be sufficient warning in itself, a sign at the T-junction where a cobbled track wound away from the road and into the woods declared that this entire area was ''Property of the State,'' patrolled and protected, and that all trespassers would be prosecuted. Motorists were not permitted to stop under any circumstances; walking in the woods was strictly forbidden; hunting and fishing likewise. Penalties would be, without exception, severe.

But for all that the place seemed deserted and lost in its own miasma of desolation, as evening grew into night and a mist came up from the streams to turn the ground to milk, so lights flickered into life behind the curtained ground-floor windows, telling a different story. In the woods, on the approach roads to the covered bridges, large black saloon cars might also appear abandoned where they blocked the way—except for the dull orange glowing of hot cigarette tips within, and the smoke curling from partly wound-down windows. It was the same inside the grounds: squat, silent shapes which might just represent men, standing in the shadowed places, their dark grey overcoats as like as uniforms, faces hidden under the brims of felt hats, shoulders robotically square . . .

In an inner courtyard of the main building, an ambulance—or maybe a hearse—stood with its back doors open, white-overalled attendants waiting and the driver seated uncomfortably at the high steering-wheel. One of the attendants played with a steel loading roller, spinning it on well-lubricated bearings at the rear end of the long, somehow sinister vehicle. Nearby, in an open-ended barnlike structure with a sagging canvas roof, a helicopter's dull paintwork and square glass windows gleamed darkly in shadow, its fuselage bearing the insignia of the Supreme Soviet. In one of the towers, leaning carefully on a low parapet wall, a figure with Army night-sight binoculars scanned the land about, particularly the open area between the perimeter wall and the central cluster. Projecting above his shoulder, the ugly blue metal snout of a specially adapted Kalashnikov rifle was limned faintly against a horizon growing steadily darker.

Inside the main building, modern soundproof partition walls now divided what had once been a vast hall into fairly large rooms, serviced by a central corridor lit with a row of fluorescent tubes strung along a high ceiling. Each room had a padlocked door and all the doors were fitted with tiny grille windows with sliding covers on the inside, and with small red lights which, when blinking, signified "No Entry—Not to be Disturbed." One of these lights, half-way down the corridor on the left, was blinking even now. Leaning against the wall to one side of the door with the blinking light, a tall, hard-faced KGB operative cradled a submachine-gun in his arms. For the moment relaxed, he was ready to spring to attention—or into action—at a

17

moment's notice. The merest hint of the door opening, the sudden cessation of the red light's blinking, and he would snap up straighter than a lamp-post. For while none of the men in that room was his real master, nevertheless one of them was as powerful as anyone in the highest ranks of the KGB, perhaps one of the ten most powerful men in Russia.

There were other men in the room beyond the door, which in fact was not one room but two, with an interconnecting door of their own. In the smaller room, three men sat in armchairs, smoking, their hooded eyes fixed on the partition wall, of which a large central section, floor to ceiling, was a one-way viewscreen. The floor was carpeted; a small wheeled table within easy reach supported an ashtray, glasses, and a bottle of high-class slivovitz; all was silent except for the breathing of the three and the faint electric whirr of the air-conditioning. Subdued lighting in a false ceiling was soothing to their eyes.

The man in the middle was in his mid-sixties, those to right and left perhaps fifteen years younger. His protégés, each of them knew the other for a rival. The man in the middle knew it, too. He had planned it that way. It was called survival of the fittest; only one of them would survive to take his place, when eventually that day came. By then the other would have been removed—perhaps politically, but more likely in some other, still more devious fashion. The years between would be their proving ground. Yes, survival of the fittest.

Completely grey at the temples, but with a broad contrasting central stripe of jet-black hair swept back from his high, much-wrinkled brow, the senior man sipped his brandy, motioned with his cigarette. The man on his left passed the ashtray; half of the hot ash found its target, the rest fell to the floor. In a moment or two the carpet began to smoulder and a curl of acrid smoke rose up. The flanking men sat still, deliberately ignoring the burning.

They knew how the older man hated fussers and fidgets. But at last their boss sniffed, glanced down at the floor from beneath bushy black eyebrows, ground his shoe into the carpet, to and fro, until the smouldering patch was extinguished.

Beyond the screen, preparations of a sort had been in progress. In the Western World it might be said that a man had been "psyching himself up." His method had been simple . . . startlingly simple in the light of what was about to occur; he had cleansed himself. He had stripped naked and bathed, minutely and laboriously soaping and scrubbing every square inch of his body. He had shaved himself, removing all surface hair from his person with the exception of the close-cropped hair of his head. He had defecated before and after his bath, on the second occasion doubly ensuring his cleanliness by washing his parts again in hot water and towelling himself dry. And then, still completely naked, he had rested.

His method of resting would have seemed macabre in the extreme to anyone not in the know, but it was all part of the preparations. He had gone to sit beside the second occupant of the room where he lay upon a not quite horizontal table or trolley with a fluted aluminum surface, and had lain his head on his folded arms where he rested them upon the other's abdomen. Then he had closed his eyes and, apparently, had slept for some fifteen minutes. There was nothing erotic in it, nothing remotely homosexual. The man on the trolley was also naked, much older than the first, flabby, wrinkled, and bald but for a fringe of grey hair at his temples. He was also very dead; but even in death his pallid, puffy face, thin mouth and dense grey inward-slanting eyebrows were cruel.

All of this the three on the other side of the screen had watched, and all had been accomplished with a sort of clinical detachment and with no outward indication of awareness from the—performer?—that they were there at all. He had simply "forgotten" their presence; his work was all-engrossing, too important to admit of outside agencies or interferences.

But now he stirred, lifted his head, blinked his eyes twice and slowly stood up. All was now in order, the inquiry could commence.

The three watchers leaned forward a little in their armchairs, automatically controlled their breathing, centred all their attention on the naked man. It was as if they feared to disturb something, and this despite the fact that their observation cell was completely insulated, soundproof as a vacuum.

Now the naked man turned the trolley carrying the corpse until its lower end, where the clay-cold feet projected a little way and made a "V," overhung the lip of the bath. He drew forward a second, more conventional trolley-table and opened the leather case which lay upon it, displaying scalpels, scissors, saws—a whole range of razor-sharp surgical instruments.

In the observation cell, the man in the centre allowed himself a grim smile which his subordinates missed as they eased back fractionally in their chairs, satisfied now that they were about to see nothing more spectacular than a rather bizarre autopsy. Their boss could barely contain the chuckle rising from his chest, the tremor of ghoulish amusement welling in his stocky body, as he anticipated the shock they had coming to them. He had seen all of this before, but they had not. And this, too, would serve as a test of sorts.

Now the naked man took up a long chromium-plated rod, needle sharp at one end and bedded in a wooden handle at the other, and without pause leaned over the corpse, placed the point of the needle in the crater of the swollen belly's navel and applied his weight to the handle.

The rod slid home in dead flesh and the distended gut vented gasses accumulated in the four days since death had occurred, hissing up into the naked man's face.

"Audio!" snapped the observer in the middle, causing the men flanking him to start in their chairs. His gruff voice was so deep in its range as to be little more than a series of glottal gurgles as he continued: "Quickly, I want to listen!" And he waggled a stubby finger at a speaker on the wall.

Gulping audibly, the man on his right stood up, stepped to the speaker, pressed a button marked "Receive." There was momentary static, then a clear *hiss* fading away as the belly of the corpse in the other room slowly settled down in folds of fat. But while yet the gas escaped, instead of drawing back, the naked man lowered his face, closed his eyes and *inhaled* deeply, filling his lungs!

With his eyes glued to the one-way screen, fumbling and clumsy, the official found his chair again and seated himself heavily. His mouth, like that of his opposite number, had fallen open; both men now perched themselves on the front edges of their chairs, their backs ramrod straight, hands gripping the wooden arm rests. A cigarette, forgotten, toppled into the ashtray on the table to send up fresh streamers of perfumed smoke. Only the watcher in the middle seemed unmoved, and he was as much interested in the expressions on the faces of his subordinates as he was in the weird ritual taking place beyond the screen.

The naked man had straightened up, stood erect again over the deflated corpse. He had one hand on the dead man's thigh, the other on his chest, palms flat down. His eyes were open again, round as saucers, but his colour had visibly changed. The normal, healthy pink of a young, recently scrubbed body had entirely disappeared; his grey was uniform with that of the dead flesh he touched. He was literally grey as death. He held his breath, seeming to

21

savour the very taste of death, and his cheeks appeared to
be slowly caving in. Then—

He snatched back his hands from the corpse, expelled
foul gas in a *whoosh*, rocked back on his heels. For a
moment it seemed he must crash over backwards, but then
he rocked forward again. And again, with great care, he
lowered his hands to the body. Gaunt and grey as stone, he
stroked the flesh, his fingers trembling as they moved with
butterfly lightness from head to toe and back again. Still
there was nothing erotic in it, but the left-hand man of the
trio of watchers was moved to whisper:

"Is he a necrophile? What *is* this, Comrade General?"

"Be quiet and learn something," the man in the middle
growled. "You know where you are, don't you? Nothing
should surprise you here. As for what this is—what he
is—you will see soon enough. This I will tell you: to my
knowledge there are only three men like him in all the
USSR. One is a Mongol from the Altai region, a tribal
witch-doctor, almost dead of syphilis and useless to us.
Another is hopelessly mad and scheduled for corrective
lobotomy, following which he too will be . . . beyond our
reach. That leaves only this one and his is an instinctive
art, hard to teach. Which makes him *sui generis*. That's
Latin, a dead language. Most appropriate. So now shut up!
You are watching a unique talent."

Now, beyond the one-way window, the "unique talent"
of the naked man became galvanic. As if jerked on the
strings of some mad, unseen puppet-master, his burst of
sudden, unexpected motion was so erratic as to be almost
spastic. His right arm and hand flailed towards his case of
instruments, almost tumbling it from its table. His hand,
shaped by his spasm into a grey claw, swept aloft as if
conducting some esoteric concerto—but instead of a baton
it held a glittering, crescent-shaped scalpel.

All three observers were now craning forward, eyes

huge and mouths agape; but while the faces of the two on the outside were fixed in a sort of involuntary rictus of denial—prepared to wince or even exclaim at what they now suspected was to come—that of their superior was shaped only of knowledge and morbid expectancy.

With a precision denying the seemingly eccentric or at best random movements of the rest of his limbs—which now fluttered and twitched like those of a dead frog, electrically coerced into a pseudo-life of their own—the arm and hand of the naked man swept down and sliced open the corpse from just below the rib-cage, through the navel and down to the mass of wiry grey pubic hair. Two more apparently random but absolutely *exact* slashes, following so rapidly as almost to be a part of the first movement, and the cadaver's belly was marked with a great "I" with extended top and bottom bars.

Without pause, the hideously automatic author of this awful surgery now blindly tossed away his blade across the room, dug his hands into the central incision up to his wrists and laid back the flaps of the dead man's abdomen like a pair of cupboard doors. Cold, the exposed guts did not smoke; no blood flowed as such; but when the naked man took away his hands they glistened a dull red, as if fresh painted.

To perform this opening of the body had required an effort of almost Herculean strength—visible in the sudden bulging of muscles across the naked man's shoulders, at the sides of his rib-cage and in his upper arms—for all the tissues fastening down the protective outer layers of the stomach must be torn at once. Also, it had been done with a fierce snarl, clearly audible over the radio link, which had drawn back his lips from clenched teeth and caused the sinews of his neck to stand out in sharp relief.

But now, with his subject's viscera entirely exposed, again a strange stillness came over him. Greyer than before, if that were at all possible, he once more straightened up, rocked back on his heels, let his red hands fall to his sides. And rocking forward again, his neutral blue eyes turned down and began a slow, minute examination of the corpse's innards.

In the other room the man on the left sat gulping continuously, his hands clawing at the arms of his chair, his face gleaming with fine perspiration. The one on the right had turned the colour of slate, shaking from head to toe, rapidly panting to compensate for a heart which now raced in his chest. But between them ex-Army General Gregor Borowitz, now head of the highly secret Agency for the Development of Paranormal Espionage, was utterly engrossed, his leonine head forward, his heavily jowled face full of awe as he absorbed each and every detail and nuance of the performance, ignoring as best he might the discomfort of his juniors where they flanked him. On the rim of his consciousness a thought formed: he wondered if the others would be sick, and which one would throw up first. And *where* he would throw up.

On the floor under the table stood a metal wastebin containing a few crumpled scraps of paper and dead cigarette ends. Without taking his eyes from the one-way screen, Borowitz reached down, lifted the wastebin up between his knees and placed it centrally on the table before him. He thought: *Let them fight it out between them.* In any case, and whichever one let the down side, his vomiting would doubtless elicit a response in the other.

As if reading his mind, the man on the right panted, "Comrade General, I do not think that I—"

"Be still!" Borowitz lashed out with his foot, catching the other's ankle. "Watch—if you can. If you can't, then be quiet and let me!"

The naked man's back was bowed now, bringing his face to within inches of the corpse's exposed organs and

24

entrails. Left and right his eyes darted, up and down, as if they sought something hidden there. His nostrils were wide, sniffing suspiciously. His brow, hitherto smooth, was now furrowed in a fantastic frown. He resembled in his attitude nothing so much as a great naked bloodhound intent upon tracking its prey.

Then . . . a sly grin tugged at his grey lips, the gleam of revelation—of a secret discovered, or about to be discovered—shone in his eyes. It was as if he said, "Yes, something is in here, *something is trying to hide!*"

And now he threw back his head and laughed—laughed out loud, however briefly—before returning to a more frantic scrutiny. But no, it wasn't enough, the hidden thing would not be exposed. It shrank down out of sight, and glee turned to rage on the instant!

Panting furiously, his grey face trembling in the grip of unimaginable emotions, the naked man snatched up a slim tool whose sharpness shone in mirror brightness. In something of an ordered manner at first, he commenced to cut out the various organs, pipes and bladders; but as his work progressed so it grew ever more vicious, and indiscriminate, until the guts as they were partially or almost wholly detached hung out of the body over the edge of the fluted metal table in grotesque lumpy rags, flaps and tatters. And still it was not enough, still the hunted thing eluded him.

He gave a shriek which passed through the speaker into the other room like chalk sliding on a blackboard, like a shovel grating in cold ashes, and grimacing hideously began to hack off the dangling gobbets and hurl them all about. He smeared them down his body, held them to his ear and "listened" to them. He scattered them wide, tossed them over his hunched shoulders, hurled them into the bath, the sink. Gore spattered everywhere; and again his cry of frustration, of weird anguish, ripped through the speaker:

"Not there! *Not there!*"

In the other room the gasping of the man on the right had turned to a wretched choking. Suddenly he snatched the wastebin from the table, lurched upright and staggered away to a corner of the room. Borowitz grudgingly gave him credit that he was reasonably quiet about it.

"My God, my God!" the man on the left had started to repeat, over and over, each repetition louder than the one before. And, "Awful, *awful!* He is depraved, insane, a fiend!"

"He is brilliant!" Borowitz growled. "See? See? Now he goes to the heart of the matter . . ."

Beyond the screen, the naked man had taken up a surgical saw. His arm and hand and the instrument itself were a blur of red, grey and silver where he sawed upwards through the centre of the sternum. Sweat rivered his gore-spattered skin, dripped from him in a hot rain as he levered at the subject's chest. It would not give; the blade of the silver hacksaw broke and he threw it down. Crying like an animal, frantic in his movements, he lifted his head and scanned the room, seeking something. His eyes rested briefly on a metal chair, widened in inspiration. In a moment he had snatched the chair up, was using two of its legs as levers in the fresh-cut channel.

In a cracking of bones and a tearing of flesh the left side of the corpse's chest rose up, was forced back, a trapdoor in the upper trunk. *In* went the naked man's hands . . . a terrible wrenching . . . and *out* they came, holding the prize aloft . . but only for a moment. Then—

Holding the heart at arms' length in both hands, the naked man waltzed it across the room, whirled it round and round. He hugged it close, held it up to his eyes, his ears. He pressed it to his own chest, caressed it, sobbed like a baby. He sobbed his relief, burning tears coursing down his grey cheeks. And in another moment all the strength seemed to go out of him.

His legs trembled, became jelly. Still hugging the heart he crumpled, plopped down on the floor, curled up into an almost foetal position with the heart lost in the curl of his body. He lay still.

"All done—" said Borowitz, "—maybe!"

He stood up, crossed to the speaker and pressed a second button marked "Intercom." But before speaking he glanced narrow-eyed at his subordinates. One of them had not moved from his corner, where he now sat with his head lolling, the wastebin between his legs. In another corner the second man was bending from his waist, hands on hips, up and down, up and down, exhaling as he went down, inhaling as he came erect again. The faces of both men were slick with sweat.

"Hah!" Borowitz grunted, and to the speaker: "Boris? Boris Dragosani? Can you hear me? Is all well?"

In the other room the man on the floor jerked, stretched, lifted his head and stared about. Then he shuddered and quickly stood up. He seemed much more human now, less like a deranged automaton, though his colour was still grey as lead. His bare feet slipped on the slimed floor so that he staggered a little, but he quickly regained his balance. Then he saw the heart still clutched in his hands, gave a second great shudder and tossed it away, wiping his hands down his thighs.

He was like (Borowitz thought) someone newly awakened from the turmoil of a nightmare . . . but he must not be allowed to come awake too rapidly. There was something Borowitz must know. And he must know it now, while it was still fresh in the other's mind.

"Dragosani," he said again, keeping his voice as soft as possible. "Do you hear me?"

As Borowitz's companions finally got themselves under

control and came to join him at the large screen, so the naked man looked their way. For the first time Boris Dragosani acknowledged the screen, which on his side was simply a lightly frosted window composed of many small leaded panes. He looked straight at them, almost as if he could actually see them, in the way a blind man will sometimes look, and answered:

"Yes, I hear you, Comrade General. And you were right: he had planned to assassinate you."

"*Hah!* Good!" Borowitz balled a meaty fist and slammed it into the palm of his left hand. "How many were in it with him?"

Dragosani looked exhausted. The greyness was going out of him and already his hands, legs and lower body had taken on a more nearly fleshly tint. Only flesh and blood after all, he seemed on the point of collapse. It was a small effort to right the steel chair where he had thrown it and to seat himself, but it seemed to consume his last dregs of energy. Placing his elbows on his knees, his head in his hands, he now sat staring at the floor between his feet.

"Well?" Borowitz said into the speaker.

"One other," Dragosani answered at last without looking up. "Someone close to you. I could not read his name."

Borowitz was disappointed. "Is that all?"

"Yes, Comrade General." Dragosani lifted his head, looked again at the screen, and there was something akin to pleading in his watery blue eyes. With a familiarity Borowitz's juniors could hardly credit, he then said: "Gregor, please do not ask it."

Borowitz was silent.

"Gregor," Dragosani said again, "you have promised me—"

"Many things," Borowitz hurriedly cut him off. "Yes, and you shall have them. *Many* things! What little you give, I shall repay many times over. What small services you perform, the USSR shall recognize with overwhelming gratitude—however long the recognition is in coming. You have plumbed depths deep as space, Boris Dragosani, and I know your bravery is greater than that of any cosmonaut. Science fiction to the contrary, there are no monsters where they go. But the frontiers you cross are the very haunts of horror! I *know* these things . . ."

The man in the other room sat up, shuddered long and hard. The greyness crept back into his limbs, his body. "Yes, Gregor," he said.

For all that Dragosani could not see him, still Borowitz nodded, saying, "Then you do understand?"

The naked man sighed, hung his head again, asked: "What is it you wish to know?"

Borowitz licked his lips, leaned closer to the screen, said, "Two things. The name of the man who plotted with that eviscerated pig in there, and proof which I can take before the Presidium. Not only am I in jeopardy without this knowledge, but you too. Yes, and the entire branch. Remember, Boris Dragosani, there are those in the KGB who would eviscerate *us*—if only they could find a way!"

The other said nothing but returned to the trolley carrying the remains of the corpse. He stood over the violated mess, and in his face was written his intent: the ultimate violation. He breathed deeply, expanding his lungs and letting the air out slowly, then repeating the procedure; and each time his chest seemed to swell just a little larger, while his skin rapidly and quite visibly returned to its deep slate-grey hue. After several minutes of this, finally he turned his gaze upon the tray of surgical instruments in its case.

By now even Borowitz was disturbed, agitated, unnerved. He sat down in his central chair, seemed to shrink into himself a little. "You, two," he growled at his subordinates. "Are you all right? You, Mikhail—is there any puke left in you? If so, stand well away." (This to the one on the left, whose nostrils were moist, flaring jet-black pits in a face of chalk.) "And you, Andrei—are you done now with your bending and ventilating?"

The one on the right opened his mouth but said nothing, keeping his wet eyes on the screen, his Adam's apple bobbing. The other said: "Let me see the beginning at least. But I would prefer not to throw up. Also, when all is done, I would be grateful for an explanation. You may say what you like of that one in there, Comrade General, but I personally believe he should be put down!"

Borowitz nodded. "You shall have your explanation in good time," he rumbled. "Meanwhile I agree with you—I, too, would prefer not to throw up!"

Dragosani had taken up what looked like a hollow silver chisel in one hand, and a small copper-jacketed mallet in the other. He placed the chisel in the centre of the corpse's forehead, brought the mallet sharply down and drove the chisel home. As the mallet bounced following the blow, so a little brain fluid was vented through the chisel's hollow stem. That was enough for Mikhail; he gulped once, then returned to his corner and stood there trembling, his face averted. The man called Andrei remained where he was, stood there as if frozen, but Borowitz noted how he clenched and unclenched his fists where they hung at his sides.

Now Dragosani stood back from the corpse, crouched down, stared fixedly at the chisel where it stood up from the pierced cranium. He nodded slowly, then sprang erect and stepped to the table with the case of instruments. Dropping the mallet on to the tough floor tiles, he snatched up a slender steel straw and dropped it expertly, with hardly a glance, into the chisel's cavity. The fine steel tube sank slowly, pneumatically down through the body of the chisel until just its mouthpiece projected.

"Mouthpiece!" Andrei suddenly croaked, turning away and stumbling blindly across the floor of the observation cell. "My God, my God—*the mouthpiece!*"

Borowitz closed his eyes. Tough as he was he could not watch. He had seen it all before and remembered it only too well.

Moments passed: Mikhail in his corner, trembling—Andrei across the room, his back to the screen—and their superior with his eyes tightly shut, squeezed down in his chair. Then—

The scream that came over the speaker was one to shatter the strongest nerves, indeed a scream to raise the dead. It was full of horror, full of monstrous knowledge, full of . . . outrage? Yes, outrage—the cry of a wounded carnivore, a vengeful beast. And hot on its heels—chaos!

As the scream subsided Borowitz's eyes shot open, his heavy eyebrows forming a peaked tent over them. For an instant he sat there, a startled owl, nerves jumping, fingers clawing at the arms of his chair. Then he gave a hoarse shout, threw up an arm before his face, hurled his heavy body backward. His chair crashed over, allowing him to roll clear, protected by the chair to the left, as the screen caved inward in a shower of glass and small, buckling strips of lead. A large hole had appeared in the screen, with the legs of the steel chair from the other room protruding half-way through. The chair was snatched back out of sight—and again driven forward, smashing out the rest of the small panes and sending fragments of glass flying everywhere.

"Swine!" Dragosani's shriek came from both the speaker and the shattered screen. "Oh, you *swine*, Gregor Borowitz! You poisoned him—an agent to rot his brain—and now, you bastard, *now I have tasted that same poison!*"

31

From behind the outraged, hate-filled voice came Dragosani himself, to stand outlined for a moment in a frame of jagged, dangling glass teeth, before hurling himself across the table and tumbled chairs at Borowitz where he floundered on the floor. In his hand something glittered, silver against the grey of his flesh.

"No!" Borowitz boomed, his bullfrog voice loud with terror in the confines of the small room. "No, Boris, you're mistaken. You're not poisoned, man!"

"*Liar!* I read it in his dead brain. I felt his pain as he died. And now that stuff is in me!" Dragosani leapt on to Borowitz where he fought to struggle to his feet, bore him down again, raised high the sickle shape of silver in his clenched fist.

The man called Mikhail had been flapping in the background like a wind-torn scarecrow, but now he came forward, his hand reaching inside his overcoat. He caught Dragosani's wrist just as it commenced its downward sweep. Expert with a cosh, Mikhail applied it at precisely the correct point, just hard enough to stun. The bright steel flew from Dragosani's nerveless fingers and he fell face down across Borowitz, who managed to roll half out of the way. Then Mikhail was helping the older man to his feet, while Borowitz cursed and raved, kicking once or twice at the naked man where he lay groaning. Up on his feet, he pushed his junior away and began to dust himself down—but in the next moment he saw the cosh in Mikhail's hand and understood what had happened. His eyes flew open in shock and sudden anxiety.

"What?" he said, his mouth falling open. "You struck him? You used that on him? Fool!"

"But Comrade Borowitz, General, he—"

Borowitz cut him off with a snarl, pushed with both hands at Mikhail's chest and sent him staggering. "Dolt! Idiot! Pray he is unharmed. If there's any god you believe in, just pray you haven't permanently damaged this man. Didn't I tell you he's unique?'' He went down on one knee, grunting as he turned the stunned man over on to his back. Colour was returning to Dragosani's face, the normal colour of a man, but a large lump was growing where the back of his skull met his neck. His eyelids fluttered as Borowitz anxiously scanned his face.

"Lights!" the old General snapped then. "Let's have them up full. Andrei, don't just stand there like—" he paused, stared about the room as Mikhail turned up the lights. Andrei was not to be seen and the door of the room stood ajar. "Cowardly dog!" Borowitz growled.

"Perhaps he has gone for help," Mikhail gulped. And continued: "Comrade General, if I had not hit Dragosani he would have—"

"I know, I know," Borowitz growled impatiently. "Never mind that now. Help me get him into a chair."

As they lifted Dragosani up and lowered him into a chair he shook his head, groaned loudly and opened his eyes. They focused on Borowitz's face, narrowing in accusation. "You!" he hissed, trying to straighten up but failing.

"Take it easy," said Borowitz. "And don't be a fool. You're not poisoned. Man, do you think I would so readily dispose of my most valuable asset?"

"But he *was* poisoned!" Dragosani rasped. "Only four days ago. It burned his brain out and he died in agony, thinking his head was melting. And now the same stuff is in me! I need to be sick, quickly! I have to be sick!" He struggled frantically to get up.

Borowitz nodded, held him down with a heavy hand, grinned like a Siberian wolf. He brushed back his central streak of jet-black hair and said, "Yes, that is how *he* died—but not you, Boris, not you. The poison was something special, a Bulgarian brew. It acts rapidly . . . and disperses just as rapidly. It voids itself in a few hours, leaves no trace, becomes undetectable. Like a dagger of ice, it strikes then melts away.''

Mikhail was staring, gaping like a man who hears something he can't believe. "What *is* this?" he asked. "How can he possibly know that we poisoned the Second in Command of the—"

"Be *quiet!*" again Borowitz rounded on him. "That loose tongue of yours will choke you yet, Mikhail Gerkhov!"

"But—"

"Man, are you blind? Have you learned nothing?"

The other shrugged, fell silent. It was all beyond him, completely over his head. He had seen many strange things since he'd been transferred into the branch three years ago—seen and heard things he would never have believed possible—but this was so far removed from anything else he'd experienced that it defied reason.

Borowitz had turned back to Dragosani, had clasped his neck where it joined his shoulder. The naked man was merely pale now, neither leaden grey nor fleshy pink but pale. He shivered as Borowitz asked him: "Boris, did you get his name? Think now, for it's very important."

"His name?" Dragosani looked up, looked sick.

"You said he was close to me, the man who plotted my assassination with that gutted dog in there. Who is he, Boris? Who?"

Dragosani nodded, narrowed his eyes, said: "Close to you, yes. His name is . . . Ustinov!"

"Wha—?" Borowitz straightened up, realization dawning.

"Ustinov?" Mikhail Gerkhov gasped. "Andrei Ustinov? Is that possible?"

"Very possible," said a familiar voice from the doorway. Ustinov stepped through it, his thin face lined and drawn, a submachine-gun cradled in his arms. He directed the weapon's muzzle ahead of him, carelessly aimed it at the other three. "Definitely possible."

"But why?" said Borowitz.

"But isn't that obvious, 'Comrade General?' Wouldn't any man who'd been with you as long as I have, want to see you dead? Too many long years, Gregor, I've suffered your tantrums and rages, all your petty little intrigues and stupid bullying. Yes, and I served you loyally—until now. But you never liked me, never let me in on anything. What have I been—what *am* I even now but a cipher of yourself, a despised appendage? Well, you'll be pleased to note that I am, after all, an apt pupil. But your deputy? No, I was never that. And I should step aside for this upstart?" he nodded sneeringly towards Gerkhov.

Borowitz's face clearly showed his disgust. "And you were the one I would have chosen!" he snorted. "*Hah!* No fool like an old fool . . ."

Dragosani groaned and lifted a hand to his head. He made as if to stand, fell out of the chair on his knees, sprawled face down on the glass-littered floor. Borowitz made to kneel beside him.

"Stay where you are!" Ustinov snapped. "You can't help him now. He's a dead man. You're all dead men."

"You'll never carry it off," Borowitz said, but the colour was draining from his face and his voice was little more than a dry rustle.

"Of course I will," Ustinov sneered. "In all this mayhem, this madness? Oh, I'll tell a good tale, be sure—of you, a raving lunatic, and of the worse than crazy people you employ—and who will there be to say any different?" He stepped forward, the ugly weapon in his hands making a harsh *ch-ching* as he cocked it.

On the floor at his feet, Boris Dragosani was not unconscious. His collapse had simply been a ploy to put him within reach of a weapon. Now his fingers closed on the bone handle of the small, scythe-like surgical knife where it had fallen. Ustinov stepped closer, grinned as he quickly reversed his weapon, slamming its butt into Borowitz's unsuspecting face. As the Head of ESP Branch flew backwards, blood smearing his crushed mouth, so Ustinov adjusted his grip on the gun and squeezed the trigger.

The first burst caught Borowitz high on the right shoulder, spun him like a top and tossed him down. It also lifted Gerkhov off his feet, drove him across the room and slammed him into the wall. He hung there for a second like a man crucified, then took a single step forward, spat out a stream of blood and fell face down. The wall was scarlet where his back had pressed against it.

Borowitz scrambled backwards, trailing his right arm along the floor, until his shoulders brought up against the wall. Unable to go any farther, he hunched himself up and sat there, waiting for it to happen. Ustinov drew his lips back from his teeth like a great shark before it strikes. He aimed at Borowitz's belly, closing his finger on the trigger. At the same time Dragosani lunged upward, his knife not quite hamstringing Ustinov behind his left knee. Ustinov screamed, Borowitz too, as bullets chewed up the wall just over his head.

Hanging onto Ustinov's coat, Dragosani hauled himself to his knees, sliced blindly upward a second time. His sickle blade cut through overcoat, jacket, shirt and flesh. It carved Ustinov's upper right arm to the bone and his useless fingers dropped the gun. Almost as a reflex action, he kneed Dragosani in the face.

Gasping his pain and terror, knowing he was badly cut, Andrei Ustinov, traitor, hobbled out of the door and slammed it shut. Another moment saw him pass through a tiny anteroom and out into the corridor. There he closed the soundproof door more quietly behind him, stepped over the body of the KGB man where it lay with lolling tongue and caved-in skull. The killing of this one was unfortunate, but it had been necessary.

Cursing and gasping his pain, Ustinov hobbled down the corridor leaving a trail of blood. He had almost reached the door to the courtyard when a sound behind him brought him up short. Turning, he brought out a compact fragmentation grenade from his inside pocket, pulled the pin. He saw Dragosani step out into the corridor, stumble over the body sprawled there and go to his knees. Then, as their eyes met, he lobbed the grenade. After that there was nothing to do but get out of there. With the grenade's bouncing ringing in his ears, and Dragosani's *hiss* of snatched breath, he opened the steel door to the courtyard, stepped through it and pulled it firmly shut behind him.

Out in the night, Ustinov mentally ticked off the seconds as he limped towards the two white-coated attendants at the rear of the ambulance. "Help!" he croaked. "I'm cut—badly! It's Dragosani, one of our special operatives. He's gone mad, killed Borowitz, Gerkhov, and a KGB man."

From behind him, lending his words definition, there came a muffled detonation. The steel door gonged as if someone had struck it with a sledgehammer; it bowed outward a little and broke a hinge, then was sucked back and open to slam against the corridor wall. Smoke, heat and a lick of red flame billowed out, all bearing the heavy stench of high explosives.

"Quick!" Ustinov shouted over the frantic questioning of the attendants and the yelling of security guards as they came clattering over the cobbles. "You, driver, get us away from here at once, before the whole place goes up!" There was little fear of that happening, but it would guarantee some action. And it would get Ustinov out of harm's way, for the moment anyway. The hell of it was that he couldn't be sure any of them back there were dead. If they

37

were he would have plenty of time to construct his story; if not he was done for. Only time would tell.

He flopped into the back of the ambulance as its engine roared into life, followed by the attendants who at once began to peel off his outer garments. Doors flapping, the vehicle pulled away across the courtyard, passed under a high stone archway and onto a track leading to the perimeter wall.

"Keep going," Ustinov yelled. "Get us away!" The driver hunched down over the wheel and put his foot down.

Back in the courtyard the security men and the helicopter pilot hopped and skittered on the cobbles, coughing in the streamers of acrid smoke from the hanging door. The fire, what little of it there had been, had died in the smoke. And now, out from behind that dense, reeking wall of smoke staggered an ashen nightmare figure: Dragosani, naked still, black-streaked over grey and gore-spattered flesh, carried a bellowing Gregor Borowitz draped in a fireman's lift across his shoulders.

"What?" the General shouted between coughs and splutters. "*What?* Where's that treacherous dog Ustinov? Did you let him get away? Where's the ambulance? What are you bloody fools doing?"

As the security men lifted Borowitz down from Dragosani's bowed back, one of them breathlessly told him: "Comrade Ustinov was wounded, sir. He went off in the ambulance."

"Comrade? *Comrade?*" Borowitz howled. "No comrade, that one! And 'wounded,' you say? Wounded, you arsehole? *I want him dead!*"

He turned his wolf's face up to the tower, yelled: "You there—do you see the ambulance?"

"Yes, Comrade General. It approaches the outer wall."

"Stop it!" Borowitz screamed, clutching at his shattered shoulder.

38

"But—"

"Blow it to hell!" the General raged.

The marksman in the tower slid his night-sight binoculars into a groove in the butt of the Kalashnikov, slapped home a mixed clip of tracers and explosive bullets. Kneeling, he picked up the vehicle again in the cross-hairs of the night-sights, aimed at the cab and bonnet. The ambulance was slowing down as it approached one of the archways through the perimeter wall, but the marksman knew it would never get there. Jamming his weapon between his shoulder and the parapet wall, he squeezed the trigger and kept it squeezed. The hosepipe of fire reached out from the tower, fell short of the vehicle by a few yards, then jumped the gap and struck the target.

The front end of the ambulance burst into white fire, exploded and hurled blazing petrol in all directions. Blown off the track, turned on its side, the vehicle ploughed to a halt in torn-up turf. Someone in white crawled away from it on hands and knees as it burned; someone else, wearing an open, flapping shirt and carrying a dark overcoat, cowered back from the flames and limped in the direction of the covered exit.

Unable to see out of the courtyard from where he stood supported by the security men, Borowitz eagerly shouted up to the tower, "Did you stop it?"

"Yes, sir. Two men at least are alive. One is ambulance crew, and I think the other is—"

"I know who the other is," Borowitz screamed. "He's a traitor! To me, to the branch, to Russia. Cut him down!"

The marksman gulped, aimed, fired. Tracers and bullets reached out, chewed up the earth at Ustinov's heels, caught up with him and blew him apart in blazing phosphorus and exploding steel.

It was the first time the man in the tower had killed. Now he put down his gun, leaned shakily against the balcony wall and called down, "It's done, sir." In the lull, his voice seemed very small.

"Very well," Borowitz shouted back. "Now stay where you are for the moment and keep your eyes open." He groaned and clutched at his shoulder again where blood seeped through the material of his overcoat.

One of the security men said, "Sir, you're hurt."

"Of course I'm hurt, fool! It can wait a little while. But for now I want everyone called in. I want to speak to them. And for the moment none of this is to be reported outside these walls. How many bloody KGB men do we have here?"

"Two, sir," the same security man told him. "One in there—"

"He's dead," growled Borowitz, uncaring.

"Then only one, sir. Out there, in the woods. The rest of us are branch operatives."

"Good! But . . . does the one in the woods have a radio?"

"No, sir."

"Even better. Very well, bring him in and lock him up for now—on my authority."

"Right, sir."

"And don't let anyone worry," Borowitz continued. "All of this is on my shoulders—which are very broad, as you well know. I'm not trying to hide anything, but I want to break it in my own time. This could be our chance to get the KGB off our backs once and for all. Right, let's see some action around here! You—" he turned to the helicopter pilot. "Get yourself airborne. I need a doctor—the branch doctor. Bring him in at once."

"Yes, Comrade General. At once." The pilot ran for his machine, the security men for their car where it was parked outside the courtyard. Borowitz watched them go, leaned on Dragosani's arm and said:

"Boris, are you good for anything else?"

"I'm still in one piece, if that's what you mean," the other answered. "I just had time to shelter in the anteroom before the grenade exploded."

Borowitz grinned wolfishly despite the terrible burning in his shoulder. "Good!" he said. "Then get back in there and see if you can find a fire extinguisher. Anything still burning, stop it. After that you can join me in the lecture room." He shook off the naked man's arm, swayed for a moment then stood rock steady. "Well, what are you waiting for?"

As Dragosani ducked back through the ruined door into the corridor, where the smoke had almost completely disappeared now, Borowitz called after him: "And Comrade, find yourself some clothes to wear, or a blanket at least. Your work is over for tonight. It hardly seems right that Boris Dragosani, Necromancer to the Kremlin—one day, anyway—should be running about in his birthday-suit, now does it?"

A week later at a special hearing held *in camera*, Gregor Borowitz defended the action he had taken at the converted Château Bronnitsy on the night in question. The hearing was to serve a double purpose. One: Borowitz must be seen to have been called to order over "a serious malfunction of the 'experimental branch' under his control." Two: he must now be allowed the opportunity to present his case for complete independence from the rest of the USSR's secret services, particularly the KGB. In short, he would use the hearing as a platform in his bid for complete autonomy.

The five-strong panel of judges—more properly questioners, or investigators—was composed of Georg Krisich of the Party Central Committee, Oliver Bellekhoyza and Karl Djannov, junior cabinet ministers, Yuri Andropov, head of the Komissia Gosudarstvennoy Bezopasnosti, the KGB, and one other who was not only "an independent observer" but in fact Leonid Brezhnev's personal representative. Since the Party Leader would in any case have the last say, his "nameless" but all-important cipher was the man Borowitz must most impress. He was also, by virtue of his "anonymity," the one who had least to say . . .

The hearing had taken place in a large room on the second floor of a building on Kurtsuzov Prospekt, which made it easy for Andropov and Brezhnev's man to be there since they both had offices in that block. No one had been especially difficult. There is an accepted element of risk in all experimental projects; though, as Andropov quietly pointed out, one would hope that as well as being "accepted," the risk might also on occasion be "anticipated," at which Borowitz had smiled and nodded his head in deference while promising himself that one day the bastard would pay for that cold, sneering insinuation of inefficiency, not to mention his smug and entirely inappropriate air of sly superiority.

During the hearing it had come out (exactly as Borowitz had reported it) how one of his junior executives, Andrei Ustinov, had broken down under the stresses and strains of his work and gone berserk. He had killed KGB Operative Hadj Gartezkov, had tried to destroy the Château with explosives, had even wounded Borowitz himself before being stopped. Unfortunately, in the process of "stopping" him, two others had also lost their lives and a third man had been injured, though mercifully none of these had been citizens of any great importance. The state would do what it could for their families.

After the "malfunction" and until all the facts in the case could be properly substantiated, it had been unfortunately necessary to detain a second member of Andropov's

KGB at the Château. This had been unavoidable; with the single exception of a helicopter pilot flying his machine, Borowitz had allowed no one to leave until all was sorted out. Even the pilot would have been kept back had the presence of a doctor not been urgently required. As for the agent's detention in a cell: that had been for his own safety. Until it could be shown that the KGB itself was not Ustinov's main target—indeed, until it was discovered that no "target" as such existed, but that a man had quite simply gone mad and committed mayhem—Borowitz had considered it his duty to keep the agent safe. After all, one dead KGB man was surely one too many; a sentiment Andropov must feel obliged to endorse.

In short, the entire hearing was little more than a reiteration of Borowitz's original explanation and report. No mention at all was made of the disinterment, subsequent evisceration and necromantic examination of a certain senior ex-MVD official. If Andropov had known of *that* then there really would have been a problem, but he did not know. Nor would matters have been improved by the fact that only eight days ago he himself had lain a wreath on that poor unfortunate's fresh-made grave—or the fact that at this very moment the body lay in a second, unmarked grave somewhere in the grounds of the Château Bronnitsy . . .

As for the rest of it: Minister Djannov had made some indelicate inquiry or other in respect of the work or the purpose of Borowitz's branch; Borowitz had looked astonished if not outraged; Brezhnev's representative had coughed, stepped in and sidetracked the question. What is the use, after all, of a secret branch or organization once it has been made to divulge its secrets? In fact, Leonid Brezhnev had already vetoed any such direct enquiries in respect of ESP Branch and its activities; Borowitz had been a sinewy old warhorse and Party man all his life, not to mention a staunch and powerful supporter of the Party Leader.

Throughout, it had been fairly obvious that Andropov was disgruntled. He would dearly have loved to bring charges, or at least press for a full KGB investigation, but had already been forbidden—or rather, he had been "convinced" that he should not follow that route. But when all was said and done and the others had left, the KGB boss asked Borowitz to stay back and talk a while.

"Gregor," he said when they were alone, "of course you know that nothing of any real importance—I mean *nothing*—is ever entirely secret from me? 'Unknown' or 'as yet unlearned' are not the same as secret. And sooner or later I learn everything. You do know that?"

"Ah, omniscience!" Borowitz grinned his wolf's grin. "A heavy load for any one man's shoulders to bear, Comrade. I sympathize with you."

Yuri Andropov smiled thinly, his eyes deceptively misty and vacant behind the lenses of his spectacles. But he made no effort to veil the threat in his voice when he said: "Gregor, we all have our futures to consider. You of all people should bear that in mind. You are not a young man. If your pet branch goes down, what then? Are you ready for an early retirement, the loss of all your little privileges?"

"Oddly enough," Borowitz answered, "there is that in the nature of my work which has assured my future—my foreseeable future, anyway. Oh, and incidentally—yours too."

Andropov's eyebrows went up. "Oh?" Again his thin smile. "And what have your astrologers read in my stars, Gregor?"

Well, he knows that much at least! thought Borowitz; but it wasn't really surprising. Any secret police chief worth his salt could get hold of that much. And so there seemed little point in denying it. "Elevation to the Politburo in two years," he said, without changing his expression by so much as a wrinkle. "And possibly, in eight or nine more, the Party Leadership."

"Really?" Andropov's smile was half-curious, half-sardonic.

"Yes, really." Still Borowitz's expression had not changed. "And I tell you it without fear that you in turn will report it to Leonid."

"Do you indeed?" answered that most dangerous of men. "And is there any special reason why I will not tell him?"

"Oh, yes. I suppose you could call it the Herod Principle. Of course, being good Party Members we don't read the so-called 'Holy Book,' but because I know you for a most intelligent man I also know that you will understand what I mean. Herod, as you will know, became a mass murderer rather than suffer the threat of a usurper on his throne—even a baby infant. You are by no means innocent as a baby, Yuri. And at the same time, of course, Leonid is no petty Herod. Still, I don't believe you'll tell him what I predict for you . . ."

After a moment's thought Andropov shrugged. "Perhaps I won't," he said, no longer smiling.

"On the other hand," said Borowitz over his shoulder as he turned and left the room, "perhaps *I* would—except for one thing."

"One thing? What thing is that?"

"Why, that we all have our futures to consider, of course! And also because I consider myself wiser far than those three foolish 'wise' men . . ."

And grimacing savagely to himself as he stamped down the corridor toward the stairs, suddenly Borowitz's wolf's grin returned as he recalled something else his seers had told him about Yuri Andropov: that shortly after attaining premiership he would sicken and die. Yes, within two or

three years at most. Borowitz could only hope it would be
so . . . or perhaps he could do better than just hope.

Perhaps he should make preparations of his own, starting right now. Perhaps he should speak to a certain chem-
ist friend in Bulgaria. A slow poison . . . undetectable
. . . painless . . . bringing on a swift deterioration of vital
organs . . .

Certainly it was worth thinking about.

On the following Wednesday evening Boris Dragosani
drove his spartan little Russian puddle-jumper the twenty-
odd miles out of the city to Gregor Borowitz's spacious
but rustic dacha in Zhukovka. As well as being pleasantly
situated on a pine-covered hillock overlooking the sluggish
Moscow River, the place was also "safe" from prying
eyes and ears—especially the electric sort. Borowitz would
have nothing made of metal in the place—with the exception of his metal-detector. Ostensibly he used this to seek
out old coins along the river-bank, especially near the
ancient fording places, but in fact it was for his own
security and peace of mind. He knew the location of every
nail in every log in his dacha. The only bugs that could get
anywhere near the place were the sort that crawled in the
rich soil in Borowitz's overgrown garden.

For all that, still the old General took Dragosani walking
in order to talk to him, preferring the outdoors to the
ever-dubious privacy of four walls however well he'd
checked them over. For even here in Zhukovka there was a
KGB presence; indeed, a strong one. Many senior KGB
officials—a few generals among them—had their dachas
here, not to mention a host of retired state-rewarded ex-
agents. None of them were friends of Borowitz; all would
be delighted to supply Yuri Andropov with whatever tidbits of information they could unearth.

"But at least the branch itself is now rid of them,"

Borowitz confided, leading the way down a path along the river bank. He took Dragosani to a place where there were flat stones to sit on, where they could watch the sun going down as the evening turned the river to a dark green mirror.

They made an odd couple: the squat old soldier, gnarled, typically Russian, all horn and yellow ivory and time-tooled leather; and the handsome young man, almost effete by comparison, delicate of features (when they were not transformed by the rigours of his work), long-fingered hands of a concert pianist, slim but deceptively strong, with shoulders broad as his smile was narrow. No, apart from a mutual respect, they seemed to have very little in common.

Borowitz respected Dragosani for his talent; he had no doubt but that it was one which could help make Russia truly strong again. Not merely "super power" strong but invulnerable to any would-be invader, indestructible to any weapons system, invincible in the pursuit of a steady, stealthy, world-enveloping expansionism. Oh, the latter was already here, but Dragosani could speed up the process immeasurably. *If* Borowitz's hopes for the branch were firmly founded. It was still espionage, yes—but it was the other side of the coin from Andropov's Secret Police. Or rather, the edge of the coin. Espionage—but with the emphasis on "Esp." That was why Borowitz "liked" the unlikeable Dragosani: he would never look right in a dark-blue overcoat and fedora, but by the same token no KGB man could ever fathom the wells of secrets to which Dragosani was privy. And of course, Borowitz had himself "discovered" the necromancer and brought him into the fold. That was another reason he liked him: he was his greatest find.

As for the paler, younger man—he too had his targets, his ambitions. What they were he kept to himself—kept them locked in that macabre mind—but they were certainly not Borowitz's visions of Russian world dominance and universal empire, of a mother Russia whose sons could never again be threatened by any nation or nations however strong.

For one thing, Dragosani did not consider himself a genuine Russian. His was a heritage older far than the oppression of Communism and the blunt tribes who used its hammer and sickle sigil not only as tools but as a banner and a threat. And perhaps that was one of the reasons he "liked" the equally unlikeable Borowitz, whose politics were quite un-politic. As for respect—there was a measure of that in him for the old warhorse, yes, but not for ancient heroics on the field of battle, or the practised ease with which Borowitz could bluff the very sting out of a scorpion's tail. Instead Dragosani respected his boss much as a steeplejack respects the higher rungs of his ladder. And much like a steeplejack, he knew he could never afford to step back and admire his work. But why should he, when one day the chimney would be built and he could stand at its top and enjoy his triumph from its own unassailable apex? Meanwhile Borowitz could instruct, guide his feet up the rungs, and Dragosani would climb—as fast and as high as the ladder could bear his weight. Or perhaps he respected him as a tight-rope walker respects his rope. And how then must he watch his step?

What friction there was between the two sprang mainly from disparate backgrounds, upbringing, loyalties and lifestyles. Borowitz was a born and bred Muscovite who had been orphaned at four, had cut bundles of firewood for a living at seven, and had been a soldier from the age of sixteen. Dragosani had been named for his birthplace on the Oltul River where it flowed down from the Carpatii Meridionali towards the Danube and the border with Bulgaria. In the old days that had been Wallachia, with Hungary to the north and Serbia and Bosnia to the west.

And that was how he saw himself: as a Wallach, or as a Romanian at the very least. And as a historian and patriot (while yet his patriotism was for a country whose name had long since faded on old maps) he knew that his homeland's history had been long and very bloody. Trace Wallachia's history and what does one find?—that it has been bartered, annexed, stolen, re-taken and stolen again, raked over and ravished and ruined—but that always it has sprung back into a being of its own. The country was a phoenix! Its very soil was alive, dark with blood, given strength by blood. Yes, the strength of the people had been in the land, and that of the land in its people. It was a land they could fight for, which by its nature could almost fight for itself. Any set of historical maps would show why this was so: in those old days, before the aeroplane and the tank—ringed about by mountains and marshes, with the Black Sea on the eastern flank, boglands to the west and the Danube in the south—the region had been almost completely insular, safe as a fortress.

And so, through his pride in his heritage, Dragosani was first a Wallach (and possibly the only surviving Wallach in the world), second a Romanian, but hardly a Russian at all. What were they after all, Gregor Borowitz included, but the settled spume of wave after wave of invaders, sons of Huns and Goths, Slavs and Franks, Mongols and Turks? Of course there'd be the blood of those dogs in Boris Dragosani, too, but mostly he was a Wallach! He could only liken himself to the older man in the one respect that they had both been orphans of sorts; but even in that area the circumstances were very different. Borowitz had at least *had* parents of his own; as a baby he had known them, even though they were now long forgotten. But Dragosani . . . he had been a foundling. Found on a doorstep in a Romanian village, little more than a day old, and brought up and educated by a rich farmer and land-owner; that had been his lot. And not a bad one overall.

"Well, Boris," said Borowitz, drawing his protégé back from his musing, "and what do you think of that, eh?"

"Of what?"

"*Huh!*" the older man snorted. "Look, I know this place is very restful, and that I'm a boring old fart at best, but for goodness' sake don't go to sleep on me! What do you think of the branch being free at last of the KGB?"

"Is it really?"

"Yes, really!" Borowitz rubbed his blunt hands together in satisfaction until they almost rustled. "We're purged, you might say. We were only obliged to suffer them in the first place because Andropov likes to have a finger in every pie. Well, this pie's no longer to his taste. It has all worked out very well."

"How did you do it?" (Dragosani knew the other was dying to tell him.)

Borowitz shrugged, almost as if to play down his own role in the affair—which in itself gave Dragosani to know that the exact opposite was the truth. "Oh, a little of this, a little of that. Should I say that I put my job on the line? That I put the branch itself on the line? I gambled, if you like—except that I knew I couldn't lose."

"Then it wasn't a gamble," said Dragosani. "What, *exactly*, did you do?"

Borowitz chuckled. "Boris, you know how I hate being exact. But yes, I'll tell you. I went to see Brezhnev *before* the hearing—and I told him how things were going to be."

"Hah!" it was Dragosani's turn to snort. "*You* told *him*? You told Leonid Brezhnev, Party Leader, how things were going to be? What things?"

Borowitz smiled his wolf's smile. "Future things!" he

said. "Things which are not yet! I told him his political billing and cooing with Nixon would take him from strength to strength—but that he should prepare for Nixon's fall three years from now, when it will be shown to the world that he is corrupt. I told him that when that is over he will be in a position of some advantage, dealing with a bumbler in the White House. I told him that in preparation for American hard-liners yet to come, next year he will sign an agreement permitting sputniks to photograph missile sites in the USA, and vice versa—that he should do it while he still had the chance and while America is ahead in the space race. Détente again, you see. He's keen on it. He's similarly keen that they shouldn't get too far ahead in that race, and so I promised him a joint space venture, which will come in 1975. As for a whole crowd of Jews and dissidents who've been giving him problems, I told him we'd be rid of a great many of them—possibly as many as 125,000—in the next three or four years!

"Oh, don't look so shocked or disgusted or whatever emotion that expression of yours is supposed to signify, Boris. We're not barbarians, my young friend. I'm not talking extermination or Siberia or pre-frontal lobotomy but eviction, emigration, kicking or allowing them to drag their arses out of here! Oh yes!

"All of these things I told him and more. And I guaranteed them—strictly between Leonid and myself, you understand—if only he'd let me do my job and get the KGB right off my back. What were these starch-faced policemen anyway but spies for their boss? And why should they spy on me, loyal as any man and a damn sight more than most? But over and above everything else, how could I hope to maintain any sort of secrecy—absolutely necessary in an organization such as ours—with members of another branch peering over my shoulder and reporting back to their master everything I was doing, who couldn't possibly understand *anything* I was doing? They would only laugh, deride what they could not hope to fathom, blow any last vestige of secrecy sky high! And yet again our foreign adversaries would forge ahead; for make no mistake, Boris, the Americans and the British—yes, and the French and the Chinese, too—they also have their mind-spies!

"But give me four years, Leonid," I said, "four years free of Yuri Andropov's monkeys, and I will give you the sprouting germ of an ESPionage network whose incredible potential you cannot possibly imagine!"

"Strong stuff!" Dragosani was suitably impressed. "And his reply?"

"He said, 'Gregor, old friend, old warhorse, old Comrade . . . all right, you shall have your four years. And I shall sit and wait and see to it that your bills are paid, and keep you and your branch in funds enough to run your Volgas and drink your vodka, and I shall watch all of these things you've promised or predicted come to pass, which will make me very grateful to you. And if in four years they have not come to pass—then I shall have your balls!' "

"And so you've put your faith in Vlady's predictions," said Dragosani, nodding. "Are you so sure, then, that this seer of ours is infallible?"

"Oh, yes!" answered Borowitz. "He's almost as good at predicting the future as you are at sniffing out the secrets of the dead."

"Huh!" This time Dragosani was not impressed. "And why then didn't he predict that mess at the Château? Surely he could have foreseen a disaster of that magnitude?"

"But he did predict it," answered Borowitz, "in a roundabout way. Two weeks ago he told me I would shortly lose both my right- and left-hand men. And I did. He also said I would appoint others—but this time from the rank and file, as it were."

Dragosani couldn't conceal his interest. "You have someone in mind?"

Borowitz nodded. "You," he answered, "and perhaps Igor Vlady himself."

"I want no rival," said Dragosani at once.

"Rivalry does not come into it. Your talents are diverse. He does not profess to be a necromancer, you cannot read the future. The reason there must be two of you is to ensure continuity if anything should happen to either one of you."

"Yes, and we had two predecessors," Dragosani growled. "What were their talents—and did they also start out without rivalry?"

Borowitz sighed. "In the beginning," he patiently began to explain, "when I was first pulling the branch together, I was short of actual effective talent in the ranks: my first troop of agents, ESPers, were untried. Those with real talent—like Vlady, who I've had from the beginning, and who improves all the time; and, more recently, like yourself—were too important to tie down with routine administration. Ustinov, also with us from the start but purely as an administrator, and later Gerkhov, fitted their positions precisely. They had no ESP-talent whatsoever but both seemed to have open minds—difficult to find in Russia these days, not that can stay on the right side of the political fence at the same time—and I had hopes that at least one of them would become as deeply interested and involved with our work as I am. When jealousy intervened and they became rivals, I decided to let them weed themselves out without intervention. Natural selection, you might say. But you and Vlady are different kettles of fish entirely. I will not permit rivalry between you. Put it out of your mind."

"Nevertheless," Dragosani insisted, "when you are gone one of us will have to take the reins."

"I do not intend to go anywhere," said Borowitz. "Not for a very long time. By then . . . we shall see what we shall see." He fell silent, musing, chin in hands, watching the river's slow swirl.

"Why did Ustinov turn on you?" the younger man finally asked. "Why not simply get rid of Gerkhov? Surely that were easier, less risky?"

"There were two reasons why he couldn't just remove his rival," said Borowitz. "First, he had been suborned by an old enemy of mine—the man you 'examined'—who I'd suspected for some time of plotting my removal. We actually hated each other, me and this old MVD torturer! It was unavoidable: he would kill me or I him. Because of this I had Vlady watch him, concentrate on him, read him. In his immediate future he read treachery and death. The treachery would be directed against me; the death would be mine or his. A pity Igor isn't more specific. Anyway, I arranged for it to be his.

"Second, killing Gerkhov—however skilfully, however carefully avoiding his own involvement in the actual 'accidental' death—would not remove the problem at its root. It would be like cutting down a weed; in time it would only spring up again. Doubtless I would elevate someone else to the post, probably an ESPer, and what hope would there be for poor Ustinov then? That was his only real problem—ambition.

"Anyway, I am a survivor, as you see. I used Vlady to foresee what that old pig of a Bolshevik arse-kicker had in store for me, and got him before he could get me, and I used you to read his dead guts and see who else was involved. Alas, it was Andrei Ustinov. I had thought perhaps Andropov and his KGB might be in on it, too. They like me about as much as I like them. But they were not involved. I'm glad about that, for they don't give in very easily. But what a world of petty feuding and vendettas we live in, eh, Boris? Why, it's only two years ago that Leonid Brezhnev himself was fired upon at the very Kremlin gates!''

Dragosani had been looking thoughtful. ''Tell me something,'' he finally said. ''When it was all over—that night at the Château, I mean—was that why you asked me if it was possible for me to read Ustinov's corpse? Or rather, the mess that was left of him? Because you thought he might have been got at by the newer KGB, as well as your retired old chum from the MVD?''

''Something like that,'' Borowitz shrugged. ''But it doesn't matter now. No, for if they'd been involved at all it would have come out at the hearing; our friend Yuri Andropov would not have been so much at ease. I'd have been able to see it in him. As it was, he was just a bit pissed off that Leonid has seen fit to haul in his leash a bit.''

''Which means he'll really be after your blood now!''

''No, I don't think so. Not for four years, anyway. And when it is shown that I'm correct—that is, when Brezhnev realizes Vlady's predictions, and so has proof positive of the effectiveness of the branch—not then either! So . . . with a bit of luck, we're free of that pack for good.''

''Hmm! Well, let's hope so. So, it would seem you've been very clever, General. But I knew that anyway. Now tell me, what other reasons did you have for calling me here today?''

''Well, I've more to tell you—other things in the pot, you know? But we can do that over dinner. Natasha is serving fish fresh from the river. Trout. Strictly forbidden. They taste all the better for it!'' He got up, began to lead the way back up the river bank. ''Also'' (over his shoulder) ''to advise you that you should now sell that box on wheels and get yourself a decent car. A second-hand Volga, I should think. Nothing newer than mine, anyway. It goes with your promotion. You can try it out when you go on holiday.''

"Holiday?'' It was all coming thick and fast now.

"Oh, yes, hadn't I told you? Three weeks at least, on the state. I'm fortifying the Château. It will be quite impossible to get any branch work done . . .''

"You're doing what? Did you say you're—''

"Fortifying the place, yes,'' Borowitz was very matter of fact about it. "Machine-gun emplacements, an electric fence, that sort of thing. They have it at Baikonur in Kazakhstan, where they launch the space vehicles—and is our work any less important? Anyway, the work has been approved, starts Friday. We're our own bosses now, you know, within certain limitations . . . inside the Château, anyway. When I'm finished we'll all have passes for access, and no way in without them! But that's for later. Meanwhile there'll be a lot of work going on, much of which I'll supervise personally. I want the place expanded, opened up, widened out. More room for experimental cells. I've got four years, yes, but they'll go very quickly. First stage of the alterations will take the best part of a month, so—''

"So while all this is going on, I'm to get a holiday?'' Dragosani was keen now, the tone of his voice eager.

"Right, you and one or two others. For you it's a reward. You were very good that night. With the exception of this hole in my shoulder, the whole thing was very successful—oh, and also the loss of poor Gerkhov, of course. My one regret is that I had to ask you to take it all the way. I know how hateful that must be for you . . .''

"Do you mind if we don't talk about it?'' Dragosani found Borowitz's sudden concern for his sensibilities a bit much—not to mention entirely out of character.

"All right, we won't talk about it,'' said the other. But

half-turning and with a monstrous grin, he added: "Anyway, fish tastes better!"

That was more like it. "You sadistic old bastard!"

Borowitz laughed out loud. "That's what I like about you, Boris. You're just like me: very disrespectful to your superiors." He changed the subject:

"Anyway, where will you spend your holiday?"

"Home," said the other without hesitation.

"Romania?"

"Of course. Back to Dragosani where I was born."

"Don't you ever go anywhere else?"

"Why should I? I know the place, and I love the people—as much as it's possible for me to love anything, anyway. Dragosani is a town now, but I'll find a place outside the town—somewhere in the villages in the hills."

"It must be very pleasant," Borowitz nodded. "Is there a girl?"

"No."

"What, then?"

Dragosani grunted, shrugged, but his eyes narrowed to slits. Walking in front, his boss didn't see the look in his face when he answered, "I don't know. Something in the soil, I suppose."

Chapter Two

HARRY KEOGH FELT THE WARM SUN ON THE SIDE OF HIS face, beating through the open classroom window. He knew the solid, near-indestructible feel of a school bench under his thighs, its surface polished by tens of thousands of bottoms. He was aware of the aggressive hum of a tiny wasp on its tour of inspection of his inkwell, ruler, pencils, the dahlias in a vase on the window ledge. But all of these things lay on the periphery of his consciousness, little more than background static. He was aware of them in the same way that he was aware of his heart hammering in his chest—hammering far too quickly and loudly for an arithmetic class on a sunny Tuesday afternoon in August. The real world was there, all right—real as the occasional breath of breeze fanning his cheek from the open window—and yet Harry craved air no less than a drowning man. Or a drowning woman.

And the sun could not warm him where he struggled under the ice, and the wasp's buzzing was almost entirely lost in the gurgle and slosh of icy water and the burble of bubbles from his nostrils and straining, silently screaming jaws! Darkness below, frozen mud and weeds; and above—

A sheet of ice, inches thick, and somewhere a hole—the hole he (she?) had fallen through—but where? Fight the river's rush! Kick against it and swim, swim! Think of Harry, little Harry. You have to live for him. For his sake. For Harry . . .

There! There! Thank God for the hole!—oh, thank God!

Clawing at the rim, the edges of ice sharp as glass. And heaven-sent hands coming down into the water, seeming to move oh so slowly—almost in slow motion—dreadfully, monstrously languid! Strong hands, hairy. A ring on the second finger of the right hand. A cat's-eye stone set in thick gold. A man's ring.

Looking up, a face all aswim, seen through the chop of wavelets and the liquid flurry of water. And through the ice, his frosty outline kneeling at the rim. Grasp his hands, those strong hands, and he'll lift you out like a baby. And he'll shake you till you're dry for frightening him.

Fight the current—grasp at the hands—kick against the river's rush. Fight, fight! Fight for Harry . . .

There! You've got the hands! Grip tight! Hold on! Try to lift your head up through the hole and breathe, breathe!

But . . . the hands are pushing you down!

Seen through the water the face wobbles, shifting and changing. The trembly jelly lips turn up at their corners. They smile—or grimace! You hang on. You scream—and water rushes in to replace the escaping air.

Cling to the ice. Forget the hands, the cruel hands that continue to hold you down. Just grab at the rim and lift your head. But the hands are there, breaking your grip. They thrust you away, under the ice. They murder you!

You can't fight the cold and the river and the hands. Blackness is roaring down on you. In your lungs, in your head, in your eyes. Stick your long fingernails into the hands, claw at them, tear the flesh from them. The gold ring comes loose, spirals down into the murk and mud. Blood turns the water red—red against the ultimate black of your dying—blood from the cruel, cruel hands.

No fight left in you. Waterlogged, you sink. The current drags you along the bottom, tumbling you. But you no longer care. Except . . . you care for Harry. Poor little Harry! Who'll care for him now? Who'll look after Harry . . . Harry . . . Harry—?

"Harry? Harry Keogh? Christ, boy!—are you here at all?"

Harry felt the elbow of his pal Jimmy Collins digging him covertly, however sharply, in the ribs, causing him to draw air explosively; he heard Mr. Hannant's rasping voice crashing in on his eardrums above the receding tumult of water. He jerked upright on his bench, gulped again at the air, thrust his hand up foolishly, as if in response to some question or other. It was an automatic reaction: if you were quick off the mark the teacher knew you knew the answer and he'd ask someone else. Except . . . sometimes it didn't work out that way, teachers didn't always fall for it. And Hannant, the maths teacher—he was nobody's fool.

Gone now the sensation of drowning; gone utterly the bitter cold of the water, the pitiless torture of thrusting, brutally inhuman hands; gone the entire nightmare—or, more properly, the daydream. By comparison the newer situation was a mere trifle. Or was it?

Harry was suddenly aware of a classroom full of eyes, all staring at him; aware too of Mr. Hannant's purple, outraged face glaring at him from out in front of the class. What had they been dealing with?

He glanced at the blackboard. Oh, yes! Formulae—areas and properties of circles—the Constant Factor(?)—diameters and radii and pi. Pi? That was a laugh! It was *all* pi to

Harry. Pie in the sky. But what had been Hannant's question? Had he even asked a question?

White-faced now, Harry peered about the classroom His was the only hand in the air. Slowly he drew it down. Beside him, Jimmy Collins sniggered, coughing and spluttering to hide it. Normally that would have been sufficient to set Harry off, too, but with the memory of the night- or day-mare so fresh in his mind, he had little difficulty staving it off.

"Well?" Hannant demanded.

"Sir?" Harry queried. "Er, could you repeat the question?"

Hannant sighed, closed his eyes, rested his great knuckles on his desk and leaned his stocky body on his straight arms. He counted ten under his breath, but loud enough for the class to hear him. Finally, without reopening his eyes, he said: "The question was, are you here at all?"

"Me, sir?"

"God, yes, Harry Keogh! Yes, you!"

"Why, yes sir!" Harry tried not to act too innocent. It looked like he might get away with it—or would he? "But there was this wasp, sir, and—"

"My *other* question," Hannant cut him short, "my *first* question—the one that made me suspect perhaps you weren't with us—was this: what is the relationship between the diameter of a circle and pi? I take it that's the one you wanted to answer? The one you had your hand up for? Or were you swatting flies?"

Harry felt a flush riding up his neck. Pi? Diameter? Circle?

The class grew fidgety; someone sniffed disgustedly, probably the bully, Stanley Green—the pushy, big-headed, swotty slob! The trouble with Stanley was that he was clever *and* big . . . What was the question again? But what difference did it make without the answer?

Jimmy Collins looked down at his desk, ostensibly at a work book there, and whispered out of the corner of his mouth: *"Three times!"*

Three times? What did *that* mean?

"Well?" Hannant knew he had him.

"Er, three times!" Harry blurted, praying that Jimmy wasn't having him on. "—Sir."

The maths teacher sucked in air, straightened up. He snorted, frowned, seemed a little puzzled. But then he said, "No!—but it was a good try. As far as it goes. Not three times but three point one four one five nine times. Ah! But times what?"

"The diameter," Jimmy whispered. *"Equals circumference . . ."*

"D-diameter!" Harry stuttered. "Equals, er, circumference."

George Hannant stared hard at Harry. He saw a boy, thirteen years old; sandy haired; freckled; in a crumpled school uniform; untidy shirt; school tie like a piece of chewed string, askew, its end fraying; and prescription spectacles balanced on a stub of a nose, behind which dreamy blue eyes gazed out in a sort of perpetual apprehension. Pitiful? No, not that; Harry Keogh could take his lumps, and dish them out when his dander was up. But . . . a difficult kid to get through to. Hannant suspected there was a pretty good brain in there, somewhere behind that haunted face. If only it could be prodded into life!

Stir him out of himself, maybe? A short, sharp shock? Give him something to think about in *this* world, instead of that other place he kept slipping off into? Maybe. "Harry Keogh, I'm not altogether sure that answer was yours in its entirety. Collins is sitting too close to you and looking too disinterested for my liking. So . . . at the end of this chapter in your book you'll find ten questions. Three of 'em concern themselves with surface areas of circles and cylinders. I want the answers to those three here on my desk first thing tomorrow morning, right?''

Harry hung his head and bit his lip. "Yes, sir."

"So look at me. *Look* at me, boy!"

Harry looked up. And now he did look pitiful. But no good going back now. "Harry," Hannant sighed, "you're a mess! I've spoken to the other masters and it's not just maths but everything. If you don't wake up, son, you'll be leaving school without a single qualification. Oh, there's time yet—if that's what you're thinking—a couple of years, anyway. But only if you get down to it right now. The homework isn't punishment, Harry, it's my way of trying to point you in the right direction.''

He looked towards the back of the class, to where Stanley Green was still sniggering and hiding his face behind a hand that scratched his forehead. "As for you, Green—for you it *is* punishment, you obnoxious wart! You can do the other seven!''

The rest of the class tried hard not to show its approval— dared not, for Big Stanley would surely make them pay for it if they did—but Hannant saw it anyway. That was good. He didn't mind being seen as a sod, but far better to be a sod with a sense of justice.

"But sir—!" Green started to his feet, his voice already beginning to rise in protest.

"Shut up!" Hannant told him sharply. "And sit *down!*" And then—as the bully subsided with a loud *huh!* "Right, what's next?" He glanced at the afternoon's programme under the glass on top of his desk. "Oh, yes—stone collecting on the beach. Good! A bit of fresh air might wake you all up. Very well, start packing up. Then you can go—but in an *orderly* manner!" (As if they'd take any notice of that!)

But—before they could commence their metamorphosis into a pencil-clattering, desk-slamming, floor-shaking horde— *"Wait!* You may as well leave your things here. The monitor takes the key and opens up again after you've brought your stones back from the beach. When you've picked up your things, then he'll lock up again. Who is the monitor this week?"

"Sir!" Jimmy Collins stuck up his hand.

"Oh?" said Hannant, raising thick eyebrows, but not at all surprised really. "Going up in the world, are we, Jimmy Collins?"

"Scored the winning goal against Blackhills on Saturday, sir," said Jimmy with pride.

Hannant smiled, if only to himself. Oh, yes, that would do it. Jamieson, the headmaster, was a fool for football—indeed for all sports. *A healthy mind needs a healthy body* . . . Still, he was a good head.

The boys were exiting now, Green elbowing his way through the crush, looking surlier than ever, with Keogh and Collins bringing up the rear; the two of them, for all their differences, inseparable as Siamese twins. And as he'd known they would, they stood at the door waiting.

"Well?" Hannant asked.

"Waiting for you, sir," said Collins. "So I can lock up."

"Oh, is that so?" Hannant aped the boy's breeziness. "And we'll just leave all the windows open, will we?"

As the two came tumbling back into the classroom he grinned, packed his briefcase, did up the top button of his shirt and straightened his tie—and still got out into the corridor before they were through. Then Collins turned the key in the lock and they were off—brushing past him, careful not to touch him, as if fearing they'd catch something—dashing after the others in a clatter of flying feet.

Maths? Hannant thought, watching them out of sight along the shining corridor, slicing through the square beams of dusty sunlight from the windows. *What the hell's maths? Star Trek on the telly and a stack of brand new Marvel comics in the newsagent's—and I expect them to study numbers! God! And just wait another year or so, till they start to notice those funny lumps on girls—as if they haven't already!* And again: *Maths? Hopeless!*

He grinned, however ruefully. Lord, how he envied them!

Harden Modern Boys' was a secondary modern school on England's north-east coast, catering to the budding minds of the colliery's young men. That did not mean a great deal: most of the boys would become miners or employees of the Coal Board anyway, like their fathers and older brothers before them. But some, a small percentage, would go on through the medium of examinations to higher education at academic and technical colleges in neighbouring towns.

Originally a cluster of two-storey Coal Board offices, the school had been given a face-lift some thirty years earlier when the village's population had suddenly grown to accommodate greatly expanded mining operations. Now, standing behind low walls just a mile from the shore to the east and half that distance from the mine itself to the north, the plain old bricks of the place and the square windows seemed to lend it an air of frowning austerity out of keeping with its prosperous self-help gardens, a cold severity not at all reflected in its staff. No, for all in all they were a good, hard-working bunch. And headmaster Howard Jamieson BA, a staunch survivor of "the Old School," saw to it that they stayed that way.

The weekly stone-gathering expedition served three purposes. One: it got all the kids out in the fresh air, allowing those teachers with a predilection for nature-rambling a rare chance to turn the minds of their wards towards

Nature's wonders. Two: it provided gratis much of the raw material for garden walls within the grounds of the school, gradually replacing the old fences and trellises, a project which naturally bore the head's stamp of approval. Three: it meant that once a month three-quarters of the masters could get away from school early, leaving their charges in the care of the dedicated ramblers.

The idea was this: that all the pupils employ Tuesday's last period to walk a mile down leafy country lanes to the beach, there to collect up large, flat, rounded stones, of which there were plenty, and to carry them back one per pupil to the school. And as stated, along the way one male teacher (usually the gym-master, who was ex-Army Physical Training Corps) and two of the school's younger, unattached female teachers would extol the glories of the hedgerows, the wonders of the wild flowers and the countryside in general. None of which was of any real interest to Harry Keogh; but he did like the beach, and anything was better than a classroom on a warm, droning afternoon.

"Here," said Jimmy Collins to Harry as they strolled, two abreast, midway in a long line of kids, down through the paths of the dene winding to the sea, "you really ought to pay attention to old Hannant, you know. I mean, not about all that "needing qualifications" stuff—that's up to you—but during lessons gen'rally. He's not a bad 'un, old George, but he could be if he decided you were just taking the mickey."

Harry shrugged dejectedly. "I was daydreaming," he said. "Actually, it's sort of funny. See, when I daydream like that, it's like I can't stop. Only old Hannant shouting—and you give me a jab—pulled me out of it."

Pulled me out . . . the strong hands reaching down into the water . . . to pull me out, or push me under?

Jimmy nodded. "I've seen you like it before, lots of times. Your face goes sort of funny . . ." He looked

66

serious for a moment, then chuckled and gave Harry a playful thump on the shoulder. "Not that that's a big deal—your face is funny *all* the time!"

Harry snorted. "Listen who's talking! Me, funny-looking? I'd play Kirk to your Spock any time! Anyway, what do you mean? I mean, *how* do I look, you know, funny?"

"Well, you just sit very still, all stary-eyed, scared-looking. But not always. Sometimes you look a bit dreamy, like. Anyway, it's like old George said: you just don't seem to be here at all. Actually, you're very weird! I mean, it's true, isn't it? How many friends have you got?"

"I've got you," Harry feebly protested. He knew what Jimmy meant: he was too deep, too quiet. But not studious, not a swot. If he'd been good at lessons, that would perhaps explain it, but he wasn't. Oh, he was clever enough (at least he *felt* he could be clever) if he wanted to concentrate on it. It was just that he found concentration very hard. It was as if sometimes the thoughts he thought weren't really his at all. Complicated thoughts and day-dreams, fancies and phantasms. His mind made up stories for him—whether he wanted it to or not—but stories so detailed they were like memories. The memories of other people. People who weren't here any more. As if his head was an echo-chamber for minds which had . . . gone somewhere else?

"Yes, you've got me for a friend," Jimmy interrupted his train of thought. "And who else?"

Harry shrugged, went on the defensive. "There's Brenda," he said. "And . . . and anyway, who needs a lot of friends? I don't. If people want to be friendly they'll be friendly. If they don't, well that's up to them."

Jimmy ignored the mention of Brenda Cowell, Harry's *grande passion* who lived in the same street. He was into sport, not girls. He'd hang himself from a goal-post before he'd be caught with his arm round a girl in the cinema when the lights went up. "You've got *me!*" he said. "And that's it. As for why I like you—I just dunno."

"Because we don't compete," said Harry, shrewder than his years. "I don't understand sport, so you enjoy explaining it to me—'cos you know I won't argue. And you don't understand me being so, well, quiet—"

"*And* weird," Jimmy interrupted.

"—And so we get along."

"But wouldn't you like more friends?"

Harry sighed. "Well, see, it's like I *have* friends. Up in my head."

"Imaginary friends!" Jimmy scoffed, but not unkindly.

"No, they're more than that," Harry answered. "And they're good friends, too. Of course they are . . . I'm the only friend they've got!"

"*Huh!*" Jimmy snorted. "Oh, you're weird, all right!"

Way up at the head of the column, "Sergeant" Graham Lane came out of the woods into bright sunlight, pausing to hasten on the double rank of kids behind him. This was the narrow mouth of the dene, also the mouth of the stream which had cut its gulley through the sea cliffs. To north and south those cliffs now rose, mainly of sandstone but layered with belts of shale and shingle, and banded with rounded stones; and here the stream passed under an old, rickety wooden bridge. Beyond lay a reedy, weedy marsh or lake of brackish water, only ever replenished by high tides or storms. A path skirted the boggy area towards the sandy beach; and beyond that, there lay the grey North Sea, growing greyer every day with debris from the pits. But today it was blue in the bright sunlight, flecked white here and there by the spray of diving gulls where they fished.

"Right!" Lane called loudly, standing arms akimbo and very much The Man, in his track-suit bottoms and T-shirt on the nearside of the bridge. "Off you go, over the bridge, round the lake and on to the beach. Find your stones and bring 'em back to me—er, no, to Miss Gower—for grading. We've a good half hour, so anyone who fancies can have a quick dip as soon as he's found his stone—*if* you've got your costumes with you. But no nude bathing if you please, remember there are other people on the beach. And stick to the pools left by the sea. You all know what the current's like just here, you young buggers!''

They knew, all right: the current was treacherous, especially on an ebb tide. People were drowned up and down this coast every year, strong swimmers too.

Miss Gower—Religious Instruction and Geography—from her position roughly half-way back along the column, had heard Lane's gravel-voiced, parade-ground instructions. She gave a little grimace. Oh, she understood well enough why she was to grade the stones: it was to allow Lane and Dorothy Hartley a bit of freedom, so they could have a little 'ramble' along the rocks and find themselves a spot for a quick hump! Purely physical, of course, for their minds were totally incompatible.

Miss Gower tilted her nose and sniffed loudly; and now, as the pace of the kids towards the front began to speed up, she called out: "All right, boys—hurry along. And remember this week's wild-life quest. We need some good razor-shells for the natural history room. Whole ones, still hinged together if you can find them. But please—*empty* ones! Let's *not* carry any rotting molluscs back, shall we?''

Farther back, along the path under the trees, where the rear was brought up by Miss Hartley and the monitors of her English and History classes, Stanley Green trudged, hands in pockets, his clever but vicious mind dark with thoughts of violence. He had heard Miss Gower's memo to the kids: no dead shellfish. No, but he'd like to fix it for a dead "Speccy" Keogh! Well, maybe not dead, but severely mauled. It was that dumb kid's fault he had those maths problems to work out tonight. Dumb shit, sitting there like a zombie, fast asleep with his eyes wide open! Well, Big Stanley would open his eyes for him, sure enough—or close them!

"Hands out of your pockets, Stanley," pretty Miss Hartley said from behind him. "It's five months yet to Christmas, not quite cold enough for snow. And why the hunched shoulders? Is something bothering you?"

"No, Miss," he mumbled in answer, his head down.

"Try to enjoy, Stanley," she told him, a little archly. "You're still very young, but if you keep on taking your spite out on the entire world you'll get old very, very quickly." And to herself she added, *like that frustrated bitch, Gertrude Gower . . . !*

Harry Keogh was not a natural born voyeur, just a curious boy. Last Tuesday down here on the beach he'd stumbled on something, and he hoped to do so again today. That was why, after he delivered up his stone to Miss Gower, he checked that no one was watching him and cut away across the dunes and round towards the other side of the reedy marsh. It was only a little more than a hundred yards, but in half that distance he'd already picked up fresh footprints in the sand. A man's and a woman's; and of course he'd seen "Sergeant" and Miss Hartley heading this way, as he'd suspected they might.

Earlier, Harry had conveniently "forgotten" his bathing briefs; this had left him free to pursue his own interests, for Jimmy had subsequently gone off to swim with the rest of the boys. What Harry was looking for was simple: he wanted pointers. Sitting next to Brenda in the cinema and pressing his knee against hers (or, when she leaned close to him, squeezing her upper arm so that his knuckles touched her small breasts through her coat and jumper) was all very well and even sort of exciting, but it seemed pretty tame when compared with the games teachers Lane and Hartley got up to!

Finally, coming over a dune and crouching down he located them sitting on a patch of sand within a semicircle of tall reeds—the same spot where he'd seen them last week. Harry backtracked and quickly chose a place at the crest of another dune where he could lie down and peer through a clump of crabgrass. Last week she (Miss Hartley) had been playing with "Sergeant's" thing, whose size Harry had found extraordinary. Her sweater had been up and "Sergeant" had had one hand up her skirt while the other fondled and tugged at her firm, large-nippled breasts. When he'd come, she had taken a handkerchief and delicately soaked up the glistening semen from his belly and chest. Then she'd kissed him on the tip of his thing— actually *kissed* him there—and started to put her clothes right while he just lay there like a dead man. Harry had tried hard to imagine Brenda Cowell doing that to him, but the picture just wouldn't develop in his mind. It was too alien.

This time it was very different. This time it was going to be what Harry really wanted to see. By the time he got himself settled down on his stomach, "Sergeant" had his track-suit bottoms right off and Miss Hartley's short white, pleated tennis skirt up around her waist. He was trying to get her knickers off, and his thing—even bigger than last week, if that was at all possible—was jerking about on its own like a puppet on some unseen string.

From beyond the dunes, far off down the beach, Harry could hear the kids shouting and laughing where they swam and splashed in one of the big tidal pools; the sun burned the back of his neck and ears where he lay perfectly still, his chin in the palms of his hands; sand fleas jumped only inches from his face. But he allowed nothing

71

to distract him; his eyes remained riveted to the sexual activity of the lovers in their reed bower.

At first she seemed to be fighting "Sergeant," trying to push his hands away. But at the same time she unbuttoned her blouse so that her breasts jutted up naked in the sunlight, their pointed tips unbelievably brown. Harry sensed a sort of panic in her, reflected in his own suddenly pounding blood. It was as if she were hypnotized, with "Sergeant's" penis a snake where it swayed over her belly—mesmerized into lifting her bottom so that her lover could remove her panties, and into bending her knees and parting her legs. In there, she was dark as night—as if she wore a smaller pair of black knickers under her white ones. Black, yes, and then pink where she put her hands under her thighs to open herself for "Sergeant."

Harry caught a glimpse of her, pink, white, curving, dark, brown, but that was all. Climbing between her legs, his incredible penis disappearing into her in a moment, "Sergeant" allowed no more. All that was left were feet and legs and the gym teacher's tight buttocks starting to lunge, shutting off the view. The watching boy gasped, felt himself grown hard inside his pants, rolled on his side to relieve the throbbing of his genitals—and spotted Stanley Green coming over the dunes, scowling, his little pig eyes full of venom!

On the trail of the lovers, Harry had found a perfect razor-shell, both halves intact and hinged together. Now he studiously scraped away sand, "found" the shell, slid down the dune holding it carefully in one hand. Aware that his complexion must be bright red, he turned his face away from Green, pretending not to see him until the youth was almost on top of him. After that there was no avoiding it. No avoiding a showdown, either.

"Hello there, Speccy," the bully growled, approaching in a half-crouch, his arms spread wide, defying Harry to

72

run. "Fancy finding you here, 'stead of pissing about with your mate the big football star. What're we doin' here then, Speccy? Found a pretty shell for Miss Gower, have we?"

"What's it to you?" Harry muttered, trying to sidestep the other, get round him and away.

Green moved closer, snatched the double shell out of Harry's hand. It was a shiny olive colour, old, brittle as a wafer. As he deliberately closed his fist on it, so it crumbled into fragments. "There," he said, his voice full of an unpleasant satisfaction. "You goin' to tell on me, Speccy?"

"No," Harry breathlessly answered, still trying to dodge past, seeing in his mind's eye "Sergeant's" backside going up and down, up and down, in the reed hollow not fifteen yards away on the other side of the dune. "I don't tell on people. And I don't bully, either."

"Bully? You?" Green found it funny. "You couldn't bully a fart out of a frog! All you're good for's falling asleep in class and acting like a big tart! That and getting people in trouble."

"You got yourself in trouble!" Harry protested. "Giggling like that."

"Giggling?" Big Stanley caught his arm, pulled him close. "Giggling? Girls giggle, Speccy. You callin' me a girl, then?"

Harry shook himself loose, put his fists up. Trembling in every limb, he said, "Piss off!"

Green's mouth fell open. "Rude, is it?" he said. Then he shrugged, half-turned, as if to go, and when Harry dropped his guard turned back and caught him a punch at the side of his mouth.

"Ow!" said Harry, spitting blood from a split lip. Off balance, he stumbled and fell; and Green was just readying a kick when "Sergeant" Lane, tucking in his T-shirt, came storming over the top of the dune scarlet with rage and frustration.

"What the bloody hell—?" he roared. He caught the flabbergasted Green by the scruff of his neck, swung him round, aimed his instep accurately at the seat of the bully's pants and let fly. Green yelped as he flew facedown in the sand.

"Up to your usual tricks, are you, Big Stanley?" "Sergeant" shouted. "And who's your victim this time? *What?* Skinny Harry Keogh? By God, you'll be strangling babies next!"

As Green scrambled to his feet, spitting sand, the PT master pushed him in the chest, sent him flying again. "See, it's not so pleasant, Stanley, when you're up against someone who's bigger. And that's how Harry feels about it. Right, Keogh?"

Still holding his mouth, Harry said: "I can look after myself."

Big Stanley, for all that he was a year older than Harry and looked older still, was on the point of blubbering. "I'll tell my dad," he said, scrambling away.

"What?" "Sergeant" laughed, hands on his hips as the bully backed off. "Tell your dad? That fat beer-gut who arm-wrestles for pints with his mates in the Black Bull? Well when you do, ask him who beat him last night and nearly broke his arm!" But Stanley was off and running.

"You all right, Keogh?" Lane helped him to his feet.

"Yes, sir. Mouth's bleeding a bit, that's all."

"Son, you stay away from that one," said the master. "He's a bad lot and he's much too big for you. When I called you skinny, I didn't mean it; it was just to point up the difference in your sizes. Big Stanley's not likely to forget this in a hurry, so look out for him."

"Yes, sir," Harry said again.

"Right, then. Off you go." Lane made as if to return

across the dune, but just then Miss Hartley appeared, looking all prim and proper. *"Shit!"* Harry heard "Sergeant" say under his breath. He wanted to grin but was afraid it would split his lip even more. So turning his face away he made for where the rest of the boys were gathering around Miss Gower, ready for the return trek.

It was the second week in August, a Tuesday evening, and it was hot. It was funny, George Hannant thought as he mopped his brow with a handkerchief, just how hot it could get on an evening like this. You'd think it would cool down, but instead the heat seemed to close in on you. During the day there had been a breeze, not much of a breeze but a breeze; now there was none, it was still as a painting out there. All the heat of the day, soaked into the earth, was coming out now, coming at you from all sides. Hannant mopped again at his brow, his neck, sipped an iced lemonade, knew that that, too, would soon start to run out of him. It was that kind of weather.

He lived alone not far from the school, but on that side of it away from the mine. The other side would have been too depressing, too oppressive. Tonight he had papers and books to mark up, lessons to plan. He didn't feel like doing either one of these things, or anything else for that matter. He could use a drink but . . . the pubs would be full of miners in their caps and shirt-sleeves, their voices coarse and guttural. There was a decent film on at the Ritz, but the sound system was deafening at the front and the courting couples in the back rows invariably annoyed him, their sweaty fumblings distracting his attention from the screen. And anyway, he had that marking to do.

Hannant's home, a semi-detached bungalow on a tiny private estate overlooking the dene and its valley where they narrowed towards the sea, was cut off from the school by the broad swath of a cemetery with its old church, well-kept plots, high perimeter walls. He usually walked through the place to school each morning, back again in the evening. There were benches circling huge, gorgeously-clad horse chestnut trees, their leaves already turning in places. He could always take his books and papers there.

Actually, it wasn't a bad idea. The occasional old-timer, a pensioned-off survivor of the colliery, would get in there to sit with his dog and stick, chewing baccy or drawing on an old pipe—and spitting, of course. Rotten lungs were a legacy of the pit; rotten lungs and spines like eggshells. But apart from the old lads it was usually quiet in there, away from the village's centre, the pubs and cinema, the main road. Oh, when the conkers began to fall there'd be kids to contend with, of course; what's a conker without its child on the end of a length of cord? That was a nice thought and Hannant smiled at it. Someone had once said that from a dog's point of view, a human was a thing to throw sticks. So why shouldn't a horse chestnut have a point of view? Which might well be that boys were for whirling them on strings—and for splitting them wide open. One thing seemed certain, boys weren't for learning maths!

Hannant showered, towelled himself slowly, methodically dry (hurrying would only produce more sweat), put on baggy grey flannels and an open-neck shirt, took up his briefcase and left his home. He walked out of the estate, into the graveyard and along the broad gravel path which bisected it. Squirrels played in the high branches of the brandy-glass-shaped trees, shaking loose the occasional leaf. The sun's rays came slanting down from across the low hills to the west, where that great brazen ball seemed permanently suspended, as if it never would relinquish the day to night. The day had been beautiful; the evening, despite the heat, was incredibly beautiful; and both of them (Hannant weighed the heavy briefcase in his hand)

76

would have been quite wasted. Or if not wasted, spent fruitlessly—if there was a difference. He snorted mirthlessly, picturing young Johnnie Miller in a couple of years' time, "down the pits," hewing coal, relieving his boredom and passing his shift by calculating surface areas of circles. What the hell was the point of it?

And as for kids like Harry Keogh—poor little sod— why, he had neither muscles for the mine nor much of a mind for anything else. Well, *perhaps* a mind, but if so a mind like an iceberg, only its tip showing. As for how much of it lay under the surface—who could say? Hannant only wished he could find a way to capsize the little bugger, while there was still time . . . He had this *feeling* about Keogh: that whatever he was going to do or going to be should begin to show in him now. Like watching a strange seed throw up a shoot, and waiting to see what the flower would be.

But talk of the devil . . . wasn't that Keogh there now, sitting on an old slab in the shade of a tree, his back to the mossy headstone? Yes, it was Keogh; the sun, glinting off his specs where it struck through the hanging foliage, had given him away. He sat there, a book open in his lap, sucking on the chewed stem of a pencil, his head back, lost in thought. And Jimmy Collins nowhere in sight; he'd be at football practice with the rest of the team, up in the recreation ground. But Keogh—he wasn't a member of any sort of team.

Suddenly Hannant felt sorry for him. Sorry, or . . . guilty? Hell, no! Keogh had got away with it for far too long. One of these days he'd go off like that—out of himself—and never make it back again! And yet—

Hannant sighed, let his feet wend him around the plots and between the rows of headstones, along ill-defined paths to where the boy sat. And as he got closer he could see that Harry was once again lost in his own thoughts, daydreaming away in the cool shade of the tree. For some probably irrational reason this made Hannant feel angry—until he saw that the book in Keogh's lap was his maths homework book, which made it seem that he was at least attempting to work out his punishment.

"Keogh? How's it going?" Hannant said, seating himself on the same slab. This corner of the cemetery wasn't unknown to the maths teacher; he'd walked here and sat here himself on many, many occasions. In fact it wasn't that he was the intruder, rather that Keogh was the odd-man-out here. But he doubted if the boy knew or would even understand that.

Harry took the pencil out of his mouth, looked at Hannant, unexpectedly smiled. "Hello, sir . . . Er, sorry?"

Er, sorry! Hannant had been right, the kid just hadn't been there. King of the daydreamers. The Secret Life of Harry Keogh! "I asked you," Hannant tried not to growl, "how it was going?"

"Oh, it's all right, sir."

"Drop the 'sir,' Harry. Save that for the classroom. Out here it makes conversation difficult. What about the problems I gave you? They're what I meant by how's it going."

"The homework questions? I've done them."

"What, here?" Hannant was surprised; and yet thinking about it, it seemed entirely fitting.

"It's quiet here," Harry answered.

"Would you like to show me?"

Harry shrugged. "If you like." He passed over the work-book.

Hannant checked it, was doubly surprised. The work was very neat, almost immaculate. There were two answers, both correct if his memory served him right. Of course the working would be equally important, but he didn't check that just yet. "Where's the third question?"

Harry frowned. "Is that the one with the grease-gun, where—?" he began.

But Hannant impatiently cut him off: "Let's not piss about, Harry Keogh. There are only three questions out of the ten which could possibly qualify. The rest concern themselves with boxes, not circles, not cylinders. Or am I being unjust? The book's a new one to me, too. Give it here."

Harry lowered his head a little, bit his lip, passed the book over. Hannant flipped pages. "The grease-gun," he said. "Yes, this one," and he stabbed at the page with a forefinger. It showed this diagram:

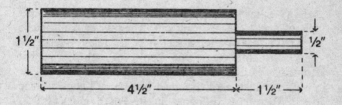

The measurements were internal; barrel and nozzle were cylindrical, full of grease; squeezed dry, how long would the line of grease be?

Harry looked at it. "Didn't think it qualified," he said.

Hannant felt angry. Two out of three wasn't good enough. Three *wrong* answers would almost be better than this crap. "Why don't you just say it was too difficult?" he tried not to bark. "I've had all I can take of bluff for one day. Why not simply admit you can't do it?"

Suddenly the boy looked sick. His face shone with sweat and his eyes seemed a little glazed through the lenses of his spectacles. "I can do it," he slowly answered; then, more quickly, with acid precision: "An idiot could do it! I didn't think it qualified, that's all."

Hannant believed his ears must be deceiving him, that he'd misunderstood the boy's answer. "What about the formula?" he rasped.

"Not required," said the other.

"Shit, Harry! It's pi times the radius squared times length equals contents. That's all you need to know. Look—" and he quickly scribbled in the workbook:

Contents of Barrel: Contents of Nozzle:

$$\frac{3.14159 \times .75 \times .75 \times 4.5}{3.14159 \times .25 \times .25} + \frac{3.14159 \times .25 \times .25 \times 1.5}{3.14159 \times .25 \times .25}$$

He gave Harry the pencil back, said: "There. After that most of it just cancels itself out. The divisor is of course the surface area of a cross-section of the line of grease."

"A waste of time," said Harry, in such a way that Hannant knew it wasn't just rank insubordination, indeed in a voice which hardly seemed like Harry Keogh's voice at all. There was authority in it. For a moment . . . Hannant almost felt intimidated! What was going on behind the kid's glasses, inside his skull? What was the meaning in his not-altogether-there eyes?

"Explain yourself," Hannant demanded. "And make it good!"

Harry glanced at the diagram, not at the teacher's suggested solution. "The answer is three and a half feet," he said. And again there was the same authority in his voice.

As Hannant had said, the text-book was new to him; he hadn't properly worked through it himself yet. But just looking at Keogh he'd be willing to bet the kid was right. Which could only mean—

"You went back to the classroom with Collins after the beach," he accused. "I'd told him to lock up, but before he did you opened my desk, looked up the answers in the answer book there. I wouldn't have believed it of you, Keogh, but—''

"You're wrong," Harry cut him short in that same flat, emotionless, *precise* voice. Now he stabbed at the diagram with *his* finger. "Look at it for yourself. The first two questions required formulas, yes, but not this one. Given a diameter to four decimals, what's the surface area? That requires a formula. Given a surface area to four decimals, what's the radius? *That* requires almost the same formula in reverse. But this? Listen:

"The barrel's diameter is three times greater than the nozzle's. The circle's *area* is therefore nine times greater. The barrel's length is three times greater. Three times nine is twenty-seven. The barrel contains twenty-seven times as much grease as the nozzle. Barrel and nozzle together therefore contain twenty-eight nozzles' worth. The nozzle is one and a half inches long. Twenty-eight times one and a half equals forty-two. And forty-two inches equals three and a half feet, sir . . .''

Hannant stared at the boy's expressionless, almost vacant face. He stared at the diagram in the book. His mind whirled and it seemed that a cold wind blew on his spine, causing him to shiver. What the hell—? For Christ's sake, *he* was the maths teacher, wasn't he? But there was no fighting Keogh's logic. The question hadn't needed formulae, hadn't needed maths at all! It was mental arithmetic—to someone who understood circles. To someone who could see past the trees to the wood. And of course his answer was, must be, right! If Hannant threw his formulae away, he would have been able to do it too—with a little thought. But Keogh's application had been instantaneous. His scorn had been real!

And now Hannant knew that if he didn't play this right, he'd probably lose this boy right here and now. He also knew that if that happened, he wasn't the only one who would lose. There *was* a mind in there, and it had . . . hell, potential! Whatever Hannant's confusion, however great, he must somehow retain his authority.

He forced a grin, said: "Very good! Except I wasn't just checking out your IQ, Harry Keogh. It was to see whether or not you knew your formulae. But now you've really puzzled me. Seeing as how you're so smart, how come your classwork has always been so lousy?"

Harry stood up. His movements were stiff, automatic almost. "Can I go now, sir?"

Hannant stood up too, shrugged and stepped aside. "Your free time's your own," he said. "But when you get five minutes, you might still bone up on your formulae."

Harry walked off, his back straight, movements stiff. A few paces away he turned and looked back. A beam of sunlight striking through the trees caught his glasses, turning his eyes to stars. "Formulae?" he said in that new, strange voice. "I could give you formulae you haven't even dreamed of."

And as the cold chill struck at his spine once more, Hannant somehow knew for a certainty that Keogh wasn't just bragging.

Then . . . the maths master wanted to shout at the boy, run at him, even strike him. But his feet seemed rooted to the spot. All of the energy had gone out of him. He'd lost this round—completely. Trembling, he sat down again on the slab, leaning back weakly against the headstone as Harry Keogh walked away. He leaned there for a moment—then jerked forward, started upright, threw himself away from the grave. He tripped and sprawled on the close-cropped grass. Keogh was disappearing, lost among the markers.

The evening was warm—no, it was damned hot, even now—but George Hannant felt cold as death. It was in the air, in his heart, freezing him. Here, in this place, of all places. And it came to him now just exactly where and when he had heard someone speak like Harry Keogh before, with his authority, his precision and logic. Thirty long years ago, almost, when Hannant had been little more than a lad himself. And the man had been more than his peer. He had been his hero, almost his god.

Still trembling he got to his feet, picked up Keogh's books and put them in his briefcase, then backed carefully away from the grave.

Cut into the headstone, lichened over in parts, the legend was simple and George knew it by heart:

JAMES GORDON HANNANT
13 June 1875–11 Sept. 1944
Master at Harden Boys' School
for Thirty Years, Headmaster
for Ten, now he Numbers
among the Hosts
of Heaven.

The epitaph had been the Old Man's idea of a joke. His principal subject, like that of his son after him, had been maths. But he had been far better at it than George would ever be.

Chapter Three

THERE WAS ONE SHORT MATHS LESSON FIRST THING ON THE following morning, but before then George Hannant had done some soul-searching, a little rationalizing; so that by the time all the kids were working away and the room was quiet bar the scratching of pens and rustling of papers, he was satisfied that he had the right answer to what had seemed the night before an incident or occurrence of some moment. Keogh was obviously one of those special people who could get right down to the roots of things, a *thinker* as opposed to a *doer*. And a thinker whose thoughts, while they invariably ran contrary to the general stream, nevertheless ran true.

If you could get him interested in a subject deeply enough to make him want to do something with it, then he'd doubtless do something quite extraordinary. Oh, he would still make errors in simple addition and subtraction—two plus two could still on occasion come out five—but solutions which were invisible to others would be instantly obvious to him. That was why Hannant had seen in the lad a likeness to his own father; James G. Hannant, too, had had that same sort of intuitive knack, had been a *natural* mathematician. And he too had had little time for formulae.

And equally obvious to Hannant was the fact that he had indeed fanned some spark into flame in Keogh's brain, for it was his pleasure to note that the boy seemed to be working quite hard—or at least he had been, for the first fifteen minutes or so of the period. After that—well, of course, he was daydreaming again. But when Hannant crept up behind him—lo and behold!—the questions he'd set were all answered, and correctly, however insubstantial the working. It would be interesting later in the week, when they got onto basic trigonometry, to see what Keogh would do with that. Now that the circle held little of mystery for him, perhaps he'd take an interest in the triangle.

But there was still something which puzzled George Hannant, and for the answer to that he must now go to Jamieson, the headmaster. Leaving the boys to work alone for a few minutes—with the customary warning about their behaviour in his absence—he went to the head's study.

"Harry Keogh?" Howard Jamieson seemed a little taken aback. "How did he do in the Technical College examination?" He took out a slim file from one of his desk drawers, flipped through it, looked up. "I'm afraid Keogh didn't take the examination," he said. "Apparently he was down with hay fever or some such. Yes, here it is: hay fever, three weeks ago; he had two days off school. Unfortunately the exams took place in Hartlepool on the second day of Keogh's absence. But why do you ask, George? Do you think he'd have stood a chance?"

"I think he'd have sailed it," Hannant answered, frank to the point of being blunt.

Jamieson seemed surprised. "Bit late in the day, isn't it?"

"To worry about it? I suppose it is."

"No, I meant this interest in Harry Keogh. I didn't know you much approved of him. Wait—" He took out another file, a thicker one, this time from a cabinet. "Last year's reports," he said, checking through the file. And this time he wasn't at all surprised. "Thought so. According to this none of your colleagues here give Keogh a cat in hell's chance at anything—and that includes you, George!"

"Yes," Hannant's neck reddened a little, "but that was last year. Also, the Technical College exams are aimed more at basic intelligence than academic knowledge. If you were to give our Harry Keogh an IQ test I think you'd be in for a surprise. Where maths is concerned, anyway. It's all instinct, all intuition—but it's there, sure enough."

Jamieson nodded. "Well, it's something when a master takes more than a grudging interest in a Harden boy," he said. "And that's not to put anyone down, not even the kids themselves—but they do have a hell of a handicap here, in background and environment, I mean. Do you know how many of our boys got through that exam, by the way? Three! Three out of that age group—which is to say one in sixty-five!"

"Four, if Harry Keogh had taken it."

"Oh?" Jamieson wasn't convinced. But he was impressed, at least. "All right," he said, "let's assume you're right about the maths side of it. And in fact you *are* right that the test is a measure of basic intelligence rather than knowledge assimilated parrot-fashion. So what about the other subjects? According to these reports Keogh is a habitual failure in just about any subject you care to mention! Bottom of his class in many of them."

Hannant sighed, nodded, said: "Look, I'm sorry I've

wasted your time on this one. Anyway, the question hardly arises since he didn't sit the exam in the first place. It's just that I feel it's a shame, that's all. I think the kid has potential.''

"Tell you what," said Jamieson, coming round his desk and moving towards the door with his hand on Hannant's shoulder. "Send him to see me during the afternoon. I'll have a word with him, see what I think. No, wait—maybe I can be a little more constructive than that. Instinctive or intuitive mathematician, is he? Very well—"

He returned to his desk, took a pen and quickly scribbled something on a blank sheet of A4. "There you go," he said. "See what he makes of that. Let him work at it through the lunch break. If he comes up with an answer, then I'll see him and we'll see how we go from there."

Hannant took the sheet of A4 and went out into the corridor, closing the door behind him. He looked at what the head had written, shook his head in disappointment. He folded the sheet and pocketed it, then took it out again, opened it and stared at it. On the other hand . . . maybe it was exactly the sort of thing Keogh could handle. Hannant was sure that *he* could do it—with a bit of thought and a spot of trial and error—but if Keogh could work it out, then they'd be on to something. His case for the boy would be proven. In the event Keogh failed, then Hannant would simply stop worrying about him. There were other kids who were equally deserving of his attention, he was sure . . .

At 1:30 P.M. sharp Hannant knocked on Jamieson's door, was through it on the instant the head called him in. Jamieson himself was just back from lunch, hardly settled down. He stood up as Hannant crossed the floor of his study, shook out the folds of the A4 and handed it to him.

87

"I did as you suggested," Hannant told the head, breathlessly. "This is Keogh's solution."

The headmaster quickly scanned the scribbled text of his original problem:

Magic Square:
   A square is divided into 16 equal, smaller squares. Each small square contains a number, 1 to 16 inclusive. Arrange them so that the sum of each of the four lines and each of the four columns, and the diagonals, is one and the same number.

The answer, in pencil—including what looked like a false start—had been drawn beneath the question and was signed Harry Keogh:

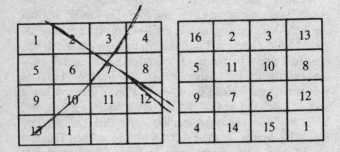

Jamieson stared at it, stared harder, opened his mouth to speak but said nothing. Hannant could see him rapidly adding up the columns, lines, diagonals—could almost hear his brain ticking over. "This is . . . *very* good," Jamieson finally said.

"It's better than that," Hannant told him. "It's perfect!"

The head blinked at him. "Perfect, George? But all

magic squares are perfect. That's the lure of them. That's their magic!''

"Yes," Hannant agreed, "but there's perfect and there's perfect. You asked for columns, lines, diagonals all totalling the same. He's given you that and far more. The corners total the same. The four squares in the middle total the same. The four blocks of four total the same. Even the opposing middle numbers at the sides come out the same! And if you look closer, that's not the end of it. No, it *is* perfect.''

Jamieson checked again, frowned for a moment, then smiled delightedly. And finally: "Where's Keogh now?"

"He's outside. I thought you might like to see him . . .''

Jamieson sighed, sat down at his desk. "All right, George, let's have your prodigy in, shall we?''

Hannant opened the door, called Keogh in.

Harry entered nervously, fidgeted where he stood before the head's desk.

"Young Keogh," said the head, "Mr. Hannant tells me you've a thing for numbers."

Harry said nothing.

"This magic square, for instance. Now, I've fiddled about with such things—purely for my own amusement, you understand—ever since, oh, since I was about your age. But I don't think I ever came up with a solution as good as this one. It's quite remarkable. Did anyone help you with it?''

Harry looked up, looked straight into Jamieson's eyes. For a moment he looked—scared? Possibly, but in the next moment he went ôn the defensive. "No, sir. No one helped me.''

Jamieson nodded. "I see. So where's your rough work? I mean, one doesn't just guess something as clever as this, does one?''

"No, sir," said Harry. "My rough work is there, crossed out."

Jamieson looked at the paper, scratched his very nearly bald head, glanced at Hannant. Then he stared at Keogh. "But this is simply a box with the numbers laid in in their numerical sequence. I can't see how—"

"Sir," Harry stopped him, "it seemed to me that was the logical way to start. When I got that far I could see what needed doing."

Again the head and the maths teacher exchanged glances.

"Go on, Harry," said the head, nodding.

"See, sir, if you just write the numbers in, like I did, all the big numbers go to the right and to the bottom. So I asked myself: how can I get half of them over from right to left and half of them from the bottom to the top? And: how can I do both at the same time?"

"That seems . . . logical." Jamieson scratched his head again. "So what did you do?"

"Pardon?"

"I said, what—did—you—*do*, boy!" Jamieson hated having to repeat himself to pupils. They should hang on his every word.

Harry was suddenly pale. He said something but it came out a croak. He coughed and his voice dropped an octave or two. When he spoke again he no longer sounded like a small boy at all. "It's there in front of you," he said. "Can't you see it for yourself?"

Jamieson's eyes bugged and his jaw dropped, but before he could explode Harry added: "I reversed the diagonals, that's all. It was the obvious answer, the only logical answer. Any other way's a game of chance, trial and error. And hit and miss isn't good enough. Not for me . . ."

Jamieson stood up, flopped down again, pointed an enraged finger at the door. "Hannant, get—that—boy—*out*—of—here! Then come back in and speak to me."

Hannant grabbed Keogh's arm, dragged him out into the corridor. He had the feeling that if he hadn't physically taken hold of the boy, then Keogh might well have fainted. As it was he propped him up against the wall, hissed *"Wait here!"* and left him there looking slightly dazed and sick.

Back inside Jamieson's study, Hannant found the headmaster soaking sweat from his brow with a large sheet of school blotting paper. He was staring fixedly at Harry's solution and muttering to himself. "Reversed the diagonals! *Hmm!* And so he has!" But as Hannant closed the door behind him Jamieson looked up and grinned somewhat feebly. He had obviously regained his self control and continued to dab away at the sweat on his forehead and neck. "This bloody heat!" he said, waving a limp hand and indicating that Hannant should take a seat.

Hannant, whose shirt was sticking to his back beneath his jacket, said, "I know. It's murder, isn't it? The school's like a furnace—and it's just as bad for the kids." He remained standing.

Jamieson saw his meaning and nodded. "Yes, well that's no excuse for insolence—or arrogance."

Hannant knew he should keep quiet but couldn't. "*If* he was being insolent," he said. "Thing is, I believe he was simply stating a fact. It was the same when I crossed him yesterday. It seems that as soon as you crowd him he gets his back up. The lad's brilliant—but he'd like to pretend not to be! He does his damnedest to keep it hidden."

"But why? Surely that's not normal. Most boys of his age like the chance to show off. Is it simply that he's shy—or does it go deeper than that?"

Hannant shook his head. "I don't know. Let me tell you about yesterday."

When he was through, the head said: "Almost exactly parallel to what we've just seen."

"That's right."

Jamieson grew thoughtful. "If he really is as clever as you seem to think he is—and certainly he seems to have an intuitive knack in some directions—then I'd hate to be the one to deprive him of a chance to get somewhere in life." He sat back. "Very well, it's decided. Keogh missed the exams through no fault of his own, so . . . I'll speak to Jack Harmon at the Tech., see if we can fix up some sort of private examination for him. Of course I can't promise anything, but—"

"It's better than nothing," Hannant finished it for him. "Thanks, Howard."

"Fine, fine. I'll let you know how I get on."

Nodding, Hannant went out into the corridor where Keogh was waiting.

Over the next two days Hannant tried to put Keogh to the back of his mind but it didn't work. In the middle of lessons, or at home during the long autumn evenings, even occasionally in the dead of night, the boy's young-old face would be there, hovering on the periphery of Hannant's awareness. Friday night saw the teacher awake at 3:00 A.M., all his windows open to let in what little breeze there was, prowling the house in his pyjamas. He had come awake with that picture in his mind of Harry Keogh, clutching Jamieson's folded sheet of A4, heading off across the schoolyard of milling boys in the direction of the back gate under the stone archway; then of the boy crossing the dusty summer lane and passing in through the iron gates of the cemetery. And Hannant had believed that he knew where Harry was going.

And suddenly, though the night had not grown noticeably cooler, Hannant had felt chilly in a way he was now becoming used to. It could only be a psychic chill, he suspected, warning him that something was dreadfully wrong. There *was* something uncanny about Keogh, certainly, but what it was defied conjecture—or rather, challenged it. One thing was certain: George Hannant hoped to God the kid could pass whatever exams Howard Jamieson and Jack Harmon of Hartlepool Tech. cooked up for him. And it was no longer simply that he wanted the boy to realize his full potential. No, it was more basic than that. Frankly, he wanted Keogh out of here, out of the school, away from the other kids. Those perfectly ordinary, *normal* boys at Harden Secondary Modern.

A bad influence? Hardly that! Who could he possibly influence—in what way?—when the rest of the kids generally considered him a weed? A corruption, then, a taint which might somehow spread—like the proverbial rotten apple at the bottom of the barrel? Perhaps. And yet that simile didn't exactly fit either. Or maybe, in a way, it did. For after all, it makes little difference that an apple can't appreciate its own rottenness: the corruption spreads anyway. Or was that too strong? How could it even be possible that there was something, well, *wrong* with Harry Keogh, something of which even he was unaware or lacked understanding? Actually the whole thing was becoming distinctly ridiculous! And yet . . . what was it about Keogh which so worried Hannant? What was *in* him, seeking a way out? And why did Hannant feel that when it finally emerged it would be terrible?

It was then that Hannant decided to investigate Keogh's background, discover what he could of the boy's past. Perhaps that was where the trouble lay. And then again, maybe there was nothing at all and the whole affair was simply something spawned of Hannant's own overactive imagination. It could be the heat, the fact that he was sleeping badly, the unending, unrewarding, repetitious routine of the school—any or all of these things. It *could* be—but why then did that inner voice keep insisting that

Keogh was different? And why on occasion would he find Keogh staring at him with eyes which might well be those of his own dead and buried father . . . ?

Ten days and two Tuesdays later, tragedy struck. It happened when the boys, PTI Graham Lane, and the Misses Dorothy Hartley and Gertrude Gower went off on their end-of-day stone-gathering trek to the beach. "Sergeant," ostensibly to collect specimens of some rare wild flower, but more likely to impress his lady love, had climbed the beetling cliffs. When he had been more than half-way up the treacherous face of the cliff, projecting stones had given way under his feet, pitching him down to the boulder- and scree-clad beach below. He had tried to cling to the crumbling surface even as he fell, but then his feet had struck a narrow ledge, breaking it away, and he had been set spinning free in air. He had landed on his chest and face, crushing both and killing himself outright.

The affair was made more especially gruesome in light of the fact that "Sergeant" and Dorothy Hartley, only the night before, had announced their engagement. They were to have been married in the spring. As it was, the following Friday saw "Sergeant" buried. It would have been better for him, Hannant later remembered thinking, as he watched Lane's coffin being lowered into a fresh plot of earth in the old cemetery, if he'd stayed in the Army and taken his chances there.

Afterwards, there had been sandwiches, cakes and coffee in the staff-room at the school, and a nip of something stronger for those who fancied it. And of course, Dorothy Hartley to console as best she could be consoled. So that none of the teachers had been there to see the grave filled in, or, after the gravedigger was through and the wreaths lay in position, the last lone mourner where he sat on a slab nearby, chin in the palms of his hands and lacklustre eyes staring from behind his spectacles, fastened mourn-fully—curiously? expectantly?—upon the mound.

Meanwhile, Howard Jamieson had not been remiss in seeking to get Harry Keogh a post-examination place at the Tech. in Hartlepool; or if not an actual place, at least the opportunity to win one for himself. The private exami-nation—in the main an IQ test consisting of questions designed to measure verbal, numerical and spatial percep-tion and aptitude—was to take place at the college in Hartlepool under the direct supervision of John ("Jack") Harmon, the headmaster. Wind of it had got out, however, along the Harden Boys' School grapevine, and Harry had become something of a target for various jibes and japes.

He was no longer simply "Speccy" for instance but had acquired other nicknames including "the Favourite"—which meant that Big Stanley had been putting it about that Harry was some sort of teacher's or headmaster's pet. And with the help of a twisted sort of logic, of which Stanley was a past-master—not to mention the threat in his pudgy but hard-knuckled fists—it hadn't taken long to convince even the more liberal-minded lads that there was definitely some-thing fishy about Keogh's belated emergence as someone who was a bit more than just "ordinary."

Why, for instance, should Speccy—or "the Favourite" —why should he alone get this crack at a special Tech. examination? Other kids had been sick that day, too, hadn't they? And were they being given special treatment? No they weren't! It was just because that dreamy little fart got on well with the teachers, that was all. Who was it went digging up stupid, smelly shells for that old bag Miss Gower? Speccy Keogh, that was who—and hadn't old Sergeant always used to stick up for him? Of course he had! And now, since he'd suddenly started being a bit clever at maths and so on, even snotty old Hannant was on his side. Oh, he was "the Favourite," all right—the four-eyed little fart. But not with Big Stanley Green he wasn't!

It had all sounded very logical; to which add the now sullen voices of the others who, through no fault of their own, had missed the exam, and soon the bully had a fair-sized crowd of like-minded boys on his side. Even Jimmy Collins seemed of the opinion that something "niffed a bit."

Then Tuesday came around, one week exactly after the gym-teacher's death, when once more the school trooped down to the beach for what was hopefully to be the last stone-gathering expedition of the season. The idea had been a novelty at first, but now boys and teachers alike were fed up with it; Lane's death had soured it for everyone. Miss Gower was present, as usual, with Jean Tasker of Science (a little older than Gower but much less frumpish) taking the place of Dorothy Hartley who had been given leave of absence. George Hannant was also there, replacing Graham Lane.

As usual, after the stones had been collected and piled up, the boys were allowed to do their own thing for an hour before carrying their booty back to the school. "Gee-gee" Gower, (as her pupils sometimes called her, referring to her equine aspect as much as her initials) was giving instructions to a bunch of reluctant non-swimmers in a tidal pool; George Hannant and Jean Tasker stood down by the edge of the sea, gathering shells and bright pebbles, chatting and generally passing the time of day. That was when Big Stanley, who could no longer contain his vindictiveness, saw his opportunity to "teach Keogh a lesson."

Harry had been off on his own, head down, hands behind his back, beachcombing; but as he returned to the pile of stones he looked up and spotted Green and a large handful of the others waiting for him.

"Well, well!" sneered the bully, pushing his way to the

front of the crowd. "And if it isn't our little teacher's pet—little skinny Speccy Keogh—with a fistful of pretty shells for daft old Gee-gee! How's things then, Speccy? How d'you fancy your chances with this 'special' exam they've fixed it for you to take, eh?"

"Reckon you'll pass it, do you then, Speccy?" said another, his voice hard-edged. "They'll push you through it, will they?"

"Oh, he's 'favourite,' all right!" said a third. "What, him? Teacher's pet and all—how can he fail?"

Jimmy Collins, towelling himself dry as he came up the beach, saw the mood of the crowd at once but said nothing. Instead he went to the rear of the group, wrapped a towel round his waist and started to dress.

"Well?" Green prodded Harry in the chest. "How about it, four-eyes? Are the nice teachers going to let you pass your little exam, then—so you can get away from all us nasty rough boys and go to school in Hartlepool with the rest of the fairies?"

Harry staggered backward from the other's shoving, dropping the shells he'd collected. Big Stanley gave a *whoop*, jumped forward, crushed them to dust under his shoes and ground them into the sand. Harry swayed, looked sick, began to turn away. His eyes were suddenly misty behind his spectacles; his face, which wasn't tanned like the faces of the rest, turned even paler.

"Shitty little cowardly teacher's pet!" Green crowed maliciously. "Old Man Jamieson's little 'Favourite,' eh, Speccy? And is that you crying, then? Tears, is it? Wetting ourself, are we? You four-eyed little—"

"Shut it, shithead!" Harry growled, turning back and facing the bully. "You're ugly enough without me making it worse!"

"Wha—?" Green couldn't believe his ears. What was that Keogh had said? No, it couldn't have been. Why, it hadn't even sounded like him. He must have a frog in his throat, or he was all choked up with fear.

"Whyn't you leave him alone?" said Jimmy Collins, pushing through the crowd. Three or four of them grabbed him, held him back.

"Stay out of it, Jimmy," said Harry in his new, gritty voice. "I'm all right."

"All right, is it?" cried Big Stanley. "I'll say you're *not*, Speccy my son. I'll say you're—in—the—*shit!*"

With his last word he swung his fist for the smaller boy's head. Harry ducked easily, stepped forward, jabbed with a straight arm, fingers straight and stiff. Big Stanley folded in the middle, jack-knifed, his face coming down on Harry's knee—which was coming up! The crack was like a pistol shot. Green straightened up and flew backward, his arms straight out from his shoulders. And down he crashed on the sand.

Harry stepped close. Seconds passed but Green just lay there. Then he sat up, shook his head groggily. His nose was the wrong shape, bleeding profusely; his eyes were glassy behind welling tears of pain. "You . . . you . . . *you!*" he spat blood.

Harry bent over him, showed him a white, knobbly fist. "You what?" he growled, the corner of his mouth lifting from his teeth. "Go on, Bully, say something. Give me a reason to hit you again."

Green said nothing, reached up a trembling hand to touch his broken nose, his split mouth. Then he started to cry real tears.

But Harry wasn't finished with him. He wanted him to remember. "Listen, shithead," he said. "If ever—if you ever once—call me Speccy or Favourite or any other bloody funny name again—if you even *speak* to me, I'll hit you so hard you'll be shitting teeth for a month! Have you got that, shithead?"

Big Stanley turned on his side in the sand and cried even harder.

Harry looked up, glared at the rest of them. He took off his spectacles, put them in a pocket, scowled. He didn't squint, didn't look as though he'd needed the glasses at all. His eyes were bright as marbles, full of sparks. "What I said to this shit goes for the rest of you. Or if any of you fancies his chances here and now——?"

Jimmy Collins stepped beside him. "Or any two of you?" he said. The crowd was silent. As a man, all their mouths were wide, their eyes even wider. Slowly they turned away, began talking, nervously laughing, fooling about as if nothing had happened. It was over—and strangely, they were all glad it was over.

"Harry," said Jimmy quietly out of the corner of his mouth, "I never seen anything like that! Not ever. Why, you did it like—like—like a man! Like a grown man! Like old "Sergeant" when he used to shadow-fight in the gym. Unarmed combat, he called it." He elbowed his pal in the ribs—but gingerly. "Hey, you know something?"

"What?" Harry asked, trembling all over, his voice his own again.

"You're weird, you are, Harry Keogh. You're really weird!"

Harry Keogh sat his examination a fortnight later.

The weather had changed in the first week of September, since when it had grown progressively worse until the sky seemed permanently filled with rain. It rained on the day of the examination, too, a downpour which washed the windows of the head's study where Harry sat at a huge desk with his papers and pens.

Jack Harmon himself invigilated, seated behind his own desk, reading the minutes of (and adding his comments and recommendations to) the observations and notes of the last Staff Meeting. But while he worked, occasionally he would look up, glance at the boy, wonder about him.

Actually, Harmon didn't particularly want Harry Keogh at the Tech. Not for any personal motive—not even because he half felt that he'd been pushed into this unheard-of situation: that of being obliged to test a boy who had, quite simply, already missed his chance—but because it might set an unfortunate precedent. Time was precious enough without extra work of this sort being found or manufactured. Exams were exams: they were held annually and the colliery boys who passed them had the opportunity to finish their final years of schooling here, where perhaps they could go on to better things than their fathers had known. The system was long-established and worked very well. But this new thing—Howard Jamieson pushing the Keogh boy forward like this . . .

On the other hand, the headmaster at Harden Modern Boys' *was* a proven friend from the old days, and it was also true that Harmon owed him a favour or two. Even so, when Jamieson had first approached him on the subject, Harmon had been cool about it; but the other had persisted. Finally Harmon's curiosity had been aroused: he'd wanted to see this 'teenage prodigy' for himself. At the same time, however, and as stated, he had not wanted to set any sort of precedent. He had looked for an easy way out and believed he'd found one. He himself had set the questions, choosing only the most difficult problems from the last six years' examination papers. No boy of Keogh's educational background could possibly hope to answer them (not all of them, anyway, and certainly not correctly) but while the examination itself would almost constitute a farce, still Harmon would be able to look at examples of Keogh's work and so satisfy his curiosity. Jamieson, too, would have been mollified, at least in respect of his request that the boy be tested; Keogh's failure would destroy the credibility of any further, like requests in the future. And so Jack Harmon invigilated, keeping an eye on the boy while he worked at the papers.

An hour had been allowed for each subject; there were to be ten-minute breaks between subjects; tea and biscuits would be served right here in the head's study during the breaks, and a staff toilet was right next door. The first paper had been the English exam, following which Keogh had sat quietly drinking his tea, staring pallidly at the rain beyond the windows. Now he was half-way into the maths paper—or should be. That was a moot point.

Harmon had watched him. The boy's pen had seemed barely to scratch the answer paper; or if it had, then it was during those moments when the Tech's headmaster had been busy with his own work. Oh, the boy had been hard enough at it through the first hour, the first test: the English paper had seemed to interest him, he'd done a lot of frowning and pen-chewing and had written and rewritten—indeed he'd still been working when Harmon had called time—but the maths paper obviously had him stumped. He made the occasional, sporadic attempt at it, Harmon must give him that much (and there he went again, even now, his pen flying, scratching away) but after only a moment or two he'd sit back, stare out of the windows, go pale and quiet again, almost as if he were exhausted.

Then he would appear to pick up, glance at the next question, scribble away at frantic speed, as if inspired—before pausing again, exhausted—and so on. Harmon could well understand his tension or anxiety or whatever it was: the questions were *very* difficult. There were six of them, each one of which would normally take at least a quarter of an hour to complete—and only then if the boy's aptitude was well in advance of his years and present level of education at Harden Modern.

What Harmon couldn't understand was why he bothered at all, why he kept making these furious attacks on the paper, only to sit back each time after a little while, frustrated and tired. Wasn't it obvious to him that he couldn't win? What were his thoughts as he gazed out of the windows? Where *was* he when his face took on that blank, almost vacant expression?

Maybe Harmon should stop this now, put an end to it. Plainly the lad wasn't getting anywhere . . .

They were now (the headmaster glanced at his watch) thirty-five minutes into the maths section. As the boy sat back yet again, his arms dangling and his eyes half-closed behind the lenses of his spectacles, so Harmon quietly stood up and approached him from the rear. Outside, the rain was blowing in gusts against the windowpanes; in here, an old clock ticked on the wall, pacing the head's breathing. He glanced over Keogh's shoulder, not really knowing what he expected to see.

His glance became a fixed stare. He blinked, blinked again, and his eyes opened wide. His eyebrows drew together as he craned his neck the better to see. If Keogh heard his gasp of astonishment he made no sign, remained seated, continued to gaze blearily at the rain rivering the windows.

Harmon took a step backwards away from the boy, turned and went back to his desk. He seated himself, slid open a drawer, held his breath and took out the answers to the maths section. Keogh had not only answered the questions, he'd got them right! All of them! That last frenzied burst of work had been him working on the sixth and last. Moreover he'd accomplished it with the very minimum of rough work and hardly any use at all of the familiar and accepted formulae.

Finally the head allowed himself a deep, deep breath, gawped again at the printed answer sheets in his hand—the masses of complicated workings and neatly resolved solutions—then carefully placed them back in the drawer and slid it shut. He could hardly credit it. If he hadn't been sitting here through the entire examination, he'd swear the boy must have cheated. But quite obviously, that was not the case. So . . . what did Harmon have here?

"Intuitive," Howard Jamieson had called the boy, an "intuitive mathematician." Very well, Harmon would see how well (if at all) this intuition of his worked with the next paper. Meanwhile—

The headmaster rubbed his chin and stared thoughtfully at the back of Keogh's head. He must speak to both Jamieson and young George Hannant (who'd first brought the boy to Jamieson's attention, apparently) at greater length. These were early days, of course, but . . . intuition? It seemed to Harmon that there just might be another word for what Keogh was, one which the teachers at Harden simply hadn't thought to apply. Harmon could well understand that, for he too was reluctant.

The word in Harmon's mind was "genius," and if this was so then certainly there was a place for Keogh at the Tech. Harmon would soon discover if he was right.

And of course he was. It was only in his application that he was wrong. Keogh's "genius" lay in an entirely different direction.

Jack Harmon was short, fat, hirsute and generally apish. He would be quite ugly except that he exuded a friendliness and an aura of well-being that cut right through his outer guise to show the man inside for what he really was: one of Nature's truest gentlemen. He also had a quite brilliant mind.

In Harmon's younger days he had known George Hannant's father. That was when J. G. Hannant had been head at Harden and Harmon had taught elementary Maths and Science at a tiny school in Morton, another colliery village. On and off over the intervening years he'd met the younger Hannant and so watched him grow up. It had come as no great surprise to him to learn that George Hannant, too, had finally come into "the business" —teaching must be as much a part of him as it had been of his father.

"Young Hannant," Harmon had always thought of him. Ridiculous—for of course George had been a teacher now for almost twenty years!

Harmon had called the maths teacher down from his own school to Hartlepool in order to talk to him about Harry Keogh. It was the Monday following Keogh's "examination" and they had met at the Tech. Harmon lived close by and had taken the younger man home with him for a lunch of cold meats and pickles. His wife, knowing it was business, served the food then went shopping while the two men ate and talked. Harmon opened with an apology:

"I hope it isn't inconvenient for you, George, to be called away like this? I know Howard keeps you pretty busy up there."

Hannant nodded. "No problem at all. 'Himself' is standing in for me this afternoon. He likes to take a crack at it now and then. Says he 'misses' the classroom. I'm sure he'd swap that study of his—and the admin that goes with it—for a classroom full of boys any time!"

"Oh, he would, he would! Wouldn't we all?" Harmon grinned. "But it's the money, George, it's the money! And I suppose the prestige has a little to do with it, too. You'll know what I mean when you're a 'head' in your own right. Now then, tell me about Keogh. You're the one who discovered him, aren't you?"

"I think it's truer to say he discovered himself," Hannant

answered. "It's as if he's only recently woken up to his own potential. A late starter, so to speak."

"But one who's all set to overtake the rest of the runners in a flash, eh?"

"Ah!" said Hannant. Since Harmon hadn't yet said anything about the results of Keogh's tests, he had half-feared that the boy had failed. Being called down here had reassured him a little, and now Harmon's remark about Keogh "overtaking the rest" had clinched it. "He passed then?" Hannant smiled.

"No," Harmon shook his head. "He failed—miserably! The English paper let him down. He tried hard, I believe, but—"

Hannant's smile faded. His shoulders slumped a little.

"—but I'm taking him anyway," Harmon finished, grinning again as Hannant's wide eyes came up once more to meet his. "On the strength of what he did with the other papers."

"What he did with them?"

Harmon nodded. "I admit that I gave him the most difficult questions I could find—and he made mincemeat of them! If he has any fault at all, I'd say it was his unorthodox approach—*if* that in itself is a fault. It's just that he seems to dispense with all the customary formulae."

Hannant nodded, made no comment, thought: *I know exactly what you mean!* And when he saw that Harmon was waiting, he said out loud, "Oh, yes—he does that."

"I thought it might just be Maths," said the other, "but it was just the same with the other paper. Call it 'IQ' or 'spatial' or whatever, it's mainly designed to test the *potential* of the intellect. I found his answer to one of the questions especially interesting; not the answer itself, you understand, which was absolutely correct anyway, but the way he arrived at it. It concerned a triangle."

"Oh, yes?" *Ah! Trig,* Hannant thought, forking a piece

of chicken into his mouth. *I wondered how he'd do with that.*

"Of course, it could have been solved with simple trigonometry," (Harmon had almost read his mind,) "or even visually—it was *that* simple. Indeed it was the only simple question in the batch. Here, let me show you:"

He pushed his plate aside, took out a pen and sketched on a paper napkin:

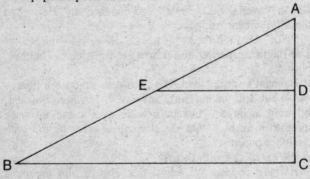

"Where AD is half AC, and AE is half AB, how much greater is the larger triangle than the smaller?"

Hannant dotted the diagram so:

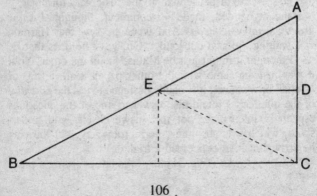

and said: "Four times greater. Visual, as you said."

"Right. But Keogh simply wrote down the answer. No dotted lines, just the answer. I stopped him and asked: 'How did you do that?' He shrugged and said: 'A half times a half is a quarter—the smaller triangle is one quarter as great as the big one.'"

Hannant smiled, shrugged. "That's typical of Keogh," he said. "It's what first attracted me to him. He ignores formulae, jumps gaps in the normal reasoning process, leaps from terminal to terminal."

Harmon's expression hadn't changed. It was a very serious expression. "What formulae?" he asked, "Has he done Trig yet?"

Hannant's smile slipped. He frowned, paused with his fork half-way to his mouth. "No, we were just starting."

"So he wouldn't have known this formula anyway?"

"No, that's true," Hannant's frown deepened.

"But he does now—and so do we!"

"Sorry?" Hannant had been left behind somewhere.

Harmon went on: "I said to him, 'Keogh, that's all very well, but what if it wasn't a right-angled triangle? What if it was like . . . this?'"

Again he sketched:

"And I said to him," Harmon continued, " 'this time AD is half AB, but BE is only quarter of BC.' Well, Keogh just looked at it and said: 'One eighth. Quarter times a half.' And then *he* did this:"

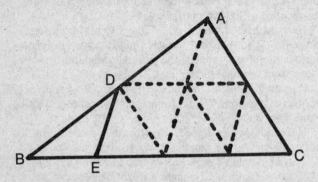

"What point are you trying to make?" Hannant found himself fascinated by the other's tense expression, if not by his subject. What was Harmon getting at?

"But isn't it obvious? This *is* a formula, and he'd figured it out for himself. And he'd done it *during* the examination!"

"It may not be as clever or inexplicable as you think," Hannant shook his head. "As I said, we were going to be starting on Trig in the near future. Keogh knew that. He may have done some reading in advance, that's all."

"Oh?" said Harmon, and now he beamed, reached across the table and punched the other on the shoulder. "Then do me a favour, George, and send me a copy of the text-book he's been swotting from, will you? I'd very much like to see it. You see, in all my years of teaching, that's a formula I never came across. Archimedes might well have known it, Euclid or Pythagorus, but I certainly didn't!"

"What?" Hannant stared again at the diagram, stared harder. "But surely I know this? I mean, I understand Keogh's principle. Surely I've seen it before? I must have—Christ, I've been teaching Trig for twenty years!"

"My young friend," said Harmon, "so have I, and longer. Listen: I know all about sines, cosines, tangents—I fully understand trigonometrical ratios—I am as familiar with all the common or garden mathematical formulae as you yourself are. Probably more familiar. But I never saw a principle so clearly set forth, so brilliantly logical, so expertly . . . *exposed!* Exposed, yes, that's it! You can't say Keogh invented this because he didn't—no more than Newton invented gravity—or 'discovered' it, as they say. No, for it's as constant as pi: it has always been there. But it took Keogh to show us it was there!" He shrugged defeatedly. "How might I explain what I mean?"

"I know what you mean," said Hannant. "No need to explain further. It's what I told Jamieson: this thing of Keogh's for seeing right through the trees to the wood! But a formula . . . ?" And suddenly, in the back of his mind:

Formulae? I could give you formulae you haven't even dreamed of . . .

". . . Oh, but it is!" Harmon insisted, cutting in on Hannant's wandering thoughts. "For a specific sort of question, certainly, but a formula nevertheless. And I ask myself, where to from here? Are there any more 'basic principles' in him—principles we simply never stumbled on before—just waiting for the right stimulus? That's why I want him here at the Tech. So that I can find out."

"Actually, I'm glad you're taking him," said Hannant after a moment. He found himself on the verge of mentioning his disquiet concerning Keogh, then changed his mind and deliberately lied: "I . . . don't think he can realize his full potential at Harden."

"Yes, I see that," Harmon answered, frowning. And

then, a little impatiently: "But of course we've already made that point. Anyway, you can rest assured that I shall do my utmost to develop his potential here. Indeed I will. But come on now, tell me about the lad himself. What do you know of his background?"

On his way back to Harden, at the wheel of his '67 Ford Cortina, Hannant reflected on what he'd told Harmon of Keogh's origins and upbringing. Most of it he'd had from the boy's aunt and uncle, with whom Keogh lived in Harden. His uncle had a grocery shop in the main street; his aunt was mainly a housewife, but she also helped out in the shop two or three days a week.

Keogh's grandfather had been Irish, moving from Dublin to Scotland in 1918 at the end of the war and working in Glasgow as a builder. His grandmother had been a Russian lady of some note, who fled the Revolution in 1920 and took up residence in an Edinburgh house close to the sea. There Sean Keogh met her, and in 1926 they'd been married. Three years later Harry's uncle Michael was born, and in 1931 his mother, Mary. Sean Keogh had been hard on his son, apparently, bringing him into the building business (which he'd hated) and working him hard from the age of fourteen; but by comparison he had seemed literally to dote on his daughter, for whom nothing had ever been good enough. This had caused some jealousy between brother and sister, which came to an end when Michael was nineteen and ran off south to set himself up in a business of his own. Michael was the uncle Harry Keogh now lived with.

By the time Mary Keogh was twenty-one, however, her father's doting had turned to a fierce possessiveness which totally shut her off from any sort of social life, so that she stayed mainly at home and helped with the housework, or assisted her aristocratic Russian mother in the small psychic circle she had built up, where she would attend and regularly take part in those séances for which Natasha Keogh had become something of a local celebrity.

Then, in the summer of '53, Sean Keogh had been killed when an unsafe wall he was working on fell on him. His wife, who for all that she was not yet fifty was already ailing, had sold the business and gone into semi-retirement, holding the occasional séance to eke out her living, which now mainly derived from the interest on banked money. For Mary, on the other hand, the death of her father had heralded a hitherto undreamed-of freedom; quite literally, a "coming out."

For the next two years she enjoyed a social life limited only by her tiny allowance, until by the winter of '55 she had met and married an Edinburgh man twenty-five years her senior, a banker in the city. He was Gerald Snaith, and he and Mary had been very happy for all the gap in their age groups, living in a large house in its own private grounds not far from Bonnyrigg. Unfortunately, by then Mary's mother was rapidly sickening and her doctors had diagnosed cancer; so that Mary lived half of her time at Bonnyrigg, and the rest of it looking after her mother, Natasha, at the seaside house in Edinburgh.

Harry 'Keogh' was therefore born Harry Snaith just nine months after his grandmother died in 1957—and just a year before his banker father would follow her, dying from a stroke in his office at the bank.

Mary Keogh was a strong girl and still very young. She had already sold the old family house by the sea and now found herself sole beneficiary of her husband's not inconsiderable estate. Deciding to get away from Edinburgh for a little while, in the spring of '59 she had come down to Harden and hired a house until the end of July, spending a lot of time in becoming reconciled with her brother and in getting to know his new wife. During that time she saw

111

how his business was declining and helped out with sufficient hard cash to tide him over.

It was then, too, that Michael first detected an aura of sadness or hopelessness about his sister. When he asked what was bothering her (other, of course, than the recent death of her husband, which still weighed heavily) she reminded him of their mother's "sixth sense," her psychic sensitivity. She believed she had inherited something of it; it "told" her that she would not have a long life. That didn't worry her unduly—what would be would be—but she did worry about little Harry. What would become of him, if anything should happen to her while he was still a child?

It was unlikely that Michael Keogh and his wife, Jenny, would be able to have children of their own. They had known this when they married, but mutually agreed that it was not a matter of overriding importance; their feelings for each other came first. Later, when their small business was better established, there would be time enough to consider adoption. In these circumstances, however, and *if* anything should "happen" to Mary—a prediction which, while her brother himself put little store by it, Mary seemed strongly inclined, indeed resolved, towards—then she would not need to let it concern her. Of course her brother and his wife would bring up little Harry as their own. The "promise" was made more to put her mind at rest than as a real promise as such.

When Harry was two his mother met and was "swayed" by a man only two or three years older than herself, one Viktor Shukshin, an assumed dissident who had made his way to the West in pursuit of a political haven, or at least political freedom, such as Mary Keogh's mother had done in 1920. Perhaps Mary's fascination with Shukshin was due to this "Russian connection," but whichever, she married him late in 1960 and they lived at the house near

Bonnyrigg. A linguist, Harry's new stepfather had been giving private lessons in Russian and German in Edinburgh for the last two years; but now, all financial problems set aside, he and his new wife gave themselves over to a life of leisure and personal interests and inclinations. He, too, was greatly interested in the "paranormal," encouraging his wife in her psychic pursuits.

Michael Keogh had met Shukshin at his sister's wedding, and again, briefly, while on a touring holiday in Scotland—but after that . . . only at the inquest. For in the winter of '63 Mary Keogh died, as she had predicted, at only thirty-two years of age. Of Shukshin himself Hannant had only ascertained that the Keoghs hadn't liked the man. There had been that about him which alienated them; probably the same thing which had attracted Michael's sister.

As to Mary's death:

She had been a skater, had loved the ice. A river within view of the house near Bonnyrigg had claimed her, when she had apparently fallen through thin ice while skating and been swept away. Viktor had been with her but had been unable to do anything. Distraught—almost out of his mind with horror—he had gone for help, but . . .

Beneath the ice, the river had been swollen, rushing, at the time of the accident. Downriver were many little backwaters where Mary's body might have been washed up under the ice, remaining there until the thaw. Lots of mud had been washed down out of the hills, too, and this had doubtless covered her. At any rate, her body was never found.

Within six months Michael had fulfilled his promise; Harry "Keogh" had gone to live with his uncle and aunt in Harden. This had suited Shukshin; Harry had not been his child, and he was in any case middling with children and did not feel inclined to bring the boy up on his own.

Mary's will had made good provision for Harry; the house and the rest of her estate went to the Russian. To Michael Keogh's knowledge, Shukshin lived there yet; he had not re-married but gone back to giving private tuition in German and Russian. He still gave lessons at the house near Bonnyrigg, where he apparently lived alone. Not once over the years had he asked to see Harry, nor even enquired about him.

Dramatic as his family history might seem, still, all in all, Harry Keogh's beginnings had not been very remarkable. The only matter which had made any real impression on Hannant had been Keogh's grandmother's and mother's predilection for the paranormal; but that in itself was not very extraordinary. Or there again . . . perhaps it was. Mary Shukshin had seemed convinced that Natasha's "powers" had been passed down to her, and what if she in turn had passed them down to Harry? Now *there* was a thought! Or there might be one, if Hannant believed at all in such things.

But he did not.

It was an evening some three weeks later, four or five days after Keogh had left Harden Modern Boys' for the Tech., when Hannant stumbled across one final "oddity" concerning the boy.

Up in Hannant's attic he'd long kept an old trunk of his father's containing one or two books and bundles of old papers, dusty bits of bric-à-brac and various mementoes of the old man's years of teaching. Having gone up there to fix a tile loosened in a brief storm off the North Sea, he had seen the trunk and admired it. Stoutly constructed, its dark body and brass hasps and hinges retained an olde-worlde appeal. It would create a very handsome effect beside the bookshelves in Hannant's front room.

Dragging the trunk downstairs, he had started to empty

it, glancing again at old photographs unseen for many a year, and putting aside items which might be useful at school (several old text-books, for example) until he'd come across a large leatherbound notebook full of notes and jottings in his father's hand. Something about the pattern and layout of his father's work had held his eye for a moment . . . until it dawned on him just exactly what it was—or what he thought it was.

In the next moment that awful inexplicable chill had come again to strike Hannant's spine, causing him to tremble where he sat holding the book open in his lap, stiffening his back with shock. Then . . . he had snapped the book shut, carried it through to his front room where a coal fire blazed beneath the wide chimney-piece. There, without even glancing at the book again, he thrust it into the flames and let it burn.

That same day Hannant had collected Keogh's old Maths books from the school for forwarding on to Harmon at the Tech. Now, taking the most recent one, he let its pages fall open for one last glance, then closed it with a shudder and let it join his father's old book in the flames.

Prior to Keogh's—awakening?—his work had been scruffy, lacking in order, by no means precise. Afterwards, for the last six or seven weeks . . .

Well, the books were gone now, roared up in a sheet of flame and lost in the chimney, lost to the night.

There was no comparing them now, and that was probably the best way. To consider that there might be any real comparison would be too gross, too grotesque. Now Hannant could put the whole thing out of his mind forever. Thoughts like that had never belonged in any completely sane mind in the first place.

Chapter Four

IT WAS THE SUMMER OF 1972 AND DRAGOSANI WAS BACK IN Romania.

He looked very trendy in a washed-out blue open-necked shirt, flared grey trousers cut in Western style, shiny black shoes with sharply pointed toes (unlike the customary square-cut imported Russian footwear in the local shops) and a fawn-chequered jacket with large patch pockets. In the hot Romanian midday, especially at this farm on the outskirts of a tiny village some way off the Corabia-Calinesti highway, he stood out like the proverbial sore thumb. Leaning on his car and scanning the huddled roof-tops and snail-shell cupolas of the village, which stood a little way down the gently sloping fields to the south, he could only be one of three things: a rich tourist from the West, one from Turkey, or one from Greece.

But on the other hand his car was a Volga and black as his shoes, which suggested something else. Also, he didn't wear the wide-eyed, wary/innocent look of the tourist but a self-satisfied air of familiarity, of belonging. Approaching him from the farmhouse yard where he'd been feeding chickens, Hzak Kinkovsi, the "proprietor," couldn't make up his mind. He was expecting tourists later in the week, but this one had got him beat. He sniffed suspiciously. An official, maybe, from the Ministry of Lands and Properties? Some snotty lackey for those stone-faced Bolshevik industrialists across the border? He'd have to watch his step here, obviously. At least until he knew who or what the newcomer was.

"Kinkovsi?" the young man inquired, eyeing him up and down. "Hzak Kinkovsi? They told me in Ionestasi that you have rooms. I take it that place—" (a nod towards a tottering three-storeyed stone-built house by the cobbled village road) "—is your guesthouse?"

Kinkovsi deliberately looked blank, feigned a lack of understanding, frowned as he stared at Dragosani. He didn't always declare his earnings from tourism—not all of them, anyway. Finally he said: "I am Kinkovsi, yes, and I do have rooms. But—"

"Well, can I stay here or can't I?" the other seemed tired now, and impatient. Kinkovsi noted that his clothes, at first glance smart and modern, actually looked crumpled, much-travelled. "I know I'm early by a month, but surely you can't have that many guests?"

Early by a month! Now Kinkovsi remembered.

"Ah! You must be the Herr from Moscow? The one who made inquiry in April? The one who booked lodgings— but sent no money in advance! Is it you, then, that Herr Dragosani who has the name of the town down the highway? But you are indeed early—though welcome for all that! I shall have to prepare a room for you. Or perhaps I can put you in the English room, for a night or two anyway. How long will you stay?"

"Ten days at least," Dragosani answered, "if the sheets

117

are clean and the food is at all bearable—and if your Romanian beer is not too bitter!" His glance seemed unnecessarily severe; there was that in his attitude which got Kinkovsi's back up.

"Mein Herr," he began with a growl, "my rooms are so clean you could eat off the floor. My wife is an *excellent* cook. My beer is the best under all the Carpatii Meridionali! What's more, our manners are good up here—which seems to be more than can be said of you Muscovites! Now, do you want a room or don't you?"

Dragosani grinned and held out his hand. "I was pulling your leg," he said. "I like to find out what people are made of. And I like a fighting spirit! You are typical of this region, Hzak Kinkovsi: you wear a farmer's clothes but you're a warrior at heart. But me, a Muscovite? With a name like mine? Why, there are some who'd say that you're the foreigner here, 'Hzak Kinkovsi!' It's in your name, your accent, too. And what of your use of 'Mein Herr'? Hungarian, aren't you?"

Kinkovsi briefly studied the other's face, looked him up and down, decided he liked him. The man had a sense of humour, anyway, which in itself made a welcome change. "My grandfather's grandfather was from Hungary," he said, taking Dragosani's hand and giving it a firm shake, "but my grandmother's grandmother was a Wallach. As for the accent, it's local. We've absorbed a good many Hungarians over the decades, and a good many settled here. Now?—I'm a Romanian no less than you. Only I'm not as rich as you!" He laughed, showing yellow, worndown teeth in a face of creased leather. "I suppose you'd say I'm a peasant. Well, I'm what I am. As for 'Mein Herr'—would you prefer me to call you 'Comrade'?"

"Heavens, no! Not that!" Dragosani answered at once. " 'Mein Herr' will do nicely, thanks." He too laughed. "Come on, show me this English room of yours . . ."

Kinkovsi led the way from the big Volga to the tall, high-peaked guesthouse. "Rooms?" he grumbled. "Oh, I've plenty of rooms, all right! Four to each floor. You can have a whole suite of rooms if you like."

"One will be fine," Dragosani answered, "as long as it has its own bath and toilet."

"Ah—*en suite*, is it? Well, then, that's the top floor. A room with its own loo and bath up under the roof. Very modern."

"I'm sure," said Dragosani, not too drily.

He saw that the ground floor walls of the house had been rendered and pebble-dashed on top of the sand-coloured cement. Rising damp, probably. But the upper levels showed their original stone construction. The house must be three hundred years old if it was a day. Very suitable. It took him back in time—back to his roots and beyond them.

"How long have you been away?" Kinkovsi asked, letting him in and showing him to a room on the ground floor. "You'll have to stay here for now," he explained, "until I can get the upstairs room ready. An hour or two, that's all."

Dragosani kicked off his shoes, hung his jacket over a wooden chair, dropped onto a bed in a square of sunlight where it came through an oval window. "I've been away half of my life," he said. "But it's always good to come back. I've been back for the last three summers now, and four more to go."

"Oh? Got your future all planned out, have you? Four more to go? That sounds sort of final. What do you mean by it?"

Dragosani lay back, put his hands behind his head, looked at the other through eyes slitted against the glancing sunlight. "Research," he finally said. "Local history. At only two weeks each year, it should take me another four years."

"History? This country is steeped in it! But it's not your job, then? I mean, you don't do it for a living?"

"No," the man on the bed shook his head. "In Moscow I'm . . . a mortician." That was close enough.

"Huh!" Kinkovsi grunted. "Well, it takes all kinds. Right, I'm off now to sort out your room. And I'll make arrangements for a meal. If you want the loo, it's just out here in the corridor. Just take it easy . . .."

When there was no answer he glanced again at Dragosani, saw that his eyes were closed—the warm sunshine and the quiet of the room. Kinkovsi picked up his guest's car keys from where he'd tossed them down at the foot of the bed, quietly left the room and eased the door shut behind him. One last glance as he went; the rise and fall of Dragosani's chest had taken on the slow rhythm of sleep. That was good. Kinkovsi nodded to himself and smiled. Obviously he felt at home here.

Dragosani chose new lodgings each time he came here. Always in the vicinity of the town he called home—within spitting distance—but not so close to the last place that he'd be remembered from the previous year. He had thought of using an assumed name, a pseudonym, but had thrown the idea out untried. He was proud of his name, probably in defiance of its origin. Not in defiance of Dragosani the town, his geographical origin, but the fact that he'd been *found* there. As for his parents: his father was that almost impregnable mountain range up there to the north, the Transylvanian Alps, and his mother was the rich dark soil itself.

Oh, he had his own theories about his real parents; what they'd done had probably been for the best. The way he imagined them, they had been Szgany, "Romany," Gipsies; young lovers out of feuding camps, their love had not had the power to reconcile old slights and spites. But they had loved, Dragosani had been born, and he had been left. As to actually tracking them down, those unknown parents: he had thought to do that three years ago and had come here for precisely that reason. But . . . it had been utterly hopeless. A task enormous, impossible. There were as many gipsies in Romania now as ever there had been in the old days. Despite their "satellite" designation, old Wallachia, Transylvania, Moldavia and all the lands around had retained something of autonomy, of self-determination. Gipsies had as much right to be here as the mountains themselves.

These had been the thoughts in Dragosani's mind as he drifted into sleep, but the dream he dreamed then was not of his parents at all but of scenes from his childhood, before he'd been sent out of Romania to complete his education. He had been a loner even then, had kept himself to himself, and sometimes he'd wandered where others feared to go. Or where they had been forbidden to go . . .

The woods were deep and dark on hillsides steep and winding as fairground Figures-of-Eight. Boris had only ever seen a Figure-of-Eight once, three days ago on his seventh birthday (his seventh "found" day, as his foster-father would have it) when his treat had been to go in to Dragosani and visit the little picture house there. A short Russian film had been shot entirely from fairground rides, and the Figure-of-Eight had been so real that Boris had actually suffered from vertigo, so that he'd nearly fallen out of his seat. It had been very frightening, but exciting, too; so much so that he'd devised his own game to simulate the thrill of the ride. It wasn't as good and it was hard work, but it was better than nothing. And you could do it right here, on the slopes of the wooded hills not a mile from the estate.

This was a place where no one ever went, a completely

121

lonely place, which was why Boris liked it so much. The woods had not been cut here for almost five hundred years; no gamekeeper had penetrated the pine-grown slopes, where only the rarest sunbeams ever cut through to lighten the dusty gloom; only the muted cooing and occasional flapping of wood pigeons disturbed the deep silence, and the rustle of small, creeping creatures; it was a place of dancing dust motes, of pine cones and needles, of fungi and a few fleet, strangely silent squirrels.

The hills were on the old Wallachian plain, sloping down from the foothills of the Alps forty-five miles away. They were shaped like a crucifix, with the central spine almost two miles long from north to south and the crossbar a mile long east to west. Around them were fields, divided by walls, hedges and fences, and occasionally narrow avenues of trees; but the fields in the immediate vicinity of the hills which formed the cross were untilled, where wild grasses grew long and thistles stood tall and gleamed green and lush. Now and then Boris's foster-father would let horses or cattle graze there, but not often. Even the animals shunned the place; they shied a lot for no reason and sometimes broke down fences or jumped hedgerows to be away from those wild, too quiet fields.

But for little Boris Dragosani the place was something else entirely. He could hunt big game there, penetrate to the unexplored interior of the Amazon, search for the lost cities of the Incas. He could do all of these things and more—provided that he never told his foster-family about his games. Or rather, where he played them. But for all that they were forbidden, the woods fascinated him. There was that in them which drew him a like a magnet.

It was there now as he clambered up the steep slope near the centre of the cross, clawing his way upward from close-grown tree to tree, puffing and panting and dragging behind him the big cardboard box which was his vehicle, his Figure-of-Eight car without wheels. A long climb, yes, but worth it. He would have one last ride, this time from the very top, before setting off for home. The sun was low in the sky now and it seemed likely that he was in trouble already for being late, so one more ride couldn't hurt.

At the top he paused to draw breath, sat for a moment swatting at midges in the pale beams of sunlight lancing down through tall, dark pines, then dragged the box along the crest of the ridge to a place where he could see a track running clear to the bottom. In some forgotten yesteryear, a fire-break had been cut here before the lumbermen had remembered or been told about the nature of the place; since then saplings had sprung up once more to almost but not quite obscure the scar. Now that scar was to become the track of Boris's daredevil ride.

And balancing his "car" on the rim, he jumped aboard and clutched the sides, tilting the box forward until it began to ride.

The box rode smoothly and well at first, slipping easily over a bed of pine needles and coarse grasses, between low bushes and slender saplings, following the old scar of the fire-break. But . . . Boris was a child. He had seen no danger, had not reckoned on the steepness of the slope or rate of acceleration.

Now the box picked up speed, and now his ride more closely approximated the terrifying, dizzy rush of the car on the Figure-of-Eight. He hit a hummock of grass and the box jumped clear of the slope. It came down, struck a glancing blow at a sapling, shot off sideways into the denser pines where they marched breakneck down the almost sheer hillside alongside the scar.

There was no controlling the careening ride of his "car" now. Boris had no brakes, no guidance system. He could only go where the box took him.

With many a jolting crash and sideways slide, more

bruised and shaken with every passing second, he was rattled in his box like a loose pea in a pod. And now, away from the scar of the fire-break, the failing light was shut out almost completely; so that Boris ducked his head, a precaution against unseen, whipping branches, as his nightmare descent continued. But with the trees grown so close, it could only go on for a little while longer.

At last, in a place where the ground beneath the trees was of sliding shale and scree, where their humped roots stuck up above the surface like thick-bodied serpents, suddenly the ride as such came to a halt. With a jarring crash the bottom of the box was ripped out from beneath Boris and the sides quite literally disintegrated in his clutching, terrified fingers. He was thrown not quite head-on into the bole of a tree and sent spinning. Tumbling head over heels, bouncing and sliding, Boris hardly felt the many brittle branches flying into shards as he plunged through them; he was aware only of glimpses of a whirling sky scanned through the tops of frowning pines, of a sick plunging and jolting that seemed to go on forever, and finally of shooting over a lip or ledge of rock and hurtling into dark, dusty space.

Then the impact and after that nothing. Nothing for a time, anyway . . .

Boris might have been out for one minute, for five, or fifty. Or he might not have been out at all. But he was shaken up, and badly. If he hadn't been, then what happened next could easily have killed him. He might have died of fright.

"Who are you?" *asked a voice in his reeling head.* "Why have you come here? Do you . . . offer yourself to me?"

The voice was evil, utterly evil. In it were elements of everything horrific. Boris was only a boy; he did not understand words like bestial, sadistic, diabolic, or the meaning of phrases like "the Powers of Darkness," or the Acts by which such Powers are invoked. To him there was fear in a creaking tread on a dark landing; there was terror in the tapping of a twig on his bedroom window, when all the house was asleep; there was horror in the sudden squirm or hop of a toad, or the startled freezing of a cockroach when the light is switched on, and especially in its scurrying when it knows *it is discovered!*

Once, in the deepest cellar under the farm, where his foster-father kept wines in racks and cheeses wrapped in muslin on cool shelves, Boris had heard the rustling cheep of crickets. In the beam of a tiny torch he'd seen one, leprous grey from the lightlessness of its habitation. As he moved closer, to step on it, the insect jumped and disappeared. He found another and the same thing happened. And another, and so on. He saw a dozen and stepped on none. They had all vanished. Climbing the steps out of the place, as daylight filtered down from above, a cricket had jumped from Boris's shorts. They were on *him! They had jumped* onto *him! That way he couldn't step on them. And oh how Boris had* danced *then!*

That was his *idea of nightmare: the knowledge of sly intelligence where none should be. Just as it should not be here . . .*

"Ah!" said the voice, stronger now. "Ah!—so you are one of mine! And because you are one of mine, you came here. Because you knew where to find me . . ."

It was then that Boris knew he was conscious and that the voice in his head was real! And its evil was the slimy touch of a toad, the leaping of crickets in darkness, the slow tick of a hated clock, which seems to talk to you in the night and chuckle at your fears and your insomnia. Oh, and it was much worse than that, he was sure—except he didn't have the words or knowledge or experience to describe it.

But he could picture the mouth which spoke those guttural, clotted, sly and insinuating words in his head. And he knew why it was clotted and gurgling. In his mind's eye the picture was vivid and monstrous: the mouth dripped blood like liquid rubies, and its gleaming incisors were pointed as those of a great hound!

"What . . . is your name, boy?"

"*Dragosani,*" *Boris answered, or at least thought the answer, for his throat was too dry for speech. In any case, it was enough.*

"Ahhhh! Dragosani!" *The voice was a hoarse sigh now, like autumn leaves skittering on cobbles. A sigh of dawning realization, of understanding, of satisfaction.* "Then indeed you are one of mine. But alas, too small, too small! You have not the strength, boy. A child, a mere child. What can you do for me? Nothing! Your blood runs like water in your veins. It has no iron . . ."

Boris sat up, stared frightenedly about in the gloom, his eyes darting and his head reeling. He was more than halfway down the hillside on a sort of flat ledge of rock beneath the trees. He had never been here before, never guessed the place existed. Then, as his eyes became more accustomed to the gloom and his senses returned to him more fully, he saw that in fact he sat upon lichen-clad stone flags before what could only be—a mausoleum!

Boris had seen the like before; his uncle (at least, his foster-father's brother) had died a month ago and had been interred in just such a place; but that had been in holy ground, in the churchyard in Slatina. This place, on the other hand . . . this was not a holy place. No, not by any stretch of the imagination . . .

Unseen presences moved here, stirring the musty air without stirring the festoons of cobwebs and fingers of dead twigs that hung down from above. Here it was cold—

clammy cold—where the sun had not broken through for five hundred years.

Behind Boris, hewn from a great outcrop of rock, the tomb itself had long since caved in, its roof of massive slabs lying in a tangle of masonry. In his hurtling rush from above, Boris must have flown over that jumble of stone, or doubtless he'd have brained himself. Perhaps he had anyway, for certainly he was feeling and hearing things where there was nothing to be felt or heard. Or where there should not be anything.

He pricked up his ears and squinted his eyes in the dusk of this enclosed place, but . . . there was nothing.

Boris tried to stand up, managed it on his third attempt. He leaned his trembling weight on a sloping slab which had once formed the front lintel of the tomb's door. Then he listened and looked again, straining ears and eyes in the gloom. But no voice now, no mouth dripping blood in the mirror of his mind. He sighed his relief, his breath rasping in his throat.

A thickly matted crust of dirt, lichens and pine needles fell away from the slab beneath his hands, partly revealing a motif or coat of arms. Boris cleared away more of the grime of centuries, and—

He snatched away his hands at once, reeled back, tripped and sat down again, gasping. The arms had consisted of a shield bearing in bas-relief a dragon, one forepaw raised in threat; and riding upon its back, a bat with triangular eyes of carnelian; and surmounting both of these figures, the leering horned head of the devil himself, forked tongue protruding and dripping gouts of carnelian blood!

All three symbols—dragon, bat, devil—now came together in Boris's mind. They became amalgamated as the author of the voice in his head. The voice which chose that precise moment of time to speak to him yet again:

"Run, little man, run . . . begone from here. You are

too small, too young, *too* innocent, and I am far too weak and oh so very old . . ."

On legs that trembled so fearfully he was sure he would fall, Boris stood up, backed away. Then he turned and fled the place full tilt—away from the pine-needle-strewn flagstones, which the gnarled roots of centuries were pushing upward; away from the tumbled tomb and whatever buried secrets it contained; away from the gloom of the place, so menacing as to seem to have physical substance.

And as he went—under the dark, uncut trees and down the steep hillside, torn by whipping branches and bruised from fall after fall, so the voice chuckled in his mind like a file on glass or chalk on a blackboard, obscene in its ancient knowledge. "Aye, run—run! But never forget me, Dragosani. And be sure I shall not forget you. No, for I shall wait for you while you grow strong. And when your blood has iron in it and you know what you do—for it must be of your own free will, Dragosani—then we shall see. And now I must sleep . . ."

Bursting from the trees at the foot of the hill, bounding a low fence where the top bar was broken down, Boris flew forward into long grass and thistles, and blessed, blessed light! But even then he did not pause, but scrambled to his feet and ran for home. Only in the middle of the field, with no breath left in him to carry him on, did he stop, collapse to the earth, turn his face and look back at the looming hills. Away in the west the sun was setting, its last lances of fire turning the topmost pines to gold; but Boris knew that in the secret place, the tree-shrouded glade of the tomb, all was clammy and crawly and dark with dread. And only then did he think to ask:

"What . . . who . . . who are you?"

And as if from a million miles away—carried on the evening breeze, which has blown over the hills and fields

*of Transylvania since remembered time began—the answer
came to him in the back of his mind:*

"Aaahhh!—but you know that, Dragosani. You know
that. Ask not 'who are you' but 'who am I.' But what does
it matter? The answer is the same. I am your past,
Dragosani. And you . . . are . . . my . . . fuuutuuure!"

"Herr Dragosani?"

"What . . . who . . . who are you?" Repeating his
question from the dream, Dragosani came awake. Eyes
gazed at him, almost triangular, unblinking, searing in the
unexpected gloom of the room; so that for a moment, a
single second, he almost fancied himself back in the glade
of the tomb. But they were green eyes, like a cat's.
Dragosani stared at them and they stared back, unabashed.
They were framed by a white face in an oval of raven-
black hair. A female face.

He sat up, stretched, swung his feet down to the floor.
The owner of the eyes curtsied peasant fashion—inelegantly,
Dragosani thought. He sneered at her. Rising from sleep,
he was always testy; waking before his time, as by an
intrusion, like now, he was especially so.

"Are you deaf?" he stretched again, pointed directly at
her nose. "I said who are you? Also, why have I been
allowed to sleep so late?" (He could also be contrary.)

His rigidly pointing finger didn't seem to impress her at
all. She smiled, one eyebrow arching delicately, almost
insolently. "I'm Ilse, Herr Dragosani. Ilse Kinkovsi. You've
been asleep for three hours. Since you were obviously very
tired, my father said I should leave you sleeping and
prepare your room in the garret. That has been done."

"Oh? So? And what do you want of me now?" Dragosani
refused to be gracious. And this wasn't the same game
he'd played with her father; no, for there was that about
her which genuinely irritated him. She was far too self-

assured, too knowing, for one thing. And for another she was pretty. She must be, oh . . . twenty? It was odd she wasn't married, but there was no ring on her finger.

Dragosani shivered, his metabolism adjusting, not yet fully awake. She saw it, said: "It's warmer upstairs. The sun is still on the top of the house. Climbing the stairs will get your blood going."

Dragosani looked about the room, used his delicate fingertips to brush the crusts of sleep from the corners of his eyes. He stood up, patted the pocket of his jacket where it hung over the back of the chair. "Where are my keys? And . . . my cases?"

"Yes," she nodded, smiling again, "my father has taken your cases up for you. Here are your keys." When her hand touched his it was cool, his was suddenly feverish. And this time when he shivered she laughed. "Ah! A virgin!"

"What?" Dragosani hissed, probably giving himself away completely. "What—did—you—say?"

She turned towards the door, walked out into the hall and towards the stairs. Dragosani, furious, snatched up his coat and followed her. At the foot of the wooden stairs she looked back. "It's a saying hereabouts. It's just a saying . . ."

"What is?" he snapped, following her up the stairs.

"Why, that when a boy shivers when he's hot, it's because he's a virgin. A reluctant virgin!"

"A bloody stupid saying!" Dragosani scowled.

She looked back and smiled. "With you it doesn't apply, Herr Dragosani," she said. "You are not a boy, and you don't look at all shy or virginal to me. And anyway, it's just a saying."

"And you are too familiar with your guests!" he grumbled, feeling that he'd been let off the hook, as if she'd taken pity on him.

On the first landing she waited for him, laughed and said: "I was being friendly. It's a cold greeting when people don't talk to each other. My father told me to ask you: will you eat with us tonight, since you're the only one here, or will you have a meal in your room?"

"I'll eat in my room," he growled at once. "If we ever get to it!"

She shrugged, turned and started up the second flight. Here the stairs climbed more steeply.

Ilse Kinkovsi was dressed in a fashion quite out of date in the towns but still affected in the smaller villages and farming communities. She wore a slightly longer than knee-length pleated cotton dress, gathered in tightly at the waist, a short-sleeved black bodice buttoned down the front, with puffs at the shoulders and elbows, and (ridiculously, as Dragosani thought) calf-boots of rubber; but doubtless they were fine in the farmyard. In winter she would also wear stockings to the tops of her thighs. But it was not winter . . .

He tried to avert his eyes but there was nowhere else to look. And, damn it, she flounced! A narrow black "V" separated the swivelling white globes of her buttocks.

At the second landing she paused, deliberately turned to wait for him at the head of the stairs. Dragosani stopped dead in his tracks, held his breath. Looking down at him—and looking as cool as ever—she leaned her weight on one foot more than the other, rubbed at the inside of her thigh with her knee, flashed her green eyes at him. "I'm sure you'll like it . . . here," she said, and slowly shifted her weight to the other foot.

Dragosani looked away. "Yes, yes—I'm sure I . . . I—"

Ilse took note of the fine film of sweat on his brow. She turned her face away and sniffed. Perhaps she had been right about him in the first place. A pity . . .

Chapter Five

WITHOUT ANY MORE DELAY, ILSE KINKOVSI NOW TOOK Dragosani straight to the garret, showed him the bathroom (which, surprisingly, *was* quite modern) and made as if to leave. The rooms were very pretty: whitewash and old oak beams, with varnished wooden corner cupboards and shelves, and Dragosani was beginning to feel much better about things. As the heat went out of the girl, so he warmed a little towards her—or more properly towards the as yet unseen Kinkovsi family in its entirety. It would be extremely gauche of him to eat here, alone in his room, after the Kinkovsis, father and daughter both, had shown him such hospitality.

"Ilse," he called after her on impulse. "Er—Miss Kinkovsi—I've changed my mind. I would like to eat at the farm, yes. Actually, I lived on a farm when I was a boy. It won't be strange to me—and I'll try not to be too strange to the family. So . . . when do we eat?"

Descending the stairs she looked back over her shoulder. "As soon as you can wash and come down. We're waiting for you." There was no smile on her face now.

"Ah!—then I'll be two minutes. Thank you."

As her footsteps on the stairs faded into silence, he quickly took off his shirt, snapped open one of his cases and found shaving gear, towel, clean, pressed trousers and new socks. Ten minutes later he hurried downstairs, out of the guesthouse, and was met by Kinkovsi at the farmhouse door.

"I'm sorry, I'm sorry!" he said. "I hurried as fast as I could."

"No matter," the other took his hand. "Welcome to my house, please enter. We'll eat at once."

Inside, it was just a little claustrophobic. The rooms were large but low-ceilinged and the decor was dark and very "old" Romanian. In the dining-room, at a huge square deal table which could have seated a dozen easily, Dragosani found himself with a side of his own, facing a window. The light was such that the face of Ilse, who, after she had helped her mother serve, sat opposite, was set in a vague semi-silhouette. To Dragosani's right sat Hzak Kinkovsi, with his wife when her duties were done, and to his left two sons of maybe twelve and sixteen years respectively. A small family by farming community standards.

The meal was simple, abundant, deserving of an accolade. Dragosani said as much and Ilse smiled, while her mother Maura beamed delightedly across the table at him, saying: "I thought you would be hungry. Such a long journey! All the way from Moscow. How long did it take you?"

"Oh, well I did stop to eat," he answered, smiling. And then, remembering, he frowned. "I ate twice, and both meals were unsatisfactory and very expensive! I even slept for an hour or two, in the car, just this side of Kiev.

And of course I came via Galatz, Bucharest and Pitesti, chiefly to avoid the mountain passes.''

"A long way, yes," Hzak Kinkovsi nodded. "Sixteen hundred kilometres."

"As the crow flies," said Dragosani. "But I'm not a crow! More than two thousand kilometres, according to my car's instruments."

"And all this way just to study a little local history," the farmer shook his head.

They had finished their meal now. The old boy (not really old, more weathered than withered) sat back with a clay-pipeful of fragrant tobacco; Dragosani lit a Rothmans, one of a pack of two hundred Borowitz had purchased for him back in Moscow at a "special" store for the party élite; the two boys left to tend to evening chores, and the women went off to wash dishes.

Kinkovsi's remark about "local history" had taken Dragosani a little by surprise, until he remembered that was his assumed reason for being here. Drawing on his cigarette, he wondered how much he dare say. On the other hand, he was also supposed to be a mortician; perhaps it would not seem too strange if his inclinations ran altogether morbid.

"Local history in a way, yes—but I might just as easily have gone into Hungary, or cut short my journey in Moldavia, or gone on across the Alps to Oradea. Or Yugoslavia for that matter, or as far east as Mongolia. They all hold a common interest for me, but more so here for this is my birthplace."

"And what is this interest, then? Is it the mountains? Or perhaps the battles, eh? My God—this country has known some fighting!" Kinkovsi was not merely polite but genuinely interested. He poured more farm-brewed wine (made from local grapes and quite excellent) into Dragosani's glass and topped up his own.

134

"The mountains are part of it, I suppose," the younger man answered. "And in this part of the world, the battles, certainly. But the legend in its entirety is far older than any history we can hope to remember. It's possibly as old as the hills themselves. A very mysterious thing—and very horrible!"

He leaned across the table, stared fixedly into Kinkovsi's watery eyes.

"Well, go on, don't keep me in suspense! What is this mysterious passion, this ancient quest of yours?"

The wine was very heady and had robbed Dragosani of most of his natural caution. Outside, the sun had gone down and dusk lay everywhere like a mantle of blue smoke. From the kitchen came the clinking of dishes and soft, muted voices. In another room, an old clock ticked throatily. It was the perfect setting. And these country folk being so superstitious and all—

Dragosani couldn't resist it. "The legend of which I speak," he said, slowly and distinctly, "is that of the *vampir!*"

For a moment Kinkovsi said nothing, looked stunned. And then he rocked back in his chair, roared with laughter and slapped his thigh. *"Hah!*—the *vampir*—I should have known it! Every year there are more of you, and all looking for Dracula!"

Dragosani sat astounded. He was not sure what reaction he'd expected, but certainly it was not this. "More of us?" he said. "Every year? I'm not sure I understand . . ."

"Why, now that the restrictions have been relaxed," Kinkovsi explained. "Now that your precious 'iron curtain' has been opened up a little! They come from America, from England and France, even one or two from Germany. Curious tourists, mainly—but at other times learned men and scholars. And all of them hunting this same lie of a 'legend.' What? Why, I've pulled a dozen legs here in this very room, by pretending to be afraid of this . . . this 'Dracula.' But what fools! Surely everyone knows—even 'ignorant peasants' like myself—that the creature is only a character in a story by a clever Englishman, written at the turn of the century? Yes, and not more than a month ago there was a film of the same title at the picture house in town. Oh, you can't fool me, Dragosani. Why, it wouldn't surprise me at all to discover that you're here as a guide for my English party. They're due in on Friday. And yes, they too are searching for the big bad *vampir!*''

''Scholars, you say?'' Dragosani fought hard to hide his confusion. ''Learned men?''

Kinkovsi stood up, switched on the dim electric light where it hung in a battered lampshade from the centre of the ceiling. He sucked at his pipe and got it going again. ''Scholars, yes—professors from Köln, Bucharest, Paris. For the last three years. All armed with their notebooks, photocopies of mouldy old maps and documents, their cameras and sketchbooks and—oh, all sorts of paraphernalia!''

Dragosani had recovered himself. ''And their chequebooks, too, eh?'' he feigned a knowing smile.

Again Kinkovsi roared. ''Oh, yes, of course! Their money, too. Why, I've heard that up in the mountain passes there are little village shops which actually sell tiny glass bottles of earth from this Dracula's castle! My god! Can you believe it? It'll be Frankenstein next! I've seen him on film, too, and he's *really* frightening!''

Now the younger man began to feel angry. Irrationally, he felt himself to be the butt of Kinkovsi's joke. So the snag-toothed simpleton didn't believe in vampires; they made him roar with laughter; they were like the Yeti or the Loch Ness Monster: tourist attractions born out of myths and old wives' tales . . .

. . . And right there and then Dragosani made himself a promise that—

"What's all this talk about monsters?" Maura Kinkovsi came in from the kitchen, drying her hands on her apron. "You be careful, Hzak! Mind how you speak of the devil. And you, Herr Dragosani. There are still things in the lonely places that people don't understand."

"What lonely places, woman?" her husband chuckled. "Here's a man come down from Moscow in little more than a day—a journey which once would have taken a week and more—and you talk about lonely places? There's no room for lonely places any more!"

Oh, but there is, Dragosani thought. *It's a terribly lonely place in your grave. I've felt it in them: a loneliness they don't even know is there—until they waken to my touch!*

"You know what I mean!" Kinkovsi's wife snapped. "It's rumoured that in the mountains there are still villages where they yet put stakes through the hearts of people taken too young or dead from no obvious cause—to make sure they don't come back. And no one thinks ill of it." (this last to Dragosani) "It's just custom, so to speak, like doffing your hat to a funeral procession."

Now Ilse also appeared. "What? And are you a *vampir*-hunter, too, Herr Dragosani? But what a dark, morbid lot they are! Surely you can't be one of them?"

"No, no, of course not," Dragosani's feigned smile was fixed now, frozen on his face. "I was just having a laugh with your father, that's all. But my joke seems to have backfired." He stood up.

"Eh?" said Kinkovsi, obviously disappointed. "Early night, is it? I suppose you're still tired. Pity, I was looking forward to talking to you. Never mind, I've jobs a-plenty to get on with. Maybe tomorrow."

"Oh, we'll find time for talking, I'm sure," said Dragosani as he followed his host to the door.

"Ilse," said Kinkovsi, "take a torch and see the Herr to the guesthouse, will you? The dusk is worse than darkest midnight when you're not sure of your step."

The girl did as she was told and guided Dragosani across the farmyard, out of the gate and into the guesthouse. There she switched on the lights for the stairs. Before saying goodnight, she told him:

"Herr Dragosani, there is a button beside your bed. If you require anything in the night just press it. Unfortunately, it will probably wake up my parents, too. A better way would be to open your curtains half-way—which I would see from my own bedroom window . . ."

"What?" said Dragosani, pretending to be slow on the uptake. "In the middle of the night?"

But as to her meaning, Ilse Kinkovsi left little doubt of that. "I don't sleep very well," she said. "My room is on the ground floor. I like to open my window and smell the night air. Sometimes I even go out that way and walk in the silver moonlight—usually about 1:00 A.M."

Dragosani nodded his head but made no answer. She was standing very close to him. Before she could further clarify the situation he turned away from her and hurried up the stairs. He could feel her mocking eyes on him until he turned the corner onto the first landing.

In his room Dragosani quickly closed the curtains at the window, unpacked his cases, ran himself a bathful of water. Heated by a gas jet, the water steamed invitingly. Adding salts, Dragosani stripped himself naked.

In the bath he lay and soaked, luxuriating in the heat and languid swirl of the water when he moved his arms. In what seemed a very short while he found himself nodding, his chin on his chest, the water growing cold. Stirring himself, he finished bathing and prepared for bed.

It was only 10:00 P.M. when he slipped between the sheets, but within a minute or two he was fast asleep.

Just before midnight he woke up, saw a vertical white band of moonlight, deep and inches wide, like a luminous shaft, streaming into the room where the curtains missed coming together. Remembering what Ilse Kinkovsi had said, he got up, took a safety pin and firmly pinned the curtains shut. He half-wished it could be different, more than half, but . . . it couldn't.

It wasn't that he hated women or was frightened of them, he didn't and wasn't. It was more that he couldn't understand them, and with so many other things to do—so much else to learn and try to understand—he simply had no time to waste on dubious or untried pleasures. Or so he told himself. And anyway, his needs were different to those of other men, his emotions less volatile. Except when he needed them to be. But what he'd lost in common sensuality, he more than made up for in uncommon sensitivity. Though even that would seem a paradox to anyone who knew his work.

As for those other things he had to learn or at least try to understand—they were legion. Borowitz was happy with him the way he was, yes, but Dragosani was not. He felt that at the moment his talent was one-dimensional, that it lacked any real depth. Very well, he would give it the very greatest depth, a depth unplumbed for half a millennium! Out there in the night lay one who had secrets unique, one who in life commanded monstrous magics, and who even now, in death, was undead. And there, for Dragosani, lay the fount of all knowledge. Only when he had drained that well would there be time for the rest of his sorely neglected "education."

It was midnight now, the witching hour. Dragosani

wondered how far the sleeper's dreams reached out beyond the borders of the dark glade, wondered if they might meet half-way. The moon was up and full, and all the stars were bright; high in the mountains wolves prowled and howled even now, as they had five hundred years ago; all the auspices were right.

He lay back in his bed, lay very still, and pictured the shattered tomb where roots groped like fossil tentacles and the trees leaned inward to hide their secret. He pictured it, and out loud but also in his mind said:

"Old one, I've come back. I bring you hope in return for knowledge. It's the third year, and only four remain. How goes it with you?"

Outside in the night a wind sprang up, blowing down from the mountains. Trees soughed as their branches bowed a little, and Drangosani heard a sighing behind the rafters over his head. But as quickly as it had risen the wind fell, and in its place:

Ahhh! Dragosaaani! Is it you, my son? Are you then returned to me in my solitude, Dragosaaani . . . ?

"Who else would it be, old devil? Yes, it is Dragosani. I have grown stronger, I am become a small power in the world. But I want more! You hold the ultimate secrets of power, which is why I have returned and why I will continue to return, until . . . until . . ."

Four more years, Dragosani. And then . . . then you shall sit upon my right hand, and I shall teach you many things. Four years, Dragosani. Four years. Ahhh!

"Long years for me, old dragon, for I must wake each morning and sleep each night and count all the hours between. And time is slow. But for you . . . ? How has it been, old one, this last year?"

It would have been the merest moment, fleeting, speeding, gone!—had you not disturbed me, Dragosani. But you have given me . . . yearnings. Here I lay and for fifty

140

years hated, and lusted for revenge on them that put me here. And for fifty more I desired only to be up and about my business, which is to put down my enemies. And then . . . then I thought me: but my murderers are no more. They are bones in graves of their own now, or dust blown on the winds. And in another hundred years . . . what of even the sons of my enemies then? Ah! Well might I ask! What of the legions who came up against these mountains in ages past and met my father's fathers waiting? What of the Lombard and the Bulgar, the Avar . . . and the Turk? Ah!—a brave fighter in his time, the Turk—he was my enemy, but no more. And so five hundred years fleeting by, for I was forgetting the glories just as a grandfather forgets his own infancy, until I had forgotten— almost. Until I was forgotten—almost! And what then, when there was nothing left of me but a word in a book, and when the book itself crumbled to dust? Why, then surely I would have no reason to be at all! And perhaps glad of it. And then you came, a mere boy, but a boy whose name . . . was . . . Dragosaaaniiii . . .

As the voice faded so the wind sprang up again, the two merging and dying away together. Dragosani thought of what was to be done and shivered in his bed. But this was his chosen course, this his destiny. And fearing that he had lost the other, he called out urgently:

"Old one, you of the Dragon-banner, of the bat and the dragon and the devil—are you there?"

Where else would I be, Dragosani? the voice seemed to mock. *Yes, I am here. I quicken in my forsaken place, in this earth which was my life. I thought I was forgotten, but a seed was sown and blossomed, and you remembered and knew me. And by your name, so I knew you, Dragosaaaniiii . . .*

"Tell me again!" Dragosani was eager. "Tell me how

it was. My mother, my father, their coming together. Tell me it.''

Twice you have heard it, the voice in his head sighed. *And would you hear it again? Do you hope to seek them out? Then I cannot help you. Their names were of no importance to me; I knew them not, knew nothing of them except the heat of their blood. Aye, and of that I tasted the merest drop, a small pink splash. But afterwards there was that of them in me, and that of me in them—which came out in you. Don't ask after them, Dragosani. I am your father . . .*

''Would you walk on earth, and breathe, and slake your thirst again, old one? Would you slaughter your enemies and drive them back as before—as your ancestors before you—and this time as your own man, not merely a sellsword to ungrateful Dracul princelings? If you would, then trade with me. Tell me of my parents.''

Sometimes a bargain sounds more like a threat, Dragosani. And would you threaten me? The voice hissed in his head like ice on the strings of an ill-tuned violin. *You dare speak to me—you dare remind me—of Vlads, Radus, Draculs and Mirceas? You call me a sellsword? Boy, in the end my so-called ''masters'' feared me more than the Turk himself! Which is why they weighed me down in iron and silver and buried me in this secret place, in these same cruciform hills which I had defended with my blood. For them I fought, aye—for the sake of their ''Holy cross,'' their ''Christianity''—but now I fight to be free of it. Their treachery is my pain, their cross the dagger in my heart!*

''A dagger which I can draw for you! Your enemies have come again, old devil, and none to drive them out save you. And there you lie, impotent! The crescent of the Turk is grown into the sickle of another, and what he cannot cut down he hammers flat. I am a Wallach no less than you, whose blood is older than Wallachia itself. Nor

will I suffer the invader. Well, and now there's a new
invader and our leaders are puppets once more. So how is
it to be? Are you content, or would you fight again? The
bat, the dragon, the devil—against the hammer and the
sickle!''

(A sigh, whispering with the wind in the rafters.) *Very
well, I will tell you how it was, and how you . . . became.*

*It was . . . springtime. I could feel it in the soil. The
growing time. The year . . . but what are years to me? A
quarter-century ago, anyway.*

"It was 1945," said Dragosani. "The war would soon
be at an end. The Szgany were here, fled into the mountains for their refuge, as they've done right down the
centuries. Refugees from the German war machine, they
were here in their thousands. And the Transylvanian pla-
teau shielded them, as always. The Germans had been
rounding them up—Szgany, Romany, Szekely, Gipsy, call
them what you will—all over Europe, for slaughter along
with the Jews in the death-camps. Stalin had deported
many minority peoples, alleged 'collaborators,' from the
Crimea and Caucasus. That's when it was, and that's when
it stopped. Spring 1945, but we had surrendered more than
six months earlier than that. Anyway, the end was in sight,
the Germans were on the run. By the end of April, Hitler
had killed himself . . .''

*I know only what you have told me of that. Surrender,
you say? Hah! I am not surprised. But 1945? Aieee! More
than four and a half centuries, and still the invader came—
and I was not there to drink the wine of war. Oh, yes, you
stir old yearnings in me, Dragosani.*

*Anyway, it was springtime when these two came. I
suspect that they were in flight. Perhaps from war, who
can say? Anyway, they were very young and of the old
blood. Gipsies? Aye. In my day, as a great Boyar, thousands such had worshipped me, owed me allegiance more*

143

than the puppet Basarabs and Vlads and Vladislavs. And would they worship me still? I wondered. And did I yet have influence over them?

My tomb was broken down then just as it is now, unvisited since the day I was interred—except in the first half-century, by priests who cursed the ground where I lay. And so they came, one night as the moon rose over the mountains. Young ones, Szekely, a boy and a girl. It was spring and warm, but the nights were cold. They had blankets and a small lamp with oil. Also, they had fear. And passion. It was that, I think, which stirred me from my slumbers. Or perhaps I had been half awake anyway. After all, engines of war were rumbling, and their thunder was in the earth. Perhaps it was that which stirred these old bones . . .

I felt what they were doing. In four and a half centuries and more I had learned to recognize the fall of a leaf from a tree, the timid landing of a woodcock's feather. They put a blanket across two leaning slabs, forming a shelter. They lit the lamp to see each other, also for warmth. Hah! Szekely? They didn't need a lamp to be warm.

They . . . interested me. For years I had called, for centuries, and no one came, no one answered. Perhaps they were kept away by priests, by warnings, by myths that had grown into legends down the long years. Or—perhaps in life my excesses had been . . .

You have told me, Dragosani, how many of my greatest deeds are now accorded to the Vlads, and how I am reduced to a ghost for frightening children. More than this, my very name will have been stricken from the old records, for that was their way in those days. If they feared something they destroyed it and pretended it had never been. Ah, but did they think I was unique of my sort? I was not—I am not! I was one of a few who once were a great many. Aye, and word of my plight must *surely have found its way to the others? For hundreds of years it had angered me that someone had not come to release or at least avenge me! And when at last someone did come . . . gipsies, Szekelys!*

The girl was frightened and he could not calm her. I calmed her. I crept inside her mind, gave her strength to face her fears, whatever they were, and to meet him in a hot collision of flesh. Ahhh!

Yes, and she was a virgin! Her maidenhead was intact. I might have died again, in my grave, from lusting after it! A maidenhead, intact! To quote an old, old book of lies: how are the mighty fallen! I had broken two thousand in my day, one way or another. Ha, ha, ha! *And they called young Vlad "the Impaler"!*

So . . . they were lovers, but not yet in the fullest sense of the word. He was a boy—a mere pup, and never breached a bitch—and she a virgin. And so I got into his mind, too. Ah!—and I bequeathed the night to them. I drew strength from them and they from me. One night they had from me, just one, for before the dawn they left. After that—(a mental shrug)—*I knew no more of them . . .*

"Except that she bore me," said Dragosani, "and left me on a doorstep to be found."

The answer to that was a while in coming, sighing in a wind little more than a breeze now. The old one in the ground was tired; he had little more of strength left in him, not even for thinking; the earth held him in its hardpacked womb and turned on its inexorable axis and lulled him. But at last, sighingly:

Yesss. Yes, but at least she knew where to bring you. She was a Gipsy, remember? A wanderer. And yet when you were born she brought you back here. She brought you . . . home! She did that because she knew your real father, Dragosani! You might say that of my whole life, which was bloody beyond measure, that one night was a

145

true labour of love. Aye, and my only tribute a single splash of blood. The merest drop, Dragosaaaniiii . . .

"My mother's blood."

Your mother's, splashed on the earth where I lay. But such a precious drop! For it was your blood, too, and runs in your veins even now. And then, as a child, it brought you back to me.

Dragosani was quiet, his head full of thoughts, visions, pseudo-memories evoked of the other's words in his head. Finally he said, "I'll come to you tomorrow. We'll talk more then."

As you will, my son.

"Sleep now . . . father."

A last gust of wind rattling a loose tile, and with it a long, last sighing.

Sleep well, Dragosaaaniiii . . .

And some ten minutes later down in the farmhouse, Ilse Kinkovsi got out of bed, went to her window and looked out. She thought it was the wind that woke her up, but there wasn't the slightest breath of breeze. It made no difference, she had intended to wake up just before 1:00 A.M. anyway. Outside all was silvery moonlight—but in the guesthouse garret Boris Dragosani's curtains were drawn tighter than she'd ever seen them. And his light was out.

The next day was Wednesday.

Dragosani ate a quick breakfast and drove off in his car before 8:30 A.M. He took the road which led him close to the hills in the shape of a cross. Down in a wide depression to the west of those hills lay the farm where he'd spent his childhood. New people had it now, for the last nine or ten years. Dragosani found a vantage point on a little-used track and looked at the place for a while. It no longer did anything for him. Maybe a very small lump in his throat—which was probably dust or pollen from the dry summer air.

Then he turned his back on the farm and looked at the hills. He knew exactly where to look. As if his eyes were the lenses of binoculars, they seemed to focus on the place, blowing it up large and with incredible clarity and detail. He could almost see *beneath* the green canopy of the trees to the tumbled slabs and the earth beneath. And if he tried hard enough, maybe even deeper than that.

He dragged his eyes away. It would be useless to go there anyway, before nightfall. Or late evening at the earliest.

And then he remembered another evening, when he had been a small boy . . .

After that first time when he was seven, it had been six months before he went to the place again. He had been out with his sledge, a dog bounding by his side. Bubba was a farm dog, really, but where Boris went he always had to be. There was a slope on the other side of the farm towards the village, a place where the kids snowballed and sledged each winter. Boris should be there, but he knew where there was a better run: the fire-break, of course. He also knew—as he had always known—that these hills were forbidden, and since the summer he had known why. People sometimes dreamed funny things there, things that stuck in their minds and came back in the night to bother them. That must be it. But knowing it didn't stop him. Rather it drew him on.

Now, with the snow deep and crisp, the hills didn't look so forbidding and the fire-break made for near-perfect sledging. Boris was good at it. He'd come here last winter, too, alone, and even the winter before that, when he was very small. But today he used the slope only once, and then half-way down he'd looked across to his right to see if he could pick out the spot under the trees. After that he left the sledge at the bottom of the hill, and he and Bubba had climbed up under the pines, stark black against the snow. He was going back to the tomb (he told himself) to satisfy himself that that was *all* it was: just the burial place of some old and long-forgotten landowner, and nothing more. That first time had been a bad dream, after he'd bumped his head when he was thrown from his cardboard cart. And anyway he now had Bubba for company and for his protection.

Or would have Bubba, except the dog gave a whining, worried bark as they approached the secret place and ran off. After that Boris saw him once through a break in the trees, down at the bottom of the slope near the sledge, wagging his tail nervously, in sporadic bursts, and offering up the occasional bark.

Then at last he was there and the place was just as he remembered it. If anything it was even darker, for snow on the higher branches shut out most of what little light would normally penetrate; and here where the winter had been kept out, the ground was black to eyes used to a white glare. Airless as ever, the place seemed; and what air there was, as before, seemed stirred by unseen shapes and presences. Oh, certainly, it was a place for bad dreams. Especially in the evening. And evening approached even now . . .

Distantly, heard with only the edge of his conscious mind (for he was absorbed with the place, its *genius loci*) Boris was aware of Bubba's occasional barking like frozen gunshots cracking the air. Wishing the dog would be quiet, he scrambled to where the slabs leaned and the fallen lintel bore the ancient shield.

Now that this eyes were growing accustomed to the gloom, and with his cold fingers to help him trace the bat-dragon-devil symbols carved in the stone, he remembered the voice of uttermost evil which he had thought to hear the last time he stood in this place. A dream? But such a real dream: it had kept him from the wooded slope for half a year!

And what was he afraid of, anyway? An old tomb, broken down? The whispers of ignorant peasants, their mumblings and obscure signs? A fancied voice, like the taste of something rotten in his mind? Rotten, yes, but *so* insistent! And how often since then had it come to him in the night, in his dreams, when he was safe in his bed, whispering, "Never forget me, Dragosaaniiii . . ."

On impulse, out loud, he suddenly called out: "See, I didn't forget. I came back. I came here. To your place. No, to *my* place. My secret place!"

His breath plumed in the air in bursts which turned white and drifted away, dispersing. And Boris listened with every fibre of his being. Blue icicles depended from the rim of a leaning slab like gleaming teeth; the pine needles formed a frozen crust beneath his pigskin-booted feet; his last breath fell to earth in frozen crystals before he drew another. And still he listened. But . . . nothing.

The sun was sinking. Boris must go. He turned from the tomb. His words, caught in the frozen crystals of his breath, sent down their message into the earth.

Ahhh! It might have been the sighing of a wind in the high branches, but it rooted Boris to the spot like nails through his feet.

"You . . . !" he heard himself saying to no one, to nothing, to the gloom. "Is it . . . you?"

Ahhh! Dragosaaniiii! And has the iron crept into your blood then, boy? Is that why you've returned?

Boris had rehearsed this moment a hundred times: his response, his reaction, should the voice ever speak to him again in the secret place. Bravado, he remembered none of it now.

Well? And has the winter frozen your tongue to your

teeth? Say it in your head if you can't speak it, boy. What, are you a vacuum? The wolves howl over the passes even now, the winds likewise above the seas and mountains. Even the snow in its falling seems to sigh. And you, so full of words—bursting with questions, thirsting for knowledge— are you struck dumb?

Boris had meant to say: "These hills are mine. This place is mine alone. You are merely buried here. So be quiet!" And he had meant to say it boldly, just as he'd rehearsed it. But now what he said, and stumblingly, was this: "Are you . . . real? Who—what—*how* are you? How can you be?"

How can the mountains be? How can the full moon be? The mountains grow and are eroded. The moon waxes and wanes. They are, and so am I . . .

For all that he failed to understand, Boris grew bolder. He at least knew where this being was—in the ground— and how could he harm anyone from down there?

"If you are real, show yourself to me."

Do you play with me? You know it cannot be. Would you have me put on flesh? I cannot do that. Not yet. Also, I see that your blood is yet water. Yes, and it would freeze like the ice on my tomb, if you saw me, Dragosani.

"Are you . . . a dead thing?"

I am an undead thing.

"I know you!" Boris suddenly clapped his cold hands. "You're what my step-father calls 'imagination.' You're my imagination. He says I have a strong one."

And so you have, but my nature is . . . other than that. No, I am not merely a thing of your mind. Do not flatter yourself.

Boris tried hard to understand. Finally he asked: "But what do you do?"

I wait.

"For what?"

For you, my son.

"But I'm here!"

It grew darker in a moment, as if the trees had leaned closer together, shutting out the light. The touch of the unseen presences was feather-light but suddenly bitter as rime. Boris had almost forgotten his fear, but now it flooded back. And because it is a true adage that familiarity breeds contempt, he had almost forgotten just how much evil that voice in his head contained. Now he was reminded of that, too:

Child, do not tempt me! It would be quick, it would be sweet, and it would be futile. There is not enough of you, Dragosani, and your blood lacks substance. I hunger and would feast—and what are you but a nibble?

"I . . . I'm going now . . ."

Aye, begone. Come back when you're a man and not merely an irritation.

And over his shoulder as he quickly, tremblingly left the place and headed for the clean snow of the fire-break, Boris called back: "You're only a dead thing. You know nothing! What can you tell me?"

I am an undead thing. I know everything that needs to be known. I can tell you everything.

"About what?"

About life, about death, about undeath!

"I don't want to know those things!"

But you will, you will.

"And when will you tell me these things?"

When you can understand, Dragosani.

"You said I was your future. You said you were my past. That's a lie. I have no past. I'm just a boy."

Oh? Ha, ha, ha! So you are, so you are. But in your thin blood runs the history of a race, Dragosani. I am in you and you are in me. And our line is . . . ancient! I know all you want to know, all you will want to know.

Aye, and this knowledge shall be yours, and you shall be one of an élite and ancient order of beings.

Boris was half-way to the break now. Until this point and from the moment he fled, his conversation had been part bravado, part terror, like a man whistling in the dark. Now, feeling safer, he became curious again. Clinging to the bole of a tree and turning to look back, he asked: "Why do you offer anything to me? What do you want of me?"

Nothing which you will not give freely. Only that which is offered freely. I want something of your youth, your blood, your life, Dragosani, that you may live in me. And in return . . . your life shall be as long, perhaps even longer, than mine.

Boris sensed something of the lust, the greed, the eternal endless craving. He understood—or misunderstood—and the darkness behind him seemed to swell, expand, rush upon him like some black poisonous cloud. He turned from it, fled, saw ahead the dazzling white of the fire-break through the black boles of trees. "You want to kill me!" he sobbed. "You want me dead, like you!"

No, I want you undead. There is a difference. I am that difference. And so are you. It's in your blood—it's in your very name—Dragosaaniiii . . .

And as the voice faded to silence Boris emerged into the open space of the fire-break. In the fading light he felt fear falling from him like a weight, felt strangely—uplifted?—so that he held himself erect as he descended to the foot of the hill and found his sledge.

Bubba had waited there, patiently, but when Boris reached out a hand to pat him the dog snarled and drew back, the hair rising in a stiff ridge all along his back.

And after that Bubba would have nothing at all to do with him . . .

Under Dragosani's gaze the snow faded from memory

and the slopes turned green again. The old scar of the fire-break was there still, but merging into the natural contours of the hill under the weight of almost twenty years of growth. Saplings were grown into trees now, their foliage thickening, and in another twenty years it would be difficult to tell that the fire-break had ever been there in the first place.

Dragosani supposed that somewhere in the land ordinances governing these parts, there must be a clause which still forbade farming or hewing or gaming on the green cross of the hills. Yes, for despite old Kinkovsi's lack of more typical peasant superstition (which was doubtless a direct spin-off from the recent tourist boom) the old fears still lived. The taboos were still there, even if their origins were forgotten. They still existed, as surely as the thing in the ground existed. Laws which were intended to isolate it now protected it, preserved it.

The thing in the ground. That was how he thought of it. Not as "he" but "it." The old devil, the dragon, the *vampir*. The real vampire and not merely a creature of sensational novels and films. Still there, lying in the ground, waiting.

Again Dragosani let his mind slip back through the years . . .

When he was nine the local school in Ionesti had closed and his step-father had boarded him out to a school in Ploiesti. There in a very short time it had been discovered that his intelligence was of a high order, and the State had stepped in and sent him to a college in Bucharest. Always on the lookout for talent in the young of their satellite nations, Soviet officials from the Ministry of Education had eventually found him there and "recommended" that he go on to higher education in Moscow. What they meant by "higher education" was in fact intensive indoctrination, following which he would one day be sent back to Romania as a puppet official in a puppet government.

But before that—when he had first learned that he was to board in Ploiesti, and that he could only come home once or twice a year—then he had gone back to the dark glade under the trees to ask the advice of the thing in the ground. Now he went there again, on the wings of memory, and saw himself as he had been: a boy, sobbing into his hands where he kneeled beside a broken slab and poured his tears over the bas-relief motif of bat–dragon–devil.

What? Knowing I seek iron and strong meat, you offer me salt and gruel? Can this be you, Dragosani, who has the seed of greatness in him? Was I mistaken, then? And am I doomed to lie here forever?

"I'm to go to school in Ploiesti. I'm to live there and only come back now and then."

And this is the cause of your grief?

"Yes."

Then you are a girl! How would you hope to learn the ways of the world here in the shadow of the mountains? Why, even the birds that fly see more and farther than you have seen! The world is wide, Dragosani, and to know its ways you must walk them. And Ploiesti? But I know this Ploiesti: it is distant by only a hard day's riding—two at most! And is this a good reason to weep?

"But I don't want to go . . ."

I did not want to be put in the ground, but they put me here. Dragosani, I have seen a sister with her head cut off, with a stake through her breast and her eyes hanging on her cheeks, and I did not weep. No, but I pursued her slayers and skinned them and made them eat their skins. And I raped them with hot irons and before they could die soaked them in oil and put them to the torch and hurled them from the cliffs at Brasov! Only then did I cry—tears

154

of sheerest joy! What? And did I call you my son, Dragosani?

"I'm not your son!" Boris snapped, tears angrily flying. "I'm no one's son. And I have to go to Ploiesti. And it's not two days away but only three or four hours, in a car! You pretend you know so much, but you've never even seen a car, have you?"

No, I never have—until now. Now I see it, in your mind, Dragosani! I've seen a great many things in your mind. Some have surprised me, but none have awed me. So, your step-father's "car" will make it easier for you to get to Ploiesti, eh? Good! And it will make it easier for you to come back again when the time comes . . .

"But—"

Now listen: go to school in Ploiesti—become as clever as your teachers, more clever—and when you return, come back as a scholar. And as a man. I lived for five hundred years and was a great scholar. It was necessary, Dragosani. My learning stood me in good stead then, and will again. One year after I rise, I shall be the greatest power in this world! Oh, yes! Once I would have been satisfied with Wallachia, Transylvania, Rumania, call it what you will— and before that it was enough that the mountains were mine, which no one else wanted—but the world is a smaller place now and I would be greater. When I took part in man's wars I learned the joy of the conqueror, so that next time I would conquer all. And you, too, shall be great, Dragosani—but all in good time.

Something of the importance of what the voice said got through to Boris. Behind its words, he sensed the raw power of the creature which issued them. "You want me to be . . . a scholar?"

Yes. When I walk this world again I would speak with learned men, not village idiots! Oh, I shall teach you, Dragosani—and far more than any tutors in Ploiesti. Much knowledge you shall have from me—and in my turn I shall doubtless learn from you. But how shall you teach me if you yourself are ignorant?

"You've said as much before," said Boris. "But what can you teach me? You know so little of things as they are now. How can you know more? You've been dead—undead—in the ground, anyway—for five hundred years, you said so yourself!"

There came a throaty chuckle in Boris's head. *No fool you, Dragosani. Well, and perhaps you are right. Ah, but there are other seats of knowledge, and other sorts of knowledge! Very well, I have a gift for you. A gift . . . and a sign that indeed I can teach you things. Things you cannot possibly imagine.*

"A gift?"

Indeed. Go, quickly now, and find me a dead thing.

"A dead thing?" Boris shivered. "What sort of dead thing?"

Any sort. A beetle, a bird, a mouse. It makes little difference. Find me a dead thing—or kill me a live thing—and bring the body to me. Give it to me as a gift, and you in turn shall have your gift.

"I saw a dead bird at the foot of the slope. A pigeon chick, I think. It must have fallen from the nest. Will that do?"

Hah! And what dire secret has a pigeon chick, pray tell? But . . . yes, it will suffice. If only to prove a point. Bring it to me.

In twenty minutes Boris was back, laying the poor limp body on the dark earth near the broken, fallen slabs.

And again the cynical snort heard in his head: *Hah! Small tribute indeed. But no matter. Now tell me, Dragosani, would you learn the ways of this small dead thing?*

"It has no ways. It's dead."

Before it died. Would you know the things it knew?

"It knew nothing. It was a fledgling. What could it know?"

It knew many things! Now listen carefully: spread the wings, pluck out the down and small feathers and feel them, smell them, rub them between your fingers and listen to them. Do it . . .

Boris did as instructed, but clumsily, without feeling or expectation. Mites and fleas and a beetle scurried, fleeing the small corpse.

No, no! Not like that. Close your eyes, let me more fully into your mind. Now, like this . . . there!

Boris was in a high place; he felt a swaying and heard the soughing of high branches. Overhead the beckoning blue vault of the sky opened outward forever. He felt he could fall upward into the sky and never stop. Vertigo overtook him; he fell back to his own mind, dropped the dead bird and clutched at the earth.

Ah-hahhh! said the devil in the ground. And again: *Ah-hahhh! What? And was the nest not to your liking, Dragosani? But no, don't stop, there's more. Take up the bird, squeeze its body, feel it pliant in your hands. Feel the small bones under the skin, the tiny skull. Lift it to your face. Open your nostrils. Smell it, breathe it in, let it instruct you! Here, let me help . . .*

Boris was not alone—he was a twin-thing—and he was not Boris! The sensation was weird, frightening. He clung tightly to the memory of Boris, rejected the other.

No, no! Let yourself go. Enter the thing. Be one with it. Know what it knew. Like this:

There was warmth . . . a hard firm platform beneath, soft warm down overhead . . . sky no longer bright and blue but dark . . . many white pricks of light, which were stars . . . the night was still . . . a warm weight pressing down, wings covering . . . the twin-thing snuggling . . . something close by, a sound, a hooting! . . . the warm body above—the parent body—pressing down protectively, wings closing tighter, trembling . . . a slow, heavy beating of the air, growing louder, passing, fading, growing faint . . . again the hooting, farther afield . . . the owl hunted smaller prey tonight . . . the parent body relaxing a little, her rapidly beating heart slowing . . . bright points of light filling the sky . . . soft down . . . warmth.

Now break the body, Dragosani! Tear it open! Crush the skull between your fingers and listen to the vapours of the brain! Look at it in your hands, the entrails, the guts and feathers and blood and bones! Taste it, Dragosani! Use all your senses: touch, taste, see, hear, smell! Use all five—and you will discover a sixth!

Time to fly! . . . time to go . . . the air calling, lifting the small new feathers and beckoning . . . and the twin-being already gone, flown . . . the parent beings eager, frustrated, fluttering, gliding, calling, "come, fly, like this, like this!" . . . The earth a dizzy distance below, and the nest swaying in the wind.

Part of the fledgling, Boris launched himself with it from the shuddering platform of twigs which was the nest. For one brief moment he knew the triumph of flight . . . and in the next knew failure. A squally, blustery day, the wind caught him unawares, side on. After that: utter confusion rapidly turning to nightmare! Spinning, tumbling—an untried wing catching in the fork of a branch, twisting and breaking—the agony of hanging by a broken wing, and then of falling, fluttering, plummeting—and the final sharp crack of a small skull upon a stone . . .

Boris snapped back into himself, snapped out of the spell, saw the mess of a thing he held in his hands.

There! said the old devil in the ground. *And do you still think I can teach you nothing, Dragosani? How is this for knowledge, and was there ever a rarer gift? In all my lifetime I knew only a handful with a talent such as this.*

And you have taken to it as a—why, as a fledgling takes to flight! Welcome to a small, ancient, very select fraternity indeed, Dragosani.

The mess slid from Boris's hands, stained the earth, left slime on his palms and slim fingers. "What?" he said, his jaw hanging open, clammy sweat suddenly starting from his brow. "What . . . ?"

Boris Dragosani (answered the devil in the ground)—*necromancer!*

Then, the horror of the thing bursting over him, Boris had screamed long and loud; and once more he'd fled, and fled in such panic that later he could remember very little of it except the pounding of his feet and heart.

But he couldn't run from his "gift," which from that moment on had gone with him.

Or perhaps it wasn't the horror of what *he* had done (or the suspicion of what he had become) which robbed his mind of the memory of his terror-flight that time, but something else, which came between his screaming and the flight proper. At any rate, vague pictures of that *something* had remained in his mind ever since, and would spring to its surface on occasion when he least expected them—as now:

The gloomy glade of the tomb, and the shattered corpse spread in a welter of feathers and guts and limbs wrenched from their sockets. And a thin and leprous tentacle thrusting upward through the scummy earth, pushing aside soil, pine needles, clots of lichen and chips of stone. Leprous, yes, and composed of something other than flesh, but with scarlet veins pulsing:

And then . . . and then . . . a crimson eye forming in its tip and avidly scanning the ground. The eye dissolving away and a reptilian mouth and jaws taking its place, so that now the tentacle seemed a blind, smooth, mottled snake. A snake whose forked scarlet tongue flickered over the pitiful remains, whose fangs gleamed white and needle sharp, and whose jaws chomped slaveringly until every last morsel was devoured!

Then the swift withdrawal and the spell broken as the pulsing, sickening member was *sucked* back down out of sight into the naked earth.

A "small tribute," the thing in the ground had called it . . .

When Dragosani was done with memories and daydreams he drove into the town whose name he bore. Between the railway stockyards and the river on the outskirts of town, he found the trade and barter market which had flourished there on Wednesdays since a time when the town was the merest huddle of shacks; indeed Dragosani might well have sprung up from this marketplace, this meeting place. And more than that, it had been a fording place. Now there were bridges across the river, several, but in olden times the crossing had been by ford.

It was here those long centuries ago that the invading Turk, pillaging and burning as he came from the east, met the river where it flowed down out of the Carpatii Meridionali to meet the Danube. Here, too, the *Hunyadi*, and after him the Princes of Wallachia, had come down from their castles to call together the fighting men under their banners and set territorial *Voevods* over them, warlords to defend the lands against the incursion of the marauding Turk. The banner these warlords had fought under was that of the Dragon—immemorial seal and sigil of a defender, especially a Christian defender against the Turks—and now Dragosani found himself wondering if that were perhaps the source of the town's name. Certainly it was the source of the dragon on the shield in the place of the forgotten tomb.

In the marketplace he bought a live piglet which he took

away in a sack with holes for ventilation. He took it back
to his car and put it in the boot, then drove back out of
town and found a quiet track off the main road. There he
opened the sack a little way, broke a chloroform capsule
into the boot, slammed the lid shut and left it that way for
a count of fifty. Another ten minutes saw the boot flushed
out (he used the car vacuum-cleaner, reversed, to disperse
the fumes), following which the unfortunate pig went back
inside again. Dragosani certainly didn't want the animal
dying on him. Not just yet, anyway.

By early afternoon he had driven back up out of the
low-lying river valley and into the foothills, where once
again he parked the car within a few hundred yards of the
forbidden cruciform hills. In bright sunlight, but keeping
low and sticking to a hedgerow, he made his way to the
densely wooded slopes and began to climb. There, under
the cover of the frowning pines, he felt more at ease as he
toiled towards the secret place. The piglet in its sack was
slung over his shoulder, completely oblivious to a world
from which it would soon depart.

At the site of the tomb, Dragosani laid the doped animal
in a hollow between twining roots, tethered it to the bole
of a tree and tossed the sack over it for warmth. There
were plenty of wild pigs in the hills; if the piglet came to
in his absence and made a commotion, anyone hearing it
would believe it to be one of the wild variety. Not that that
was likely; just as in Dragosani's boyhood, the fields were
deserted and grown wild for a mile and more around.

At any rate that was where he left the piglet, returning
to his lodgings in mid-afternoon, booking an early evening
meal, and sleeping through the rest of the day. There was
still more than an hour's light when Ilse Kinkovsi woke
him with a substantial meal on a tray, leaving him on his
own to enjoy it and wash it down with a quart of local
beer. She hardly spoke to him at all, seemed surly, glanced

at him with a sort of sneer. That was all right; indeed it was very much to his liking—or so he tried to tell himself.

But as she left his room his eyes were drawn to the jiggle of her hips and he was given to reconsider his attitude. For a peasant she was a very attractive woman. And again he wondered why she hadn't married. Surely she was too young to be a widow? And even then she'd still wear her ring, wouldn't she? It was curious . . .

Chapter Six

TWENTY MINUTES BEFORE SUNDOWN DRAGOSANI WAS BACK in the secret place. The piglet had regained consciousness but did not yet have the strength to stand up. Wasting no time and wanting no distractions, Dragosani knocked the struggling animal out again with a single blow of a KGB-issue cosh. Then he settled down and waited, smoked a cigarette, watched the light fading as the sun sank lower and lower. Here where the pines grew straight as spears in a ring about the ancient tomb, the only real light came from directly overhead, and that was filtered down through an interlacing mesh of branches; but as night drew on so the first stars began to come out, visible in advance to Dragosani, much as they would be to a man in a deep well.

And at last, as he ground out his cigarette and the gloom closed that much more tightly around him:

Ahhh! Dragosaaniiii!

The unseen presences were there as always, springing

up from nowhere, invisible wraiths whose fingers brushed Dragosani's face as if seeking to know him, to be sure of his identity. He shivered and said: "Yes, it's me. And I've brought something for you. A gift."

Oh? And what is this gift? And what would you have from me in return?

Now Dragosani was eager and made no effort to hide it. "The gift is . . . a small tribute. You shall have it later, before I go. As for now:

"'I've talked to you in this place, old dragon, many times—and yet you've never really told me anything. Oh, I'm not saying that you've deceived or misled me, just that I've learned very little from you. Now that may well have been my own fault, I may not have asked the right questions, but in any case it's something I want to put right. There are things you know which I desire to know. There once was a time when you had . . . *powers!* I suspect you've retained many of them, which I don't know about."

Powers? Oh, yes—many powers. Great powers . . .

"I want the secret of those powers. I want the powers themselves. All that you knew and know now, I want to know."

In short, you desire to be . . . Wamphyr!

The word and the way it was uttered in his mind were such that Dragosani could not suppress a shudder. Even he, Dragosani himself—necromancer, examiner of the dead—felt its alien awe, as if the word in itself conveyed something of the awful nature of the being or beings it named. "Wamphyr . . ." he repeated it, and then:

"Here in Romania," he quickly went on, "there have always been legends, and in the last hundred years they've spread abroad. Personally, I've known what you are for many years now, old devil. Here they call you *vampir,* and in the Western world they call you a vampire. There you're a creature in tales to be told at night by the fireside, stories to frighten the children to bed and stir the morbid imagination. But now I want to know what you *really* are. I want to separate fact from fiction. I want to take the lies out of the legend.''

He sensed a mental shrug. *Then, I say it again, you would be Wamphyr. There is no other way to know it all.*

''But you have a history,'' Dragosani insisted. ''Five hundred years you've lain here—yes, I know that—but what of the five hundred before you died?''

Died? But I did not die. They might have murdered me, yes, for it was in their power to do so. But they chose not to. The punishment they chose was greater far. They merely buried me here, undead! But that aside . . . you want to know my history?

''Yes!''

It's a long one, and bloody. It will take time.

''We have time, plenty of it,'' said Dragosani—but he sensed a restlessness, frustration in the unseen presences. It was as if something warned him not to try his luck too far. It was not in the undead thing's nature to be pressured.

But finally: *I can tell you something of my history, yes. I can tell you what I did, but not how it was done. Not in so many words. Knowing my origins, my roots, will not help you to be of the Wamphyri, nor even to understand them. I can no more explain how to be Wamphyr than a fish could explain how to be a fish—or a bird how to be a bird. If you tried to be a fish you would drown. Launch yourself from the face of a cliff, like a bird, and you would fall and be crushed. And if the ways of simple creatures such as these are unknowable, how then the ways of the Wamphyri?*

''May I learn nothing of your ways, then?'' Dragosani was growing angry. He shook his head. ''Nothing of your powers? I don't think I believe you. You showed me how to speak to the dead, so why can't you show me the rest of it?''

Ah! No, you are mistaken, Dragosani. I showed you how to be a necromancer, which is a human talent. It is in the main a forgotten art among men, to be sure, but nevertheless necromancy is an art old as the race itself. As for speaking *to the dead: that is something else entirely. Very few men ever mastered that for a skill!*

"But I talk to you!"

No, my son, I talk to you. Because you are one of mine. And remember, I am not dead. I am undead. Even I could not talk to the dead. Examine them, yes, but never talk to them. The difference lies in one's approach, in their acceptance of one, and in their willingness to converse. As for necromancy: there the corpse is unwilling, *the necromancer extracts the information like a torturer, like a dentist drawing good teeth!*

Suddenly Dragosani felt that the conversation was going in circles. "Stop!" he cried. "You are deliberately obscuring the issue!"

I am answering your questions as best I might.

"Very well. Then don't tell me how to be a Wamphyr, but tell me what a Wamphyr is. Tell me your history. Tell me what you did in your life, if not how you did it. Tell me of your origins . . ."

After a moment:

As you will. But first . . . first you tell me what you know—or think you know—of the Wamphyri. Tell me about these "myths," these "old wives' tales" which you've heard, on which you appear to be something of an authority. Then, as you say, we shall separate the lies from the legend.

Dragosani sighed, leaned his back against a slab, lit another cigarette. He still felt he was getting the runaround, but there seemed little he could do about it. It was dark now but his eyes were accustomed to the gloom; anyway, he knew every twisted root and broken slab. At his feet the piglet snorted fitfully, then lay still again. "We'll take it step by step," he growled.

A mental shrug.

"Very well, let's start with this: A vampire is a thing of darkness, loyal subject of Satan."

Ha, ha, ha! Shaitan was first of all the Wamphyri—in our legends, you understand. Things of darkness: yes, in that night is our element. We are . . . different. But there is a saying: that at night all cats are grey! Thus, at night, our differences are not so great—or are not seen to be so great. And before you ask it, let me tell you this: that because of our proclivity for darkness, the sun is harmful to us.

"Harmful? It would destroy you, turn you to dust!"

What? That is a myth! No, nothing so terrible—but even weak sunlight will sicken us, just as strong sunlight sickens you.

"You fear the cross, symbol of Christianity."

I hate the cross! To me it is the symbol of all lies, all treachery. But fear it? No . . .

"Are you telling me that if a cross were held against you—a holy crucifix—it wouldn't burn your flesh?"

My flesh might burn with loathing—in the moment before I struck dead the one who held the cross!

Dragosani took a deep breath. "You wouldn't deceive me?"

Your doubts tax my patience, Dragosani.

Cursing under his breath for a moment, finally Dragosani continued: "You cast no reflection. Neither in a mirror, nor in water. Similarly, you have no shadow."

Ah! A simple misconception—but not without its sources. The reflection I cast is not always the same, and my shadow does not always conform to my shape.

Dragosani frowned. (He remembered the leprous tentacle from that time almost twenty years ago.) "Do you mean that you are fluid, unsolid? That you can change your shape?''

I did not say that.

"Then explain what you did say."

Now it was the turn of the old one in the ground to sigh. *Will you leave nothing of mystery, Dragosani? No, I'm sure you won't . . .*

But now Dragosani was doing some thinking for himself. "I believe this may answer two questions in one," he said while the other pondered. "Your ability to change into a bat or a wolf, for example. That's part of the legend, too. If it is legend. *Are* you a shape-changer?''

He sensed the other's amusement. *No, but I might seem to be such a creature. In fact there is no such thing as a shape-changer, not that I ever encountered . . .*

Then . . . it seemed that the old one had come to a decision. *Very well, I will tell you: what do you know of the power of hypnotism?*

"Hypnotism?" Dragosani repeated, continuing to frown. But then his jaw fell open as he saw the truth, or what might be the truth, in a sudden flash of realization. "Hypnotism!" he gasped. "Mass hypnotism! That's how you did it!''

Of course. But while it fools the mind it cannot fool a mirror. And while I might appear *to be a fluttering bat or loping wolf, still my shadow is that of a man. Ah! The mystique falls away, eh, Dragosani?*

Dragosani remembered the leprous tentacle again but said nothing. He had long ago decided that dead (or undead) things which talked in men's minds might also be masters of deception. Anyway, he had other questions to ask:

"You can't cross running water. It drowns you."

Hmmm! I may have an answer for that one, too. In my life I was a mercenary Voevod. And aye, I would not *cross running water! It was my strategy. When the invader came*

*I waited and let him cross the water—and slaughtered him
on my side. Perhaps this is where this legend arose, on the
banks of the Dunarea, the Motrul and the Siretul. And I
have seen those rivers run red, Dragosani . . .*

While the other offered his explanation, Dragosani had
been building up to the big one. Now, without pause, he
tossed it in: "You drink the blood of the living! It is a lust
in you, which drives you on. Without blood you die. Your
utterly evil nature demands that you feed on the lives of
others. The blood is the life."

*Ridiculous! As for evil: it is a state of mind. If you
accept evil you must accept good. Perhaps I am out of
touch with your world, Dragosani, but in mine there was
very little of good! And as for drinking blood: do you take
meat? And wine? Of course you do! You devour the flesh
of beasts and the blood of the grape. And is that evil?
Show me a creature which lives, which does not devour
lesser lives. This legend springs from my cruelties, which I
admit, and from all the blood I spilled in my lifetime. As to
why I was so cruel: it seemed to me that if my enemies
believed I was a monster, then they would be reluctant
to come against me. And so I was a monster! If my legend
has lasted so long and grown so fraught with terror, who
may say I was wrong?*

"That doesn't answer my question. I—"

*And I . . . am tired now. Do you know what it takes
from me, this sort of inquisition? And do you think I am
one of your corpses, Dragosani? A suitable case for necromantic examination?*

At that a thought came into Dragosani's mind—but he
suppressed it at once. "One last question," he said darkly.

Very well, if you must.

"The legend has it that the vampire's bite turns ordinary
men into vampires. If you were to draw my blood, old
one, would I become as you—undead?"

A long pause, through which Dragosani sensed something of confusion, a mental scrabbling for an answer. And finally: '

There was a time in the world's youth when the forests were alive with great bats, as they were with all sorts of creatures. Disease destroyed most of them—a specific disease, and horrible—but some learned to live with it. In my day a species existed which drew the blood of other animals, including men. Since the bats were carriers of the disease, they passed it on to those they bit, and the infected victims were seen to take on certain characteristics which—

"Stop!" said Dragosani. "You mean the vampire bat, which still exists in Central and South America even today? Obviously you do. The disease is rabies. But . . . I don't see the connection."

The thing in the ground chose to ignore his scepticism, said: *America?*

"A new land," Dragosani explained. "They hadn't found it in your day. It's vast and rich and . . . very, very powerful!"

Ah? You say so? Well! And you must describe this entire new world of yours in more detail—but on some other occasion. As for now . . . I am tired, and—

"Not so fast!" cried Dragosani, aware that the conversation had strayed. "Are you saying I wouldn't become a vampire if you bit me? Are you trying to say that the legend is unfounded, except upon this supposed connection with vampire bats? That won't wash, old devil! No, for the bat was named after you, not you after the bat!"

Another pause—but not so long as to give the other too much time to think over what he had said—and Dragosani quickly continued: "You asked me if I desired to be of the Wamphyri. And how would you make me a Wamphyr if not in this way? Could I be 'invested' with it, then, as

170

you were once invested with the Order of the Dragon? *Hah!* No more lies, old devil. I want only the truth. And if you really are my 'father,' why do you hold the truth back? What do you fear?''

Dragosani felt the disapproval of the unseen presences, sensed them drawing back from him. In his mind the other's voice was indeed tired now—and accusing. *You promised me a gift, a small tribute, and brought me only weariness and torment. I am a spark that grows dim, my son, an ember that expires. You have kept the flickering flame alive, and would you now snuff it out? Let me sleep now, if you would not . . . exhaust . . . me . . . utterly . . . Dragosaaniiii . . .*

Dragosani clenched his teeth, growled his frustration low in his throat, snatched up the piglet by its hind legs. He jumped to his feet, took out a switchblade and snapped it open. The blade glittered sharp as a razor. ''Your gift!'' he snapped.

The piglet struggled, squealed once. Dragosani slit its throat, let the scarlet blood spray out, then drain onto the dark earth. A wind at once sprang up that sighed in the pines with a voice not unlike that of the thing in the ground: *Ahhh!*

Dragosani tossed the piglet's corpse down in tangled rootlets, stepped back from it, took out a handkerchief and cleaned his hands. The unseen presences crept forward.

''Back!'' Dragosani snapped, turning on his heel to leave. ''Back, you ghosts of men. It's for him, not you.''

Descending through the pines in total darkness, Dragosani was sure-footed as a cat. In his way, he too was a creature of the night. But a live one. And thinking of life, death, undeath, he smiled an emotionless smile into the darkness as he considered again the one question he had not asked: How might one kill a vampire? Kill it dead.

No, he had not asked the thing in the ground that

question—not in a place such as this, during the hours of darkness. For who could gauge what the reaction might or might not be? It could be a very dangerous question indeed.

And anyway, Dragosani believed he already knew the answer.

The next day was Thursday. Dragosani had spent a poor night with very little sleep, and he was up early. Looking out of his window, he saw Ilse Kinkovsi feeding chickens where they had wandered out of the farmyard and on to the grass verge of the country road. Out of the corner of her eye she saw his movement at the window and turned her face up to him.

Dragosani had thrown the windows wide, was breathing the morning air deeply into his lungs. Leaning on the sill, leaning out into the light, his flesh was pale as snow. Ilse looked at his naked chest. When he breathed in deeply like that, the muscles under his arms where they V-ed down into his back seemed to swell out like air sacs. He was deceptive, this one. She suspected he would be very powerful. "Good morning!" she called up.

For an answer he nodded, and staring at her knew now why he'd slept so badly. She was the reason . . .

"Is that good?" she asked, her teeth white where she deliberately licked them.

"What?" he went on the defensive again—and at once silently cursed himself for an immature child. Yes, *him*, Dragosani!

"The air on your skin like that. Does it feel good? But look at you, so pale! You could use some sunlight, too, Herr Dragosani."

"Yes, you could . . . could be right," he stuttered, and withdrew from the window to get dressed. Angrily tugging his clothes on, he thought: *women, females, sex! So . . .*

172

ugly? Is it? So un-*natural! And so . . . necessary? Is this what I lack?*

Well, there was a way to find out. Tonight. It would have to be tonight, for tomorrow the English were coming. He made up his mind and went back to the window.

Ilse had gone back to feeding her chickens. Hearing his cough, she looked up to see him buttoning his shirt, staring down at her. For a long moment their eyes met; then, stumblingly, he said:

"Ilse, does it get chilly still? Er, in the night, I mean . . ."

She frowned, wondering what he was getting at. "Cold? Why, no, it's summer."

"Then tonight," he blurted, "I believe I'll leave my window—and my curtains—open."

Her frown lifted. She tossed her head and laughed. "That's very healthy," she answered after a moment. "I'm sure you'll feel better for it."

Embarrassed now, Dragosani once more withdrew, closed the window and finished dressing. For a moment or two he regretted what he had done—this rendezvous so simply arranged, which in fact seemed to have been arranged for him—but finally he shrugged the feeling off. It was done now. What would be would be. And anyway, it was time he lost his virginity.

Lost his virginity, indeed! It made him sound like a young girl! And yet there was a touching naïvety about that phrase, unlike the blunt delivery of his undead mentor. How had the old devil in the ground put it that time? "A mere pup who never breached a bitch . . ."

Yes, that was it—and he'd been referring to Dragosani's father. His true father. *And so I got into his mind . . . and I bequeathed the night to them!*

He got into his mind—to show him how to do it . . .

Dragosani started as a pebble clattered against his window. He had been sitting on his bed, lost in thought. Now he got up, opened the window again. It was Ilse.

"Breakfast in your room, Herr Dragosani?" she called up, "or will you eat with us?" The emphasis she put on "in your room" was unmistakable, but Dragosani ignored it. No, for first he must speak to the old dragon.

"I'll come down," he answered, and narrowed his eyes thoughtfully at the disappointment which instantly registered in her face. Oh, yes, he would need assistance with this one, this time, this first time. She would know exactly what she was about, and he knew nothing. But . . . the Wamphyr knew everything. And Dragosani suspected that there were certain secrets which even that devious old one wouldn't mind divulging. No, not at all . . .

Dragosani's sexual problem—rather, the mental block which had until now checked his psychological development in this area—had been implanted in puberty, at a time when other boys went on to steal their first kisses and explore their first soft bodies with hot, groping, inexperienced fingers. It had happened during his third year in Bucharest while he was boarding at the college there.

He had been thirteen and looking forward to the summer break. Then his step-father's letter had arrived telling him not to come home. There was disease on the farm; the animals were being slaughtered; visitors were forbidden and even Boris would not be allowed onto the estate. The fever was virulent; people could easily spread it about on their feet, their shoes; the entire area for twenty miles around was under quarantine.

A disaster, apparently—but it need not prove to be one for Boris. He had an "aunt" in Bucharest, his step-father's younger sister, and could stay at her house for the break. It was better than nothing; at least he would have somewhere to go and not be stuck in an outbuilding of the old college, cooking his own food on a tiny stove.

His Aunt Hildegard was a young window with two daughters only a year or so older than Boris himself, Anna and Katrina, and they lived in a large, rambling wooden house on the Budesti road. Oddly, they had never been much mentioned at home and Boris had only ever met them on their very infrequent visits to the Romanian countryside. He had always found his aunt very affectionate, perhaps too much so—and his cousins a little sickly and giggly in the way of young girls, except that there were also undercurrents of a sly sensuality beyond their years— but hardly darkly suspicious or especially odd. Yet he gained the impression from his step-father's attitude towards them that his aunt was something of a black sheep, or at least a lady with a terrible secret.

In the three weeks he lived with her and her precocious daughters, when the college closed down for the summer break, Boris had discovered all he believed he needed to know of her "oddness," of sex and the perverse ways of females, and his experiences had turned him off for all the years in between—until now. For the simple fact of the matter had been that his aunt was a nymphomaniac. Recently set free by the death of her husband, she had allowed her sexual obsession to get out of hand; and her daughters, apparently, were cut of pretty much the same cloth. Even when her ailing husband had been alive she had been notorious for her lovers. Word of her affairs had often got back to her brother in the country, so bringing about his aloofness, his disapproval. He was no prude himself, but he considered her little more than a whore.

Just how far she had carried her excesses was beyond her brother's power to know, especially now that he had broken off almost all contact with her. If he had known, then he would have made other arrangements for the youth;

but his adopted son was, after all, barely a boy; he would surely stand exempt from the woman's vices.

Boris had known none of this but was to find out about it soon enough.

To begin with, there had been no locks on any of the interior doors in his aunt's house. Neither the bedrooms nor the bathroom had locks, not even the toilets. Aunt Hildegard had explained that there were no secret places here—nowhere for the performance of secret deeds—and that secret things in general were not tolerated. Which made it hard for Boris to understand the secretive or mischievously furtive looks which often passed between mother and daughters when he was present.

As for privacy: there was likewise absolutely no need for privacy in a place where nothing was forbidden, nothing frowned upon. Enquiring as to his aunt's philosophy, Boris had been told that this was "a house of Nature," where the human body and its functions were things of Nature given us to "explore, discover, understand and enjoy to their full, without conventional restrictions." Provided that he respect the house and property of his hostess, there was nothing he could not do here and welcome; but he must similarly respect the "natural" behaviour of the resident females of the house, whose ways he would find entirely open and unrestricted. As for philosophy as such: there was too little love in the world and too much hatred; if the lusts of the body and fires of the spirit could be quenched, sated in the pleasurable violence of embraces instead of war, then surely it would be a better place. Perhaps Boris would not understand immediately, but his aunt was sure that he would in a little while . . .

After an early supper on the first evening, Boris had gone up to his room to read. He had brought some of his own books with him from the college, but at the foot of the stairs leading to his bedroom was a tiny room set aside by his aunt as her "library." Looking in, Boris had found the shelves full of erotica and sexual perversions and abnormalities, some of which were so fascinating that he took several of the illustrated volumes upstairs with him. They were unlike anything he had ever seen before, even in the College library which was fairly comprehensive.

In his bedroom he had become engrossed with one of the books (which purported to be factual but was so "improbable" to Boris's mind that he "knew" it must be a spoof, a work of highly imaginative fiction; though how some of the alleged photographs had been produced was quite beyond him) and, like any boy of his age, soon found himself aroused. Masturbation was not unknown to Boris—he relieved himself that way from time to time as most young men do—but here in his aunt's house he hadn't felt secure or private enough to do so. To avoid further frustration, he had taken the books back downstairs to the library.

Earlier, while reading, he had heard a car pull up to the house and the arrival and entry of some visitor or other, someone obviously popular with the household, but had paid no heed. As he deposited the books back in the library, however, he now heard laughter and the sounds of physical activity and apparent enjoyment from the main living-room—a room he had been shown and in which he'd admired the mirrors set all about and the curiously mirrored ceiling—and was drawn to see what was taking place. The door stood a little ajar, and from within as he approached in silence Boris could hear a guttural male voice, straining in something of exertion, plus the now coarsened and urgent voices of his step-aunt and -cousins. It was then that he had started to suspect that something very much out of the ordinary must be going on in there. Boris paused at the door to stare in through the inches-wide gap and and was shocked almost rigid by what he saw. Far from being "fantastic" as he had supposed, the book he had been reading had contained nothing comparable with this! The man—a stranger to Boris, bearded, pockmarked, huge in the belly and hairy—was quite repulsive in his looks and almost malformed in his body. Also, he was naked. What Boris could not know was that he was a satyr, which by this house's standards more than compensated for his ugliness and malformation.

Viewing the interior of the room through a mirror which stood just inside the door, therefore not directly, Boris could not see the entire performance, but what he could see was more than enough. The three females were taking turns with their playmate, urging him to greater efforts, working on him with their hands and mouths and bodies in a frenzy of sexual excess.

He lay on his back upon a divan, while the younger of the sisters, Anna, kneeled astride him and literally bounced herself up and down on him. With each upward bound of her body she revealed most of the great length and thickness of him, shiny with the liquids of their throbbing bodies. With each brief appearance of that slippery pole of flesh, Boris could see Katrina's tiny and almost fragile hand locked tightly around its girth between the two where they continued to collide, working at it no less than her sister's jolting body. As for the mother of the girls, "Aunt" Hildegard, a woman of perhaps thirty-four: she kneeled at the head of the couch and flopped her great loose breasts upon his feverish face, so that her nipples dangled alternately into his gaping, gasping mouth. Occasionally, apparently lost in her ecstasy, she would stretch up, thrusting her pubic region against his quivering lips and tongue.

The women were not naked but all the more lewd for their garments, loose, baggy white things which were open and allowed their breasts and buttocks to be fondled, and all parts of them to be touched at will. What transfixed

Boris most, riveting him to the spot, was not so much that this was sex—of which he knew very little in any case—but that all four participants seemed so utterly involved and engrossed, each enjoying not only the rewards of his/her own facet of the performance, whatever the part being played, but also the cavorting of the others!

But as they changed places and positions before his eyes, and almost without pause commenced a new series of intricate exertions (this time with the man mounted atop his aunt like some awful dog, while the girls played lesser roles), so Boris had begun to understand. No one was neglected here; each became the aggressor in turn, so that all received maximum satisfaction. Or, in Boris's fevered eyes, so that all seemed equally disgusting.

In any event, while he believed that he now understood something of what he was seeing, still he did not quite believe that he was actually *seeing* it. It was the central character—the man, the awful spurting machine—which he couldn't fathom.

Boris knew how exhausted he always felt after masturbating, so how must this hairy animal in the room of mirrors feel? He seemed to be hosing out semen almost continually, and groaning with the intensity of the pleasure given him by each fresh burst; except that it hardly seemed to weary him at all but only served to drive him to greater excess. Surely he must collapse at any moment now!

And as Boris had finally got his legs going and backed away from the door—and as if his aunt had been thinking almost precisely the same thing as Boris himself—he heard her gaspingly say: "Now, now, you two! Let's not weary Dmitri so quickly. Why don't you go and play with Boris, eh? But not too fiercely or else you might frighten him. Poor lamb, he looks the sort who'd frighten very easily. About as lusty as a lettuce!"

That had been enough to send Boris scrambling frantically upstairs to his room, out of his clothes in a flash and into bed. There he lay and cringed—knowing his door was unlocked, that it couldn't *be* locked—waiting for . . . sometimes he daren't even essay a guess at. If he had been alone with one cousin, one normal girl, then perhaps things might have been different. Perhaps then there might have been a shy, gradual, fumbling introduction to sex—to normal sex—with Boris himself taking the stumbling initiative.

For until now Boris's dreams and fancies in this respect had been fairly ordinary. He had even entertained fantasies of being alone with his aunt—of smothering himself in her soft breasts, her white body—and had not found them especially abhorrent or shameful. Not before.

But now he had *seen!* Any innocence his fantasies might have contained was gone now, wrenched out of him. What could there possibly be of normal, healthy sex now? Was there any such thing? He had seen, yes.

Downstairs in this very house he had seen three women (he could no longer think of his cousins as girls) coupling with a seemingly inexhaustible beast. He had seen the beast's great pole of lusting flesh. And should he compare himself with that? Did he as a male even *exist* after that? A twig against a branch? And must he be a party to orgies such as that—like one small hare amongst a pack of hounds? The mere thought of contact with the beast was sickening!

These had been his thoughts as his cousins came looking for him where he lay wrapped in sheets and blankets, absolutely still and breathless in his bed. He had heard them enter, had tried not to twitch when Anna had giggled throatily and asked: "Boris, are you awake?"

"Is he? Is he?" Katrina had eagerly wanted to know.

"No, I don't think so." (Disappointed.)

"But . . . his light is on!"

"Boris?" (Anna's weight pressing down on his bed beside him.) "Are you *sure* you're asleep?"

Feigning sleep, his heart hammering, Boris had turned a little where he lay, grumbled, said: "Wha-? What? Go away. I'm tired."

It was a mistake. Both of them giggled now, their voices still coarse and full of lust. "Boris, won't you play a game with us?" said Katrina. "Stick your head out, at least. We've something . . ." (more giggles) ". . . something to show you!"

He couldn't breathe. He'd tugged his bedclothes so close and tight that he'd shut out the air. He would have to come out in a moment, whether he wanted to or not. "Please go away and let me sleep."

"Boris" (Anna again, and a vision of her with her dainty hands on the beast's belly, jolting up and down on that pink pole) "if we put the lights out will you come out?"

For a moment—the merest moment—a gulp of air—just long enough to fill his lungs! "Yes," he had gasped.

Then he'd heard the click of the light switch and felt Anna stand up, lifting her weight from his bed. "There, it's out!"

It *was* out, as Boris discovered a moment later when, having struggled to free his head, he thrust it into darkness and breathed air deeply into his starved lungs—and almost gagged!

And at once, with more giggles from across the room, the light came on again.

Which of the girls it was, he couldn't tell, but one of them had been standing beside his bed with her loose cassock thing over his head like a tent. The musty smell of the body had been beating into his face, and he had seen the dark V of her pubic patch dewed with a string of milky semen pearls. The light through her garment wasn't good, but it was good enough for Boris to see, when she deliberately bowed her legs outward a little, what looked to him like the parting of that patch into a greedy vertical grin!

"There!" Boris had dimly remembered a husky voice saying, through a rising gale of coarse laughter. "And didn't we *tell* you we had something to show you?"

But that was all that was said, for suddenly beside himself in a panic of loathing, that was when Boris had lashed out. Later he remembered little of it—only the giggles turning to screams, and the dull pain in his fists and skinned knuckles—but he did remember how, the next day, his tormentors had kept well away from him; and how both of them had sported blue bruises, while Anna had a split lip and Katrina a great black eye! Perhaps his aunt had been correct to liken him to a lettuce—in one direction. But for tenacity and ferocity—Boris had lacked neither one.

That next day had been nightmarish. Exhausted after a night of wakefulness, barricaded in his room against all entreaty to come out, Boris had had to suffer his aunt's wrath and (from a safe distance) the accusations of her oversexed daughters. Aunt Hildegard would not feed him, starving him for punishment, and she swore that she would complain to his father if he didn't come to his senses at once. By that she meant that he should come out of his room and talk to her, apologize to the girls, and generally pretend that nothing had happened. He would have none of it, remaining in his room except for short and hurried excursions to the toilet and bathroom, determined that before nightfall he would flee the house and make his way back to Bucharest.

The only trouble with that scheme was that his father was bound to find out and would want to know why, and Boris would simply not be able to tell him. He'd never been an easy man to talk to, and this—this had been simply unbelievable. And even then, assuming his stepfather *did* believe and accepted all that had happened, mightn't there still be doubts about Boris's own—participation? His active, perhaps his willing participation . . .

There were other difficulties, too. Boris had no money and no arrangements had been made for him at the college. Which was why, when evening came around again and when his aunt's threats turned to pleading, he had dragged his bed and dresser away from the door and allowed her to take him downstairs.

She was sorry, she said, that the girls had teased him so badly the night before, and that he'd been so alarmed. What they could possibly have done to offend him so— that he should have reacted so violently—was quite beyond her powers of understanding. But whatever, it was all over now and Boris should try to forget it. It could only cause trouble between herself and her brother if he learned of it—whatever it had been. Oh, yes, for he always blamed her for everything.

Boris had silently agreed with her. It would cause trouble, yes—and even more so if there should be mention of the beast! But his aunt didn't know he knew about that, and it was best that she shouldn't. Otherwise . . . the entire charade would fall apart. Anyway, the satyr was no longer in the house and Boris had hoped he wouldn't be back; Aunt Hildegard had fed Boris, and later he'd heard her telling Anna and Katrina to leave him completely alone, that he wasn't for them, and this must all be handled very delicately; the thing had seemed to be finished with, for which Boris had been grateful.

Until that night . . .

Exhausted, Boris had slept in his bed against the door, his own weight replacing that of the dresser; but that had not been enough. At about 3:00 A.M., aware of some sort of erratic, intermittent motion, he had come half-awake to hear his aunt's voice clumsily hushing and lulling him back to sleep, or at least attempting to. Her voice had been slurred and her breathing very heavy; she had been drinking and was naked, as he discovered when he put out his hand in the darkness. That had instantly shocked him fully awake, aware that this insatiable woman was trying to get into bed with him. And at that, immediately and like a cool, salving hand on his hot brow, an icy anger had come over him to oust and completely replace all fear.

"Aunt Hildegard," he had said into the darkness, sitting up and averting his face from the alcohol on her breath, "please put the light on."

"Ah! Dear boy! You're awake and want to see me. But . . . why! I've been to bed, Boris, and I'm afraid I've no clothes on. So *hot*, these summer nights! I got up for a little drink of water, and must have stumbled in here by mistake." As she finished speaking, her breasts had brushed his face.

Gritting his teeth and again turning his face away, Boris had repeated, "Put on the light."

"But that's very naughty of you, Boris!" she'd girlishly pretended to protest, at the same time finding the light switch. And momentarily dazzled, there she had stood quite naked where she'd forced the bed back from the open door. And smiling a little drunkenly at him, which had the effect of making her look utterly stupid and disgusting, she'd moved towards him and reached out her arms.

Then, seeing that he was fully dressed, and for the first time noting the strange look on his face, her hand had flown to her mouth. "Boris, I—"

"Aunt," he had swung his legs out of bed and slipped his feet into his shoes, "you will get out of this room now, please, and stay out. If you do not, *I* shall leave, and if the door downstairs is locked then I'll break a window. Then, as soon as I'm able, I shall tell my step-father exactly what goes on in this house, and—''

"Goes on?" she was sobering rapidly, trying to catch hold of his hand, beginning to look worried.

"About the men who come here, to fuck you and my cousins—like the great bulls which service my step-father's cows!"

"Why, you—!" She had staggered back from him, her eyes wild in a suddenly white face. "You *saw!*"

"Get out!" Boris had sneered at her then, a withering look which he would employ from that day forward when dealing with women, and tried to thrust her from the door.

At that her eyes had narrowed to slits and she'd spat at him: "So that's the way it is, is it? The big boys at the college got to you first, did they? You like them better than girls, do you?"

Boris had turned towards the window then, picking up a chair. "Go on," he'd snapped, "out! Or I leave at once, right now. And not only will I tell my father, but also every policeman I meet between here and Bucharest. I'll tell them about the library of dirty books you keep—which alone might get you a term in prison—and about your daughters, who are little more than girls and already worse than whores—"

"Whores?" she had cut him off with such a hiss that he'd thought she would fly at him.

"—but who could never be as totally rotten as you!" he'd finished.

Then she had broken down, bursting into tears and letting him shove her from the room without further protest. And for the rest of the night he'd slept soundly and completely undisturbed.

That had been the end of it. At midday the next day, while Boris was enjoying his lunch in silence and on his own, his step-father had arrived to take him home. The trouble with the animals was over; it had not been so serious after all, thank God! Never had Boris been so glad to see anyone in his whole life, and he'd had to fight hard not to show it too much. While he got his things together Aunt Hildegard spent an apparently cordial if careful half-hour with her brother, who made a point of asking after his nieces, neither of them being present. Then, with brief farewells, Boris and his step-father had left to begin their trip back into the country.

At the gate as they got into the car, Aunt Hildegard had managed to catch Boris's eye. Her look, just for a second, before she began to wave them goodbye, was pleading. Her eyes begged his silence. In answer he had once more shown her that sneer, that look far worse than any snarl or threat, which said more of what he thought of her than any thousand words ever could.

In any event, he had never spoken of that awful visit to anyone. Nor would he ever, not even to the thing in the ground.

The thing in the ground . . . the old devil . . . the Wamphyr.

He was waiting (what else could he do but wait?) when Dragosani arrived in the gloomy glade of the tomb just before dusk with another piglet in a sack. He was awake, angry, lying there in the ground and fuming. And as the sun's rim touched the rim of the world and the far horizon turned to blood, he was the first to speak:

Dragosani? I smell you, Dragosani! And have you come to torment me? With more questions, more demands? Would you steal my secrets, Dragosani? Little by little, piece by piece, until there's nothing left of me? And then what? When I lie here in the cold earth, how will you reward me? With the blood of a pig? Ahaaa! I see it's so. Another piglet—for one who has bathed in the blood of men and virgins and armies! Often!

"Blood is blood, old dragon," Dragosani answered. "And I note you're more agile tonight for what you drank last night!"

For what I drank? (Scorn, but feigned or genuine?) *No, the earth is the richer, Dragosani, not these old bones.*

"I don't believe you."

And I don't care! Go, leave me be, you dishonour me. I have nothing for you and will have nothing from you. I do not wish to talk. Begone!

Dragosani grinned. "I've brought you another pig, yes— for you or for the earth, whichever—but there's something more, something rare. Except . . ."

The old one was interested, intrigued. *Except?*

Dragosani shrugged. "Perhaps it has been too long. Perhaps you're not up to it. Perhaps it's impossible—even for you. For after all, what are you but a dead thing?" And before the other could object: "Or an undead thing, if you insist."

I do insist . . . Are you taunting me, Dragosani? What is it you bring me this night? What would you give me? What do you . . . propose?

"Maybe it's more what we can give each other."

Say on.

Dragosani told him what was in his mind, exactly what it was he was willing to share.

And you would trade? What would you have from me in return for this . . . sharing? (Dragosani could almost sense the Wamphyr licking its lips.)

"Knowledge," Dragosani answered at once. "I'm just a man, with a man's knowledge of women," he lied, "and—" He paused in confusion, for the old one was chuckling! It had been a mistake to lie to him.

Oh? A man's knowledge of women? A "complete" man's knowledge, eh, Dragosani?

He gritted his teeth, choked out: "There hasn't been

187

time . . . my work, studies . . . the opportunity hasn't
arisen."

*Time? Studies? Opportunity? Dragosani, you are not a
child. I was eleven when I tore through my first maidenhead, a thousand years ago. After that—virgin, bitch,
whore, what did it matter? I had them all, in all ways—
and always wanted more! And you? You have not tasted?
You have not soaked yourself in the sweat and the juice
and the hot sweet blood of a woman? Not one? And you
call me a dead thing!*

The old one laughed then, laughed uproariously, out-
rageously, obscenely. He found it all so ecstatically ridiculous! His laughter went on and on, became a deluge, a
tidal wave, a howling ocean of laughter in Dragosani's
head, threatening to drown him.

"Damn you!" He stood up and stamped on the earth,
spat on it. "Damn you!" He shook his knotted fists at the
black soil and tumbled slabs. "Damn you, damn you,
damn you!"

The old one was quiet in a moment, oozing like some
nightmare slug in Dragosani's mind. *But I'm already
damned, my son*, he said, after a little while. *Yes, and so
are you . . .*

Dragosani snatched out his knife, reached for the stunned
piglet.

*Wait! Not so hasty, Dragosani. I have not refused. But
tell me: since it would appear that like some puny priest
you've abstained for all these long years, why now?*

Dragosani thought about it, decided he might as well tell
the truth. The old devil in the ground had probably seen
through him, anyway. "It's the woman. She aggravates
me, taunts me, flaunts her flesh."

Ahhh! I know the sort.

"Also, I believe she thinks I've been with men—or at
least she has wondered about it."

Like the Turks? The old one's mental response was sharp, touched with hatred. *That is an insult!*

"I think so too," Dragosani nodded. "So . . . will you do it?"

You are inviting me into your mind, am I correct? Tonight, when this woman comes to you?

"Yes."

And it is an invitation, made of your own free will?

Dragosani grew wary. "Just this once," he answered. "It will have no permanence."

Again you flatter yourself, the other chuckled. *I have—or will have—my own body, Dragosani, which is nothing so weak as yours!*

"And you can do it? And will I learn from it?"

Oh, I can do it, my son, yeessss! Have you forgotten the fledgling? And did you learn something that time, too? Who made you a necromancer, Dragosani? Yes, and this time you will learn . . . much!

"Then I want nothing more from you—for now, anyway." He began to back away from the tomb, moving downhill, away from that place of centuried horror. And—

But what of the piglet? asked the thickly glutinous voice in his head. And more hurriedly: *For the earth, Dragosani, for the earth.*

In the deep, unquiet gloom, Dragosani narrowed his eyes. "Oh, yes, I very nearly forgot," he said, his tone not quite sarcastic. "The piglet, of course. For the earth . . ." Quickly he returned, slit the insensate animal's throat, tossed its pink body down. And then, without looking back, he made silently away.

A little way down the slope, against the bole of a tree where great roots forked, trapped there and unable to roll any farther, he saw something strange and stooped to pick it up. It was last night's offering, or what remained of it. A tightly interwoven ball of pink skin and crushed bones, all dry as crumpled cardboard. A beetle crawled on it, seeking in vain for some morsel of sustenance. Dragosani let it fall and roll out of sight.

Oh, yes, he thought—but guarded his thoughts carefully there in the darkness beneath the pines—*oh, yes. For the earth. Only for the earth . . .*

Dragosani got back to the Kinkovsi place in time to eat supper with the family again; for the last time, though he couldn't know that then. During the meal Ilse showed little or no interest in him, which was as well for he felt tense and on edge. He was not sure he'd done the right thing; the old devil in the ground was no fool and had stressed that this would be at Dragosani's own invitation; his old revulsion was gradually mounting in him as the time approached; but at the same time his body ached for release from years of sexual self-denial. For the first time since his arrival here the food seemed tasteless to him, and even the beer was flat and lifeless.

Later, in his room, he paced and fantasised, growing ever more angry with himself and fretful as the hours slipped by. For the third or fourth time since supper he took out the half-dozen volumes he'd brought with him on vampirism, read through the relevant passages, put the books away again, out of sight in a suitcase. According to legend, one must never accept any invitation from a vampire; and, equally important, one must never invite a vampire to do anything! In this the conscious will of the victim (by accepting or making an invitation) was all-important. It meant in effect that it was his decision *to be* a victim. The will was like a barrier in the mind of the victim which the vampire was reluctant, even unable, to surmount without the aid of the victim himself. Or perhaps, psychologically, it was a barrier the victim must surmount: before he could become a victim, he must first believe . . .

In Dragosani's case it was a question of the depth of his belief. He *knew* the thing in the ground was there, so that didn't come into it. But as yet he did not know what power—or the extent of the power—the creature could exert externally. Perhaps even more important, now that he had "invited it in," as it were, he didn't know the limits of his own resistance, or if he would be able to resist at all. Or if he would want to . . .

Well, doubtless he would find out soon enough.

The hour between midnight and 1:00 A.M. passed incredibly slowly, and as the trysting time approached Dragosani began to hope that Ilse would think better of it and stay away. She might be sound asleep even now, with no intention of meeting him here. It could simply be a game she played with all of her father's guests—to make them look and feel foolish! In fact, she might well feel the same way about men as Dragosani—until now—had been caused to feel about women.

A half-dozen and more times the thought had come to him that she was making an utter fool of him, and each time he had gone to the open window to close it and draw his moon-silvered curtains. But on every occasion he had paused, something had stopped him, and he'd snarled silently at his own incompetence in this thing and gone back to sit on his bed in the darkness of the room.

Now, at two minutes past the hour, cursing himself for a buffoon and rushing to the window yet again, he was on the point of slamming it shut when—

Down there in the moonlit farmyard, making its way like a shadow amongst shadows, a figure, dark and gauzy, fleeting—and Ilse Kinkovsi's bedroom window open a little way, seeming to smile up at him with her face, her knowing eyes. She was coming!

God, how Dragosani needed the old one now! And how

he did not want him. *Did* he need him, really? But . . .
dare he make do without him?

Elation vied with terror in Dragosani and was very
nearly overwhelmed at the first pass. Terror born not alone
of the tryst itself, nor even the purpose of the tryst, but
perhaps more out of his own ability—or inability?—to
carry it through. He was a man now, yes, but in matters
such as this still a boy. The only flesh he had known,
whose secrets he had delved, had been cold and dead and
unwilling. But this was live and hot and all *too* willing!

Revulsion climbed higher in him, coursed through him
like a flood. He had been a boy, just a boy . . . pictures
filled his head in bestial procession, which he had thought
were forgotten, thrust out . . . the visit to his aunt's house
. . . his cousins . . . the beast-thing which he knew had
been only a rutting man! God, that—had—been—a—
nightmare!

And was it to be like that all over again? And himself
the lusting, slavering beast?

Impossible! He couldn't!

He heard the creak of a stair down in the bowels of the
guesthouse, flew to the window and stared wild-eyed out
into the night. Another creak, closer, sent him flying to the
light switch. She was out there, on the landing, coming to
his door!

A gust of wind moaned into the room, billowing the
curtains, striking at—*into*—Dragosani's heart. In a moment all fear, all uncertainty was gone. He stepped out of
the moonlight into shadow and waited.

The door opened silently and she came in. Trapped in a
shaft of moonlight the grey veil-like garment she wore was
almost transparent. She closed the door behind her, moved
towards the bed.

"Herr Dragosani?" she said, her voice trembling just a
little.

"I'm here," he answered from the shadows.

She heard but didn't look his way. "So . . . I was wrong about you," she said, raising her arms and drawing off the gauzy shift. Her breasts and buttocks were marble where the moon caressed them.

"Yeesss," he whispered, stepping forward.

"Well," now she turned to him, "here I am!"

She stood like a statue carved of milk, gazing at him with nothing at all of innocence. He came forward, a dark silhouette, reaching for her. In daylight she had thought his eyes a trifle weak, a watery blue—a soft, almost feminine, filmstar blue—but now . . .

The night suited him. In the night his eyes were feral—like those of a great wolf. And as he bore her down on to the bed, only then did she feel the first niggling doubt in the back of her mind. His strength was—enormous!

"I was very, *very* wrong about you," she said.

"*Aahhh!*" said Dragosani.

The following morning, Dragosani called for his breakfast early. He took it in his room, where Hzak Kinkovsi found him looking (and feeling) more fully alive than he had thought possible. The country air must really agree with him. Ilse, on the other hand, was not so fortunate.

Dragosani didn't need to enquire after her: her father was full of it, grumbling to himself as he served up a substantial breakfast on a tray. "That woman," he said, "my Ilse, is a good strong girl—or should be. But ever since her operation—" and he had shrugged.

"Her operation?" Dragosani had tried not to seem too interested.

"Yes, six years ago. Cancer. Very bad for a young girl. Her womb. So, they took it away. That's good, she lives. But this is farming country. A man wants a wife who'll give him children, you know? So, she'll be an old maid—

maybe. Or perhaps she'll go and get a job in the city. Strong sons are not so important there.''

It explained something, possibly. "I see," Dragosani nodded; and, carefully: "But this morning . . . ?''

"Sometimes she doesn't feel too good, even now. Not often. But today she really isn't up to much. So, she stays in her room for a day or two. Curtains drawn, dark room, all wrapped up in her bed, shivering. Just like when she was a little girl and sick. She says she doesn't want a doctor, but—" he shrugged again. "—I worry about her.''

"Don't," said Dragosani. "I mean, don't worry about her.''

"Eh?" Kinkovsi looked surprised.

"She's a full-grown woman. She'll know what's best for her. Rest, quiet, a nice dark room. Those are the right things. They're all I need when I'm a bit down.''

"Hmm! Well, perhaps. But still it's worrying. And a lot of work to be done, too! The English come today.''

"Oh?" Dragosani was glad that the other had changed the subject. "Maybe I'll meet them tonight.''

Kinkovsi nodded, looked gloomy. He gathered up the empty tray. "Difficult. I don't know a lot of English. What I know I learned from tourists.''

"I know some English," said Dragosani. "I can get by.''

"Ah? Well, at least they'll be able to talk to someone. Anyway, they bring good money—and money talks, eh?" he managed a chuckle. "Enjoy your breakfast, Herr Dragosani.''

"I'm sure I will.''

Beginning to grumble again under his breath, Kinkovsi left the garret room and made his way downstairs. Later, when Dragosani went out, both Hzak and Maura were readying the lower rooms for their expected English guests.

*   *   *

By midday Dragosani had driven into Pitesti. He did not know why exactly, except that he remembered the town had a small but very comprehensive reference library. Whether or not he would have gone to the library—or what he would have done there—is academic. The question did not arise for he was not given the chance to go there; the local police found him first.

Alarmed at first and imagining all sorts of things (worst of all, that he had been watched and followed, and that his secret—concerning the old devil in the ground—had been discovered), he calmed down as soon as he found out what the trouble really was: that Gregor Borowitz had been trying to track him down since the day he left Moscow and finally had succeeded. It was a wonder Dragosani hadn't been stopped at the border where he'd crossed into Romania at Reni. The local law had tracked him to Ionestasi, from there to Kinkovsi's, finally to Pitesti. In fact it was his Volga they'd tracked: there weren't many of those in Romania. Not with Moscow plates.

Finally the policeman in charge of the patrol vehicle which had stopped him apologized for any inconvenience and gave Dragosani a "message"—which was simply Borowitz's Moscow telephone number, the secure line. Dragosani went with them at once to the police station and phoned from there.

On the other end of the line, Borowitz came right to the point: "Boris, get back here a.s.a.p."

"What is it?"

"A member of the staff at the American embassy has had an accident while touring. A fatal accident: wrecked his car and gutted himself. We haven't identified him yet—not officially, anyway—but we'll have to do it soon. Then the Americans will want his body. I want you to see him first—in your, er, specialist capacity . . ."

"Oh? What's so important about him?"

"For some time now we've suspected him and one or

two others of spying. CIA, probably. If he's one of a network, it's something we should know about. So get back quickly, will you?''

"I'm on my way."

Back at Kinkovsi's Dragosani tossed his things into the car, paid what he owed and a little more, thanked Hzak and Maura and accepted sandwiches, a flask of coffee and a bottle of local wine. But for all that they gave him these parting gifts, it was obvious that Hzak had some misgivings about him.

"You told me you were a mortician," he complained. "The police laughed when I told them that! They said you're a big man in Moscow, an important man. It seems a great shame that an important man would want to make a fool out of a fellow countryman—an unimportant man!"

"I'm sorry about that, my friend," said Dragosani. "But I *am* an important man and my job is very special— and very tiring. When I come home I like to forget my work completely and just take it easy, and so I became a mortician. Please forgive me."

That seemed to suffice; Hzak Kinkovsi grinned and they shook hands, and then Dragosani got into his car.

From behind her drawn curtains Ilse watched him drive away and breathed a sigh of relief. It was unlikely she'd ever meet another like him, and maybe that was as well, but . . .

Her bruises were blooming now but would soon fade, and anyway she could always say she had suffered a dizzy bout, tripped and fallen. The bruises would disappear, yes, but not the memory of how she had got them.

She sighed again . . . and shivered deliciously.

Interval One:

On the top floor of a well-known London hotel, in a suite of private office, Alec Kyle sat at the desk of his ex-boss and scribbled frantically in shorthand. The "ghost" (he couldn't help thinking of it that way) which stood facing him across the desk had been speaking rapidly, in soft, well-modulated tones, for more than two and a half hours now. Kyle's wrist felt cramped; his head ached from the myriad weird pictures implanted there; he had no doubt at all but that the "ghost" spoke the truth, the whole truth, and etc . . .

As to how it (*he!*) knew these matters he so fluently related, or why he related them—who is to say what knowledge such a creature should or shouldn't have and tell? But one thing Kyle knew for certain was this: that the information to which he now found himself privy was vastly important, and that he must also consider himself privileged to be the medium through which it was imparted.

As a pain suddenly shot up his forearm from his wrist, causing him to drop his pencil and clutch at his hand as it went into a brief spasm, so his unearthly visitor paused. It was as good a juncture as any, Kyle thought, and he was grateful. He massaged his hand and wrist for a minute, then took up a sharpener and renewed the pencil's point for what must be the ninth or tenth time at least.

"Why not use a pen?" the ghost asked, in such a perfectly natural and inquiring tone that Kyle found himself answering without even considering that he talked to something far less substantial than smoke.

"I prefer pencils. Always have. Just a quirk, I suppose.

197

Anyway, they don't run out of ink! I'm sorry I stopped just then, but my wrist feels mangled!''

"We've a way to go yet."

"I'll manage somehow."

"Look, go and get yourself another coffee. Have a cigarette. I realize how strange all this must be for you. It's strange for me, too—but if I were you my nerves would be leaping! I think you're doing remarkably well. And we're getting on fine. I was fully prepared, before I came here, to allow several visits just to let you adjust to me. So as you can see, we're well ahead.''

"Yes, well it's time that's worrying me." Kyle answered, lighting up and drawing luxuriously on the smoke, saturating his lungs with it. "You see, I've a meeting to attend at 4:00 P.M. It's then that I'm to try to convince some rather important people that they keep the branch open and allow me to take over from Sir Keenan and run it. So you see, I'd like to be finished before then.''

"Don't let it concern you," the other smiled his wan smile. "Consider them convinced.''

"Oh?" Kyle got up and went through into the main office, put money into the coffee machine. This time the ghost followed him, stood behind him. When he turned from the machine it was there, office furniture visible right through it. It was less than a holograph, less than a bubble, ectoplasm. Kyle started and slopped a little coffee, edged around the other and went back into Gormley's office.

"Yes," the ghost continued, back where it had been, "I believe we'll be able to 'sway' your superiors in your favour.''

"We?" said Kyle.

The other merely shrugged. "We'll see. Anyway, I want to tell you a little more about Harry Keogh now, before returning to Dragosani. Sorry to jump about like this, but it's better if you see a complete picture.''

"Anything you say."

"Are you ready?"

"Yes," Kyle took up his pencil. "Except . . ."

"Well?"

"It's just that I was wondering where you fit into all of this?"

"Me?" the ghost raised its eyebrows. "I suppose I'd have been disappointed if you hadn't asked. Since you have: if things work out the way I hope, I'll be your future boss!"

Kyle's face twitched and he grinned lopsidedly. "A . . . ghost? My future boss?"

"I thought we'd been through that once," said the other. "I'm not a ghost and never have been. Though I'll admit I came pretty close. But we'll get to that, you'll see."

Kyle nodded.

"Can we get on now?"

And Kyle nodded again.

Chapter Seven

HARRY KEOGH WAS MILES AWAY, HIS THOUGHTS LOST IN the clouds that drifted like puffs of cotton wool on the blue ocean of a summer sky. Hands behind his head, a blade of sweet grass standing straight up like a tiny mast, its white tip trapped in his teeth, he hadn't said a word since they'd made love. Seagulls cried where they made white splashes in the shallows, diving for fish, and their somehow plaintive songs came up off the sea on a breeze that moved the grass on the dunes like a caress.

A caress, too, Brenda's hand where she stroked him, even though she no longer commanded the full attention of his flesh. In a little while he might want her again, but if not it wouldn't matter. In fact she liked him like this: quiet, verging on sleep, with all of his strangeness sucked out of him. He *was* strange, yes, but that was all part of his fascination. It was one of the reasons she loved him. And sometimes she fancied that he loved her, too. It was difficult to tell, with Harry. Most things were difficult to tell with him.

"Harry," she said, gently tickling his ribs. "Anybody in?"

"Umm?" the grass in his teeth gave a feeble twitch. She knew he wasn't ignoring her, knew that he simply wasn't here. Not here at all—not all of him—but somewhere else, somewhere very different. Now and then she would try to find out about that place, Harry's secret place, but so far he'd kept mum.

She sat up, buttoned her blouse, straightened her skirt, brushed sand from its pleats. "Harry, you should do yourself up. There are people down on the beach. If they walked this way they'd see."

"Umm," he said again.

She did it for him, then curled beside him and kissed his forehead. Tugging his ear, she asked: "What are you thinking? Where *are* you, Harry?"

"You don't want to know that," he said. "It's not always a nice place. I'm used to it, but you wouldn't like it."

"I'd like it if you were there," she said.

He turned his face towards her, squinted a little, frowned seriously. He could look very serious, she thought, sometimes—in fact most of the time. Now he shook his head. "No, you wouldn't like it if I was there," he said. "You'd hate it."

"Not if I were with you."

"It's not a place where you can be with someone," he told her, which was as close to the truth as he had ever come on this subject. "It's a place for being entirely alone."

She wanted to know more. "Harry, I—"

"Anyway, we're here," he cut her off. "Nowhere else. We're here and we've just made love."

Knowing that if she tried to probe deeper he would only

retreat, she changed the subject. "You've made love to me," she said, "eight hundred and eleven times."

"I used to do that," he said, presently.

It stopped her dead in her tracks. After a moment's thought, she said: "Do what?"

"Count things. Anything. Tiles on a toilet wall. You know, while I was sitting there."

She sighed, exasperated. "I was talking about making love, Harry! Sometimes I think there isn't an ounce of romance in you."

"There isn't now," he agreed. "You just had it all!" That was better. He was away from his morbid turn. That was how Brenda thought of it when Harry was vague and strange in that way of his: "a morbid turn." She went along with it, wrinkled her nose playfully, was glad for his humour.

"Eight hundred and eleven times," she repeated, "in just three years! That's a lot. Do you know how long we've been going out?"

"Since we were kids," he answered. His eyes were on the sky again and she could see he was only half interested in what she was saying. There was something on his mind, hovering on the periphery of his awareness. Knowing him, she knew it was there. Maybe one day she'd know what it was. All she knew now was that it came and went, and that this time it seemed to be taking its time going.

"But how *long?*" she insisted. She caught his chin in a delicate hand, turned his face towards hers.

He stared at her blankly, let his eyes focus of their own accord. "How long? Four or five years, I suppose."

"Six," she said. "Since you were twelve and I was eleven. At twelve you took me to the pictures and held my hand."

"There you go," he said, making an effort and coming

back to earth. "And you just accused me of being unromantic!"

"Oh?" she said. "But I bet you can't remember the film we saw. It was *Psycho*. I don't know which of us was the most frightened!"

"I was," he grinned.

"Then," she continued, "when you were thirteen, we made a picnic in the field on Ellison's Bank. After we had eaten we fooled about a bit and you put your hand on my leg under my dress. I shouted at you and you pretended it was an accident. But the next week you did it again and I wouldn't speak to you for a fortnight."

"I should be so unlucky now!" Harry sighed. "Anyway, you soon enough came back for more."

"Then you started going to school in Hartlepool and I didn't see so much of you. The winter was a long one. But the next summer was a good one—for us, anyway. One day we got a changing tent on the beach at Crimdon and went swimming. Afterwards, in the tent, when you were supposed to be drying my back, you touched me."

"And you touched me," he reminded her.

"And you wanted me to lie down with you."

"But you wouldn't."

"Not until the next year. Harry, I wasn't even fifteen! That was terrible!"

"Oh, it wasn't so bad," he grinned. "Not the way I remember it. But do you remember that first time?"

"Of course I do."

"What a mess!" he chuckled ruefully. "Like trying to pick a lock with a piece of wet blotting paper."

She had to smile. "You got good at it very quickly, though," she said. "I always wondered where you learned it all. I suppose I really wondered if someone else had shown you how."

He had been smiling but now the smile fell from his

face in a moment. "What do you mean by that?" he said sharply.

"Why, another girl, of course!" She was startled by his abrupt change of mood. "What did you think I meant?"

"Another girl?" he was frowning still. But slowly his look turned first to a sour smile, then an amused grin, and at the last a shaky laugh. "Another girl!" he said again, laughing outright now. "What, when I was eleven?"

Relieved, Brenda laughed with him. "You're funny," she said.

"You know," he answered, "it seems that all my life people have been telling me the same thing: that I'm funny. I'm not really, you know. God, sometimes I wish I knew how to be: how to have a good laugh! It's as if I don't have time, as if I've never had time. Did you ever get the feeling that if you don't laugh soon you'll scream? It's a feeling I get, I promise you."

She shook her head. "Sometimes I think I'll never understand you. And sometimes I think you don't want me to." She sighed. "It would be nice if you wanted me as much as I want you."

He stood up, drew her to her feet and kissed her on the forehead, his way of changing the subject. "Come on, let's walk all the way along the beach into Hartlepool. You can catch a bus back to Harden from there."

"Walk into Hartlepool? That'll take all day!"

"We'll stop for a coffee on the beach at Crimdon," he said. "And we can have a swim from the sands a bit farther along. Then we'll go to my place. You can stay until this evening if you like—unless you've other plans?"

"No, I haven't—you know I haven't—but . . ."

"But?"

Suddenly she was upset, a touch of anxiety. "Harry, what's going to happen to us?"

"How do you mean?"

"Do you love me?"

"I think so."

"But don't you know? I mean, I know I love you."

They began to walk along the dunes, gradually making for the damp sands where the sea was retreating. There were people swimming in the sea down there but not many; the beach was dirty with all the debris of the coalmines to the north, a problem which had been growing for a quarter of a century. Black lorries trundled at the waterline like great amphibious beetles, where their crews shovelled up rounded nuggets of washed sea-coal like black gold. A few miles south of here it was a little cleaner, but as far as Seaton Carew coal and slag deposits marred the clean white sands. Farther south still the damage was much less, but since the mines were almost exhausted Nature would soon begin to put things right again. Still, it would take a long time for the beaches to return to their former beauty. Perhaps they never would.

"Yes," Harry finally answered, "I think I do love you. I mean, I know I do. It's just that I've a lot on my mind. Is that what you mean? That I don't show it enough? See, I don't know what you want me to say. Or I haven't the time to think of the right things to say."

She clung to his arm, snuggled closer as they walked. "Oh, you don't have to say anything. It's just that I'd hate it to end . . ."

"Why should it end?"

"I don't know, but I worry about it. We don't seem to be getting anywhere. My parents worry, too . . ."

"Oh," he said, glumly nodding. "Marriage, you mean?"

"No, not really," she sighed again. "I know how you feel about that: not yet, you keep saying. And: we're too young. I agree with you. I think my mother and father do, too. I know you like to be on your own a lot; and you're right: we *are* too young!"

"You keep saying that," he said, "but still we end up going round in circles."

She looked downcast. "It's just that . . . well, the way you are, I never know what's what. If only you'd tell me what it is that preoccupies you so. I know there's something, but you won't say."

He looked about to say something, changed his mind. Brenda held her breath, let it go when it became apparent he'd backed off. She tried elimination.

"I know it's not your writing, because you were like this long before you started to write. In fact, as long as I've known you. If only—"

"Brenda!" he stopped, grabbed her in his arms, dragged her to a halt. He seemed breathless, unable to speak, to say what he wanted to say. It frightened her.

"Yes, Harry? What is it?"

He gulped, drew breath, started to walk again. She caught up with him, grabbed his hand. "Harry?"

He wouldn't look at her, but he said:

"Brenda, I . . . I want to talk to you."

"But I *want* you to!" she said.

Again he stopped walking, drew her into an embrace, stared out to sea over her shoulder. "It's a queer subject, that's all . . ."

She took the initiative, broke away, led him by the hand along the beach. "Right. We walk, you talk, I listen. Queer subject? I don't mind. There, I've done my bit. Your turn."

He nodded, glanced at her out of the corner of his eye, coughed to clear his throat and said: "Brenda, have you ever wondered what people think about when they're dead? I mean, what their thoughts are when they lie there in their graves."

She felt goose-flesh come up on her neck and at the top of her spine. Even with the sun hot on her, the utterly emotionless tone of his voice coupled with what he had said chilled her to the marrow. "Have I ever wondered—?"

"I said it was a queer subject," he hurriedly reminded her.

She didn't know what to say to him, how to answer him. She gave an involuntary shudder. He couldn't be serious, could he? Or was this something he was working on? That must be it: it was a story he was writing!

Brenda was disappointed. A story, that's all. On the other hand, perhaps she had been wrong to neglect his writing as the source of his moodiness. Maybe he was that way *because* there was no one to talk to. Everyone knew that he was precocious; his writing was brilliant, the work of a mature man. Was that it? Was it simply that he had too much bottled up inside, and no way to let it out?"

"Harry," she said, "you should have told me it was your writing!"

"My writing?" his eyebrows went up.

"A story," she said. "That's what it is, isn't it?"

He began to shake his head, then changed it to a nod. And smiling, he nodded more rapidly. "You guessed it," he said. "A story. But a weird one. I'm having difficulty pulling it together. If I could talk about it—"

"But you can, to me."

"So let's talk. It might give me some more ideas, or tell me what's wrong with the ideas I've got now."

They carried on walking, hand in hand. "Right," she said, and after frowning for a moment, "happy thoughts."

"Eh?"

"The dead, in their graves. I think they'd think happy thoughts. That would be the equivalent of heaven, you know."

"People who were unhappy in their lives don't think anything," he told her, matter-of-factly. "They're just glad to be out of it, mostly."

"Ah! You mean that you're going to have categories of dead people: they won't be all the same or think the same thoughts."

He nodded. "That's right. Why should they? They didn't think the same thoughts when they were alive, did they? Oh, some of them are happy, with nothing to complain of. But there are others who lie there sick with hatred, because they know the ones who killed them live on, unpunished."

"Harry, that's an awful idea! What sort of story is it, anyway? It has to be a ghost story."

He licked his lips, nodded again. "Something like that, yes. It's about a man who can talk to people in their graves. He can hear them, in his head, and know what they're thinking. Yes, and he can talk to them."

"I still think it's terrible," she said. "I mean, it's horrible! But the idea is good. And these dead people actually talk to him? But why would they want to?"

"Because they're lonely. See, there's no one else like this man. As far as he knows, he's the only one who can do it. They don't have anyone else to talk to."

"Wouldn't that drive him mad? I mean, all those voices in his head at the same time, all yammering for his attention?"

Harry gave a wry smile. "It doesn't happen like that," he said. "See, normally they just lie there, thinking. The body goes—I mean, you know, it rots—eventually becomes dust. But the mind goes on. Don't ask me how, that's something I won't try to explain. It's simply that the mind is the conscious and the subconscious control centre of a person, and after he dies it carries on—but only on the subconscious level. Like he's sleeping; and in fact he *is* sleeping, in a way. It's just that he won't wake up again. So you see, the necroscope only talks to the people he wants to talk to."

"Necroscope?"

"That's my name for such a person. A man who looks into the minds of the dead . . ."

"I see," said Brenda, frowning. "At least, I think I do. So happy people just lie there remembering all the good things, or thinking happy thoughts. And unhappy people, they just switch off?"

"Something like that. Malicious people think bad things, and murderers think murderous thoughts, and so on: *their* own particular sorts of hell, if you like. But these are the ordinary people, with ordinary thoughts. I mean, their thoughts run on a low level. Let's say that in life their thoughts were pretty mundane. I'm not putting them down; they just weren't very bright, that's all. But there are extraordinary people, too: creative people, great thinkers, architects, mathematicians, authors, the real intellectuals. And what do you suppose they do?"

Brenda looked at him, trying to gauge his thoughts. She paused to pick up a bright, sea-washed pebble. And in a little while: "I suppose they'd go on doing their thing," she said. "If they were, say, great thinkers in their lives, then they'd just go on sort of thinking their special thoughts."

"Right!" said Harry emphatically. "That's exactly what they do. The bridge-builders go on building their bridges—in their heads. Beautiful, airy things that span entire oceans! The musicians write wonderful songs and melodies. The mathematicians develop abstract theories and polish them until they are crystal things even a child could understand, and yet so astonishing that they hold the secrets of the universe. They *improve* upon what they were doing when they were alive. They carry their ideas to the limits of perfection, finishing all the unfinished thoughts they never had time for when they lived. And no distractions, no outside interference, no one to bother or confuse or concern them."

"The way you tell it," she said, "it sounds nice. But do you think that's how it really is?"

"Of course," he nodded, and quickly checked himself. "In my story, anyway. I mean, how would I know what it's really like?"

"I was just being silly," she told him. "Of course it's not really like that. Anyway, I still don't see why these dead people would want to talk to your, er, necroscope. Wouldn't he be a distraction? Wouldn't he annoy them, butting in like that on all their great schemes?"

"No," Harry shook his head. "On the contrary. It's human nature, see? What's the good of doing something wonderful if you can't tell or show anyone what you've done? That's why they enjoy talking to the necroscope. He can appreciate their genius. He's the *only* one who can do that! Also, he's sympathetic—he *wants* to know about their wonderful discoveries, the fantastic inventions they've designed, which won't be invented in the real world for a thousand years!"

Brenda suddenly saw something in what he'd said. "But that's a wonderful idea, Harry! It's not morbid at all, as I first thought. Why, the necroscope could "invent" their inventions for them! He could build their bridges, make their music, write their unwritten masterpieces! Is that what's going to happen? In your story, I mean?"

He turned his face away, stood gazing far out to sea, and said: "Something like that, I suppose. That's what I haven't worked out yet . . ."

Then for a while they were silent, and shortly afterwards they came to Crimdon and stopped for a coffee in a little café at the foot of the beach banks.

Harry lay sleeping on his bed, stark naked, the sheets thrown back. It was a very warm evening and the sun, sinking, continued to stream its golden fire in through the high windows of his tiny flat. Seeing the fine sheen of sweat where it made his brow damp, Brenda drew the thin curtains across the garret windows to cut down on the sunlight. As the shadow fell across his face he groaned and mumbled something, but Brenda couldn't catch what he said. Quietly dressing, she thought back on the day. She thought back to other times, too, allowing her memory full rein as she examined the years she and Harry had known each other.

Today had been good. And at last Harry had talked to her about . . . well, about things. He'd opened up a little and got some of it off his chest and out of his system. And since their long talk about his story he'd been a lot easier in himself, happy almost. Just what it would take to make him truly happy—Brenda could hardly imagine the nature of such a thing. He said it was that he had "a lot on his mind." A lot of what? His writing? Possibly. But she had never known him to be truly happy. Or if he had been it hadn't shown much . . .

But there, she'd side-tracked herself. She went back to today.

After Crimdon they'd walked on for another mile to a more or less deserted part of the beach where they'd gone swimming in their underwear. From a distance no one would be able to tell; it would be thought they wore costumes. After a little while, as they fooled about in the water, some old beach-combing tramp had come on the scene and it had been time to go. Dressing before the old boy could get really close, they'd dried out as they covered the last leg of their walk. In Hartlepool, a bus ride from the old part of the town to the "new" had carried them almost to the door of the three-storey Victorian house where Harry had his garret flat, and there Brenda had made sandwiches for them before they'd showered and made love. The sex they'd shared had been delicious, with both of them still tasting a little of the sea's salt, all glowing from the sun and radiating their heat, and all seeming very right and natural. She liked Harry best in the summer, for then he wasn't so pale and his thin frame seemed somehow more muscular.

Not that he was in any way weak or weedy; Harry was well able to look after himself and hardly the type to accept sand kicked in his face. Twice Brenda had seen him deal with would-be bullies, and they had been the ones to go away nursing cuts and bruises. She secretly prided herself that on both occasions she had been the spur to his anger. Harry was indifferent towards jibes aimed at himself—he could always ignore them, put them down to the ignorance of louts—but he would not accept insults or insinuations directed at Brenda, or at himself when she was with him. At times like that he seemed almost to become another person, a harder, faster, more capable person entirely. And yet even his mastery of self-defence mystified her; it was just another of those things in which he had grown inexplicably expert.

Like his lovemaking, and his writing. Brenda looked at them in that order:

Harry had been sixteen when he first made love to her—when they first did it properly, anyway—but he'd been eager for it long before that. And as she had pointed out on the beach, he had very quickly got to be very good at it. Innocent in all such things, Brenda had thought there was only one way to do it, but Harry's sexual repertoire had seemed inexhaustible. And it was perfectly true: she *had* often wondered if someone else had shown him how. In the end she'd stopped worrying about it, putting it down to the fact that he was precocious. For some unexplained reason there were skills in which Harry Keogh excelled—in which he excelled *naturally*, without any prior knowledge or intensive instruction.

His writing:

Harry had once admitted that his English had used to let him down badly; it had very nearly stopped him going on to the Tech. to complete his schooling, when he'd completely messed up the English examination paper. Well, however much that had been the case then, it certainly wasn't so now. Perhaps it was that he'd worked hard at it, but when? Brenda had never seen him studying or swotting-up his English; he had never seemed to study anything much. And yet here he was, eighteen years old and an author, and so prolific that he was published under four pseudonyms! Only short stories so far, but three a week at least—and all of them snapped up—and she knew that he was now working on a novel.

His battered, second-hand typewriter stood on a small table close to the window. Once when she'd dropped in to see him unexpectedly, Harry had been working. It was one of the few occasions when Brenda had actually seen him at work. Coming upstairs, she had heard the intermittent clatter of the keys of his machine, and creeping into his tiny entrance hall she'd poked her head round the door. Lost in thought, smiling to himself—even muttering to himself, she'd fancied—Harry's chin had been propped in his hands where he sat at the table. Then he had straightened up to tap out a few more two-fingered lines, only pausing to nod and smile at some private thought, and gaze out of the garret window and across the road.

Then she had knocked on the door, startling him, and entered the room; Harry had greeted her, put away his work and that had been that—except that she had glanced at the sheet of paper in the typewriter and had seen typed at its head: *Diary of a Seventeeth-Century Rake*.

It was only later that she'd wondered what Harry could

possibly know about the seventeenth century (what, Harry? with his limited knowledge of history, which as it happened had always been his very worst subject?) or, for that matter, rakes . . .

She was all done with dressing now and tip-toed across the room to apply a little make-up to her face in front of a wall mirror. This took her close to his table, and again she glanced at the typewriter and the uncompleted sheet it contained. Obviously he was still hard at his novel: the A4 sheet was numbered P.213 and in the left-hand upper corner bore the legend *Diary of . . . etc.*

Brenda wound the sheet up a little and read what was written—or at least started to. Then, blushing, she averted her eyes, stared out the window. It was hot stuff: very polished, very stylish, extremely randy! Out of the corner of her eye she glanced at the sheet again. She loved seventeenth-century romances and Harry's style was perfect—but this wasn't a romance and his material was frankly pornographic.

Only then did she notice what she was looking at through the window: the old cemetery across the road. The graveyard, four hundred years old, with its great horse-chestnuts, glossy shrubbery and flower borders, its leaning, weathered headstones and generally well-tended pebble plots. And as she gazed, so she wondered at Harry's choice of a dwelling-place. There were better flats around, all over town, but he had told her that he "liked the view." And it was only now that she'd realized what the view was. Oh, pretty enough in the summer, certainly, but a graveyard for all that!

Behind her Harry once again mouthed something and turned on his side. She crossed to where he lay and smiled gently down on him, then drew a sheet over his lower half. In the shade now, he was starting to shiver a little. In any case, she would soon have to wake him; it was time she got on her way. Her parents liked her to be in while it was still daylight, on those occasions when they didn't know where she was. But first she would make some coffee. As she began to turn away Harry spoke yet again, and this time his words were very clear:

"Don't worry, Ma. I'm a big boy now. I can take care of myself. You can rest easy . . ." He paused and even sleeping seemed to adopt an attitude of listening. Then:

"No, I've told you before, Ma—he didn't hurt me. Why should he? Anyway, I went to Auntie and Uncle. They looked after me. Now I'm grown up. And very soon now, maybe when you know I'm okay, then you'll be able to rest easy . . ."

Another pause, a brief period of listening, and: "But why can't you, Ma?"

Then more incoherent mumbling before ". . . I *can't!* Too far away. I know you're trying to tell me something but . . . just a whisper, Ma. I hear some of it but . . . don't know what . . . make out what you're saying. Maybe if I come to see you, come to where you are . . ."

Harry was restless now and sweating profusely for all that he shivered. Looking at him, Brenda became a little worried. Was it some kind of fever? Sweat gathered in the hollow above the middle of his upper lip; it formed droplets on his forehead and made his hair damp; his hands jerked and twitched beneath the sheet.

She reached out a hand and touched him. "Harry?"

"What!" he burst awake, his eyes snapping open and staring fixedly, his entire body going rigid as an iron bar. "Who . . . ?"

"Harry, Harry! It's only me. You were nightmaring." Brenda cradled him in her arms and he let her, curling up and throwing his arms about her. "It was about your Mam, Harry. Listen, you're all right now. Let me go and make some coffee."

She hugged him tighter for a moment, then gently released herself and stood up. His eyes, still wide open, followed her as she moved to the alcove where he had his rudimentary kitchen. "About my mother?" he said.

Spooning instant coffee into mugs, she nodded. She filled the electric kettle and switched it on. "You called her 'Ma,' and you were talking to her."

He uncurled himself and sat up, brushing his fingers dazedly through his hair. "What did I say?"

She shook her head. "Nothing much. Mainly mumbo-jumbo. You told her you were grown up now, and that she should rest easy. It was just a nightmare, Harry."

By the time the coffee was ready he had dressed himself. They said no more about his nightmare but drank their coffees; then he walked her down to the bus-stop for Harden, where they waited in silence until the bus came. At the last, before she boarded, he kissed her lightly on the cheek. "See you soon," he said.

"Tomorrow?" Tomorrow was Sunday.

"No, during the week. I'll come up for you. 'Bye, love."

She got a seat at the back of the bus and watched Harry through the rear window where he stood alone at the stop. As the bus began to round a bend he turned on his heel and walked along the pavement away from his flat. Wondering where he was headed, Brenda kept watching him as long as she could. The last she saw of him was when he turned in through the gates of the cemetery, with the sun's last rays burning in his hair.

Then the bus was round the bend and Harry was out of sight.

Harry did not come to see her during the week, and Brenda's work began to suffer at the ladies' hairdressing salon in Harden. By Thursday she was thoroughly worried about him; on Friday night she cried and her father said she was a fool for him. "That lad's bloody weird!" he declared. "Our Brenda, you must be soft!" And he wouldn't hear of her going down to Hartlepool that night. "Not on a Friday night, my girl, when all the lads have their beer money. You can go and see your daft Harry tomorrow!"

Tomorrow seemed ages coming and Brenda hardly slept at all, but Saturday morning bright and early she took a bus in to town and went up to Harry's flat. She had her own key and let herself in but he wasn't to be found. In the typewriter was a sheet of paper with yesterday's date and a simple message:

Brenda—

I've gone up to Edinburgh for the weekend. I've people to see up there. I'll be back Monday at the latest and I'll see you then—promise. Sorry I didn't see you during the week—I had a lot on my mind and wouldn't have been much fun.

Love, Harry

The last two words meant a lot to her and so she forgave him the rest. Anyway, Monday wasn't so very far away—but who could he possibly have to see in Edinburgh? He had a step-father up there, who hadn't once seen him since he was a child, but who else? No one that Brenda knew of. Other relatives that she didn't know of? Maybe. And then there had been his mother, except she had been drowned when he was little more than a baby.

Drowned, yes, but Harry had been talking to her in his sleep . . .

Brenda shook herself. Why, some of her ideas were almost as morbid as Harry's! All graveyards and death and maggots. No, of course he wouldn't be going to see his mother, for they'd never found her body. There would be no grave for him to visit.

The thought didn't improve Brenda's state of mind. Instead it drove her to do something she would never normally consider. She carefully went through Harry's file of manuscripts, checking every story whether it was complete or barely started. She didn't really know what she was looking for, but by the time she was through she knew what she had failed to find.

Nowhere in all his work had she come across a story about a necroscope.

So, either Harry hadn't started the story yet—

Or he was a liar—

Or—

Or what was bothering her was something entirely different.

As Brenda Cowell stood in a shaft of morning sunlight in Harry's flat, pondering the strangeness of the man she was involved with, one hundred and twenty miles away Harry Keogh himself stood in the same sunlight on the banks of a drowsy river in Scotland and looked across it at the big house where it stood at the head of a large, overgrown garden. There had been a time when the place was well maintained, but that was a long time ago and Harry couldn't remember it. He had been too young, an infant, and there were many things he couldn't remember. But he remembered his mother. Somewhere, deep in his subconscious mind, he had never forgotten about her—and she had never forgotten about him. And she still worried about him.

Harry stared at the house for a long time, then at the river. Its waters moved slowly, swirling, cool and inviting. Or inviting to most. A grassy bank with a few reeds; deep green water, and just here, a pebbly bottom; and somewhere down there, lodged in the slime-slick pebbles where it had lain for most of Harry's years—

A ring. A man's ring. A cat's-eye stone set in thick gold. Harry staggered at the river's edge. He deliberately flopped down to save himself from falling. The sun shone on him but he was cold. The blue sky reeled, became the grey, liquid flurry of slushy water.

He was under the water, trying to fight his way up through a hole in the ice.

Then the face seen through the ice, its trembling jelly lips turning up at their corners in a grimace—or a smile! The hands coming down into the water, holding him under— and on one of them that ring. The cat's-eye ring, on the second finger of the right hand! And Harry tearing at those hands, clawing at them, ripping the strong flesh in his frenzy. The gold ring coming loose, spiralling down past him into the murk and the icy deeps. Blood from the torn hands turning the swirling water red—red against the black of Harry's dying.

No, not his dying, hers! His mother's!

Waterlogged, he/she sank; and the current dragging them along under the ice, turning and tumbling them; and who'll look after Harry now? Poor little Harry . . .

The nightmare receded, its rush and gurgle diminishing in his mind, leaving him gasping for air where he clawed at the grassy bank. Then he curled on his side and was violently ill. This was it; it was here. This was where it had happened. This was where she had died. Where she had been murdered. Right *here!*

But—

Where was she now?

Harry allowed his feet to lead him, following the course of the river downstream. Where the channel narrowed a little, he crossed a small wooden bridge and continued on down the bank. Garden hedges came down close to the river's edge here, so that he walked a narrow, often overgrown path between fences on the one hand and reeds and water on the other. And in a little while he came to a place where the bank had been worn away, forming an overhanging bite not ten feet across. Above the still water in the pool, the path ended where the fence leaned dangerously riverward, but Harry knew he need look no further. This was where she lay.

Anyone watching him from the bank opposite would have seen the beginning of a strange thing then. Harry sat down with his feet dangling over the shallow, muddy pool, put his chin in his hands, stared deep into the water. And minutes later, if anyone had been closer, he would have been witness to something stranger still: tears from this young man's staring, unblinking eyes which dripped from the tip of his nose in a steady stream to add their substance to the river's.

And for the first time in his adult life Harry Keogh met his mother, talked to her "face to face," and was able to verify the terrible things his dreams and her restless messages had caused him to more than suspect for so many years. And while they talked he cried—tears of sadness, and some of gladness at first; then of remorse and frustration, that he'd had to wait so long for this day; then of white anger as things began to make more sense to him. Finally he told her what he intended to do.

Upon which the wondering observer, had there been one, would have seen the strangest thing of all. For when Mary Keogh knew her son's plans she became even more afraid for him and voiced her fears, and she made Harry promise that he would do nothing rash. He couldn't deny her pleading, answered with a nod of his head. She didn't believe him, cried out after him as he stood up and moved away. And for a moment—the merest second—it seemed the bottom of the pool shuddered, shaking the water and sending ripples coursing outward from its centre. Then the pool was still again.

Harry didn't see this for already he was making for the bridge, returning to the spot where it had happened all those years ago. The place where his gentle mother had been murdered.

He found a place where the reeds grew tall, checked that he was completely alone, stripped down to his shorts and stepped to the river's edge. A moment later he was in the water, diving deep, then making for the middle where the current ran swiftest. Even there the river's pull was barely noticeable, and after twenty minutes of diving and delving amongst the pebbles of the bottom he found what he was looking for. It lay within a few inches of the spot where he'd first thought it might be, tarnished and a little slimy, but unmistakably a ring. The gold gleamed through on the instant he rubbed it, and the cat's-eye stone held its cold, unwinking stare as of old. Harry had never actually seen the ring before that moment when his groping fingers found it—not consciously, anyway—but he knew it at once. It was that familiar. Nor did it seem odd to him that he'd known where to look. Stranger far if the ring had not been there.

On the bank of the river he finished cleaning it, slid it on to the index finger of his left hand which it fitted a little loosely but was not so slack that he might lose it, and turned it thoughtfully between his fingers, getting the feel of it. It felt cold even under the hot sun, cold as the day its owner had lost it.

Then Harry dressed and headed for Bonnyrigg. From there he'd catch a bus into Edinburgh and take the first train home to Hartlepool. His work here was done—for now.

Now that he had found his mother he would have no trouble reaching her again, no matter how far he wandered, and he would be able to calm her fears and give her a little of the peace she'd sought for so long. She would no longer need to worry about little Harry.

Before leaving the spot by the river, however, he paused to look again at the big house where it stood well back from the opposite bank; and he stared at its old gables and wild gardens for long, long moments. His step-father still lived and worked there, he knew. Yes, and it would not be too long before Harry paid him a visit.

But before that there was much he would have to do. Viktor Shukshin was a dangerous man, a murderer, and Harry must be careful how he approached him. He intended that his step-father should pay the price for his mother's death—that he must be punished in full—but the punishment would have to fit the crime. And no use at all to simple accuse the man, for what proof was there after all these years? No, Harry must set a trap, and bait it, and Shukshin must find it irresistible. But no hurry, none at all, for Harry had time on his side. Time would allow him to become expert in many things, and indeed he had much to learn. For what good to be a necroscope if he could make no use of it? As to how he would use his talent after he had avenged his mother's death: that remained to be seen. It would be as it would be.

But right now his instructors were waiting for him and they were the best in the world. Yes, and they knew far more now than ever they had known when they were alive.

Chapter Eight

The summer of 1975.

THREE YEARS SINCE DRAGOSANI'S LAST TRIP HOME, AND ONLY a year short of that time when the old thing in the earth had promised to deliver up his secrets to Dragosani, the secrets of the Wamphyri. In return for which, Dragosani would give him back his life—or rather, he would return him to renewed undeath, to walk the earth again.

Three years, and the necromancer had gone from strength to strength until his position as Gregor Borowitz's right-hand man now seemed virtually unassailable. When the old man went, Dragosani would be the one to replace him. After that, with the entire Soviet ESP organization at his command, and with all the knowledge of the Wamphyri in his hands and mind—the possibilities were vast.

What had once seemed an impossible dream might still come to pass, when old Wallachia would once more become a mighty nation—the mightiest nation of all. Why not, with Dragosani to lead the way? A mortal man can achieve very little in his short span of years, but an immortal man might achieve anything. And with that thought in mind, a question Dragosani had often asked himself cropped up yet again: if it was true that longevity meant power, and immortality ultimate power, why had the Wamphyri themselves failed? Why weren't vampires the leaders and rulers of this world?

Dragosani had long since worked out something of an answer; right or wrong he could not yet say:

To man the concept of a vampire is abhorrent—the very *concept* itself! If men believed—if they were given indisputable proof of vampiric infestation—then they would seek the creatures out and destroy them. This had been the way of it since time began, since a time when men really did believe, and it had limited the vampire in his scope. He dare *not* reveal himself, must *not* be seen to be different, to be alien. He must control as best he might his passions, his lusts, his natural craving for the sheer power he knows his evil arts could bring him. For to have power, whether political or financial or of any other sort, is to be scrutinized—which is the one thing above all others that a vampire dreads! For under prolonged scrutiny he must be discovered and destroyed.

But if a mere man could control a vampire's arts—a living man, as opposed to an undead Thing—he would suffer no such restrictions. Having nothing to hide but his dark knowledge itself . . . why, he could achieve almost anything!

That was why Dragosani had journeyed yet again to Romania; conscious of the fact that his duties had kept him away for far too long, he wished to speak once more with the old devil and offer him small favours, and learn whatever there was to be learned before next summer, when the time appointed would be at hand.

The time appointed, yes—when all the vampire's secrets would lie naked before him, open and revealing as an eviscerated corpse!

Three years had flown by since last he was here, and they had been busy years. Busy for Dragosani because over that entire period Gregor Borowitz had driven all of his ESPers, including the necromancer, to the limits of their capabilities. Of course he had: to ensure that in the four years Leonid Brezhnev had allowed him, in which he must turn a profit, his branch would become so firmly entrenched as to be indispensable. And now the Premier had seen that it was indeed *utterly* indispensable. What's more, it was the most secret of all his secret services and by far the most independent—which was the way Gregor Borowitz wanted it.

Through Borowitz's advance warning, Brezhnev had been fully prepared for the fall from grace of his one-time political pal Richard Nixon in the USA. And where Watergate might have hindered or even ruined many another Russian premier, Brezhnev had actually managed to reap some benefits from it—but only by virtue of Borowitz's (or more properly Igor Vlady's) predictions. "A pity," Brezhnev had told Borowitz at the time, "that Nixon didn't have you working for him, eh, Gregor?"

Similarly, and also as predicted, the Premier now found himself advantageously placed in his dealings with the presidential "stand-in," at best a bumbler; and before Nixon's fall, as early as 1972, knowing in advance that there were American hard-liners still to come, Brezhnev had taken Borowitz's advice and signed satellite agreements with the USA. Moreover, and especially since America was so far advanced in space technology, he had also been quick to put his signature to the ultimate "détente" coup of his career: a joint Skylab space venture, which even now was coming to fruition.

Indeed, the Soviet premier had taken the initiative on these and many other ESP-Branch suggestions or prognoses—including the expulsion of many dissidents and the "repatriation" of Jews—and every step he had taken so far had been completely successful in bolstering his already awesome position as Leader. And much if not all of the credit due directly to Borowitz and his branch, so that Brezhnev had been pleased to honour his and Borowitz's agreement of 1971.

Thus, as Brezhnev and his regime prospered, so prospered Gregor Borowitz; likewise Boris Dragosani, whose loyalty to the branch seemed unquestionable. And in fact it *was* unquestionable—for the moment . . .

While Gregor Borowitz had secured the permanence of his branch and climbed in Leonid Brezhnev's esteem, however, his relationship with Yuri Andropov had deteriorated at a directly proportionate rate; there was no overt hostility, but behind the scenes Andropov was as jealous and scheming as ever. Dragosani knew that Borowitz continued to watch Andropov closely. What the necromancer did not know was that Borowitz also watched him! Oh, Dragosani was not under any sort of surveillance, but there was that in his attitude which had been worrying his boss for quite some time. Dragosani had always been arrogant, even insubordinate, and Borowitz had accepted that and even enjoyed it—but this was something else. Borowitz suspected it was ambition; which was fine, as long as the necromancer didn't become too ambitious.

Dragosani too had noticed the change in himself. Despite the fact that one of his oldest inhibitions, his greatest "hangup," was now extinct, he had grown if anything colder still towards members of the opposite sex. When he took a woman it was invariably brutally, with little or nothing of love in it but purely as a release for his own pent-up emotional and physical needs. And as for ambition: at times he had difficulty controlling his frustration and could hardly wait for the day when Borowitz would be out of his way. The old man was past it, a dodderer, his usefulness was on the wane. This was not in fact the case, but such was Dragosani's own energy—the rapid acceleration and growth of his drive and character—that it seemed that way to him. And that was another reason why he had returned this time to Romania: so that he might obtain the counselling of the Thing in the ground. For like it or not, Dragosani had begun to accept the vampire as a sort of father-figure. Who else could he talk to, in absolute confidence, of his ambitions and his frustrations? Who else if not the old dragon? No one. In a way the vampire was like an oracle . . . but in another way he was not. Unlike an oracle, Dragosani could never be sure of the validity of any of his statements. Which meant that while he had felt himself drawn back here, to Romania, still he must be careful of his dealings with the Thing in the ground.

These were some of the thoughts which passed through his mind as he drove up through the old country from Bucharest towards Pitesti; and as his Volga passed a signpost which stated that the town was sixteen kilometres ahead, he remembered how three years ago he had been on his way to Pitesti when Borowitz had recalled him to Moscow. Strangely, he had not given thought to the library in Pitesti from that day to this, but now he felt himself drawn again to visit the place. He still knew so very little about vampirism and the undead, and what knowledge he did have was dubious in that it had come from the vampire himself. But if ever a library were the seat of local lore and legend, then surely the reference library in Pitesti was that one.

Dragosani remembered the place from his years at the college in Bucharest. The college had often used to borrow old documents and records concerning Wallachian and ancient Romanian matters from Pitesti, for a great amount of historical material had been taken there for safety from Ploiesti and Bucharest during World War II. In the case of Ploiesti this had been a wise move, for the city had suffered some of the worst bombing of the war. In any case, much of the material had not found its way back to the original museums and libraries but remained in Pitesti even now. Certainly it had been there as recently as eighteen or nineteen years ago.

So . . . the old Thing in the ground could wait a little longer on Dragosani's return. He would go first to the library in Pitesti, have lunch later in the town, and only then carry on into the heart of his homeland . . .

By 11:00 A.M. Dragosani was there, had introduced himself to the librarian on duty, asked to be allowed to see any documents pertaining to boyar families, lands, battles, monuments, ruins and burial grounds, or any records at all for the regions comprising Wallachia and Moldavia—and especially local areas—circa the mid-fifteenth-century. The librarian seemed agreeable enough and only too pleased to assist (despite the fact that he appeared to find Dragosani's request a little amusing, or sufficiently so to cause him to smile) but after he had taken his visitor to the room which housed those old records . . . then Dragosani had been able to appreciate the funny side of it for himself.

In a room of barnlike dimensions he found shelves containing sufficient books and documents and records to fill several large army trucks, all of it relating to his inquiry! "But . . . isn't it catalogued?" he asked.

"Of course, sir," the young librarian told him, smiling again; and he produced an armful of catalogues whose reading alone—if Dragosani had been willing to contemplate such a task—would have taken several days in itself; and that without taking down one of the listed items from its shelf.

"But it would take a year or more to sift through this lot!" he finally complained.

"It has already taken twenty," the other told him, "and that was simply for the purpose of cataloguing—or mainly for that purpose. But that is not the only difficulty. For even if you could afford so much time, still you would not be allowed it. At last the authorities are splitting it up; much is returning to Bucharest, a large amount is scheduled for Budapest, even Moscow has made application. It will be moved, most of it, some time in the next three months."

"Well you're right," said Dragosani. "I haven't years or months but just a few days. So . . . I wonder if there's some way I might narrow my search down?"

"Ah!" said the other. "But then there's the question of language. Do you wish to see Turkish language records? . . . Hungarian? . . . German? Is your interest purely Slavicist? Is it Christian or Ottoman? Do *you* have any specific points of reference—landmarks, as it were? All of the material here is at least three hundred years old, but some of it dates back seven centuries and more! As I'm sure you're aware, the central span—which seems to be the seat of your interest—covers many decades of constant flux. Here are the records of foreign conquerors, yes, but we also have the records of those who thrust them out. Are you capable of understanding the texts of these works? They are, after all, half a millennium old. If you can understand them, then you're a scholar indeed! I certainly can't, not with any degree of accuracy—and I've been trained to read them . . ."

And then, seeing Dragosani's look of helplessness, he had added: "Sir, perhaps if you could be more specific . . . ?"

Dragosani saw no reason for subterfuge. "I'm interested in the vampire myth, which seems to have had its roots right here—in Transylvania, Moldavia, Wallachia—and dates back, so far as is known, to the fifteenth century.''

The librarian took a pace back from him, lost his smile. Suddenly he seemed wary. ''But you are surely not a tourist?''

''No, basically I'm Romanian, now living and working in Moscow. But what's that got to do with it?''

The librarian, perhaps three or four years younger than Dragosani and obviously a little awed by his almost cosmopolitan appearance, seemed to be giving the matter a deal of consideration. He chewed his lip, frowned and was silent for long moments. But at last he said, ''If you'll take a look at them, you'll note that those catalogues I gave you are mainly handwritten and penned in one uniform hand throughout. And I've already told you that there's at least twenty years of work in them. Well, the man who did that work is still alive and lives not far away, in Titu. That's towards Bucharest, about twenty-five miles.''

''I know the place,'' said Dragosani. ''I drove through there not half an hour ago. Do you think he could help me?''

''Oh, yes—if he wanted to.'' That sounded cryptic.

''Well, go on—?''

The librarian seemed unsure, looked away for a moment. ''Oh, I made a mistake two or three years ago, sent a couple of American ''researchers'' to see him. He wanted no truck with them, threw them out! A bit eccentric, you see? Since that time I'm more careful. We've had a good many requests of this nature, you understand. This 'Dracula' thing is something of an industry, apparently, in the West. And it's this commercial aspect that Mr. Giresci is anxious to avoid. That's his name, by the way: Ladislau Giresci.''

''Are you telling me that this man is an expert on vampirism?'' Dragosani felt his interest quickening. ''Do you mean to say that he's been studying the legends, tracing their history through these documents, for twenty-odd years?''

"Well, among other things, yes, that's what I'm saying. It's been what you might call a hobby—or perhaps an obsession—with him. But a very useful obsession where the library has been concerned.''

"Then I have to go and see him! It might save me a great deal of time and wasted energy.''

The librarian shrugged. "Well, I can give you directions, and his address, but . . . it will be entirely up to him whether or not he'll see you. It might help if you took him a bottle of whisky. He's a great whisky man, when he can afford it—but the Scottish sort and not that filth they brew in Bulgaria!''

"You just give me his address," said Dragosani. "He'll see me, all right. Of that I can assure you.''

Dragosani found the place just as the librarian had described it, on the Bucharest road about a mile outside of Titu. On a small estate of wooden, two-storey houses set back from the road in a few acres of woodland, Ladislau Giresci's place was conspicuous by its comparative isolation. All of the houses had gardens or plots of ground surrounding them and separating them from their neighbours, but Giresci's house stood well away from all others on the rim of the estate, lost in a stand of pines, hedgerows run wild amid untended shrubbery and undergrowth.

The cobbled drive leading to the house itself had been narrowed by burgeoning hedges, where leafy creepers were throwing their tendrils across the cobbles; the gardens were overgrown and slowly returning to the wilderness; the house was visibly affected by dry rot in a fairly advanced state, and wore an atypical air of almost total neglect. By comparison, the other houses on the estate were in good order and their gardens well maintained. Some small effort had been made at maintenance and repair, however, for here and there at the front of the house an old board had been removed and a new one nailed in place, but even the most recent of these must be all of five years old. The path from the garden gate to the front door was likewise overgrown, but Dragosani persisted and knocked upon panels from which the last flakes of paint were fast falling.

In one hand he carried a string bag containing a bottle of whisky bought from the liquor store in Pitesti, a loaf of bread, a wedge of cheese, some fruit. The food was for himself (his lunch, if nothing else was available) and the bottle, as advised, for Giresci. If he was at home. As Dragosani waited, that began to seem unlikely; but after knocking again, louder this time, finally he heard movement from within.

The figure which finally opened the door to him was male, perhaps sixty years of age, and fragile as a pressed flower. His hair was white—not grey but white, like a crest of snow upon the hill of his brow—and his skin was even paler than Dragosani's own, with a shine to it as if it were polished. His right leg was wooden, an old peg as opposed to any sort of modern prosthetic device, but he seemed to handle his disability with more than sufficient agility. His back was a little bent and he held one shoulder gingerly and winced when he moved it; but his eyes were keen, brown and sure, and as he enquired as to Dragosani's business his breath was clean and healthy.

"You don't know me, Mr. Giresci," said Dragosani, "but I've learned something of you, and what I've learned has fascinated me. I suppose you could say I'm something of a historian, whose special interest lies way back in old Wallachia. And I've been told that no one knows the history of these parts better than you."

"Hmm!" said Giresci, looking his visitor up and down. "Well, there are professors at the university in Bucharest who'd dispute that—but I wouldn't!" He stood blocking the way inside, seemingly uncertain, but Dragosani noted that his brown eyes went again to the string bag and the bottle.

"Whisky," said Dragosani. "I'm partial to a drop and it's hard stuff to come by in Moscow. Maybe you'll join me in a glass—while we talk?"

"Oh?" Giresci barked. "And who said we were going to talk?" But again his eyes went to the bottle, and in a softer tone: "Scotch, did you say?"

"Of course. There's only one real whisky, and that's—"

"What's your name, young man?" Giresci cut him off. He still blocked the way into his house, but his eyes held a look of interest now.

"Dragosani. Boris Dragosani. I was born in these parts."

"And is that why you're interested in their history? Somehow I don't think so." From frank and open scrutiny, now his eyes took on a look of wary suspicion. "You wouldn't be representing any foreigners, would you? Americans, for example?"

Dragosani smiled. "On the contrary," he said. "No, for I know you've had trouble with strangers before. But I'll not lie to you, Ladislau Giresci, my interest is probably the same as theirs was. I was given your address by the librarian in Pitesti."

"Ah?" said Giresci. "Is that so? Well, he knows well enough who I'll see and who I won't see, so it seems your credentials must be all right. But let's hear it from you now—from your own lips—and no holding back: just what *is* your interest?"

"Very well" (Dragosani could see no way round it, and little point in hedging the matter anyway), "I want to know about vampires."

The other stared hard at him, seemed not at all surprised. "Dracula, you mean?"

Dragosani shook his head. "No, I mean *real* vampires. The *vampir* of Transylvanian legend—the cult of the Wamphyri!"

At that Giresci gave a start, winced again as his bad shoulder jumped, leaned forward a little and grasped Dragosani's arm. He breathed heavily for a moment and said: "Oh? the Wamphyri, eh? Well—perhaps I will talk to you. Yes, and certainly I'd appreciate a glass of whisky. But first you tell me something. You said you wanted to know about the real vampire, the legend. Are you sure you don't mean the myth? Tell me, Dragosani: do you believe in vampires?"

Dragosani looked at him. Giresci was watching him keenly, waiting, almost holding his breath. And something told Dragosani that he had him. "Oh, yes," he said softly, after a moment. "Indeed I do!"

"*Hmm!*" the other nodded—and stood aside. "Then you'd better come in, Mr. Dragosani. Come in, come in—and we'll talk."

However dilapidated Giresci's place might look from outside, inside it was as clean and neat as any cripple living on his own could possibly keep it. Dragosani was pleasantly surprised at the sense of order he felt as he followed his host through rooms panelled in locally crafted oak, where carpets patterned in the old Slavic tradition kept one's feet from sliding on warmly glowing, age-polished pine boards. However rustic, the place was warm and welcoming—on the one hand. But on the other—

Giresci's *penchant*—his all-consuming "hobby" or obsession—was alive and manifest in every room. It saturated the atmosphere of the house in exactly the same way as mummy-cases in a museum inspire a sense of endless ergs of sand and antique mystery—except that here the picture was of bitter mountain passes and fierce pride, of cold wastes and aching loneliness, of a procession of endless wars and blood and incredible cruelties. The rooms *were* old Romania. This *was* Wallachia.

The walls of one room were hung with old weapons, swords, pieces of armour. Here was an early sixteenth-century arquebusier, and here a vicious barbed pike. A black, pitted cannonball from a small Turkish cannon held open a door (Giresci had found it on an ancient battlefield near the ruins of a fortress close to Tirgoviste) and a pair of ornate Turkish scimitars decorated the wall over the fireplace. There were terrible axes, maces and flails, and a badly battered and rusty cuirass, with the breastplate hacked almost in half from the top. The wall of the corridor which divided the main living-room from the kitchen and bedrooms was hung with framed prints or likenesses of the infamous Vlad princes, and with boyar family genealogies. There were family crests and motifs, too, complicated battle maps, sketches (from Giresci's own hand) of crumbling fortifications, tumuli, earthworks, ruined castles and keeps.

And books! Shelf upon shelf of them, most of them crumbling—and many quite obviously valuable—but all rescued by Giresci wherever he had found them over the years: in sales, old bookshops and antique shops, or from estates fallen into poverty or ruin along with the once-powerful aristocracy. All in all, the house was a small museum in itself, and Giresci the sole keeper and curator.

"This arquebusier," Dragosani remarked at one point, "must be worth a small fortune!"

"To a museum or a collector, possibly," said his host. "I've never looked into the question of value. But how's this for a weapon?" And he handed Dragosani a crossbow.

Dragosani took it, weighed it in his hand, frowned. The weapon was fairly modern, heavy, probably as accurate as a rifle, and very deadly. The interesting thing was that its "bolt" was of wood, possibly lignumvitae, with a tip of polished steel. Also, it was loaded. "It certainly doesn't fit in with the rest of your stuff," he said.

Giresci grinned, showing strong square teeth. "Oh but it does! My "other stuff," as you put it, tells what was, what might still be. This crossbow is my answer to it. A deterrent. A weapon against it."

Dragosani nodded. "A wooden stake through the heart, eh? And would you really hunt a vampire with this?"

Giresci grinned again, shook his head. "Nothing so foolish," he said. "Anyone who seeks to hunt down a vampire has to be a madman! I am merely eccentric. Hunt one? Never! But what if a vampire decided to hunt me? Call it self-protection, if you will. Anyway, I feel happier with it in the house."

"But why would you fear such a thing? I mean—all right, I'm in agreement with you that such creatures have existed and still do, possibly—but why would one of them bother itself with you?"

"If you were a secret agent," said Giresci, (at which Dragosani smiled inside) "would you be happy—would you ever feel safe—knowing that some outsider knew your business, your secrets? Of course you wouldn't. And what of the Wamphyri? Now . . . I think that perhaps the risk is a very small one—but twenty years ago when I bought this weapon I wasn't so sure. I had seen something which would stay with me for the rest of my life. Such creatures really were, yes, and I knew about them. And the more I looked into their legend, their history, the more monstrous they became. In those days I could not sleep for my nightmares. Buying the crossbow was like whistling in the dark, I suppose: it might not keep away the dark forces, but at least it would let them know that I wasn't afraid of them!"

"Even if you were?" said Dragosani.

Giresci's keen eyes looked deep into his own. "Of

course I was," he finally answered. "What? Here in Romania? Here under these mountains? In this house, where I've amassed and studied the evidence? I was frightened, yes. But now . . ."

"Now?"

The other pulled a half-disappointed face. "Well I'm still here, alive after all these years. Nothing has "happened" to me, has it? And so now . . . now I think that maybe they are, after all, extinct. Oh, they existed—if anyone knows that, I do—but perhaps the last of them has gone forever. I hope so, anyway. But what about you? What do you say, Dragosani?"

Dragosani gave the weapon back. "I say keep your crossbow, Ladislau Giresci. And I say look to its maintenance. Also, I say be careful who you invite into your house!"

He reached into his inside pocket for a packet of cigarettes, froze as Giresci aimed the crossbow directly at his heart across a distance of only six or seven feet and took off the safety catch. "But I am careful," said the other, still staring directly into his eyes. "We apparently know so much, you and I. I know why *I* believe, but what of you?"

"Me?" inside his jacket, Dragosani slipped his issue pistol from its under-arm holster.

"A stranger in search of a legend, apparently. But such a *knowing* stranger!"

Dragosani shrugged, palmed the grip of his gun, began to turn its muzzle towards Giresci. At the same time he turned slightly to the right. Perhaps Giresci was insane. A pity. Also a pity that there would be a hole right through Dragosani's jacket and powder burns on the lining, but—

Giresci put on the crossbow's safety, set it down on a small table. "Too cool by far," he laughed, "for a vampire faced with a wooden stake! And you know: the pressure on that wooden bolt is set to transfix a man but not pass right through him and out the back. That would be no good. Only when the stake is in place is the creature truly immobilized, and—'' His eyes went wide and his jaw dropped.

Grey as death, Dragosani had taken out his gun, applied the safety, placed it beside the crossbow on the table. "The pressure on *that*," he rasped, "is sufficient to blow your heart right out through your backbone! I also saw the mirrors on the walls of the corridor—and the way you looked into them as I passed. Too many mirrors by far, I thought. And the crucifix on the door, and doubtless another around your neck—for all the good they'd be. Well, and am I a vampire then, old man?''

"I'm not sure what you are," the other shook his head. "But a vampire? No, not you. You came in out of the sun, after all. But think: a man, seeking me out, specifically desiring to know about the Wamphyri—even *knowing* that name: Wamphyri, which few if any others in the whole world know! Why, wouldn't you be cautious?''

Dragosani breathed deeply, relaxed a little. "Well, your 'caution' nearly cost you your life!' he said bluntly. "So before we go any further, are there any more tricks up your sleeve?''

Giresci gave a shaky laugh. "No, no," he said. "No, I think we understand each other now. Come, let's leave it at that for the moment. And here, let's see what else you have in that bag of yours." He took the string bag from Dragosani and directed him to sit at a dining table close to an open window. "It's shady there," he explained "Cooler."

"The whisky's yours," said Dragosani. "The rest was for my lunch—except I'm not sure now that I feel like eating! That crossbow of yours is a bloody thing!''

"Of course you can eat, of course you can! What? Cheese for lunch? No, I wouldn't hear of it. I've woodcocks in the oven, done to a turn by now. A Greek recipe. Delicious. Whisky as an aperitif; bread to soak up the fat of the birds; cheese for afterwards. Good! An excellent lunch. And while we eat, I'll tell you my story, Dragosani.''

The younger man allowed himself to be placated, accepted a glass which the other produced from an old oak cabinet, allowed him to pour him a liberal whisky. Then Giresci hobbled off for a moment to the kitchen, and soon Dragosani began to sniff the air as the sweet odour of roasting meat slowly filled it. And Giresci had been right: it was delicious. Another moment and he was back with a smoking oven tray, directing Dragosani to get plates from a drawer. He tipped a brace of small birds on to his guest's plate, one on to his own. There were baked potatoes, too, and again Dragosani got the lion's share.

Impressed by Giresci's generosity, he said: ''That's hardly fair on you.''

''I'm drinking your whisky,'' the other replied, ''so you can eat my birds. Anyway, I can shoot more any time I want them—right out of that window there. They're easy to get, but whisky's harder to come by! Believe me, I'm getting the best of the bargain.''

They began to eat, and between mouthfuls Giresci started to tell his tale:

''It was during the war,'' he said. ''When I was a boy, I hurt my back and shoulder very badly, which did away with any question of my being a soldier. But I wanted to do my bit anyway and so joined the Civil Defence. 'Civil Defence'—*Hah!* Go to Ploiesti, even today, all these years later, and mention Civil Defence. Ploiesti burned, night after night. It just burned, Dragosani! How does one 'defend' when the sky rains bombs?

''So I simply ran around with hundreds of others, dragging bodies out of burning or blasted buildings. Some of them were alive but most were not, and others would have been better off dead anyway. But it's amazing how quickly you get used to it. And I was very young and so got used to it all the more quickly. You're resilient when you're young. You know, in the end all the blood and the pain and the death didn't even seem to matter very much. Not to me, nor to the others who were doing the same job. You do it because it's there—like climbing a mountain. Except this was one where we could never get to the top. So we just kept on running around. Me, running! Can you picture that? But in those days I had both my legs, you see?

"And then . . . then there was this night when it was very bad. I mean, it was bad almost every night, but this one was—" He shook his head, lost for words.

"Outside Ploiesti, towards Bucharest, there were a good many old houses. They were the homes of the aristocracy, from the old days when there really *was* an aristocracy. Most of them were run down because people hadn't had the money to keep them going. Oh, the people who lived in them still had some money, land, but not that much. They were just hanging on, gradually decaying, falling apart along with their old houses. And that night, that's where a stick of bombs fell.

"I was driving an ambulance—a converted three-tonner, actually—between the city and the outskirts where they'd rigged up hospitals in a couple of the larger houses. Up to then, you see, most of the bombing had been in the middle of town. Anyway, when that stick fell I was blown right off the road. And I thought I was a goner . . . done for. This is how it happened:

"One minute I was driving along—with the old rich houses on my right behind high walls, and the sky to the east and the south ruddy where the fire was reflected from the underside of the clouds—and the next all hell erupting from the very earth, it seemed! My ambulance was empty, thank God, for we'd just completed one trip and unloaded a half-dozen badly injured people at one of the makeshift hospitals. There was just me and my co-driver, on our way back into Ploiesti, the truck bumping over old cobbled roads where debris was piled at every corner. And then the bombs came.

"They came marching across the rich old estates, thundering like berserker demons, blowing everything up into the air in great sheets of blinding light and sprays of brilliant red and yellow fire! They would have been awesomely beautiful, if they weren't so hellishly ugly! And they marched, yes, with the precise paces of soldiers, but gigantic. Three hundred yards away, the first one, behind the private estates: a dull boom and a sudden glare, a volcanic spout of fire and mud, and the earth shuddering under my speeding truck. Two hundred and fifty yards, the second, flinging blazing trees and earth up to the sky high over the rooftops. Two hundred, and the fireball rising higher than the old stone walls, higher than the houses themselves. And each time the earth shuddering that much stronger, that much closer. Then the house on my immediate right, set back from the road at the head of a cobbled drive, seeming almost to jump on its foundations. And I knew where the next one would land. It would hit the house! And what about the one after that?

"And I was right—almost. For a split second the house was thrown into silhouette, lit up from behind, and the light so bright that it seemed to burn through stone and all, making of the gaunt old building a stony skeleton. Downstairs, behind bay windows, a figure stood with its arms held high, shaking them as in a great and terrible anger. Then, as the glare of that bomb faded and smoking earth rained out of the night, the next one hit the house.

"That was when hell came. As the roof was blasted off and the walls flew outward in ruin and belching fire and smoke, so the road in front of my truck seemed to bend up and back on itself like a wounded snake, whipping cobbles through my windscreen. And after that . . . everything was spinning, and everything was burning!

"The ambulance was like a toy in some mad child's fist: picked up, twirled around and hurled aside, off the road, blazing. I was unconscious only for a couple of seconds—maybe not even that, perhaps it was only shock or nausea—but when I came to my senses and crawled from the blazing vehicle it was with only seconds to spare. Mere seconds, and then . . . BOOM!

"As for my partner, the man in the truck with me: I didn't even know his name. Or if I ever did, I've since forgotten it. I'd met him just that night, and now said goodbye in a holocaust. He had a hook nose, that's all I remember. I hadn't seen him in the truck when I got out of there; if he was still in there, well that was the end of him. Anyway, I never saw him again . . .

"But the bombs were still raining down, and I was shivering, miserable, shocked and vulnerable. You know how vulnerable you really are when you've just lost someone, even if you never knew him.

"Then I looked towards the house that was hit before the bomb landed on the road in front of me. Amazingly, some of it was still standing. The downstairs room with the bay windows was still there—no windows, just the room—or the shell of the room, anyway. But everything else was gone—or soon would be. The place was burning furiously.

"And that was when I remembered the angry figure I'd seen silhouetted in that bay window, shaking its arms in fury. If the room was still there, mightn't the figure—mightn't he—also be there? It was instinct, the job, the unclimbable mountain. I ran towards the house. Maybe it was self-preservation, too, for one bomb had already landed on the house; it seemed unlikely that another would follow suit. Until the raid was over, I would be as safe there as anywhere. In my dazed condition I hadn't taken into account the fact that the place was burning, that its fires would be a beacon for the next wave of planes.

"I got to the house safely, climbed through the shattered bays and into what had been a library, found the angry man—or what was left of him. What *should* have been left of him was a corpse, but that wasn't how it was. I mean, the state he was in . . . well, he should have been dead. But he wasn't. He was undead!

"Now Dragosani, I don't know how much you know about the Wamphyri. If you know a great deal, then the rest of what I have to say may not surprise you greatly. But *I* knew nothing, not then, and so what I saw—what I heard, the whole experience—was for me simply terrifying. Of course, you aren't the first to hear this story; I told it afterwards, or rather babbled it, and have told it several times since. But each time I've been more reluctant, knowing that if I do tell it, it will only be greeted with scepticism or downright disbelief. However, since my experience was the initial jolt—the shock which set my search, research, and yes, obsession, in motion—it remains the single dominant memory of my entire lifetime, and so *must* be told. Although I've drastically narrowed down my possible audiences over the years, still it must be told. Indeed you, Dragosani, will be the first to have heard it for seven years. The last one was an American who later wanted to re-write it and publish it as a sensational "true story," and I had to threaten him with a shotgun to change his mind. For obvious reasons I do *not* wish to draw attention to myself, which is precisely what his scheme would have done!

"Anyway, I can see how you're growing impatient, so let me get on:

"At first I could see nothing in that room but debris and

damage. I didn't really expect to see anything. Nothing alive, anyway. The ceiling had caved in to one side; a wall had been split and buckled by the blast and was about to go; bookshelves had been tumbled everywhere and scattered volumes lay about in disarray, some burning and adding to the smoke and the fumes and the chaos. The reek of the bomb was heavy in the air, acrid and choking. And then there came that groan.

"Dragosani, there are groans and there are groans. The groans of men exhausted to the point of collapse, the life-giving groans of women in childbirth, the groans of the living before they become the dead. And then there are the groans of the undead! I knew nothing of it then: these were simply the sounds of agony. But *such* an agony, such an eternity of pain . . .

"They came from behind an old, overturned desk close to the blown-out bays where I stood. I clambered through the rubble, hauled at the desk until I could drag it upright on to its short legs and away from the riven wall. There, between where the desk had been tossed by the blast and the heavy skirting-board, lay a man. To all intents and purposes he was a man, anyway, and how was I to know different? You must judge for yourself, but let 'man' suffice for now.

"His features were imposing; he would have been handsome but his face was contorted by agony. Tall, too, a big man—and strong! My God, how strong he must have been! This was what I thought when I saw his injuries. No man ever suffered such injuries before and lived—or if he did, then he was not a man.

"The ceiling was of age-blackened beams, a common enough feature in some of these old houses. Where it had caved in, a massive beam had snapped and its broken ends had fallen. One of these—a great splinter of age-brittled pine—had driven its point into and through the man's chest, through the floorboards beneath him, too, pinning him down like a beetle impaled on the spent stalk of a match. That alone should have killed him, must have killed any other but one of his sort. But that was not all.

"Something—the blast, it must have been, which can play weird tricks—had sliced his clothes up the middle like a great razor. From groin to rib-cage he was naked, and not only his clothes had been sliced. His belly, all trembling, a mass of raped and severed nerves, was laid back in two great flaps of flesh; all the viscera visible. His very guts were there, Dragosani, palpitating before my horrified eyes; but they were not what I expected, not the entrails of any ordinary man.

"Eh? What? I see the questions written in your face. What am I saying? you ask yourself. Entrails are entrails, guts are guts. They are slimy pipes, coiled tubes and smoking conduits; oddly shaped red and yellow and purple loaves of meat; strangely convoluted sausages and steamy bladders. Oh, yes, and indeed these things were there inside his ruptured trunk. But not alone these things. Something *else* was there!"

Dragosani listened, rapt; breathless; but while his interest was keen, with all his attention focused upon Giresci's story, still his face showed little or no true emotion or horror. And Giresci saw this. "Ah!" he said. "And you're not without strength yourself, my young friend, for there are plenty who would turn pale or puke at what I've just said. And there's a lot more to be said yet. Very well, let's see how you take the rest . . .

"Now, I've said there was something else inside this man's body cavity, and so there was. I caught a glimpse of it when first I saw him lying pinned there, and thought my eyes must be playing tricks with me. Anyway, we saw each other simultaneously, and after our eyes met for the first time the thing inside him seemed to shrink back and disappear behind the rest of his innards. Or . . . perhaps I had simply imagined it to be there in the first place, eh? Well, as to what I *thought* I had seen: picture an octopus or a slug. But big, with tentacles twining round all the body's normal organs, centering in the region of the heart or behind it. Yes, picture a huge tumour—but mobile, sentient!

"It was there, it wasn't there, I had imagined it. So I thought. But there was no imagining this man's agony, his hideous wounds, the fact that only a miracle—many miracles—had so far saved his life. And no imagining that he had more than minutes or even seconds to live, either. Oh, no, for he was certainly done for.

"But he was conscious! Conscious, think of it! And try to imagine his torment, if you can. I could, and when he spoke to me I almost fainted from the shock of it. That he could think, have any sort of ordered thought processes left in him, was . . . well, unthinkable. And yet he maintained something of control over himself. His Adam's apple bobbed, bulged, and he whispered:

" 'Pull it out. Drag it out of me. The point of the beam, draw it from my body.'

"I recovered my senses, took off my jacket and put it carefully across his burst gut. This was for my good more than for his, you understand. I could have done nothing while his innards were exposed like that. Then I took hold of the beam.

" 'It'll do no good,' I told him, nervously licking my lips. 'Look, this will kill you outright! If I can get it out—and that's a big if—you'll die at once. I wouldn't be doing you any favours if I told you anything else.'

"He managed to nod. 'Try, anyway,' he gasped.

"And so I tried. Impossible! Three men couldn't have shifted it. It was literally jammed right through him and down into the floor. Oh, I moved it a little, and when I did great chunks of the ceiling came down and the wall settled ominously. Worse, a pool of blood welled up in the depression in his chest where the beam impaled him.

"At that he started groaning and rolling his eyes to set my teeth grating, and his body started vibrating under my jacket like someone had sent a jolt of electricity through him. And his feet, drumming the ground in an absolute *fit* of pain! But would you believe it?—even while this was going on his shivering hands came up like claws to grab that splintered stump where it pinned him, and he tried to add his own weight to mine as I strained to free him!

"It was all a waste of effort and both of us knew it. I told him:

" 'Even if we could draw it out, it would only bring the whole place down on you. Look, I have chloroform here. I can knock you out so you won't have the pain. But I have to be honest with you, you won't be waking up.'

" 'No, no drugs!' he gasped at once. 'I'm . . . immune to chloroform. Anyway I have to stay conscious, stay in control. Get help, more men. Go—go quickly!'

" 'There's no one!' I protested. 'Who would there be out here? If there are any people around they'll be busy saving their own lives, their families, their property. This whole district has been bombed to hell!' And even as I spoke there came the loud droning of bombers and, in the distance, the thunder of renewed bombing.

" 'No!' he insisted. 'You can do it, I know you can. You'll find help and come back. You'll be well paid for it, believe me. And I won't die, I'll hang on. I'll wait. You . . . you're my one chance. You can't refuse me!' He was desperate, understandably.

"But now it was my turn to know agony: the agony of frustration, of complete and utter impotence. This brave, strong man, doomed to die here, now, in this place. And looking about me, I knew that I wouldn't have time to find anyone, knew that it was all over.

"His eyes follow my gaze, saw the flames where they were licking up outside the demolished bay windows. The smoke was getting thicker by the second as books burned freely, setting fire to tumbled shelves and furniture. Smoke was starting to curl down from the sagging ceiling, which even now settled a little more and sent down a shower of dust and plaster fragments.

" 'I . . . I'll burn!' he gasped then. For a moment his eyes were wide and bright with fear, but then a strange look of peaceful resignation came into them. 'It . . . is finished.'

"I tried to take his hand but he shook me off; and once more he muttered, 'Finished. After all these long centuries . . .'

" 'It was finished anyway,' I told him. 'Your injuries . . . surely you must have known?' I was anxious to make it as easy as possible for him. 'Your pain was so great that you've crossed the pain threshold. You no longer feel it. At least there's that to be thankful for.'

"At that he looked at me, and I saw scorn staring out of his eyes. 'My injuries? My pain?' he repeated. *'Hah!'* And his short bark of a laugh was bitter as a green lemon, full of acid and contempt. 'When I wore the dragon-helm and got a lance through my visor, which broke the bridge of my nose, shot through and smashed out the back of my skull, that was pain!' he growled. 'Pain, aye, for part of me—the real ME—had been hurt. That was Silistria, where we crushed the Ottoman. Oh, I know pain, my friend. We are old, old acquaintants, pain and I. In 1204 at Constantinople it was Greek fire. I had joined the Fourth Crusade in Zara, as a mercenary, and was burned for my trouble at the height of our triumph! Ah, but didn't we make them pay for it? For three whole days we pillaged, raped, slew.

248

And I—in my agony, half eaten away, burned through almost to the very heart of ME—I was the greatest slayer of all! The human flesh had shrivelled but the *Wamphyri* lived on! And now this, pinned here and crippled, where the flames will find me and put an end to it. The Greek fire expired at last, but this one will not. Human pain and agony, I know nothing of them and care less. But *Wamphyri* pain? Impaled, burning, shrieking in the fire and melting away layer by layer? No, that must not be . . .'

"These were his words as best I remember them. I thought he raved. Perhaps he was a historian? A learned man, certainly. But already the flames were leaping, the heat intolerable. I couldn't stay with him—but I couldn't leave him, not while he was conscious, anyway. I took out a cotton pad and a small bottle of chloroform, and—

"He saw my intention, knocked the unstoppered bottle from my hand. Its contents spilled, were consumed in blue flames in an instant. 'Fool!' he hissed. 'You'd only deaden the human part!'

"My clothes were beginning to feel unbearably hot and small tongues of fire were tracing their way round the skirting-board. I could barely breathe. 'Why don't you die?' I cried then, unable to tear myself away from him. 'For God's sake, die!'

" 'God?' he openly mocked me. 'Hah! No peace for me there, even if I believed. No room for me in your heaven, my friend.'

"On the floor amongst other debris from the desk lay a paperknife. One edge of its blade was unusually keen. I took it up, approached him. My target would be his throat, ear to ear. It was as if he read my mind.

" 'Not good enough,' he told me. 'It has be the whole head.'

" 'What?' I asked him. 'What are you saying?'

"Then he fixed me with his eyes. 'Come here.'

"I could not disobey. I leaned over him, gazed down on him, held out the knife. He took it from me, tossed it away. 'Now we will do it my way,' he said. 'The only sure way.'

"I stared into his eyes and was held by them. They were . . . magnetic! If he had said nothing but merely held me with those eyes, then I would have remained there and burned with him. I knew it then and know it now. Crippled, crushed, opened up like a fish for the gutting, still he had the power!

" 'Go to the kitchen,' he commanded. 'A cleaver—the big one—fetch it. Go now.'

"His words released my limbs but his eyes—no, his *mind*—remained fastened on my mind. I went, through gathering smoke and flame, and returned. I showed him the cleaver and he nodded his satisfaction. The room was blazing now and my outer clothes were beginning to smoke. All the hair of my head felt singed, crisped.

" 'Your reward,' he said.

" 'I want no reward.'

" 'But I want you to have it. I want you to know who you have destroyed this night. My shirt—tear it open at the neck.'

"I began to do so, and leaning over him thought for a single moment that something other than a tongue moved in the partly open cavern of his mouth. His breath in my face was a stench! I would have turned away but his eyes held me until the job was done. And around his neck on a chain of gold, there I found a heavy golden medallion. I unclasped it, took it, placed it in my pocket.

" 'There,' he sighed. 'Payment in full. Now finish it.'

"I lifted the cleaver in a trembling hand, but—

" 'Wait!' he said. 'Listen: the temptation is on me to kill you. It is what you would call self-preservation, which runs strong in the *Wamphyri*. But I know it for false hope.

The death you offer will be clean and merciful, the flames slow and intolerable. But for all that, still I might strike at you before you strike me, or even in the moment of the striking. And then both of us would die most horribly. Therefore . . . stay your blow until I close my eyes—then strike hard and true—then flee! Strike, and put distance between. Do you understand?'

"I nodded.

"He closed his eyes.

"I struck!

"In the moment the straight, shiny blade bit into his neck—even before it passed through and the head was severed—his eyes shot open. But he had warned me, and I had taken note. As his head shot free and blood spurted from his body I leaped backward. The head bounced, rolled, fell among blazing books. But God help me, I swear that however it flew, at whichever angle, those awful eyes turned to follow me, full of accusation! And oh!—the *mouth*—his mouth and what it contained, that forked tongue, like a snake's, slithering and flickering over lips that drained in an instant from scarlet to deathly white!

"And as bad or worse than all of this, the head itself had changed. The skin had seemed to tighten on the skull, which in turn had elongated to that of a great hound or wolf. The glaring eyes, previously dark, had turned to the colour of blood. The upper teeth had clamped down on to the lower lip, trapping the scarlet forked tongue there, and the great incisors were curved and sharp as needles!

"It is true! I saw it. I *saw* it—but only in that moment before the whole head began a swift decomposition. It was the heat; it could only be that the flesh was blistering and melting; but the sheer horror of it sent me stumbling away from it. Stumbling, yes, and then leaping—away from that staring, alien rotting head, but likewise from his decapi-

251

tated body—*in which there had now commenced the most awful commotion!* A commotion . . . and a collapse. My God, yes! Oh, yes . . .

"You'll recall I had lain my jacket across his exposed guts? Now the jacket was gripped by some invisible force from beneath, torn apart and tossed violently, in two pieces, to the ceiling. Following it, lashing wildly, a single tapering tentacle of leprous flesh burst upward from his stomach, twisting and writhing in a grim paroxysm. Like a devilish whip it thrashed the air of the room, snaking through the smoke and the flames as if searching!

"As the tentacle fell to the floor and began a systematic if spastic examination of the blazing room, only recoiling from the flames themselves, I stepped up on to a chair and crouched there transfixed with terror. And from that slightly elevated vantage point I saw what was left of the corpse falling in upon itself and becoming first putrefaction, then bones with the flesh sloughed off, finally dust before my eyes. As this happened the tentacle grew leaden, retracted, drew itself back to where the host body had lain, to the dust and the last crumbling relics of centuried bones . . .

"And all of this, you understand, taking place in mere moments, swifter far than I can possibly tell it. So that to this day I could not swear my soul on what I saw. Only that I *believe* I saw it.

"Anyway, that was when the ceiling caved in and hurled me from my chair, and the entire area of the room where the horror had been burst into flames and hid whatever remained of it. But as I staggered from the place—and don't ask me how I got out again into the reeking night air, for that's gone now from my memory—there rose up from the inferno such a protracted cry of intense agony, so piteous and terrible and savagely *angry* a wailing, as ever I had heard and hope never to hear again.

"Then—

"The skies rained bombs once more and I knew nothing else until I regained consciousness in a field hospital. I had lost a leg, and, or so they later told me, something of my mind. Shell shock, of course; and when I saw how futile it was to try to tell them otherwise, then I decided simply to let it stand at that. Mind and body, both were merely victims of the bombing . . .

"Ah! But amongst my belongings when they released me was that which told the true story, and I have it still."

Chapter Nine

ACROSS GIRESCI'S WAISTCOAT HE WORE A CHAIN OF GOLD. Now he took from the left-hand waistcoat pocket a silver fob watch completely out of keeping with the antique chain, and from the right the medallion of which he had spoken, holding the jewellery up for Dragosani's inspection. Dragosani caught his breath and held it, ignored the watch and chain but took hold of the medallion and stared at it. On one face of the disc he saw a highly stylized heraldic cross which could only be that of the Knights of St. John of Jerusalem, but which had been scored through again and again with some sharp instrument and thoroughly defaced; and on the other side—

Somehow Dragosani had expected it. In harsh, almost crude bas-relief, a triple device: that of the devil, the bat, and the dragon. He knew the motif only too well, and the question it prompted came out in a rush of breath which surprised him more than Giresci:

"Have you tracked this down?"

"The device, its heraldic significance? I have tried. It has a significance, obviously, but I've so far failed to discover the origin of this specific coat or chapter. I can tell you something of the symbolism, in local history, of the dragon and the bat; but as for the devil motif, that is rather . . . obscure. Oh, I know what *I* make of it, all right, but that's a personal thing and purely conjectural, with little or nothing to sub—"

"No," Dragosani impatiently cut him off. "That wasn't my meaning. I know the motif well enough. But what of the man—or creature—who gave you the medallion? Were you able to trace *his* history?' He stared at the other, eager for the answer without quite knowing what had prompted the question. Asking it had been an almost involuntary action, the words simply springing from his tongue—as if they'd been waiting there for some trigger.

Giresci nodded, took back the medallion, watch and chain. "It's curious, I know," he said, "but after an experience like mine you'd think I'd steer clear of all such stuff, wouldn't you? You certainly wouldn't think it would start me off on all those long years of private search and research. But that's what it did; and where better to start, as you seem to have worked out for yourself, than with the name and family and history of the creature I had destroyed that night? First his name: it was Faethor Ferenczy."

"Ferenczy?" Dragosani repeated, almost tasting the word. He leaned forward, his fingertips white where they pressed down on the table between them. The name meant something to him, he felt sure. But what? "And his family?"

"What?" Giresci seemed surprised at something. "You don't find the name peculiar? Oh, the surname is common enough, I'll grant you—it's chiefly Hungarian. But Faethor?"

"What of it?"

Giresci shrugged. "I only ever came across it on one

other occasion: a ninth-century White Khorvaty princeling. His surname was pretty close, too: Ferrenzig.''

Ferenczy, Ferrenzig, thought Dragosani. *One and the same.* And then he checked himself. Why on earth should he jump to a conclusion like that? And yet at the same time he knew that he had not merely "jumped to a conclusion" but that he had known the duality of the *Wamphyri* identity for a fact. Dual identity? But surely that too was a conclusion drawn in haste. He had meant only that the *names* were the same, not the men, or man, who had borne the names. Or had he in fact meant more than that? If so it was an insane conclusion—that those two Faethors, one a ninth-century Khorvatian prince and the other a modern Romanian landowner, should be one and the same man—or should be insane, except that Dragosani knew from the old Thing in the ground that the concept of vampiric and undead longevity was far from insane.

"What else did you learn of him?" he finally broke the silence. "What about his family? Surviving members, I mean. And his history, other than this tenuous Khorvaty link?"

Giresci frowned and scratched his head. "Talking to you," he growled, "is an unrewarding, even frustrating game. I keep getting this feeling that you already know most of the answers. That perhaps you know even more than I do. It's as if you merely use me to confirm your own well-established beliefs . . ." He paused for a moment, and when Dragosani offered no reply, continued: "Anyway, as far as I'm aware Faethor Ferenczy was the last of his line. None survive him."

"Then you're mistaken!" Dragosani snapped. He at once bit his lip and lowered his voice. "I mean . . . you can't be sure of that."

Giresci was taken aback. "Again you know better than me, eh?" He had been drinking Dragosani's whisky steadily but seemed little affected. Again he poured shots before suggesting: "Let me tell you just exactly what I found out about this Ferenczy, yes?"

"The war was over by the time I got started. As for making a living: I couldn't complain. I had my own place, right here, and was "compensated" for my lost leg. This plus a small disability pension rounded things off; I would get by. Nothing luxurious, but I wouldn't starve or go in need of a roof over my head. My wife—well, she had been another victim of the war. We had no family and I never remarried.

"As to *how* I became engrossed with the vampire legend: I suppose it was mainly that I had nothing else to do. Or nothing else that I wanted to do. But this drew me like some monstrous magnet . . .

"All right, I won't bore you; I explain all of this simply to put you in the picture. And as you know, my investigations started with Faethor Ferenczy. I went back to where it had happened, talked to people who might have known him. Most of that neighbourhood had been reduced to rubble but a few houses still stood. The actual Ferenczy house was just a shell, blackened inside and out, with nothing at all to show who or what had lived there.

"Anyway, I had his name from various sources: postal services, Lands and Property Registry, missing-believed-dead list, war casualty register, etc. But other than this handful of responsible authorities, no one seemed to know him personally. Then I found an old woman still living in the district, a Widow Luorni. Some fifteen years before the war she'd worked for Ferenczy, had been his cleaner lady. She went in twice weekly and kept his place in good order. She'd done that for ten years or more, until she'd grown disenchanted with the work. She wouldn't say why specifically, but it was obvious to me that the trouble was Ferenczy himself, something about him. Something that had gradually grown on her until she couldn't take any more of it. At any rate, she never once mentioned his name without crossing herself. Yes, but still she managed to tell me some interesting things about him . . . I'll try to cut it short for you:

"There were no mirrors in his house. I know I don't have to explain the significance of that . . .

"The Widow Luorni never saw her employer outside the place in daylight; she never saw him outdoors at all except on two occasions, both times at evening, in his own garden.

"She never once prepared a meal for him and never saw him eat anything. Not ever. He had a kitchen, yes, but to the old lady's knowledge never used it; or if he did, then he cleared up after himself.

"He had no wife, no family, no friends. He received very little mail, was often away from home for weeks on end. He did not have a job and did not appear to do any work in the privacy of his home, but he always had money. Plenty of it. When I checked, I was unable to discover anything by way of a bank account in his name. In short, Ferenczy was a very strange, very secretive, very reclusive man . . .

"But that's not all, far from it. And the rest is even stranger. One morning when she went to clean, the old girl found the local police there. Three brothers, a well-known gang of burglars working out of Moreni—a brutish lot that the police had been after for years—had been apprehended at the house. Apparently they'd broken into the place in the wee small hours of the morning. They had thought the house was empty; a bad mistake indeed!

"According to statements they later made to the police, Ferenczy had been dragging one of them and herding the other two to the cellar when his attention was arrested by the arrival of horsemen outside the house. Remember, in those days the local police still used horses in the more isolated regions. It was them, all right; they had been alerted by reports of prowlers in the area, the brothers, of course. And never were three criminals more glad to be given over into the hands of the law!

"Thugs they were, by all means, but they'd been no match for Faethor Ferenczy. Each of them had a broken right arm and a broken left leg, and their intended victim was responsible! Think of his *strength* Dragosani! The police were too grateful to him to go into the matter too deeply, Widow Luorni said—and after all, he had only been protecting his life and property—but she was there when the brothers were carted away a few hours later, and it was plain to her that her employer had scared the daylights out of them.

"Anyway, I've said that Ferenczy was in the act of taking his captives to the cellar. For what purpose? A place to detain them until help arrived? Possibly . . ."

"Or a place to keep them, like a cool pantry, until they were . . . required, eh?" said Dragosani.

Giresci nodded. "Exactly! Anyway, shortly after that the Widow stopped working there."

"Hmm!" Dragosani mused. "It surprises me he let her go. I mean, she must have suspected something. You said yourself that she was "disenchanted," that a feeling of unease had grown in her until she could take no more. Wouldn't he worry that she'd talk about him?"

"Ah!" Giresci answered. "But you've forgotten something, Dragosani. What about the way he controlled me—with his eyes and his mind—on the night of the bombing, the night he died?"

"Hypnotism," said the other at once.

Giresci smiled grimly, nodded. "It is an art of the vampire, one of many. He simply commanded her that so long as he lived she would remain silent. *While he lived,* she would simply forget all about him, forget that she had ever seen anything sinister in him.''

"I see," said Dragosani.

"And so strong was his power," the other continued, "that she actually *did* forget—until I questioned her about him all those years later. For, of course, by then Ferenczy was dead.''

Giresci's manner was beginning to irritate Dragosani. The man's air of self-satisfaction—his smugness—his obviously high opinion of his own detective skills. "But of course this is all conjecture," the necromancer finally said. "You don't know any of it for a certainty."

"Oh, but I do," answered the other at once. "I know it from the Widow herself. Now don't get me wrong: I'm not saying that she simply volunteered all of this. It wasn't that we had a good gossip session or anything like that. Far from it. No, for I had to really sit down with her and *ask* her about him, repeatedly, until I'd dug it all out. He was dead and his power gone, certainly, but still something of it lingered over, do you see?''

Dragosani grew thoughtful. His eyes narrowed a little. Suddenly, surprisingly, he felt threatened by this man. He was too clever by far, this Ladislau Giresci. Dragosani resented him—and at once wondered why. He found it hard to understand his own feelings, the sudden surge of emotion within. It was too enclosed in here, claustrophobic. That must be it. He shook his head, sat up straighter, tried to concentrate. "Of course, the Widow is long dead now."

"Oh, yes—years ago."

"So you and I, we're the only ones who know anything at all about Faethor Ferenczy?"

Giresci peered at the younger man. Dragosani's voice had sunk so low that it was little more than a growl, almost sinister. There seemed something wrong with him.

Even under Giresci's questioning gaze he gave himself another shake, rapidly blinking his eyes.

"That's right," Giresci answered, frowning. "I've told no one else in—oh, longer than I can remember. No point telling anyone else, for who'd believe? But are you all right, my friend? Are you well? Is something bothering you?"

"Me?" Dragosani found himself leaning forward, as if drawn towards Giresci. He deliberately forced himself upright in his chair. "No, of course not. I'm a little drowsy, that's all. My meal, I suppose. The good food you've served me. Also, I've driven a long way in the last few days. Yes, that's it: I'm tired."

"You're sure?"

"Yes, quite sure. But go on, Giresci, don't stop now. Please tell me more. About Ferenczy and his forebears. About the Ferrenzigs. The Wamphyri in general. Tell me anything else you know or suspect. Tell me everything."

"Everything? It could take a week, longer!"

"I have a week," Dragosani answered.

"Damn, I believed you're serious!"

"I am."

"Well now, Dragosani, doubtless you're a nice enough young fellow, and it's good to talk to someone who's genuinely interested and knows something about one's subject—but what makes you think I'd care to spend a whole week like that? At my age time's important. Or maybe you think I have the same kind of longevity Ferenczy had, eh?"

Dragosani smiled, but thinly. On the point of saying, *you can talk to me here or in Moscow,* he checked himself. That wasn't necessary. Not yet, anyway. And it might let Borowitz in on his big secret: how he came to be a necromancer in the first place. "Then how about the next hour or two?'' he compromised. ''And, since you've suggested it, we can start with Ferenczy's longevity.''

Giresci chuckled. ''Fair enough. Anyway, there's whisky left yet!'' He poured himself another shot, made himself comfortable. And after a moment's thought:

''Ferenczy's longevity. The near-immortality of the vampire. Let me tell you something else the Widow Luorni said. She said that when she was a small girl, her grandmother had remembered a Ferenczy living in the same house. And *her* grandmother before her! Nothing strange about that, though—son follows father, right? There were plenty of old Boyar families round here whose names went back to time immemorial. There still are. What's strange is this: to the Widow's knowledge there had never been any female Ferenczys. And how does a man pass on his name if he never takes a wife, eh?''

''And of course you looked into it,'' said Dragosani.

''I did. Records were scarce, however, for the war had destroyed a great deal. But certainly the house had been the seat of the Ferenczys as far back as I could trace it, and never a woman among 'em! A celibate lot, eh?''

Without understanding his outrage, Dragosani suddenly felt that he himself had been insulted. Or perhaps it was only his natural intelligence which felt slighted. ''Celibate?'' he said stiffly. ''I think not.''

Giresci nodded. In fact he was well aware of the Wamphyri's rapacious nature. ''No, of course not,'' he confirmed Dragosani's denial. ''What? A vampire celibate? Ridiculous? Lust is the very force that drives him. Universal lust—for power, flesh, blood! But listen to this:

''In 1840 one Bela Ferenczy set off across the Meridionali to visit a cousin or other relative in the mountains of the northern Austro-Hungarian borders. Now this much is well documented; indeed, old Bela seems to have gone to a deal of trouble to let people know he was going visiting. He installed a man to look after the place while he was away—not a local man, incidentally, but someone of gipsy stock—hired a coach and driver for the early stages of the journey, made reservations for connections through the high passes, and completed all of the preparations necessary to travel in these parts in those days. And he put it about locally that this was to be a journey of valediction. He had seemed to grow very old very quickly in the last year or two, and so it was accepted that he went to say his last farewell to distant relatives.

"Now remember, we were still very much Moldavia-Wallachia at that time. In Europe the Industrial Revolution was in full swing—everywhere but here! Insular as ever, we were so backward as to seem almost retarded! The Lemberg–Galatz railway, skirting the mountains, was still more than a decade away. News travelled extremely slowly, and records were hard to keep. I mention this to highlight the fact that in this case there was good communication, and that a record did survive."

"Case?" Dragosani queried. "What case are you talking about?"

"The case of Bela Ferenczy's sudden death when his coach and horses were hurled into a precipice by an avalanche in one of the high passes! News of the 'accident' got swiftly back here; the old man's Szgany retainer took Ferenczy's sealed will to the local registrar; the will was posted without delay, showing that the Ferenczy house and grounds were to pass to a 'cousin,' one Giorg, who had, apparently, already been appraised of the situation and his inheritance."

Dragosani nodded. "And of course this Giorg Ferenczy later turned up and took possession. He would be—or he would appear to be—younger far than Bela, but the family resemblance would be unquestionable."

"Good!" Giresci barked. "You follow my reasoning

precisely. Having lived here for fifty years, which would normally make him an old man, Bela had decided it was high time he "died" and made way for the next in line."

"And after Giorg?"

"Faethor, of course," Giresci scratched his chin reflectively. "I've often wondered," he said. "if I had not killed him on the night of the bombing—if he had survived that night—what his next incarnation would have been? Would he have shown up after the war in some new Ferenczy guise, to rebuild the house and carry on as before? I think the answer is probably yes. They are territorial, the Wamphyri."

"And so you're convinced that Bela, Giorg, and Faethor were all one and the same?"

"Of course. I thought that was understood. Didn't he tell me as much himself, when he raved of the battles at Silistria and Constantinople? And before Bela there was Grigor, Karl, Peter and Stefan—oh, and the Lord knows how many others—all the way back to Faethor Ferrenzig the princeling and probably beyond! This was his territory, do you see? He held bloody dominion here. And in the olden times, as princelings or Boyars, my *God* but the Wamphyri were fierce about their holdings! That was why he joined the Fourth Crusade, to keep olden and future enemies off his lands. *His* lands, you understand? No matter what king or government or system is in power, the vampire considers his home ground to be his. He fought to protect himself, his monstrous heritage, and not for a mangy pack of scummy foreigners out of the West! You've seen the defaced Crusader cross on the reverse of my medallion—*hah!* When they dishonoured him he scorned them, spat on them!"

"And have you actually traced his name that far back? To Constantinople, I mean, in 1204?" Something of his awe of the vampire—or his envy?—was evident in Dragosani's voice.

Giresci cocked his head a little on one side. "Dragosani, how's your history?"

"Hardly brilliant. Fair, I suppose."

"Hmm! Well, many names came down from the Fourth Crusade, but you'll be hard put to find a Ferenczy or Ferrenzig amongst them. He was there, though, be sure of it! How do I know? Well, it's possible that you're talking to the world's foremost authority on that particular blood-bath, and I've discovered things which I'm sure many other historians have overlooked. Of course, I had the advantage of knowing what I was looking for—my objectives were specific—but in the process of tracking down the vampire I've naturally covered a deal of extraneous ground. Man, I could write a book on the Fourth Crusade—certainly from Hungary to Constantinople! And talking of Constantinople: Lord, what a hell *that* must have been! What a battle! And sure enough, right there in the thick of it—wherever the fighting raged fiercest—there was this man and the brutish horde he commanded. He was there too when the city fell, when he and his band of mercenary berserkers rampaged, utterly out of control. Yes, and his excesses spread like a cancer; the entire army joined in; they raped, pillaged and massacred for three long days . . .

"Pope Innocent III had called the Crusade; now, aghast at what it had turned into, he was unable to regain control. The Crusaders had vowed to take the Holy Land, but Innocent and his legate were obliged to absolve them from that vow. He as good as washed his hands of the affair; but in secret communiques he exercised what little control remained to him, ordering that those directly responsible for 'gross acts of excessive and unnatural cruelty' must gain 'neither glory nor rich reward' for their barbarism but that 'their names shall not be mentioned, nor shall they be offered respect or high regard.'

"Well, no need to look far for a scapegoat: a certain 'bloodthirsty Wallach recruited in Zara' would fit the bill nicely. Nor was he blameless. At first the Crusaders had honoured and elevated him—perhaps, secretly, they'd even envied or feared him—but now he found himself stripped of all honours and disgraced, and his name was stricken from all records. In return he scorned them for their duplicity, and defacing the sigil of their campaign—the cross on his medallion—he took his band and went home, proud and fierce under the banner of the devil, the bat and the dragon."

Dragosani chewed on his lip for a moment before saying: "Let's assume that to all intents and purposes all of this is true, or at least based on the truth to the best of your knowledge. Still there are several important questions remaining to be answered."

"Such as?"

"Ferenczy was a vampire. A vampire takes victims. When the hunger is on him he'll kill as ruthlessly as a fox kills chickens, and just as thoughtlessly. Yet it seems his sheet was clean. How could he possibly live here through all those centuries without once arousing suspicion? Remember, Ladislau Giresci, the blood is the life! Were there no cases of vampirism?"

"Around Ploiesti? None—not one—not as long as they've kept records, so far as I can discover." Giresci smiled grimly and leaned forward. "But if you were a vampire, Dragosani, would you take victims right on your own doorstep?"

"No, I don't suppose I would," Dragosani frowned. "Where, then?"

"North, my friend, in the Meridionali itself! Where else but the Transylvanian Alps, where all vampire stories seem to have their roots? Slanic and Sinaia in the foothills, Brasov and Sacele beyond the pass. And none of them more than fifty miles distant from Ferenczy's house, and all shunned for their evil reputations.''

"What, even now?'' Dragosani feigned surprise, but he remembered what Maura Kinkovsi had had to say on the subject three years ago.

"Stories linger down the years, Dragosani. Especially ghost stories. They take no chances, the mountain folk. If you die young up there and there's no simple explanation, it's the stake for you for sure! As to actual case histories: the last child to die of a vampire's bite did so in Slanic in the winter of forty-three. Yes, and she was buried with a stake through her heart, like a great many innocents before her. What? There had been eleven that year alone, in the villages around!''

"In forty-three, you say?''

Giresci nodded. "Oh, yes, and I see you've already made the connection. That's right, it was just a few months before Ferenczy died. She was his last victim, or at least the last we know of. Of course, with the war going on he'd be far less restricted, his victims more readily disposed of. He may well have taken many we don't know about, people who simply 'went missing' during air-raids in the countryside around—and there were plenty of those, believe me.'' He paused. "Any more questions?''

"You said that those towns you named were up in the mountains, fifty miles from Ploiesti. That's rough country; the ground rises rapidly, through two thousand feet in places; so how did Ferenczy do it? Did he become a bat and fly to his hunting grounds?''

"Folklore says he has that power. Bat, wolf, wraith— even flea, bug, spider! But . . . I think not. There's no hard evidence anywhere to be found. But you ask, how did he get to his kill? I don't know. I have my own ideas . . . but no proof at all."

"What ideas?" Dragosani asked, and waited half-anxiously for Giresci to answer. He already knew the correct answer to the question—or believed he did—but now he would discover just how clever Giresci really was. And how dangerous . . . *What?* He once again propped himself upright in his chair. *What the hell was going wrong with his thought processes?*

"A vampire," the other slowly answered, carefully formulating his thoughts, "is not human. I saw enough on the night Ferenczy died to convince me of that. So what is he? He is an alien creature, a co-habitant of man's body and mind. He is at best symbiotic, a *gestalt*-creature, and at worst a parasite, a hideous lamprey."

Correct! Dragosani snapped his agreement—but silently, to himself. And at once he felt dizzy and confused. He had known for a fact that Giresci was right in his assessment of the vampire—but *how* had he known? And even as he wondered what was happening to him, now Dragosani heard himself say:

"But isn't he supernatural? Surely he would need to be, to go about his business and still escape detection down all the years."

"Not supernatural, no," Giresci shook his head. "Superhuman! Hypnotic, magnetic! Creature of illusion, in no way a magician but in every way a great trickster! Not a bat but *silent* as a bat! Not a wolf, but *swift* as a wolf! Not a flea but a monster with a flea's appetite for blood—on a scale unprecedented! That's my idea of the vampire, Dragosani. Fifty miles to a creature like that? A healthy evening's walk! He would be able to compel his human shell to excesses of effort undreamed of . . ."

All correct, all of it, Dragosani mentally agreed, and out loud: "The name, Ferenczy. You say it's common enough. Why, being so clever, and taking into account all your research and what have you, haven't you tracked down other Ferenczys? You say that the vampire is territorial, and this region belonged to Faethor. Surely then there must have been other territories—and who lords or lorded it over them, eh?''

His voice was a rasp, harsh as a file. Once more Giresci was a little taken aback. "Why, you've pre-empted me!" he finally answered. "Shrewd stuff, Dragosani. Very astute. If Faethor Ferenczy had single-handedly held Moldavia and eastern Transylvania in his thrall for seven hundred years and more, what of the rest of Romania? Is that what you're saying?''

"Romania, Hungary, Greece—wherever vampires still dwell.''

" 'Still' dwell, Dragosani? God forbid!''

"Have it your own way," Dragosani snapped. "Where they used to dwell, then.''

Giresci drew back from him a little way. "A Castle Ferenczy in the Alps blew itself right off the mountain back in the late Twenties. That was put down to marsh-gas, methane, accumulated in the vaults and dungeons. An ill-regarded place, no one missed it. Anyway, so far as is known, its owner went with it. A baron or count or some such, his name was Janos Ferenczy. But documentation? History? Records? Forget it! That one's page in history has been erased even more surely than old Faethor's in the Fourth Crusade. Which in my book, of course, only serves to make him more suspect.''

"Rightly so," Dragosani agreed at once. "He was blown to hell, eh, old Janos? Good! And have you tracked down any other vampires, Ladislau Giresci? Come, tell me now: were there no Ferenczys who paid for their crimes and were put down in their heyday? How say you? What of the Western Carpatii, say beyond the Oltul?''

"Eh? But that should be familiar ground for you, Dragosani," said the other. "You were born there, after all. Knowing as much as you do, and being so 'clever' in your own right—yes, and with this keen interest of yours in vampires—surely by now you'll have made your own investigations and searches?"

Dragosani nodded. "Indeed, indeed! And five hundred years ago in the west there was such a creature; he butchered the vile Turk in his thousands and was slain for his so-called 'unnatural' zest!"

"Good!" Giresci thumped the table, no longer seeming to notice the change which had come over his guest. "Yes, you're right: his name was Thibor, a powerful Boyar, destroyed in the end by the Vlads. He had great power over his Szekely followers—too much power—so that the princes feared and were jealous of him. Also, it's likely they suspected he was one of the Wamphyri. It's only us modern, sophisticated men who doubt such things. The primitive and the barbarian, they know better."

"What else do you know of this one?" Dragosani growled.

"Not much," (Giresci gulped more whisky, his eyes less sharp and his breath beginning to reek,) "not yet. He's to be my next project. I know that he was executed—"

"Murdered!" Dragosani cut in.

"Murdered, then—somewhere west of the river, below Ionesti, and that he was staked and buried in a secret place, but—"

"And was he decapitated, too, this Thibor?"

"Eh? I found no records to that effect. I—"

"He was not!" Dragosani hissed from between clenched teeth. "They weighted him down with silver and iron chains, put a stake in his vitals and entombed him. But they let him keep his head. You of all people should know what that means, Ladislau Giresci. He was not dead. He was undead. *He still is!*''

Giresci struggled upright in his chair. Finally he had sensed that something was desperately wrong. His eyes had been a little glazed but now they came back into focus. Seeing the snarl on Dragosani's face, he began to tremble and pant. "It's far too dim in here," he gasped. "Far too close . . ." And he reached out a fluttering hand to swing back a shutter on the window. The sun at once streamed in.

Dragosani had risen to his feet, was leaning forward in a half-crouch. Now his hand reached across the table and trapped Giresci's wrist in a band of steel-like fingers. His grip was ferocious. "Your next project, you old fool? And if you had found him—found the vampire's grave—what then, eh? Old Faethor showed you how to do it, didn't he? And would you do it again, Ladislau Giresci?"

"What? Are you mad?" Giresci drew back more yet, inadvertently dragging the younger man's hand and arm into the beam of sunlight. Dragosani at once released him, snatched himself upright and reeled away into the room's cool shadows. He had felt the sunlight on his arm like acid, and in that moment he had *known!*

"Thibor!" He spat the word out like a vile taste. "You!"

"Man, you're ill!" Giresci was struggling to stand up.

"You old bastard—you old devil—you ancient Thing in the earth! You would have used me!" Dragosani raved, as if to himself. But in the back of his mind, at the edge of his awareness, something chuckled evilly and shrank back, shrank down.

"You need a doctor!" Giresci gasped. "A psychiatrist, anyway."

Dragosani ignored him. He understood all now. He crossed to the small occasional table, took up his gun from where he'd placed it, jammed it firmly into its under-arm holster. He made to stride from the room, stopped and turned back. Giresci cringed away from him as he approached.

"Too much!" the oldster was babbling. "You know far too much. I don't know who you are, but—"

"Listen to me," said Dragosani.

"—I don't even know *what* you are! Dragosani, I—"

Dragosani back-handed him, bruising his mouth and jerking his head round on his scrawny neck. "Listen, I said!"

When Giresci turned his watering eyes back to Dragosani, they had gone wide with shock. "I . . . I'm listening."

"Two things," Dragosani told him. "One: you will tell no one else about Faethor Ferenczy or what you've discovered of him. Two: you will never mention the name of Thibor Ferenczy again, or ever attempt to learn more than you already know of him. Is this understood?"

Giresci nodded, and in the next second his eyes went wider still. "Y—*you?*" he said.

Dragosani laughed, however shrilly. "Me? Man, if I were Thibor you'd be dead now. No, but I know of him—and now he knows of you!" He turned towards the door, paused and tossed back over his shoulder: "It's possible you'll be hearing from me. Till then, goodbye. And Giresci—mark well what I've said."

Leaving the house and moving into sunlight, Dragosani groaned and gritted his teeth . . . but the sun did him no harm. Still, he doubted if he would ever feel entirely comfortable under its rays again. It was not Dragosani who had felt the sun's sting in Giresci's house but Thibor, the old devil in the ground. Thibor, who in that moment of time had been ascendant, in control! But even knowing that it was so, still Dragosani was glad to get out of the direct sunlight and into his car. The interior of the big Volga was like a furnace, but the heat was in no way supernatural. As Dragosani wound the windows down and pulled away, heading for the main road, so the temperature dropped and he breathed easier.

And only then did he reach into his mind to dig out the leech-thing which was still hiding there. For he knew that if Thibor could reach him, then surely he could reach Thibor.

"Oh, yes, I know your name now, old devil," he said. "It was you, Thibor, wasn't it, back there at Giresci's? It was you, guiding my tongue, asking him those questions?"

For a moment there was nothing. Then:

I won't deny it, Dragosani. But let's be reasonable: I did little to hide the fact of my presence. And no harm done. I was merely—

"You were testing your power!" Dragosani snapped. "You tried to usurp my mind! You've been trying to do so for the last three years—and might have succeeded if I hadn't been so far away! I see it all now."

What? Accusations? Remember, Dragosani, it was you came to me that time. Of your own free will, you invited me into your mind. You asked for my help with the woman, and I gave it willingly.

"Too willingly!" Dragosani was bitter. "I hurt that girl—or you did, through me. Your lust in my body . . . I could barely control it. I might easily have killed her!"

You enjoyed it. (A sly whisper.)

"No, *you* enjoyed it! I was carried along by it. Well, and maybe she deserved it—but I don't deserve you sneaking into my mind like a thief to steal my thoughts. And your lust has *stayed* in my body—which you must have known it would. My invitation wasn't permanent, old dragon. Anyway, I've learned my lesson. You're not to be trusted. Not in any way. You're treacherous."

What? the voice in Dragosani's head made mock of him. *I, treacherous? Dragosani, I am your father . . .*

"Father of lies!" Dragosani answered.

How have I lied?

"In many ways. You were weak three years ago, and I brought you food. I gave you back a measure of your strength. You scorned pig's blood and said it was good only for freshening the earth. A lie! It freshened you. It gave you a lasting strength sufficient that you could reach out your mind to me even these three years later and in the full light of day! Well, I'll feed you no more. Also, you said sunlight would merely irritate you. Another lie, for I've felt how it burns you. And how many other lies have you told to me? No, Thibor, you do nothing except for your own advantage. I always guessed it, but now I know for sure."

And what will you do about it? (Did Dragosani detect a tremor of fear in the mental voice? Was the Thing in the ground worried?)

"Nothing," he answered.

Nothing? (Relief.)

"Nothing at all. Perhaps I made a mistake, seeking to be as you were, desiring to be one of the Wamphyri. Perhaps I'll now go away from here—and this time stay away—and let the years complete their work on you. I may have temporarily given your stinking bones something of flesh, something of life, but the centuries will take it all back again, I'm sure."

Dragosani, no! (Real fear now, panic.) *Listen: I wasn't testing my power. I wasn't testing anything. Do you remember how I told you I was not unique, that others of the Wamphyri were extant even now? I said that for centuries I had waited for them to come and release or avenge me, and they came not. Do you remember that?*

"Yes, what of it?"

Why, can't you see? If our roles were reversed, would you have been able to resist? You gave me the opportunity to

274

find out about those others, to learn what had become of them. Old Faethor, who was my father, dead at last! And Janos, a brother of mine who always hated me, exploded in the gasses of what he kept in his dungeons. Aye, dead and gone, both of them—and I for one glad of it! What? Didn't they leave me rotting in the earth for half a millennium? Oh, they heard me calling down all those bitter nights, be sure of it—but did they come to set me free? Not them! So Ladislau Giresci fancies himself a tracker of vampires, does he? But I would have shown him how to track them, who left me to the dirt and the worms and the seep of centuries, when I rise up from this place! Ah, well, they are gone now, and my vengeance with them . . .

Dragosani smiled grimly. "I can't help asking myself, Thibor, *why* they deserted you and left you to your fate? Your own father, for instance, Faethor Ferenczy: who would know you better than him? And *why* did your brother, Janos, hate you so? There's more to you than meets the eye, eh, Thibor? A black sheep among vampires! Who ever heard of such a thing? But why not?—you yourself have mentioned your excesses more than once. And I have personal recollections of them. Do the things you've done bother even your conscience? Or are the Wamphyri, and you in particular, without conscience?"

You make much of very little, Dragosani.

"Oh? I don't think so. I'm only just beginning to learn about you, Thibor. When you aren't lying outright, then you're obscuring the truth. It's the way you are; you don't know any other way."

The vampire was furious. *You find it easy to insult me because you known I may not strike you! How have I obscured the truth?*

"How? Haven't you said that I 'gave' you the opportunity to discover what had become of these kin of yours? But in fact you made your own opportunity. It wasn't my intention when I started out from Moscow to go to the library in Pitesti, Thibor, so who put that thought in my head again, eh? And when you learned of Ladislau Giresci, why, I just had to go and see him, didn't I?''

Listen, Dragosani—

"No, you listen. You used me. Used me just as the vampire of popular fiction uses his human vassals, just as you used your Szekely serfs five hundred years ago. But I'm no serf, Thibor Ferenczy, and that's your big mistake. It's one you'll come to regret, too."

Dragosani, I—

"I'll hear no more talk, old dragon, not from your forked tongue. There's only one thing you can do for me now: get yourself out of my mind!"

Dragosani's mind was fully developed now, trained, sharp as one of his own scalpels. Case-hardened by the necromancy which this very vampire had inspired in him, its cutting edge was swift and deadly. In its action it was keener than an ordinary man's is over that of a mongol—but how strong was it? Now Dragosani put it to the test. He squeezed with his mind, thrusting the monster out, driving him away.

Ingrate! Thibor accused, retreating. *But don't think it ends here. One day you'll need me, and then you'll return. Only don't wait too long, Dragosani. A year at most, and after that put aside all thoughts of ever acquiring Wamphyri knowledge, for you'll be too late. A year, my son, and no more than a year. I'll be waiting, and perhaps by then I will . . . have . . . forgiven you . . . Dragosaaniiii . . . !*

Then he was gone.

Dragosani relaxed, breathed deeply, suddenly felt exhausted. It had been no easy thing, exorcizing Thibor. The vampire had resisted, but Dragosani had been stronger. The real problem had not lain in getting him out—it would lie in keeping him out. Or perhaps not. Now that Dragosani knew Thibor was able to secretly insinuate himself in his being, he could maintain a watch for the old devil.

But as for his Romanian "holiday": that was over before it had begun. Cursing, he savagely applied the brakes and slewed the Volga round in a half circle, then started back the way he had come. He was tired but sleep would have to wait. All Dragosani wanted now was to put distance between himself and the Thing in the ground.

Dragosani stopped just outside Bucharest for petrol and tried to raise Thibor. It was still full daylight but he got something: a faint response, a shiver in his mind that echoed like a coffin and wriggled like a graveworm. In Braida in the dusk he tried again. The presence was stronger as night drew on. Thibor was there and might have responded if Dragosani had given him the opportunity. He did not but closed his mind and drove on. At Reni, after passing through Customs, he let down all his defences and literally invited Thibor in. It was full night now but the whisper in his mind was faint, as if it came from a million miles away:

Dragosaaaniiii. Coward! You flee from me. An old creature trapped in the earth.

"I'm no coward, old one. And I'm not fleeing but putting myself outside your range, where you can't reach me. And if you do manage to reach me, next time I'll know. You see, Thibor, you need me more than I need you. Now you can just lie there and think it over. I may come back one day and I may not. But when, *if* I do, it will be on my terms."

Dragosani (the whisper was faint but urgent) *I—*

"Goodbye, Thibor."

And behind him, Thibor Ferenczy's mental whisper was eaten up along with all the miles, and in a little while Dragosani felt safe to stop and sleep.

And dream his own dreams.

277

Chapter Ten

The spring of '76 . . .

VIKTOR SHUKSHIN WAS RUNNING CLOSE TO BROKE. HE HAD
frittered away his inheritance from Mary Keogh-Snaith's
estate on various business ventures which had fallen through;
rates on the big house near Bonnyrigg were high; the
money he made from his private tutoring was insufficient
to keep him. He would sell the house but it had fallen into
such a state of disrepair that it would no longer realize a
high price; also, he needed the seclusion that the place
gave him. To let some of the rooms would likewise dimin-
ish his privacy, and in any case the structural and decora-
tive repairs necessary before any letting could even be
considered were quite beyond his means.

His linguistic talent was not the only one he commanded, however, and so, over the period of the last few
months, he had made several discreet trips into London to
follow up and check out certain points of information he

had acquired in the years he had been domiciled in the British Isles—information which should be worth a deal of money to certain very interested foreign parties.

In short, Viktor Shukshin was a spy—or at least, it had been intended that he should become one when Gregor Borowitz first sent him out of the USSR, in 1957. Of course, there had been a hardening of East-West relationships at that time—and a general hardening of Russia's policy towards her dissidents—so that it hadn't been too difficult for Shukshin to get into Great Britain in the guise of a political refugee.

After that, and especially after meeting, marrying and murdering Mary Keogh, Shukshin had found himself so well-fixed that he had reneged on his Soviet boss and settled to actual citizenship. Still, he had not forgotten his original reason for coming to Great Britain, and as a hedge against the future had long since set about amassing information which might eventually be useful to his mother country. It was only recently, though, because of his financial difficulties, that he had begun to realize what a good position he was in. If the Soviets would not pay him the price he demanded for his information, then he could threaten them with the release to the British of his knowledge of a certain Russian organization.

Which was why, this sparkling May morning, Shukshin had written a carefully coded letter to an old "pen-friend" in Berlin—one who had not heard from him in over fifteen years, and had thought never to hear from him again—who would forward his letter through East Germany and on to Gregor Borowitz himself in Moscow. That letter was in the post even now, and Shukshin had just returned home in his battered Ford from the Bonnyrigg post office.

But coming across the river on the stone bridge that led to his driveway, Shukshin had been startled to feel in himself a strange churning which he'd at once recognized of old, a weird energy which turned his spine chilly and tugged at his hair like static electricity. On the bridge, leaning over the parapet and staring into the river's slow swirl, a slim young man in a scarf and overcoat had lifted his head and stared at Shukshin's car. His pale blue serious eyes had seemed to burn right through the car's bodywork, touching Shukshin with their cold gaze. And the Russian had known that the stranger was endowed with more than Nature's ordinary talents, that he commanded more than man's normal powers of perception. He had known it *absolutely*, for Shukshin, too, was gifted. He was a "spotter": his talent lay in the instant recognition of another ESP-endowed person.

As to who the youth could be, the significance of his appearing here at this time: there were several possibilities. It could be coincidence, an accidental meeting; this would not be the first time nor even the fiftieth that Shukshin had stumbled across such a person. But ESP came in a range of strengths and colours, and this one had been strong indeed and scarlet—a red-tinged cloud in Shukshin's mind. Or his presence here could be deliberate: he may have been sent here. The British branch must also have its spotters, and Shukshin may well have been detected and trailed. In the light of his recent trips to London—and what he had subsequently discovered of the British ESPionage branch—this theory was by no means far-fetched and sent something of a panic surging through him. Panic and more than panic. There was something else in Shukshin now, something he must control. Something which made his eyes narrow as he thought how easily he might have swerved his car to crush the stranger against the parapet wall. The emotion was hatred, the deep and abiding hatred he felt towards all ESPers.

His rage slowly subsided and he looked at his hands. The knuckles of his fingers were white where he gripped

the edges of his desk. He forced himself to release his grip
and sat back, breathing deeply. It was always this way, but
he had learned how to control it—almost. But if only he
had not sent that letter to Borowitz. That might have been
a big mistake. Perhaps he should have offered his services
direct to the British instead; perhaps he still should,
and without delay. Before they could investigate him any
further . . .

Such were his thoughts when the doorbell rang, and
because they were guilty thoughts he gave a violent start.

Shukshin's study was downstairs in a room to the rear of
the house that opened through patio windows into its own
courtyard. Now he stood up from his desk, passed from
bright spring sunshine into gloom as he hurried through the
ground floor rooms and corridors towards the front, and
midway started again as the doorbell once more tore at his
nerve-endings.

"I'm coming, I'm coming!" he called ahead—but he
slowed down and came to a halt on the interior threshold
of the long, glazed porch. Out there beyond the frosted
glass stood a well-muffled figure which Shukshin knew at
once: it was that of the young man from the bridge.

Shukshin knew it in two ways, one of which was simple
observation and could be in error. The other way was more
certain, as positive as a fingerprint: he felt again the surge
of rare energy-fields and the heat of his instinctive hatred
for all such ESP-talented men. Again a tide of panic and
passion rose up in him, which he forcibly put down before
moving to the door. Well, he had wondered about the
stranger, hadn't he? Now it seemed that he was not to be
kept in suspense. One way or the other he would soon
discover what was going on here.

He opened the door . . .

"How do you do," said Harry Keogh, smiling and

extending his hand. "You must be Viktor Shukshin, and I believe you give private tuition in German and Russian?"

Shukshin did not take Keogh's hand but simply stood and stared at him. For his own part, Harry stared back. And for all that he continued to smile, still his flesh crawled in the knowledge that he now stood face to face with his mother's murderer. He put the thought aside; for the moment it was sufficient to just look at the other and absorb what he could of this stranger who he intended to destroy.

The Russian was in his late forties but looked at least ten years older. He had a paunch and his dark hair was streaked with grey; his sideburns ran into a neatly trimmed, pointed beard beneath a fleshy mouth; his dark eyes were red-rimmed and deeply sunken in a face lined and grey. He did not appear in good health, but Keogh suspected that there was a dangerous strength in him. Also, his hands were huge, his shoulders broad for all that they were a little hunched, and if he had stood upright he would be well over six feet tall. All in all, he was a grotesquely impressive figure of a man. And (Keogh now allowed himself to remember) he was a murderer whose blood was cold as ice.

"Er, you do give language lessons, don't you?"

Shukshin's face cracked into something approaching a smile. A nervous tic tugged at the flesh at the corner of his mouth. "Indeed I do," he answered, his voice liquid and deep, retaining a trace of his native accent. "I take it I was recommended? Who, er, sent you to me?"

"Recommended?" Keogh answered. "No, not exactly. I've seen your ads in the papers, that's all. No one sent me."

"Ah!" Shukshin was cautious. "And you require lessons, is that it? Excuse me if I'm slow on the uptake, but no one seems much interested in languages these days. I have one or two regulars. That's about it. I can't really afford the time to take on anyone else just now. Also, I'm rather expensive. But didn't you get enough of them at school? Languages, I mean?''

"Not school," Keogh corrected him, "college." He shrugged. "It's the old story, I'm afraid: I had no time for it when it was free, and so now I'll have to pay for it. I intend to do a lot of travelling, you see, and I thought—''

"You'd like to brush up on your German, eh?''

"And my Russian.''

Alarm bells rang in Shukshin's mind, vying with the pressures already there. This was all false and he knew it. Also, there was more to this young man than some weird ESP talent. Shukshin had the odd feeling that he knew him from somewhere. "Oh?" he finally said. "Then you're a rare one. Not many Englishmen go to Russia these days, and fewer still want to learn the language! Is your visit to be business or—?''

"Purely pleasure," Keogh cut him off. "May I come in?''

Shukshin didn't want him in the house, would greatly prefer to slam the door in his face. But at the same time he must find out about him. He stood aside and Keogh entered, and the door closing behind him sounded to him like a lid coming down on a coffin. He could almost feel the Russian's animosity, could almost taste his hatred. But why should Shukshin hate him? He didn't even know him.

"I didn't catch your name," said the Russian, leading the way to his study.

Keogh was prepared for that. He waited a moment, following on the other's heels until they reached the airy study with its natural light flooding in through the patio windows, then said:

"My name is Harry. Harry Keogh . . . Stepfather.''

In front of him, Shukshin had almost reached his desk.

Now he froze, poised for a moment as if turned to stone, then quickly turned to face his visitor. Keogh had expected a response something like this, but nothing quite so dramatic. The man's face had turned to chalk in the frame of his darker sideburns and beard. His jelly lips trembled with a mixture of fear, shock . . . and rage?

"What?" his voice was hoarse now, a gasp. "What's that you say? Harry Keogh? Is this some kind of practical—?" But now he looked closer and knew why he had thought he'd known this youth before. He had been only a child then, but the features were the same. Yes, and his mother had had them before him. In fact, now that he knew who this was, the resemblance was remarkable. What was more, the boy seemed to have acquired something of her wild talent, too.

Her talent! The boy was a psychic, a medium, inherited from his mother! *That was it!* That was what Shukshin could detect in him—echoes of his mother's talent!

"Stepfather?" said Keogh, feigning concern. "Are you all right?" He offered a hand but the other backed away from it into his desk. He clawed his way round the desk, flopped into his chair. "It's a . . . shock," he said then. "I mean seeing you, here, after all these years." He got a grip of himself, sighed his relief and breathed more deeply, more freely. "A great shock."

"I didn't mean to startle you," Keogh lied. "I thought you'd be pleased to see me, to learn how well I'm doing. Also, I thought it was time I got to know you. I mean, you're the only real link I have with my past, my early childhood—my mother."

"Your mother?" Shukshin immediately went on the defensive. His face was regaining a little of its former colour as he quickly composed himself. Obviously his fears that he'd been discovered by the British ESP Agency were unfounded. Keogh was simply paying him a belated visit, returning to his roots; he was genuinely interested in his past. But if that was so—

"Then what was all that rubbish about wanting to learn German and Russian?" he snapped. "Was it really necessary to go through all that just to get to see me?"

"Oh," Keogh answered with a shrug, "yes, I admit that was just a ploy to get to see you—but it was in no way malicious. I just wanted to see if you'd recognize me before I told you who I was." He kept the smile on his face. Shukshin was in control of himself again, his anger plain and making his face ugly. Now seemed a good time to drop a second bombshell. "Anyway, I speak both German and Russian far more fluently than you ever could, stepfather. In fact, I could instruct you."

Shukshin prided himself on his linguistic ability. He could hardly believe his ears. What was this pup talking about, he could "instruct" him? Was he insane? Shukshin had been teaching languages since before Harry Keogh was born! The Russian's pride took precedence over his churning emotions and the hatred inside him which the presence of any ESPer invariably invoked.

"Hah!" he barked. "Ridiculous! Why, I was born a Russian. I took honours in my mother tongue when I was just seventeen. I had a diploma in German before I was twenty. I don't know where you get your funny ideas, Harry Keogh, but they don't make much sense! Do you honestly think that a couple of GCEs can match the work of a lifetime? Or are you deliberately trying to annoy me?"

Keogh continued to smile, but it was now a smile with hard edges. He took a chair opposite Shukshin and smiled that hard smile right across the desk and into the other's scornful face. And he reached out his mind to an old friend of his, Klaus Grunbaum, an ex-POW who had married an English girl and settled in Hartlepool after the war. Grunbaum had died of a stroke in '55 and was buried in the Grayfields Estate cemetery. It made no difference that that was one hundred and fifty miles away! Now Grunbaum answered Harry, spoke to him—*through* him—spoke in a rapid, fluent German, directly across Viktor Shukshin's desk and into his face:

"And how's this for German, Stepfather? You'll probably recognize that this is how it's spoken around Hamburg." Harry paused, and in the next moment changed his/Grunbaum's accent: "Or perhaps you'd prefer this? It's *Hoch Deutsch,* as spoken by the sophisticated élite, the gentry, and aped by the masses. Or would you like me to do something really clever—something grammatical, maybe? Would that convince you?"

"Clever," Shukshin sneeringly admitted. His eyes had widened while Harry talked but now he narrowed them. "A very clever exercise in dialectal German, yes, and quite fluent. But anyone could learn a few sentences like that parrot-fashion in half an hour! Russian is a different matter entirely."

Keogh's grin grew tighter. He thanked Klaus Grunbaum and switched his mind elsewhere—to a cemetery in nearby Edinburgh. He'd been there recently to spend a little time with his Russian grandmother, dead some months before he'd been born. Now he found her again, used her to speak to his stepfather in his native tongue. With Natasha's unwavering *command* of the language, indeed with her mind, he commenced a diatribe on "the failure of the repressive Communist system," only pausing after several astonishing minutes when finally Shukshin cried:

"What *is* this, Harry? More rubbish learned parrot-fashion? What's the purpose of all this trickery?" But for all his bluster, still Shukshin's heart beat a little faster, a little heavier in his chest. The boy sounded so much like . . . like someone else. Someone he had detested.

Still using his grandmother's Russian but speaking now

from his own mind, Keogh answered: "Oh, and could I learn this parrot-fashion? Are you so blind that you can't see the truth when you meet it face to face? I'm a talented man, stepfather. More talented than you could possibly imagine. Far more talented than ever my poor mother was . . ."

Shukshin stood up and leaned on his desk, and the hatred washed out from him in a tide, seeming almost physically to break on Keogh like a wave. "All right, so you're a clever young bastard!" he answered in Russian. "So what? And that's twice you've mentioned your mother. What are you getting at, Harry Keogh? It's almost as if you were threatening me."

Harry continued to use Shukshin's own tongue: "Threatening? But why should I threaten you, stepfather? I only came to see you, that's all—and to ask a favour."

"What? You try to make me look like a fool and then have the audacity to ask favours? What is it you want of me?"

It was time for the third bombshell. Keogh also got to his feet. "I'm told that my mother loved to skate," he said, his Russian still perfect. "There's a river out there, down beyond the bottom of the garden. I'd like to come back in the winter and visit you again. Perhaps you'll be less excitable then and we'll be able to talk more calmly. And maybe I'll bring my skates and go on the frozen river, like my mother used to, down there where the garden ends."

Once more ashen, Shukshin reeled, clutched at his desk. Then his eyes began to burn with hatred and his fleshy lips drew back from his teeth. He could no longer contain his anger, his hatred. He must strike this arrogant pup, knock him down. He must . . . must . . . *must*—

As Shukshin began to sidle round the desk towards him, Harry realized his danger and backed towards the door of the study. He wasn't finished yet, however. There was one last thing he must do. Reaching into his overcoat pocket, he drew something out. "I've brought something for you," he said, this time speaking in English. "Something from the old days, when I was very small. Something that belongs to you."

"Get out!" Shukshin snarled. "Get out while you're still in one piece. You and your damned insinuations! You want to visit me again, in the winter? I forbid it! I want nothing more of you, step-brat! Go and make a fool of someone else. Go now, before— "

"Don't worry," said Harry, "I'm going, for now. But first—catch!" and he tossed something. Then he turned and walked through the door into the shadowy house and out of sight.

Shukshin automatically caught what he'd thrown, stared at it for a second. Then his mind reeled and he went to his knees. Long after he'd heard the front door slam he continued to stare at the impossible thing in his hand.

The gold was burnished as if brand new, and the solitary cat's-eye stone seemed to stare back at him in a cold speculation all its own . . .

From the air, the Château Bronnitsy seemed not to have changed a great deal from the old days. No one would guess that it housed the world's finest ESPionage unit, Gregor Borowitz's E-Branch, or that it was anything but a tottering old pile. But that was exactly the way Borowitz wanted it, and he silently complimented himself on work well planned and executed as his helicopter fanned low over the towers and rooftops of the place and down towards the tiny helipad, which was simply a square of white-washed concrete emblazoned with a green circle, lying between a huddle of outbuildings and the château itself.

"Outbuildings," yes—that is what they looked like from

up here—old barns or sheds long fallen into disrepair and allowed to settle and crumble until they were little more than low humps of masonry dotted about the greater mass of the château. And this, too, was precisely to Borowitz's specifications. They were in fact defensive positions, machines-gun posts, completely functional and fully efficient, giving them a total arc of fire to cover the entire open area between the château and its perimeter wall. Other pill-boxes had been built into the wall itself, whose external face could become an electrical barrier at the throw of a switch.

Second only to the space-base at Baikonur, E-Branch was now housed in one of the best-fortified installations in the USSR. Certainly it vied favourably with the joint atomic and plasma research station at Gargetya, lost in the Urals, whose chief asset was its isolation; but in one major aspect it was superior to both Baikonur and Gargetya: namely it *was* "secret" in the fullest sense of the word. Apart from Borowitz's operatives, no one but a double-handful of men even suspected that the château in its present form existed, and of these only three or four knew that it housed E-Branch. One of these was the Premier himself, who had visited Borowitz here on several occasions; another, less happily, was Yuri Andropov, who had *not* visited and never would—not on Borowitz's invitation.

The helicopter settled to its pad and as its rotor slowed Borowitz slid back his door and swung out his legs. A security man, ducking low, ran in under the whirling vanes and helped him down. Clutching his hat, Borowitz let himself be assisted away from the aircraft and through an arched doorway into that area of the château which once had been the courtyard. Now it was roofed over and partitioned into airy conservatories and laboratories, where branch operatives might study and practise their peculiar talents in comparative comfort or whatever condition or environment best suited their work.

Borowitz had been late out of bed this morning, which was why he'd called for the branch helicopter to fly him in from his dacha. Even so, he was still an hour late for his meeting with Dragosani. Passing through the outer complex of the château and into the main building, then up two flights of time-hollowed stone stairs into the tower where he had his office, he grinned wolfishly at the thought of Dragosani waiting for him. The necromancer was himself a stickler for punctuality; by now he would be furious. That was all to the good. His mind and tongue would be sharper than ever, setting the stage perfectly for his deflation. It did men good to be brought down now and then, an art in which Borowitz was past master.

Taking off his hat and jacket as he went, finally Borowitz arrived at the second-floor landing and tiny anteroom which also served as an office for his secretary, where he found Dragosani pacing the floor and scowling darkly. The necromancer made no effort to alter his expression as his boss passed through with a breezy "Good morning!" on the way to his own more spacious office. There he deftly kicked the door shut behind him, hung up his hat and jacket and stood scratching his chin for a moment or two as he pondered the best way to deliver the bad news. For in fact it was very bad news and Borowitz's temper was far shorter this morning than appearances might suggest. But as everyone who knew him was well aware, when the boss of E-Branch appeared in a good mood, that was usually when he was most deadly.

Borowitz's office was a spacious affair of great bay windows looking out and down from the tower's curving stone wall over rough grounds towards the distant woodland. The windows, of course, were of bullet-proof glass. The stone floor was covered in a fairly luxurious pile carpet, burned here and there from Borowitz's careless smoking habits, and his desk—a huge block of a thing in solid oak—stood in a corner where it had both the protection of thick walls and the benefit of maximum light from the bays.

There he now seated himself, sighing a little and lighting a cigarette before pressing a button on his intercom and saying: "Come in, Boris, will you? But do please see if you can leave your scowl out there, that's a good fellow . . ."

Dragosani entered, closing the door a little more forcefully than necessary, and crossed catlike to Borowitz's desk. He had "left his scowl out there," and in its place presented a face of cold, barely disguised insolence. "Well," he said, "I'm here."

"Indeed you are, Boris," Borowitz agreed, unsmiling now, "and I believe I said good morning to you."

"It was when I got here!" said Dragosani, tight-lipped. "May I sit down?"

"No," Borowitz growled, "you may not. Nor may you pace, for pacing irritates me. You may simply stand there where you are and—listen—to—me!"

Never in his life had Dragosani been spoken to like that. It took the wind right out of his sails. He looked as if someone had slapped him. "Gregor, I—" he began again.

"What?" Borowitz roared. "Gregor, is it? This is business, agent Dragosani, not a social call! Save your familiarity for your friends—if you've any left, with that snotty manner of yours—and not for your superiors. You're a long way off taking over the branch yet, and unless you get certain fundamentals sorted out in your hot little head you may never take it over at all!"

Dragosani, always pale, now turned paler still. "I . . . I don't know what's got into you," he said. "Have I done something?"

"You, done something?" now it was Borowitz's turn to

scowl. "According to your work sheets very little—not for the last six months, anyway! But that's something we're going to remedy. Anyway, maybe you'd better sit down. I've quite a lot of talking to do and it's all serious stuff. Pull up a chair."

Dragosani bit his lip, did as he was told.

Borowitz stared at him, toyed with a pencil, finally said: "It appears we're not unique."

Dragosani waited, said nothing.

"Not at all unique. Of course we've known for some time that the Americans were fooling about with extra sensory perception as an espionage concept—but that's all it is, fooling about. They find it 'cute.' Everything is 'cute' to the Americans. There's little of direction or purpose to anything they're doing in this field. With them it's all experimentation and no action. They don't take it seriously; they have no real field agents; they're playing with it in much the same way they played with radar before they came into World War Two—and look what that got them! In short, they don't yet trust ESP, which gives us a big lead on them. Huh! That makes a nice change."

"This is not new to me," said Dragosani, puzzled. "I know we're ahead of the Americans. So what?"

Borowitz ignored him. "The same goes for the Chinese," he said. "They've got some clever minds over there in Peking, but they aren't using them right. Can you imagine? The race that invented acupuncture doubting the efficacy of ESP? They're stuck with the same sort of mental block we had forty years ago: if it isn't a tractor it won't work!"

Dragosani kept silent. He knew he must let Borowitz get to the point in his own good time.

"Then there's the French and the West Germans. Oddly enough, they're coming along quite well. We actually have some of their ESPers here in Moscow, field agents working out of the embassies. They attend parties and functions, purely to see if they're able to glean anything. And occasionally we let them have tidbits, stuff their orthodox intelligence agencies would pick up anyway, just to keep them in business. But when it comes to the big stuff—then we feed them rubbish, which dents their credibility and so helps us keep right ahead of them.''

Borowitz was bored now with toying with his pencil; he put it down, lifted his head and stared into Dragosani's eyes. His own eyes had taken on a bleak gleam. "Of course,'' he finally continued, ''we do have one gigantic advantage. We have me, Gregor Borowitz! That is to say, E-Branch answers to me and me alone. There are no politicians looking over my shoulder, no robot policemen spying on *my* spying, no ten-a-penny officials watching my expense account. Unlike the Americans I *know* that ESP is the future of intelligence gathering. I know that it is not 'cute.' And unlike the espionage bosses of the rest of the world I have developed our branch until it is an amazingly accurate and truly effective weapon in its own right. In this—in our achievements in this field—I had started to believe we were so far ahead that no one else could catch us. I believed we were unique. And we would be, Dragosani, we would be—if it were not for the British! Forget your Americans and Chinese, your Germans and your French; with them the science is still in its infancy, experimental. But the British are a different kettle of fish entirely . . .''

With the exception of the last, everything Dragosani had heard so far was old hat. Obviously Borowitz had received disturbing information from somewhere or other, information concerning the British. Since the necromancer rarely got to see or hear about the rest of Borowitz's machine, he was interested. He leaned forward, said: ''What about the

British? Why are you suddenly so concerned? I thought they were miles behind us, like all the rest.''

"So did I," Borowitz grimly nodded, "but they're not. Which means I know far less about them than I thought I knew. Which in turn means they may be even farther ahead. And if they really are good at it, then how much do they know about us? Even a small amount of knowledge about us would put them ahead. If there was a World War Three, Dragosani, and if you were a member of British Intelligence knowing about the Château Bronnitsy, where would you advise your airforce to drop its first bombs, eh? Where would you direct your first missile?"

Dragosani found this too dramatic. He felt driven to answer: "They could hardly know that much about us. I work for you and *I* don't know that much! And I'm the one who always assumed he'd be the next head of the branch . . ."

Borowitz seemed to have regained something of his humour. He grinned, however wrily, and stood up. "Come," he said. "We can talk as we go. But let's you and me go see what we have here, in this old place. Let's have a closer look at this infant brain of ours, this nucleus. For it is still a child, be sure of it. A child now, yes, but the future brain behind Mother Russia's brawn." And shirt-sleeves flapping, the stubby boss of E-Branch forged out of his office, Dragosani at his heels and almost trotting to keep pace.

They went down into the old part of the château, which Borowitz called "the workshops." This was a total security area, where each operative as he worked was watched over and assisted by a man of equal status within the branch. It might seem to be what the western world would call the "buddy" system, but here in the château it was designed to ensure that no single operative could ever be sole recipient of any piece of information. And it was

Borowitz's way of ensuring that he personally got to know everything of any importance.

Gone now the padlocks and security guards and KGB men. There were none of Andropov's lot here now, where Borowitz's own agents themselves took care of internal security on a rota system, and the doors to the ESP-cells were controlled electrically by coded keys contained in plastic cards. And only one master card, which of course was held by Borowitz himself.

In a corridor lit by blue fluorescent light, he now inserted that key in its slot and Dragosani followed him into a room of computer screens and wall charts, and shelf upon shelf of maps and atlases, oceanographical charts, fine-detail street plans of the world's major cities and ports, and a display screen upon which there came and went a stream of continually updated meteorological information from sources world-wide. This might be the anteroom of some observatory, or the air-controller's office in a small airport, but it was neither of these things. Dragosani had been here before and knew exactly what the room held, but it fascinated him anyway.

The two agents in the room had stirred themselves and stood up as Borowitz entered; now he waved them back to work and stood watching as they took their places at a central desk. Spread out before them was a complex chart of the Mediterranean, upon which were positioned four small coloured discs, two green and two blue. The green ones were fairly close together in the Tyrhennian Sea, mid-way between Naples and Palermo. One of the blue ones was in deep water three hundred miles east of Malta, the other was in the Ionian Sea off the Gulf of Taranto. Even as Borowitz and Dragosani watched, the two ESPers settled down again to their "work," sitting at the desk with their chins in their hands, simply staring at the discs on the chart.

"Do you understand the colour code?" Borowitz hoarsely whispered.

Dragosani shook his head.

"Green is French, blue is American. Do you know what they're doing?"

"Charting the location and the movement of submarines," said Dragosani, low-voiced.

"Atomic submarines," Borowitz corrected him. "Part of the West's so-called 'nuclear deterrent.' Do you know how they do it?"

Dragosani again shook his head, hazarded a guess: "Telepathy, I suppose."

Borowitz raised a bushy eyebrow. "Oh? Just like that? Mere telepathy? You understand telepathy, then, do you, Dragosani? It's a new talent of yours, is it?"

Yes, you old bastard! Dragosani wanted to say. *Yes, and if I wanted to, right now I could contact a telepath you just wouldn't believe! And I don't need to "chart his course" because I know he isn't going anywhere!* But out loud he said: "I understand it about as much as they'd understand necromancy. No, I couldn't sit there like them and stare at a chart and tell you where killer subs are hiding or where they're going; but can they slice open a dead enemy agent and suck his secrets right out of his raw guts? Each to his own skills, Comrade General."

As he spoke one of the agents at the desk gave a start, came to his feet and went to a wall screen depicting an aerial view of the Mediterranean as seen from a Soviet satellite. Italy was covered in cloud and the Aegean was uncharacteristically misty, but the rest of the picture was brilliantly clear, if flickering a little. The agent tapped keys on a keyboard at the base of the screen and a green spot of light simulating the location of the submarine to the east of Malta began to blink on and off. He tapped more keys and as he worked Borowitz said:

"That Froggie sub has just changed course. He's putting the new course co-ordinates into the computer. He isn't much on accuracy, however, but in any case we'll be getting confirmation from our satellites in an hour or so. The point is, we had the information first. These men are two of our best."

"But only one of them picked up the course alteration," Dragosani commented. "Why didn't the other?"

"See?" said Borowitz. "You don't know it all, do you, Dragosani? The one who 'picked it up' isn't a telepath at all. He's simply a sensitive—but what he's sensitive to is nuclear activity. He knows the location of every atomic power station, every nuclear waste dumping ground, every atomic bomb, missile and ammo dump, and every atomic submarine in the world—with one big exception. I'll get on to that in a minute. But locked in that man's mind is a nuclear 'map' of the world, which he reads as clearly as a Moscow street map. And if something moves on that map of his it's a sub—or it's the Americans shuffling their rockets around. And if something begins to move very quickly on that map, towards us, for instance . . ." Borowitz paused for effect, and after a moment continued:

"It's the other one who's the telepath. Now he'll concentrate on that single sub, see if he can sneak into its navigator's mind, try to correct any error in the course his partner has just set up on the screen. They get better every day. Practice makes perfect."

If Dragosani was impressed, his expression didn't register it. Borowitz snorted, moved towards the door, said: "Come on, let's see some more."

Dragosani followed him out into the corridor. "What is it that's happened, Comrade General?" he asked. "Why are you filling me in on all these fine details now?"

Borowitz turned to him. "If you more fully understand what we have here, Dragosani, then you'll be better equipped to appreciate the sort of outfit they *might* have in England. Emphasis on might. At least, the emphasis used to be on might . . ."

He suddenly grabbed Dragosani's arms and pinioned them to his sides, saying: "Dragosani, in the last eighteen months we haven't had a single British Polaris sub on those screens in there. We just don't know where they go or what they do. Oh, the shielding's good on their engines, no doubt about it, and that would explain why our satellites can't track them—but what about our sensitive in there? What about our telepaths?"

Dragosani shrugged, but not in a way that might cause offence. He was genuinely mystified, no less than his boss. "You tell me," he said.

Borowitz released him. "What if the British have got ESPers in their E-Branch who can blank out our boys as easy as a scrambler on a telephone? For if that's the case, Dragosani, then they really are ahead!"

"Do you think it's likely?"

"Now I do, yes. It would explain a lot of things. As to what it is that's brought all this to a head—I've had a letter from an old friend of mine in England. I use the term loosely. When we go back upstairs I'll tell you all about it. But first let me introduce you to a new member of our little team. I think you'll find him very interesting."

Dragosani sighed inwardly. His boss would eventually arrive at the matter in hand, the necromancer knew that. It was just that he was so devious in everything he did, including coming to a point. So . . . better to relax and suffer in silence, and let things happen in Borowitz's own good time.

Now he let the older man usher him in through another door and into a cell considerably larger than the last. Little more than a week ago this had been a storeroom, Dragosani knew, but now there had been a number of changes. The place was much more airy, for one thing; windows had been let into the far wall and looked out just above basement level onto the grounds of the château. Also, a good ventilation system had been installed. To one side, in a sort of anteroom just off the main cell, a mini-operating theatre had been set up such as was used by veterinary surgeons; and indeed about the walls of both rooms, small cages stood on steel shelves and displayed a variety of captive animals. There were white mice and rats, various birds, even a pair of ferrets.

Talking to these creatures as he moved from cage to cage, a white-smocked figure not more than five feet three or four chuckled and joked and called them pet names, tickling them where he could with his stubby fingers through the bars. As Dragosani and Borowitz approached, he turned to face them. The man was slant-eyed, his skin a light yellowy-olive colour. Heavy-jowled, still he managed to look jolly; when he smiled his entire face seemed wreathed in wrinkles, out of which incredibly deep green eyes sparkled with a life of their own. He bowed from the waist, first to Borowitz and then to Dragosani. When he did so the ring of fluffy brown hair round the bald dome of his head looked for all the world like a halo which had slipped a little. There was something monkish about him, thought Dragosani; he would exactly suit a brown cassock and slippers.

"Dragosani," said Borowitz, "meet Max Batu, who claims he can trace his blood right back to the Great Khans."

Dragosani nodded and reached out a hand. "A Mongol," he said. "I suppose they can all trace their blood back to the Khans."

"But I really can, Comrade Dragosani," said Batu, his voice soft as silk. He took Dragosani's hand, gave it a firm shake. "The Khans had many bastards. So as not to be usurped, they gave these illegitimates wealth but no position, no power, no rank. Without rank they could not aspire to the throne. Also, they were not allowed to take wives or husbands. If they in their turn did manage to produce offspring, the same strictures were placed upon them. The old ways have come down the years. When I was born they still obeyed the old laws. My grandfather was a bastard, and my father, and so am I. When I have a child, it too will be a bastard. Yes, and there is more than this in my blood. Among the Khans' bastards were great shamans. They knew things, those old wizards. They could do things.'' He shrugged. ''I do not know a lot, for all that I am told I am more intelligent than others of my race—but there are certain things I can do . . .''

''Er, Max has a very high IQ,'' said Borowitz, smiling wolfishly. ''He was educated in Omsk, opted out of civilization and went back to Mongolia to herd goats. But then he had an argument with a jealous neighbour and killed him.''

''He accused me of putting a spell on his goats,'' Batu explained, ''so that they died. I could have done it, certainly, but I did not. I told him so but he called me a liar. That is a very bad thing in those parts. So I killed him.''

''Oh?'' Dragosani tried hard not to smile. He couldn't imagine this inoffensive little fellow killing anyone.

''Yes,'' said Borowitz. ''I read about it and was interested in the, er, nature of the murder. That is, in the method Max employed.''

''His method?'' Dragosani was enjoying this. ''He threatened his neighbor, who at once laughed himself to death! Is that it?''

''No, Comrade Dragosani,'' Batu answered for himself, his smile fixed now, square teeth gleaming yellow as ivory, ''that was not how it happened. But your suggestion is very, very amusing.''

"Max has the evil eye, Boris," said Borowitz, dropping the surname at last; which in itself would normally warn Dragosani that something unpleasant was coming. Warning bells did ring, but not quite loudly enough.

"The evil eye?" Dragosani tried to look serious. He even managed to frown at the little Mongol.

"Precisely," Borowitz nodded. "Those green eyes of his. Did you ever see such a green, Boris? They are purest poison, believe me. I intervened in the trial, of course; Max was not sentenced but came to us instead. In his way he's as unique as you are. Max—" he spoke directly to the Mongol "—could you give Comrade Dragosani something by way of a demonstration?"

"Certainly," said Batu. He fixed Dragosani with his eyes. And Borowitz was right: they were absolutely exquisite in their depth, in the completely *solid* nature of their substance. It was as if they were made of jade, with nothing of flesh about them. And now the warning bells rang a little louder.

"Comrade Dragosani," said Batu, "observe please the white rats." He pointed a stubby finger at a cage containing a pair of the animals. "They are happy creatures, and so they should be. She—on the left—is happy because she is well fed and has a mate. He is happy for the same reasons, also because he has just had her. See how he lies there, a little spent?"

Dragosani looked, glanced at Borowitz, raised an eyebrow.

"Watch!" Borowitz growled, his own eyes fixed firmly on what was happening.

"First we attract his attention," said Batu—and immediately he fell into a grotesque crouch, resembling nothing so much as a great squat frog where he confronted the cage half-way across the room. The male rat at once sprang upright, its pink eyes wide in terror. It made a leap at the bars of its cage, clung there staring at Batu. "And then—" said the Mongol "—then—we—*kill!*"

Batu had squatted even lower, almost in the stance of a Japanese wrestler before the charge. Dragosani, standing side-on to him, saw his expression change. His right eye seemed to bulge outward until it almost left its orbit; his lips drew back from his teeth in an utterly animal snarl of sheer bestiality; his nostrils gaped into yawning black pits in his face and great cords of sinew stood out on his neck and up under his jaw. And the rat screamed!

It screamed—an almost human scream of terror and agony—and vibrated against the bars as if electrocuted. Then it released its hold, shuddered, flopped over on to its back on the floor of the cage. There it lay perfectly still, blood seeping from the corners of its glazed, bulging pink eyes. The rat was quite dead, Dragosani knew it for a certainty, without closer examination. The female scurried forward and sniffed the corpse of her mate, then peered out through the bars uncertainly at the three human beings.

Dragosani did not know how or why the male rat had died. The words which now sprang to his lips were more a question than a statement of fact or any sort of accusation:

"It . . . it has to be a trick!"

Borowitz had expected that; it was typical of Dragosani to leap before looking, to rush in where angels might well fear to tiptoe. The boss of E-Branch stepped well back as Batu, still crouching, swivelled to face the necromancer. The Mongol was smiling again, holding his head questioningly on one said. "A trick?" he said.

"I meant only—" Dragosani hastily began.

"That is almost the same as calling me a liar," said Batu—and his face at once underwent its monstrous transformation. Now Dragosani got the full frontal view of what Borowitz had termed "the evil eye." And without the slightest shadow of a doubt it *was* evil! It was as if

Dragosani's blood congealed in his veins. He felt his muscles stiffening, as if *rigor mortis* were already setting in. His heart gave a massive lurch in his chest, and its pain caused him to cry out and sent him staggering. But the necromancer's reflexes were lightning itself.

Even as he reeled back against the wall his hand slid inside his jacket, came out grasping his pistol. He now knew—or at least thought—that this man could kill him. And survival was uppermost in Dragosani's mind. Quite simply, he must kill the Mongol first.

Borowitz stepped between them. "That's enough!" he snapped. "Dragosani, put it away!"

"That bastard almost finished me!" the necromancer gasped, his body trembling with reaction. He tried to move Borowitz out of his line of fire but the older man was like stone.

"I said that's *enough!*" he repeated. "What, would you shoot your partner?"

"My what?" Dragosani couldn't believe his ears. "My partner? I don't need a partner. What sort of partner? Is this some sort of joke?"

Borowitz reached out a hand and carefully took Dragosani's gun. "There," he said. "That's better. And now we can go back to my office." On their way out, as he herded a shaken Dragosani before him, he turned to the Mongol and said: "Thank you, Max."

"My pleasure," said the other, his face once more wreathed in a smile. He bowed from the waist as Borowitz closed the door on him.

Out in the corridor Dragosani was furious. He snatched back his gun and put it away. "You and your damned weird sense of humour!" he snarled. "Man, I nearly died in there!"

"No you didn't," Borowitz seemed unperturbed, "not even nearly. If you had a weak heart it would have killed

you, just as it killed his neighbour. Or if you were old and
infirm. But you're young and very strong. No, no, I knew
he couldn't kill you. He himself told me that he couldn't
kill a strong man. It takes a lot out of him to do what he
does, so much indeed that he would be the one to die, not
you, if he really tried it on you. So you see, I had faith in
your strength.''

"*You* had faith in *my* strength? You crazy old sadist—
and what if you'd been wrong?"

"But I wasn't wrong," said Borowitz, starting back the
way they had come.

Dragosani wouldn't be placated. He still felt shaken,
weak at the knees. Staggering after Borowitz, he said:
"What happened back there was a deliberate set-up and
you bloody well know it!"

His boss whirled and pointed directly at Dragosani's
chest. His grin was savage as a snarl. "But *now* you
believe, yes? Now you have seen and you have felt. Now
you *know* what he can do! You no longer think it's a trick.
It's a new talent, Dragosani, and one we haven't seen
before. And who's to say what other talents there are
throughout the world, eh?"

"But why did you let me—no, *make* me—go up against
something like that? It makes no sense."

Borowitz turned and hurried on. "It makes lots of sense.
It's practice, Dragosani, and like I'm always telling you—"

"Practice makes perfect, I know. But practice for what?"

"I only wish I knew," Borowitz tossed over his shoulder. "Who can say what you'll come up against—in
England!"

"What?" Dragosani's jaw dropped. He chased after the
older man. "England? What about England? And you still
haven't told me what you meant when you said Batu was
my partner. Gregor, I don't understand any of this."

They had reached Borowitz's offices. Borowitz swept

through the anteroom and turned on his heel just across the threshold of his private room. Dragosani came to a halt facing him, stared at him accusingly. "What is it you've got up your sleeve—Comrade?"

"So you're still accusing people of trickery, eh, Boris?" said the other. "Will you never learn your lesson the first time around? I don't need to resort to trickery, my friend. I give orders, and you obey! This is my next order: you're going back to school for a few months to brush up on your English. Not only the language but the entire English system. That way you'll fit better into the embassy over there. Max will go with you—and I'll bet he learns faster, too. After that, when we've made certain arrangements —a little field trip . . ."

"To England?"

"Exactly. You and your partner. There's a man over there called Keenan Gormley, Ex-MI5. 'Sir' Keenan Gormley, no less. Now he's the boss of their E-Branch. I want him dead! That's Max's job, for Gormley has a bad heart. After that—"

Dragosani saw it all now. "You want him 'interrogated,' " he said. "You want him emptied of secrets. You want to know all about him and his E-Branch down to the last detail."

"Right first time," Borowitz gave a sharp nod of his head. "And that's your job, Boris. You're the necromancer, inquisitor of the dead. It's what you get paid for . . ."

And before Dragosani could answer, completely expressionless for once, Borowitz closed the door in his face.

A Saturday evening in the early summer of 1976. Sir Keenan Gormley was relaxing with a book in his study at home in South Kensington, an after-dinner drink on the occasional table before him, when the telephone rang in the house proper. He heard it, and a few moments later his wife's voice calling: "Darling, it's for you."

"Coming!" he called, and sighing put down his book and went through. As he took the telephone from her, his wife gave him a smile and returned to her own reading. Gormley carried the telephone to a wicker chair and sat down before glass doors which stood open on a large, secluded garden. "Gormley here?" he said into the mouthpiece.

"Sir Keenan? This is Harmon. Jack Harmon in Hartlepool. How's the world been treating you all these years?"

"Harmon? Jack! How the devil are you!? My God! How long's it been. It must be twelve years at least!"

"Thirteen," came the answer, tinny with the effects of static. "Last time we spoke was at the dinner they threw for you when you left '*shhh!*—you know who!' And that was back in 'sixty-three."

"Thirteen years!" Gormley breathed, amazed. "Where does time go to, eh?"

"Where indeed? Retirement hasn't killed you off, then?"

Gormley chuckled drily. "Ah! Well, I only half-retired, as I believe you know. I still do this and that in the city. And you—are you still stout as ever? I seem to remember you'd got yourself the head's job at Hartlepool Tech?"

"That's right, and I'm still there. Headmaster?—Christ, it was easier in Burma!"

Gormley laughed out loud. "It's very good to hear from you again, Jack, especially since you seem in such good health. Now then, what can I do for you?"

There was something of a pause before Harmon finally answered: "Actually, I feel a bit of a fool. I've been on the point of calling you several times in the last week or so, but always changed my mind. It's such a damned strange business!"

Gormley was at once interested. He'd been dealing with

'strange businesses' for many years now. His own fine-tuned talent told him that something new was about to break, and maybe it was something big. His scalp tingled as he answered: "Go on, Jack, what is it? And don't worry that I may think it daft. I remember you for a very level-headed chap."

"Yes, but this is very—you know—difficult to put into words. I mean, I'm *close* to this thing, I've seen it with my own eyes, and yet—"

"Jack," Gormley was patient, "do you remember the night of that dinner, how you and I got talking afterwards? I'd had quite a bit to drink that night—too much, maybe—and I seem to remember mentioning things I shouldn't have. It was just that you seemed so well-placed—I mean, as a headmaster and all . . ."

"But that's exactly why I'm calling you now!" Harmon answered. "Because of that chat of ours. How on earth could you possibly know that?"

Gormley chuckled. "Call it intuition," he said. "But do go on."

"Well, you said that I'd be seeing a lot of youngsters pass through my hands, and I should keep my eyes open for any that I thought were rather . . . special."

Gormley licked his lips, said: "Hang on a moment, Jack, there's a good chap." He called out to his wife, "Jackie, be a love and fetch me my drink, would you?" And to the telephone: "Sorry, Jack, but I'm suddenly quite dry. And now you've found a kid who's a bit different, have you?"

"A bit? Harry Keogh's a lot different, you can take my word for it! Frankly, I don't know what to make of him."

"Well then, tell me and let's see what I can make of him."

"Harry Keogh," Harmon began, "is . . . one hell of a weird fellow. He was first brought to my attention by a teacher at the boys' school in Harden a little farther up the coast. At that time he was described to me as an 'instinctive mathematician.' In fact he was a near genius! Anyway, he sat a form of examination and passed it—hell, he flew through it!—and so came to the Tech. But his English was terrible. I used to get on to him about it . . .

"Anyway, when I spoke to this fellow up at Harden—the young teacher, I mean, a fellow called George Hannant—I somehow got the impression that he didn't like Keogh. Or maybe that's a bit strong; maybe Keogh simply made him uneasy. Well, I've recently had cause to speak to Hannant again, and that's how the whole thing came to light. By that I mean that Hannant's observations of five years ago match mine exactly. He too, at that time, believed that Harry Keogh . . . that he . . .''

"That he what?" Gormley urged. "What's this lad's talent, Jack?"

"Talent? My God! That's not how I would describe it."

"Well?"

"Let me tell it this way. It's not that I'm shy of my conclusions, you understand, just that I believe the evidence should be heard first. I've said that Keogh's English was bad and I used to urge him to do better. Well, he improved rapidly. Before he left the school two years ago he'd sold his first short story. Since then there have been two books full of them. They've sold right across the English-speaking world! It's a bit off-putting to say the least! I mean, I've been trying to sell *my* stories for thirty years, and here's Keogh not yet nineteen, and—''

"And is that your concern?" Gormley cut him off. "That he's become a successful author so young?"

"Eh? Heavens, no! I'm delighted for him. Or at least I was. I still would be if only . . . if only he didn't write the damn things *that* way . . .'' He paused.

"What way?"

"He . . . he has, well, collaborators."

Something about the way Harmon said the last word made Gormley's scalp tingle again. "Collaborators? But surely a lot of writers have collaborators? At eighteen years of age I imagine he probably needs someone to tidy his stuff up for him, and so on."

"No, no," said the other, with an edge to his voice that hinted of frustration, of wanting to say something outright but not knowing how to. "No, that's not what I meant at all. Actually, his short stories don't need tidying up—they're all jewels. I myself typed the earliest of them for him, from the rough work, because he didn't have a machine. I even typed up a few after he'd bought a typewriter, until he got the idea of how a good manuscript should look. Since then he's done it all himself—until recently. His new work, which he's just completed, is a novel. He's called it, of all things, *Diary of a Seventeenth-century Rake!*"

Gormley couldn't suppress a chuckle. "So he's sexually precocious too, is he?"

"Actually, I think he is. Anyway, I've worked with him quite a bit on the novel, too: that is, I've arranged it into chapters for him and generally tidied it up. Nothing wrong with Keogh's history or his use of the seventeenth-century language—in fact it's amazingly accurate—but his spelling is still atrocious and on this book at least he was repetitive and disjointed. But one thing I can promise you: it will earn him an awful lot of money!"

Now Gormley frowned. "How can his short stories be 'jewels' while his novel is repetitive and disjointed? Does that follow logically?"

"Nothing follows logically in Keogh's case. The reason the novel differs from the shorter works is simple: his collaborator on the shorts was a literary type who knew what he was doing, whereas his collaborator for the novel was quite simply . . . a seventeenth-century rake!"

"Eh?" Gormley was startled. "I don't follow."

"No, I don't suppose you do. I wish to God *I* didn't! Listen: there was a very successful writer of short stories who lived and died in Hartlepool thirty years ago. His real name doesn't matter but he had three or four pseudonyms. Keogh uses pseudonyms very close to the originals."

"The 'originals'? I still don't—"

"As for the seventeenth-century rake: he was the son of an earl. Very notorious in these parts between 1660 and 1672. Finally an outraged husband shot him dead. He wasn't a writer, but he did have a vivid imagination! These two men . . . *they* are Keogh's collaborators!"

Gormley's scalp was crawling now. "Go on," he said.

"I've talked to Keogh's girlfriend," Harmon continued. "She's a nice kid and dotes on him. And she won't hear a word against him. But in conversation she let it slip that he has this idea about something called a necroscope. It's something he presented to her as fiction, a figment of his own imagination. A necroscope, he told her, is someone—"

"—who can look in on the thoughts of the dead?" Gormley cut in.

"Yes," the other sighed his relief. "Exactly."

"A spirit medium?"

"What? Why, yes, I suppose you could say that. But a *real* one, Keenan! A man who genuinely talks to the dead! I mean, it's monstrous! I've actually seen him sitting there, writing—in the local graveyard!"

"Have you told anyone else?" Gormley's voice was sharp now. "Does Keogh know what you suspect?"

"No."

"Then don't breathe another word about this to a soul. Do you understand?"

"Yes, but—"

"No buts, Jack. This discovery of yours might be very important indeed, and I'm delighted you got in touch with me. But it must go no farther. There are people who could use it in entirely the wrong way."

"You believe me, then, about this terrible thing?" the other's relief was plain. "I mean, is it even possible?"

"Possible, impossible—the longer I live the more I wonder just what might or mightn't be! Anyway, I can understand your concern, and it's right that you should be concerned. But as for this being 'a terrible thing': I'm afraid I have to reserve my judgement on that. If you *are* correct, then this Harry Keogh of yours has a terrific talent. Just think how he might use it!"

"I shudder to think!"

"What? And you a headmaster? Shame on you, Jack!"

"I'm sorry. I'm not quite sure I—"

"But wouldn't you yourself like the chance to talk to the greatest teachers, theorists and scientists of all time? To Einstein, Newton, Da Vinci, Aristotle?"

"My God!" the voice at the other end of the line almost choked. "But surely that would be—I mean, quite literally—*utterly* impossible!"

"Yes, well you just keep believing that, Jack, and forget all about this conversation of ours, right?"

"But you—"

"Right, Jack?"

"Very well. What do you intend to—?"

"Jack, I work for a very queer outfit, a very funny crowd. And even telling you that much is to tell you too much. However, you have my word that I'll look into this thing. And I want your word that this is your last word on it to anyone."

"Very well, if you say so."

"Thanks for calling."

"You're welcome. I—"

"Goodbye, Jack. We must talk again some time."

"Yes, goodbye . . ."

Thoughtfully, Gormley put the phone down.

Chapter Eleven

DRAGOSANI HAD BEEN "BACK TO SCHOOL" FOR OVER THREE months, brushing up on his English. Now it was the end of July and he had returned to Romania—or Wallachia, as he now constantly thought of his homeland. His reason for being there was simple: despite any threats he made when last he visited, still he was aware that a year had passed, and that the old Thing in the ground had warned him that a year was all the time allowed. What he had meant exactly was beyond Dragosani to fathom, but of one thing he was certain: he must not let Thibor Ferenczy expire through any oversight on his part. If such an expiry was imminent, then the vampire might now be more willing to share a few more secrets with Dragosani in exchange for an extension on his undead life.

Because it had been getting late in the day when he drove through Bucharest, Dragosani had stopped at a village market to purchase a pair of live chickens in a wicker basket. These had gone under a light blanket on the floor in the back of his Volga. He had found lodgings in a farm standing on the banks of the Oltul, and having tossed his things into his room had come out immediately into the twilight and driven to the wooded cruciform ridge.

Now, at last light, he stood once more on the perimeter of the circle of unhallowed ground beneath the gloomy pines and surveyed again the tumbled tomb cut into the hillside, and the dark earth where grotesquely twisted roots stood up like a writhing of petrified serpents.

Past Bucharest he had tried to contact Thibor, to no avail; for all that he'd concentrated on raising the old devil's mind from the slumber of centuries, there had been no answer. Perhaps, after all, he was too late. How long might a vampire lie, undead in the earth, without attention? For all Dragosani's many conversations with the creature, and for all that he had learned from Ladislau Giresci, still he knew so little about the Wamphyri. That was restricted knowledge, Thibor had told him, and must await the coming of Dragosani into the fraternity. Oh? The necromancer would see about that!

"Thibor, are you there?" he now whispered in the gloom, his eyes attuned to the shadows and penetrating the dusty miasma of the place. "Thibor, I've come back—and I bring gifts!" At his feet the chickens huddled in their basket, their feet trussed; but no unseen presence moved in the darkness now, no cobweb fingers brushed his hair, no eager invisible muzzles sniffed at his essence. The place was dry, desiccated, dead. Dangling twigs snapped loudly at a touch and dust swirled where Dragosani placed his feet on the accumulated vegetable debris of centuries.

"Thibor," he tried again. "You told me a year. The year is past and I've returned. Am I too late? I've brought you blood, old dragon, to warm your old veins and give you strength again . . ."

Nothing.

Dragosani grew alarmed. This was wrong. The old Thing in the ground was always here. He was *genius loci*. Without him the place was nothing, the cruciform hills were empty. And what of Dragosani's dreams? Was that knowledge he had hoped to glean from the vampire gone forever?

For a moment he knew despair, anger, frustration, but then—

The trussed chickens in their basket stirred a little and one of them made a low, worried clucking sound. A breeze whirred eerily in the higher branches over Dragosani's head. The sun dipped down behind distant hills. And something watched the necromancer from behind the gloom and the dust and the old, brittle branches. Nothing was there, but he felt eyes upon him. Nothing was different, but it seemed now that the place breathed!

It breathed, yes—but a tainted breath, which Dragosani liked not at all. He felt threatened, felt more in danger here than ever before. He picked up the basket and took two paces back from the unhallowed circle until he brought up against the rough bark of a great tree almost as old as the glade. He felt safer there, more solidly based, with that tough old tree behind him. The sudden dryness went out of his throat and he swallowed hard before enquiring again:

"Thibor, I know you're there. It's your loss, old devil, if you choose to ignore me."

Again the wind soughed in the high branches, and with it a whisper crept into the necromancer's mind:

Dragosaaaniiii? Is it you? Ahhhh!

"It's me, yes," he eagerly answered. "I've come to bring you life, old devil—or rather, to renew your undeath."

Too late, Dragosani, too late. My time is come and I must answer the call of the dark earth. Even I, Thibor Ferenczy of the Wamphyri. My privations have been many and my spark has been allowed to burn too low. Now it

315

merely flickers. What can you do for me now, my son? Nothing, I fear. It is finished . . .

"No, I can't believe that! I've brought life for you, fresh blood. Tomorrow there'll be more. In a few days you'll be strong again. Why didn't you tell me things were at such a pass? I was sure you cried wolf! How could you expect me to believe when all you've ever done is lie to me?"

. . . Perhaps in that I was mistaken after all, the Thing in the ground answered in a little while. *But when even my own father and brother hated me . . . why should I trust a son? And a son by proxy, at that. There is no real flesh between us, Dragosani. Oh, we made promises, you and I, but too much to believe that anything could come of them. Still, you have prospered a little—through your knowledge of necromancy—and at least I tasted blood again, however vile. So let it be peace between us. I am too weak now to care . . .*

Dragosani took a step forward. "No!" said again. "There are still things you can teach me, show me. Wamphyri secrets . . ." (Did the ground tremble just a little beneath his feet? Did the unseen presences creep closer?) He moved back against the tree.

The voice in his mind sighed. It was the sigh of one who wearies of all earthly things, of one impatient for oblivion. And Dragosani forgot that it was the lying sigh of a vampire. *Ah, Dragosani! Dragosani!—you've learned nothing. Did I not tell you that the lore of the Wamphyri is forbidden to mortals? Did I not say that to become is to know and that there is no other way? Begone, my son, and leave me to my fate. What? And should I give you the power to rule a world, while I lie here and turn to dust? What is that for justice? Where is the fairness in that?*

Dragosani was desperate. "Then accept the blood I've brought you, the sweet meat. Grow strong again. I *will* accept your terms. If I must become one of the Wamphyri to learn all of their secrets—then so be it!'' he lied. ''But without you I cannot!''

The Thing in the ground was silent for long moments while Dragosani breathlessly waited. He fancied that the earth trembled again, however minutely, beneath his feet, but that could only be his imagination—the knowledge that something ancient and evil, rotten and undead lay buried here. Behind his back the tree stood seemingly solid as a rock, so that Dragosani hardly suspected it was eaten away at its heart. But indeed it was hollow; and now *something* gradually eased its way up through the earth and into the dry, worm-eaten wood.

Perhaps in another moment Dragosani might have sensed movement, but in that precise instant of time Thibor spoke to him again and his attention was distracted:

Did you say you had . . . a gift for me?

There was interest in the vampire's mental voice now, and Dragosani saw a ray of hope. ''Yes, yes! Here at my feet. Fresh meat, blood.'' He snatched up one of the birds and squeezed its throat so that its squawking ceased at once. And in another moment he had taken a sickle of bright steel from his pocket and sliced the chicken's gizzard. Red blood spurted and the carcass flopped a little where he tossed it, while feathers fluttered silently to the black earth.

The leaf-mould soaked up the bird's blood as a sponge soaks water—but behind Dragosani's back a pseudopod of putrefaction slid swiftly up inside the hollow tree, its leprous white tip finding a knot-hole where a branch had decayed and poking through into view not eighteen inches above his head. The tip throbbed, glistening with a strange life of its own, filled with an alien foetal urgency.

Dragosani took up the second bird by its neck, stepped two paces forward to the very rim of the ''safe'' area.

"And there's more, Thibor, right here in my hand. Only show a little trust, a little faith, and tell me something of the powers I'll command when I become as you."

I . . . I feel the red blood soaking into the ground, my son, and it is good. But still I think you came too late. Well, I will not blame you. We were at odds with one another—I was as much to blame as you—and so let the past be forgotten. Aye, and I would not have it end without showing you at least a small measure of what I've come to feel for you, without sharing at least one small secret.

"I'm waiting," Dragosani eagerly answered. "Go on . . ."

In the beginning, said the Thing in the ground, *all things were equal. The primal vampire was a thing of Nature no less than the primal man, and just as man lived on the lesser creatures about him, so too lived the vampire. We both, you see, were parasites in our way. All living things are. But whereas man killed the creatures he fed upon, there the vampire was kinder: he simply took them for his host. They did not die—indeed they became undead! In this fashion a vampire is no less natural a creature than the lamprey or the leech, or even the humble flea; except his host lives, becomes near immortal, and is not consumed as in the normal manner of massive parasitic possession. But as man evolved into the perfect host, so evolved the vampire, and as man became dominant so the vampire shared his dominance.*

"Symbiosis," said Dragosani.

I can read the meaning of the word in your mind, said Thibor, *and yes, that is correct—except the vampire soon learned to keep himself secret! For along with evolution came a singular change: where before the vampire could live apart from his host, now he was totally dependent upon him. Just as the hagfish dies without its host fish, so the vampire must have his host simply to exist. And if men discovered a vampire in one of their own sort—why, they would simply kill him! Worse, they learned how to kill the greater being within!*

Nor was this the last of the vampire's problems. Nature is a strange one when it comes to correcting errors and quite ruthless. She had not intended that any of her creations should be immortal. Nothing she makes is allowed to live forever. And yet here was a creature which seemed to defy that rigid dictum, a creature which—barring accidents— might just survive indefinitely! And furious, she took her spite on the Wamphyri. As the centuries waxed and waned and the Earth grew through all the ages towards the present day, so my vampire ancestors developed within themselves a weakness. It was bred into them—it came down the generations, down all the years. It was a stric- ture of Nature, and it was this: that since vampires 'died' so very rarely, she would allow them only rarely to be born!

"Which is why," said Dragosani, "you're dying out as a race."

As individuals, we may only reproduce once in a lifespan, no matter the great length of that span . . .

"But you're so potent! I can't see that the fault lies with your males. Is it that your females are infertile . . . I mean, that they only have the one opportunity to reproduce?"

Our "males," Dragosani? said the voice in Dragosani's mind, with a sardonically inquisitive edge that he didn't like. *Our "females" . . .?* And once again the necroman- cer stepped back against the tree.

"What are you saying?"

Males and females. Oh, no, Dragosani. If Nature had saddled us with that problem then surely were we long extinct . . .

"But you are a male. I know you are!"

My human host was a male.

Dragosani's eyes were now very wide in the dark. Something inside urged him to flee—but from what? He knew that the Thing in the ground could not—dared not—harm him. "Then . . . you're a female?"

I thought I had explained adequately. I am neither one nor the other . . .

Dragosani wasn't sure of the term. "Hermaphrodite?"

No.

"Then asexual? Agamic!"

A pearly droplet was forming on the pallid, pulsating tip of the leprous tentacle where it protruded from the hole in the tree above Dragosani's head. As it grew it became pear-shaped, hung downward, began to quiver. Above it a crimson eye formed, gazed lidlessly, full of rapt intent.

"But what of your lust on the night we took the girl?"

Your lust, Dragosani.

"And all the women you had in your life?"

My energy, but my host's lust!

"But—"

AHHHH! the voice in Dragosani's mind suddenly gave a great groan. *My son, my son—it is nearly finished! It is almost over!*

Alarmed, the necromancer advanced yet again to the edge of the circle. The voice was so weak, so despairing, so filled with pain. "What is it? What's wrong? Here, more food!" He slit the second bird's throat, threw its twitching corpse down. The red blood was sucked up by the earth. The Thing in the ground drank deep.

Dragosani waited, and: *Ahhhh!*

But now the necromancer's scalp fairly tingled. For suddenly he sensed a great strength in the vampire—and even greater cunning. Quickly he stepped back—and in that same instant of time the pearly droplet overhead turned scarlet and fell!

It landed on the back of Dragosani's neck just below the

high collar-line. He felt it. It could have been a drop of moisture fallen from the tree, except it was totally dry here; or it could be a bird dropping, if he had ever seen a bird in this place. In any case, his hand automatically went to his neck to wipe it away—and found nothing. The vampire egg needed no ovipositor. Like quicksilver it had soaked straight through the skin. Now it explored the spinal column.

In the next moment Dragosani felt the pain and bounded from the tree. He found himself within what he had thought to be the danger area—bounded again as the pain increased. This time he was incapable of directing himself; he ran from the circle, blindly colliding with the boles of trees where they stood in his path; he tripped and fell, rolling headlong. And always the pain in his skull, the pressure on his spine, the fire lancing through his veins like acid.

Panic gripped him, the worst panic he had ever known in his entire life. He felt that he was dying, that his seizure—whatever its cause—must surely kill him. It felt as though his internal organs were bursting, as though his brain were on fire!

Within him, the vampire seed had found a resting place in his chest cavity. It ceased exploring, settled to sleep. Its initial fumblings had been the spastic kicking of the newborn, but now it was warm and safe and desired only to rest.

The agony went out of Dragosani in an instant, and so great was his relief that his system completely lost its balance. Drowning in the sheer pleasure of painlessness, he blacked out.

Harry Keogh lay sprawled upon his bed, sweat plastering his sandy hair to his forehead, his limbs twitching fitfully now and then in response to a dream which was something more than a dream. In life his mother had been a psychic medium of some repute, and death had not changed her; if anything it had improved her talent. Often over the years she'd visited Harry in his sleep, even as she visited him now.

Harry dreamed that they stood in a summer garden together: the garden of the house in Bonnyrigg, where beyond the fence the river swirled its sluggish way between banks grown green with the hot sun and lush from the richness of the river. It was a dream of sharp contrasts and vivid colours. She was young again, a mere girl, and he might well be her young lover rather than her son. But in his dream their relationship was distinct, and as always she was worried for him.

"Harry, your plan is dangerous and it can't possibly work," she said. "Anyway, don't you realize what you're doing? If it does work it will be murder, Harry! You'll be no better than . . . than him!" She turned her head of golden tresses and gazed fearfully at the house through eyes of blue crystal.

The house was a dark blot against a sky so blue that it hurt the eyes. It stood there like a mass of ink frozen against a green and blue background, as if fresh spilled in a child's picturebook; and like a Black Hole of interstellar physics, no light shone out of it and nothing at all escaped its gaping, aching void. It was black because of what it housed, as black as the soul of the man who lived there.

Harry shook his head, dragging his own eyes from the house only with a great effort of will. "Not murder," he said. "Justice! Something he's escaped for almost sixteen years. I was little more than a baby, a mere infant, when he took you from me. He's got away with it until now. But now I'm a man. How much of a man will I be if I let it go at that?"

"But don't you see, Harry?" she insisted. "Taking

322

your revenge won't put it right. Two wrongs never make a right . . ." They sat down on the grass and she hugged him, stroking his hair. Harry had used to love that as a baby. He looked again at the inkblot house and shuddered, and quickly looked away.

"It's not just that I want revenge, Mother," he said. "I want to know why! Why did he murder you? You were beautiful, his young wife, a lady of property and talent. He should have adored you—and yet he killed you. He held you under the ice, and when you were too weak to fight let you go with the river. He killed you as coldly as if you were an unwanted kitten, the runt of the litter. He tore you from life like a weed from this very garden, except he was the weed and you a rose. What made him do it? Why?"

She frowned and shook her golden head. "I don't know, Harry. I've never known."

"That's what I have to find out. I can't find out while he's alive, for I know he'll never admit it. So I'll have to find out when he's dead. The dead never refuse me anything. Which means . . . I have to kill him. And I'll do it my way."

"It's a very terrible way, Harry," it was her turn to shudder. "I know!"

He nodded, his eyes cold. "Yes, you do—and that's why it must be that way . . ."

She was fearful again and clutched him to her. "But what if something goes wrong? Just knowing you're all right, I can lie easy, Harry. But if anything should happen to you—"

"Nothing will happen. It will be just the way I plan it." He kissed her worried brow, but still she clung to him.

"He's a clever man, Harry. This Viktor Shukshin. Clever—and evil! Sometimes I could sense it in him, and it fascinated me. What was I after all but a girl? And him—he was magnetic. The Russian in him, which was there in me, too; the brooding darkness of his mind, the magnetism and the evil. We were opposing magnetic poles, and we attracted. I know that I loved him at first, even though I sensed his dark heart, but as for his reason for killing me—''

"Yes?''

Again she shook her head, her blue eyes cloudy with memory. "It was something . . . something *in* him. Some madness, some unspeakable thing he couldn't control. That much I know, but what exactly—'' and once more she shook her head.

"It's what I have to find out,'' Harry repeated, "for until then I won't rest easy either.''

"*Shhh!*'' she suddenly gasped, clutched him hard. "Look!''

Harry looked. A smaller inkblot had detached itself from the great black mass of the house. Manlike, it came down the garden path, peering here and there, worriedly wringing its hands. In its black blot of a head twin silver ovals gleamed, eyes which led it towards the fence at the bottom of the garden. Harry and his mother huddled together, but for the moment the Shukshin apparition paid them no heed. He passed by, paused briefly and sniffed suspiciously—almost like a dog—then moved on. At the fence he stopped, leaned on the top rail, for long moments peered at the river's slow swirl.

"I know what's on his mind,'' Harry whispered.

"*Shhh!*'' his mother repeated her warning. "He can sense things, Viktor Shukshin. He always could . . .''

The inkblot now returned, pausing every now and then, sniffing in that strange way. Close to the pair, the Shukshin-thing seemed to stare right through them with its silver eyes. Then the eyes blinked and it moved on, back towards the house, wringing its hands as before. As it merged with the house a door slammed echoingly.

The sound repeated in Harry's head, reverberating, metamorphosing from a slam to a knock, to a series of knocks, repeating:

Rat-tat-tat! Rat-tat-tat!

"You have to go," said his mother. "Be careful, Harry. Poor little Harry . . ."

He jerked awake in his flat. From the slant of the sunlight through the window, he knew that time turned towards evening. He'd slept for three hours at least; more than he'd intended. He started as the knock came again at the door:

Rat-tat-tat!

Who could this be? Brenda? No, for he wasn't expecting her. Although it was a Saturday she was putting in some overtime, dolling up the hair of some of Harden's more "fashionable" ladies. Who, then?

Rat-tat-*tat!* Insistently.

Stiffly, Harry swung his legs off the bed, stood up and went to the door. His hair was tousled, his eyes full of sleep. Visitors were rare and he liked it that way. This was an intrusion, something to be dealt with swiftly and decisively. He zipped up his trousers, shrugged into a shirt—and the knock came yet again.

Outside the door, Sir Keenan Gormley waited, knowing that Harry Keogh was in there. He had known it coming down the street, had felt it climbing the stairs. Keogh's ESP signature was written in the very air of the place as unmistakably as a fingerprint on clear glass. For like Viktor Shukshin and Gregor Borowitz, this was Gormley's one great talent: he too was a "spotter," he instinctively "knew" when he stood in the presence of an ESPer, and Keogh's ESP-aura was more powerful than any he had ever sensed before, so that he felt he was close to some great generator as he stood there at the door on the landing at the head of the stairs.

And now Harry Keogh himself opened that door . . .

Gormley had seen Keogh before, but never so close. Over the last three weeks, while he had been staying with Jack Harmon, he'd seen him often. Gormley and Harmon, following Keogh on occasion, had kept the youth under close but discreet observation; likewise on the two occasions when George Hannant had accompanied them. And Gormley had not taken long to agree with both Harmon and Hannant that indeed Keogh was something special. Quite obviously they were correct about him; he *was* a necroscope; he did have the power of intelligent intercourse with the dead. Gormley had given Keogh's weird talent a lot of thought over the last three weeks. It was one which he would dearly love to have under his control. Now he must somehow find a way to put that idea to Keogh.

Blinking the sleep from his eyes, Harry Keogh looked his visitor up and down. He had intended to be brusque no matter who it was, to deal with the problem and be done with it, but one look at Gormley had told him this was something which wasn't going to go away. There was a quiet air of unassuming but awesome intellect about this man, and coupled with his charming smile and demanding, outstretched hand, it formed a combination which was totally disarming.

"Harry Keogh?" said Gormley, knowing of course that it was Keogh and insisting that the other take his hand by shoving it even farther forward. "I'm Sir Keenan Gormley. You won't have heard of me but I know quite a bit about you. In fact—why, I know just about everything about you!"

The landing was ill-lit and Harry couldn't quite make out the other's features, just indistinct impressions. Finally, briefly, he took Gormley's hand, then stepped aside and let him in. The contact, however brief, had told him a lot. Gormley's hand had been firm and yet resilient, cool but honest; it had promised nothing, but neither had it threatened. It was the hand of someone who could be a friend. Except—

"You know everything about me?" Harry wasn't sure he liked the sound of that. "Well that won't come to much. There's not a lot to know."

"Oh, I disagree with you," said the other. "You're far too modest."

Now, in the brighter light from the windows, Keogh looked at his visitor more closely. His age could be anything between fifty and sixty, but probably at the top end; his green eyes were a little muddied and his skin full of small wrinkles; his well-groomed hair was grey on a large, high-domed head. About five-ten in height, his well-tailored jacket just failed to hide slightly rounded shoulders. Sir Keenan Gormley had seen better days, but Harry Keogh would think he had a way to go yet.

"What do I call you?" he said. It was the first time he'd spoken to a "Sir."

"Keenan will do, since we're to be friends."

"You're sure of that? That we're to be friends, I mean? I must warn you I don't make many."

"I don't think we have any choice," Gormley smiled. "We have too much in common. Anyway, the way I hear it you have lots of friends."

"Then you've heard it wrong," Harry frowned, shook his head. "I can count my real friends on one hand."

Gormley believed he might as well get straight to the point. And anyway, he wanted to see Keogh's reaction if he was caught off balance. It might just provide the final ounce of proof. "Those are the live ones," he quietly answered, easing the smile gradually off his face. "But I think the others are rather more numerous . . ."

It hit Harry like a grenade. He'd often wondered how he

would feel if anyone should ever confront him like this, and now he knew. He felt ill.

He reeled, found a rickety easy chair, sank down into it. Pale as death he shivered, gulped, gazed at Gormley through the eyes of a cornered animal. "I don't know what you're—" he finally began to croak his denial, only to have Gormley cut him off with:

"Yes you do, Harry! You know very well what I'm talking about. You're a necroscope. And you're probably the only real necroscope in the entire world!"

"You have to be crazy!" Harry gasped desperately. "Coming in here and accusing me of . . . of things. A necroscope? There's no such thing. Everyone knows you can't . . . can't . . ." Trapped, he faltered to a halt.

"Can't what, Harry? Talk to the dead? But you can, can't you?"

Clammy sweat broke out on Harry's forehead. He gasped for air. He was caught and he knew it. Trapped like a ghoul with a dripping heart in his hands, like a rapist in the beam of a policeman's torch, gasping between his battered victim's thighs. It hadn't felt like a crime before—he'd never hurt anyone—but now . . .

Gormley stepped forward, took his shoulders, shook him where he sat. "Snap out of it, man! You look like a grubby little boy caught masturbating. You're not sick, Harry—this thing you do isn't an illness—it's a talent!"

"It's a secret thing," he protested weakly, his face shining. "I . . . I don't hurt them, I wouldn't do that. Without me, who would they have to talk to? They're so *lonely!*" He was almost babbling now, convinced that he was in deep trouble and trying to talk his way out. The last thing Gormley wanted was to alienate him.

"It's okay, son, it's okay. Take it easy—no one's accusing you of anything."

"But it's a *secret* thing!" Harry insisted, gritting his

teeth, growing angry now. "Or at least it was. But now, if people know about it—"

"They won't get to know."

"You know!"

"It's my business to know these things. Son, I keep telling you; you're not in trouble. Not with me."

He was so persuasive, so quiet. Was he a friend, a real friend, or was he something else? Harry couldn't control his panic, the shock of knowing that someone else knew. His head whirled. Could he trust this man? Dared he trust anyone? And if Gormley meant the end of him as a necroscope, what of his revenge on Viktor Shukshin? Nothing must interfere with that!

He reached out desperately with his mind, contacted a confidence trickster he knew in the cemetery in Easington.

Gormley felt the power that washed out from Harry at that moment, a raw alien energy like nothing he'd felt before, which set his scalp tingling and quickened his heart alarmingly. This was it! This was the necroscope's talent in action. Gormley knew it as surely as he was born.

In his chair Harry had gradually squeezed himself into a more compact mass, hunching down. He had been the colour of drifted snow, dripping sweat like a faulty tap. But now—

He sat up, bared his teeth and grinned a wild grin, tossed back his head and sent beads of sweat flying. He uncoiled like a spring, all of the panic going out of him in a moment. His hand hardly trembled at all as he brushed damp hair back from his forehead. Colour rapidly returned to his face. "That's it," he said, still grinning. "Interview's over."

"What?" Gormley was amazed at the transformation.

"Certainly. That's what this is all about, isn't it? You came here to find out about Harry Keogh the author. Someone mentioned to you the theme of a new story I'm writing—which no one's supposed to know about incidentally —and you just hit me with it to get my reaction. It's a horror story, and you've heard I always act out what I write. So when I act out the part of the necroscope—which is a word of my own coining, by the way—naturally I do it with authority. I'm a good actor, see? Well, you've had your free show and I've had my fun, and now the interview's over." The grin fell abruptly from his face and left it sour, sneering. "You know where the door is, Keenan . . ."

Gormley slowly shook his head. At first he'd been stunned, but now his instinct took over. And it was his instinct that told him what was happening here. "That's clever," he said, "but nowhere close to clever enough. Who are you talking to now, Harry? Or rather, who is it talking *through* you?"

For a moment defiance continued to shine in Harry Keogh's eyes, but then Gormley once more felt the flow of weird energies as the youth broke the link with his clever, dead, unknown friend. His face visibly changed; sarcasm drained away and Harry was himself again; but at least he retained something of composure. His panic had passed.

"What do you want to know?" he said, his voice flat and emotionless.

"Everything," Gormley answered at once.

"I thought you already knew everything? You said you did."

"But I want to hear it from you. I know you can't explain how you do it, and I certainly don't want to know why; it's enough to say that you found yourself with a talent you could use to improve your own life. That's understandable. No, it's the facts I want. The extent of your talent, for instance, and its limitations. Until a moment ago I didn't know you could use it at a distance—that sort of thing. I want to know what you talk about, what interests *them*. Do they see you as an intruder, or do they welcome you? Like I said: I want to know everything.''

"Or else?''

Gormley shook his head. "That doesn't even come into it—not yet."

Harry gave a sour smile. "So we're to be 'friends,' are we?"

Gormley drew up a chair and sat down facing him. "Harry, no one else is going to know about you. That's a promise. And yes, we are going to be friends. That's because we need each other, and because we in turn are needed. Okay, you probably think you don't need me, that I'm the *last* thing you need! But that's only for now. You *will* need me, I assure you."

Harry looked at him through narrowed eyes. "And just why do you need me? I think, before I tell you anything—before I even admit anything—that there are one or two things you'd better tell me."

Gormley had expected nothing less. He nodded, stared straight into the other's wary, questioning eyes, drew a deep breath. "Fair enough, I will. You know who I am, so now I'll tell you what I am and what I do for a living. More importantly, I'll tell you about the people I work with."

He did. He told Harry about the British E-Branch, and what little he knew about the American, French, Russian and Chinese equivalents. He told him about telepaths who could speak to each other across the world without a telephone, with their minds alone; about precognition, the ability to pierce the future and tell of events yet to happen; about telekinesis and psychokinesis, and men who could move solid objects with their will alone and without resorting to simple physical strength. He spoke about "far-seeing," and about a man he knew who could tell you what was happening anywhere in the world at this precise moment of time; about psychic healing and a "doctor" who could conjure the supreme power of Life into his naked hands, banishing diseases without the benefit of any form of conventional treatment; about the entire range of ESPers under his command, and how there was a place there, too, for Harry. And he told it all in such a way—with such understanding and clarity and sheer conviction—that Harry knew he spoke the truth.

"So you see," Gormley finally came to a close, "you're not a freak, Harry. Your talent may well be unique but you, as an ESPer, are not. Your grandmother was one before you and passed it down to your mother. She in turn passed a large dose of it down to you. God only knows what *your* children will be capable of, Harry Keogh!"

After a long while and as all he had been told sank in, Harry said: "And now you want me to work for you?"

"In a nutshell, yes."

"What if I refuse?"

"Harry, I found you. I'm a spotter; I have no real ESP talent myself but I can spot an ESPer a mile away. I suppose that in itself is a talent, but that's all I have. The one thing I know for sure is that there are others like me. One of them is the boss of the Russian branch. Now I've come to you and put my cards on the table. I've told you things I didn't even have the right to tell you. That's because I want you to trust me, and also because I think I can trust you. You've nothing to fear from me, Harry—but I can't promise the same for the other side!"

"You mean . . . they might find me too?"

"They get cleverer all the time, Harry," Gormley shrugged, "just as we do. They have at least one man in England. I've not met him, but I've sensed him close to me. I know he was looking at me, watching me. He's probably a spotter, too. What I'm saying is this: I found you, so how long before they do? The difference is this: with them you'll not get a choice.''

"And with you I have a choice, right?''

"Of course you do. It's entirely in your hands. You join us or you don't join us. That's your choice. So take your time, Harry, and think about it. But not for too long. Like I said, we need you. The sooner the better . . .''

Harry thought about Viktor Shukshin. He couldn't know it, but Shukshin was the man Gormley had "sensed" watching him. "There are things I have to do first,'' he said, "before making any final decision.''

"Of course, I can understand that.''

"It may take some time. Maybe five months?''

Gormley nodded. "If it has to be.''

"I think it has to be, yes.'' For the first time Harry smiled his natural, shy smile. "Hey, I'm dry! Would you like a coffee?''

"Very much,'' Gormley smiled back. "And while we drink it, maybe you'd like to tell me about yourself, eh?''

Harry felt a great weight lifted from his shoulders. "Yes,'' he sighed. "I think maybe I would.''

It was a fortnight later that Harry Keogh finished his novel and "went into training'' for Viktor Shukshin. An advance on the book gave him the financial stability he would need for the next five or six months, until the job was done.

His first step was to join a group of crazy, all-weather swimming enthusiasts who made a habit of bathing in the North Sea at least twice a week all the year round—including Christmas and New Year's Day! They had something of a reputation for breaking the ice on Harden's reservoir to do charity plunges for the British Heart Foundation. Brenda, a level-headed girl on any other subject except Harry himself, thought he was crazy, of course.

"It's fine in the summer, Harry,'' he remembered her

telling him one late August evening as they had lain naked in each other's arms in his flat, "but what about when it starts to get cold? I can't see *you* breaking the ice to go for a swim! What is this swimming craze, anyway?"

"It's just a way of staying fit and healthy," he had told her, kissing her breasts. "Don't you like me healthy?"

"Sometimes," she had answered, turning more fully towards him as he grew hard again in her hand, "I think you're far *too* healthy!"

In fact she had been happier than at any time in more than three years. Harry was much more open now, less given to brooding, more lively and exciting. Nor was his sudden interest in sports confined to swimming. He'd also taken up self-defence and joined a small Hartlepool Judo club. After only a week his coach there had been calling him a "natural" and telling him he expected big things of him. He hadn't known, of course, that Harry had another coach—a man who had once been the Judo champion of his regiment, who now had nothing better to do than pass on all his expertise to Harry.

But as for Harry's swimming:

He'd always considered himself a fair swimmer; now it appeared that was *all* he had been. At first the rest of the group were way in front of him—at least until he found himself an ex-Olympic silver medallist who had died in an automobile accident in 1960, a fact recorded on his headstone in Stockton's St. Mary's graveyard. Harry was enthusiastically received (his plan with reservations) and his new friend joined in the fun and games with great aplomb.

Even with this sort of advantage, however, there was still the physical side to overcome. Harry might let the professional swimmer's mind guide his technique, but it couldn't help with his lack of muscle; only practice could do that. Nevertheless his progress was rapid.

By September the craze was underwater swimming: that

is, seeing just how long he could stay underwater on one breath, and how far he could swim before surfacing. The first time he did two complete lengths of the pool submerged was a red-letter day for Harry; everyone in the place had stopped swimming to watch him. That was at the swimming baths at Seaton Carew, where afterwards an attendant had sidled up to ask him his secret. Harry had shrugged and answered:

"It's all in the mind. Willpower, I suppose . . ." Which was fair enough. What he did not say was that while it had certainly been his willpower, it had not entirely been his mind . . .

By the end of October Harry had let his Judo training fall off a little. His progress had been too rapid and his instructors at the club were growing wary of him. Anyway, he was satisfied that he could now look after himself perfectly well, even without "Sergeant" Graham Lane's assistance. By that time, too, he had taken up ice skating, the final discipline in his itinerary.

Brenda, herself quite capable on the ice, was astonished. She had often tried to get Harry to accompany her to the ice rink in Durham, but he had always refused. That was hardly unnatural; she knew something of how his mother had died; it was just that she believed he should face up to his fear. She couldn't know that the fear wasn't entirely his but his mother's. In the end, though, Mary Keogh was made to see the sense in Harry's preparations and at last came gladly to his aid.

At first she was frightened—the ice, the memory, the sheer horror of her death lingered still—but in a very little while she was enjoying her skating again as much as ever she had in life. She enjoyed through Harry, and in his turn he received the benefit of her instruction; so that soon he was able to lead Brenda a merry dance across the ice—much to her amazement!

"One thing I can definitely say about you, Harry Keogh," she had breathlessly told him as he expertly waltzed her round and round the rink while their breath plumed fantastically in the cold air, "is that there's never a dull moment! Why, you're an athlete!"

And at that moment it had dawned on Harry that he really could be—if there weren't other matters more pressing.

But then, in the first week in November as winter crept in, his mother had dropped something of a bombshell . . .

Harry was feeling better than he had ever felt in his life before, capable of taking on the entire world, the night she had come to him in his dreams. In his waking hours he must always contact her if he wished to speak to her, but when he slept it was different. Then she had instant access. Normally she respected his privacy, but on this occasion there was something she must talk over with him, something which could not wait.

"Harry?" she'd stolen into his dream, walking with him through a misty graveyard of great, looming tombstones standing as high as houses. "Harry, can we talk? Do you mind?"

"No, Ma, I don't mind," he'd answered. "What is it?"

She took his arm, held it tightly, and knowing now that she had firmly established rapport let her fears and her urgency spill out of her in a veritable torrent of words:

"Harry, I've been speaking to the others. They've told me there's terrible danger for you. Danger in Shukshin, and if you should destroy him terrible danger beyond him! Oh, Harry, Harry—I'm so dreadfully worried for you!"

"Danger in my stepfather?" he held her close, tried to comfort her. "Of course there is. We've always known that. But danger *beyond* him? What 'others' have you been talking to, Ma? I don't understand."

She drew back from him to arm's length, grew angry with him in a moment. "Yes, you *do* understand!" she

336

accused. "Or would if you wanted to. Where do you think you got your talent in the first place, Harry Keogh, if not from me? I was talking to the dead long before you came along! Oh, not as well as you do it, no, but well enough. All I ever managed were vague impressions, echoes, memories that lingered over—while you actually talk to them, learn from them, invite them into yourself. But things are different now. I've had sixteen years to practise my art, Harry, and I'm much better at it now than when I was alive. I *had* to practise it, you see, for your sake. How else was I going to be able to watch over you?"

He drew her close again and wrapped his arms about her, staring deep into her anxious eyes. "Don't fight with me, Ma, there's no need. But tell me now, what others are you talking about?"

"Others like myself, people who were mediums in life. Some, like me, are dead only recently in the scale of time, but others have been lying in the earth a very long time indeed. In the old days they were called witches and wizards—and sometimes they were called worse than that. Many of them died for it. These are the ones I've been speaking to . . ."

Even dreaming Harry found the idea chilling: dead people talking to other dead people, communicating between their graves, considering events in a waking, living world from which they themselves had departed forever. He shuddered a little and hoped she didn't notice. "And what have they been telling you, these others?"

"They know you, Harry," she answered. "At least, they know of you. You're the one who befriends the dead. Through you, the dead have a future—some of us, anyway. Through you, there's a chance some of us can finish the things we never finished in life. They look to you as a hero, Harry, and they too worry for you. Without you there's nothing left for their hopes, you see? They . . . they *beg* you to give up this obsession, this vendetta."

Harry's mouth hardened. "You mean Shukshin? I can't do that. He put you where you are, Ma."

"Harry, it's not . . . not so bad here. I'm not lonely any more, not now."

He shook his head and sighed. "That won't work, Ma. You're only saying that for my sake. It only makes me love and miss you more. Life's a gift and Shukshin stole it from you. Look, I know it's not a good thing I'm doing— but neither is it unjust. After this it will be different. I have plans. You *did* give me a talent, yes, and when this is finished I'll use it well. That's a promise."

"But this thing with Viktor comes first?"

"It has to."

"That's your last word?"

"Yes."

She nodded sadly, freed herself and stepped away from him. "I told them that would be your answer. All right, Harry, I won't argue it any further. I'll just go now and let you do what you must. But you should know this: there will be warnings, two of them, and they won't be pleasant. One comes from the others, and you'll find it here in this dream. The other waits in the waking world. Two warnings, Harry, and if you fail to heed them . . . it will be on your own head."

She began to drift away from him, between the towering headstones, the mist lapping at her ankles, her calves. He tried to follow her but couldn't; invisible dream-stuff stood between; his feet seemed welded to the gravel chips forming the graveyard's paths.

"Warnings? What sort of warnings?"

"Follow that path," she pointed, "and you'll find one of them there. The other will come from someone you'd do well to trust. Both are indications of your future."

"The future's uncertain, Ma!" he called after her mist-wreathed ghost. "No one sees it clearly! No one knows for sure!"

"Then call it your probable future," she answered. "Yours, and also the futures of two others. Someone you love, and someone who asked for your help . . ."

Harry wasn't sure he'd heard right. "What?" he yelled at the top of his voice. "What's that, Ma?"

But her voice and figure and mind had already merged with the swirling mist of the dream and she was gone.

Harry looked the way she had pointed.

The headstones marched like giant dominoes, towering markers whose tops were lost in billowing clouds of fog. They were ominous, brooding, and so was the path between them which Harry's mother had pointed out to him. As for her "warnings": maybe it was better if he didn't know. Maybe he shouldn't walk that way at all. But he didn't have to walk; his dream was taking him that way anyway!

Harry drifted unresisting along the gravel path between ranks of mighty tombstones, drawn by some dream-force which he knew could not be denied. At the end of the avenue of markers there was an empty space where the mist alone swirled and eddied, a cold and lonely place, and beyond that . . .

Three more markers, but somehow more ominous than all the others put together. Harry drifted across the empty place straight towards them, and as he approached them where they towered up out of the earth, so the dream-force gently set him down and gave him back his volition. He looked at the headstones and the mist which half-obscured them slowly lifted. And Harry read the warning his mother's "others" had left for him . . . in geometrically rigid characters in their surface.

The first stone said:

339

BRENDA COWELL
BORN 1958
SOON TO DIE IN CHILDBIRTH
SHE LOVED AND WAS LOVED GREATLY

The second one said:

SIR KEENAN GORMLEY
BORN 1915
SOON TO DIE IN AGONY
FIRST AND FOREMOST A PATRIOT

And the third one said:

HARRY KEOGH
BORN 1957
THE DEAD SHALL MOURN HIM

Harry opened his mouth and shouted his denial: No!''
He stumbled back from the looming markers, tripped,
threw wide his arms to break his fall—

—And knocked over a tiny bedside table. For a long
moment he lay there, shocked from sleep, his heart hammering against his ribs, then gave a second great start as
his telephone rang!

It was Keenan Gormley. Harry flopped shivering into a
chair with the phone to his ear. "Oh," he said, "it's you."

"Am I that much of a disappointment, Harry?" the
other asked, but with no trace of humour in his voice.

"No, but I was sleeping. You sort of shocked me
awake."

"Oh, well I'm sorry for that. But time is passing us by,
and I—"

"Yes," said Harry, on impulse.

"Eh?" Gormley sounded surprised. "Did you say yes?"

"I mean: yes I'll join you. At least, I'll come to see you. We'll talk some more about it." Harry had been considering Gormley's proposition for some time, just as he had promised he would; but in fact it was his dream, which of course had been more than just a dream, that finally decided him. His mother had told him there was someone he'd do well to trust, someone who had asked for his help. Who could that be but Gormley? Until now his joining Gormley's ESPers had been fifty-fifty, he might and he might not. But now, if there was any way he could change what Mary Keogh had called his "probable" future, his and Brenda's and Gormley's, then—

"But that's wonderful, Harry!" Gormley's excitement was obvious. "When will you come down? There are so many people you must meet. We've so much to show you—and so much to do!"

"But not just yet," Harry tried to put the brakes on. "I mean, I'll come down soon. When I can . . ."

"When you can?" now Gormley sounded disappointed.

'Soon,' Harry said again. "As soon as I've finished . . . what I have to do."

"Very well," said the other, a little deflated, "that will have to do. But Harry—don't leave it too long, will you?"

"No, I won't leave it too long." He put the phone down.

The phone was no sooner in its cradle than it rang again, even before Harry could turn away. He picked it up.

"Harry?" It was Brenda, her voice very small and quiet.

"Brenda? Listen, love," he said before she could speak. "I think . . . I mean, I would like . . . what I'm trying to say is . . . oh, hell! Let's get married!"

"Oh, Harry!" she sighed into her end, the sound and the feeling of her relief very close and immediate his ear. "I'm so glad you said that before—before—

341

"Let's do it soon," he cut her short, trying hard not to choke on his words as once more he saw, in his mind's eye, the legend on Brenda's marker as it had appeared to him in his dream.

"But that's why I called you," she said. "That's why I'm glad you asked me. You see, Harry, it was looking like we were going to have to anyway . . ."

Which came as no surprise at all to Harry Keogh.

Chapter Twelve

IT WAS MID-DECEMBER, 1976. FOLLOWING ONE OF THE LONG-est, hottest summers on record, now Nature was trying to even up the score. Already it promised to be a severe winter.

Boris Dragosani and Max Batu were coming to England from a place far colder, however, and in any case climate had no part in their scheme of things. It was not a consideration. If anything the cold suited them: it matched precisely the emotionless iciness of their hearts, the sub-zero nature of their mission. Which was murder, pure and simple.

All through the flight, not too comfortable in the rather stiff, unyielding seats of the Aeroflot jet, Dragosani had sat and thought morbid thoughts: some of them angry and some fearful or at best apprehensive, but all uniformly morbid. The angry thoughts had concerned Gregor Borowitz, for sending him on this mission in the first place, and the

343

fearful ones were about Thibor Ferenczy, the Thing in the ground.

Now lulled by the jet's subdued but all-pervading engine noise, and by the hiss of its air-conditioning, he sank down a little farther into his seat and again turned over in his mind the details of his last visit to the cruciform hills . . .

He thought of Thibor's story: of the symbiotic or lamprey-like nature of the true vampire, and he thought of his agony and his panic-flight before merciful oblivion had claimed him half-way down the wooded slope. That was where he had found himself upon regaining consciousness in the dawn light: sprawled under the trees at the edge of the overgrown fire-break. And yet again he had cut short a visit to his homeland, returning at once to Moscow and putting himself directly into the hands of the best doctor he could find. It had been a complete waste of time; it appeared he was perfectly healthy.

X-ray photographs disclosed nothing; blood and urine samples were one hundred per cent normal; blood-pressure, pulse and respiration were exactly what they should be. Was there any condition that Dragosani was aware of? There was not. Had he ever suffered from migraine or asthma? No. Then perhaps it had been the altitude. Had his sinuses been causing him any concern? No. Had he perhaps been overworking himself? Hardly that! Did he himself have any idea as to the source of the trouble? No.

Yes, but it didn't bear thinking about and couldn't be mentioned under any circumstances.

The doctor had given him a pain-killing prescription, against the possibility of a recurrence, and that had been that. Dragosani should have been satisfied but was not. Far from it . . .

He had attempted to contact Thibor at long range. Perhaps the old devil knew the answer; even a lie might contain some sort of clue; but—nothing. If Thibor could hear him, he wasn't answering.

He had gone over for the hundredth time the events leading up to his terrible pain, his flight, his collapse. Something had splashed on his neck from above. Rain? No: it had been a fine night, bone dry. A leaf, a piece of bark? No, for it had *felt* wet. Some filthy bird's dropping, then? No, for his hand had come away clean.

Something had landed on the top of his spine, and moments later both spine and brain had been gripped and squeezed! By something unknown. But . . . what? Dragosani believed he knew, and still hardly dared to give it conscious thought. Certainly it had invaded his sleep, bringing him endless nights filled with bad dreams—recurrent nightmares he could never remember in his waking moments, but which he knew were terrible when he dreamed them.

The whole thing had become a sort of obsession with him and there were times when he thought of little else. It had to do not only with what had happened, but also with what the vampire had been telling him *when* it happened. And it also had to do with certain changes he'd noticed in himself *since* it happened . . .

Physiological changes, inexplicable changes. Or if there was an explanation, still Dragosani was not yet ready to face up to it.

"Dragosani, my boy," Borowitz had told him not a week ago, "you're getting old before your time! Am I working you too hard or something? Maybe I'm not working you hard enough! Yes, that's probably it: not enough to keep you occupied. When did you last bloody your oh so delicate fingers, eh? A month ago, wasn't it? That French double-agent? But look at you, man! Your hair's receding—your gums, too, by their look! And with that pallid complexion of yours and your sunken cheeks, why, you could almost be anaemic! Maybe this jaunt to England will do you good . . .''

Borowitz had been trying to get a rise out of him, Dragosani knew, but for once he had not dared rise to the bait. That would only serve to draw more attention to himself, which was the last thing he wanted. No, for in fact Borowitz was more nearly correct than he could possibly guess.

His hair did seem to be receding, true, but it was not. A small birthmark on Dragosani's scalp, close to the hairline, told him that much. Its position relative to his hair had not changed in ten years at least; ergo, his hair was not receding. The change was in the skull itself, which if anything seemed to have lengthened at the rear. The same was true of his gums: they were not receding, as Borowitz had suggested, but his teeth were growing longer! Particularly the incisors, top and bottom.

As for anaemia: that was purely ridiculous. Pale he might be but not weak; indeed he felt stronger, more vital in himself, than ever before in his life. Physically, anyway. His pallor probably resulted from a fast-developing photophobia, for now he literally shunned the daylight and would not go out even in dim light without wearing dark glasses.

Physically fit, yes—but his dreams, his nameless fears and obsessions—his neuroses . . .

Quite simply, he *was* neurotic!

It shocked Dragosani to have to admit it, even though he only admitted it to himself.

One thing at least was certain: no matter the outcome of this British mission, when it was finished Dragosani intended to return to Romania at his earliest opportunity. There were matters, questions, which must be resolved. And the sooner the better. Thibor Ferenczy had had things his own way for far too long.

Beside Dragosani in the cramped three-abreast seats, but with a dividing arm up to accommodate his girth, Max Batu chuckled. "Comrade Dragosani," the squat little Mongol whispered, "I am supposed to be the one with the evil eye. Had you perhaps forgotten our roles?"

"What's that?" said Dragosani, starting up in his seat as Batu commenced speaking. He glared at his grinning companion. "What do you mean?"

"I don't know what you were thinking about just then, my friend, but I'm certain it bodes no good for someone," Batu explained. "The look on your face was very fierce!"

"Oh!" said Dragosani, relaxing a little. "Well, my thoughts are my own, Max, and none of your business."

"You are a cold one, Comrade," said Batu. "Both of us are cold ones, I suppose, but even I can feel your chill. It seeps right into me as I sit here." The grin slowly faded from his face. "Have I perhaps offended you?"

"Only with your chatter," Dragosani grunted.

"That's as may be," the other shrugged, "but 'chatter' we must. You were supposed to brief me, tie up those loose ends which Gregor Borowitz left dangling. It would be a good idea if you did it now. We are alone here—even the KGB have not yet bugged Aeroflot! Also, we have only one hour before we arrive in London. In the embassy such a conversation might prove difficult."

"I suppose you're right," said Dragosani grudgingly. "Very well, then, let me put the pieces together for you. It is perhaps preferable that you're fully in the picture.

"Borowitz first conceived of E-Branch about twenty-five years ago. At that time a large Russian group of so-called 'fringe-scientists' were starting to take a real interest in parapsychology, still largely frowned upon in the USSR. Borowitz was interested—had always been interested in ESP—despite his very much down-to-earth military background and otherwise mundane persuasions.

347

Strangely talented people had always fascinated and attracted him: in fact he was himself a 'spotter' but hadn't realized it. When finally he did realize that he had this peculiar talent, he at once applied for a position as head of our ESPionage school. It was initially a school, you see, with no real application in the field. The KGB weren't interested: all brawn and bullet-proof vests, ESP was far too esoteric for them.

"Anyway, since his Army service was coming to a close, and because he had good connections—not to mention his own not inconsiderable talent—he got the job.

"A few years later he found another spotter, but in very peculiar circumstances. It came about like this:

"A female telepath, one of the few girls on Borowitz's team, whose talent was just beginning to blossom, was brutally murdered. Her boyfriend, a man called Viktor Shukshin, was charged with the crime. His defence was that he'd believed the girl was possessed of devils. He could sense them in her. Of course, Borowitz was very much interested. He tested Shukshin and discovered that he was a spotter. More than that, the ESP-aura of psychically endowed persons actually disturbed Shukshin, unbalanced him and drove him to homicidal acts—usually directed at the ESPer him or herself. On the one hand Shukshin was drawn to ESPers, and on the other he was driven to destroy them.

"Borowitz saved Shukshin from the salt mines—in much the same way he saved you, Max—and took him under his wing. He thought he might exorcize the man's homicidal tendencies but at the same time save his talent for spotting. In Shukshin's case, however, brain-washing didn't work. If anything it only served to aggravate the problem. But Gregor Borowitz hates waste. He looked for a way to use Shukshin's aggression.

"At that time the Americans were also greatly interested

in ESP as a weapon; more recently they've taken it up again, though not nearly to the extent that we have. In England, however, a rudimentary ESP-squad already existed, and the British were rather more inclined towards the serious study and exploitation of the paranormal. So Shukshin was put through a long term of spy-school in Moscow and finally released upon the British. His cover was that of a 'defector.' ''

"He was sent over to kill British ESPers?" Batu whispered.

"That was the idea. To find them, to report on their activities, and, when the psychic stress became too great for him, to kill them if and when he had to. But after he'd been in England only a few months, then Viktor Shukshin really did defect!"

"To the British?"

"No, to the country of the British—to their political system—to safety! Shukshin didn't give a damn for Mother Russia anyway, and now he had a new country, almost a new identity. He wasn't going to make the same mistake twice, do you see? In Russia he'd come close to life imprisonment for murder. Should he do the same thing in England? He could make a decent living there, a fresh start. He was a linguist, top-flight qualifications in Russian, German, English, and more than a smattering of half-a-dozen other languages. No, he didn't defect *to* anyone, he defected *from* the USSR. He ran, escaped—to freedom!"

"You sound almost as if you approve of the British system," the Mongolian grinned.

"Don't worry about my loyalties, Max," Dragosani grated. "You won't find a man more loyal than I am." *To Romania! To Wallachia!*

"Well, that's good to know," the other nodded. "It would be nice if I could say the same. But I'm a Mongol and my loyalties are different. Actually, I'm only loyal to Max Batu.''

"Then you probably resemble Shukshin a great deal. I imagine that's how he felt. Anyway, gradually over the months his reporting fell off, and finally he dropped out of sight. It put Borowitz on the spot but there wasn't a thing he could do about it. Since Shukshin was a 'defector' he'd been granted political asylum; Borowitz couldn't very well ask for him back! All he could do was keep tabs on him, see what he was up to.''

"He feared he'd join the British ESPers, eh?''

"Not really, no. Shukshin was psychotic, remember? Anyway, Borowitz wasn't taking any chances, and eventually he tracked him down. Shukshin's plan was simple: he'd got himself a job in Edinburgh, bought a tiny fisherman's cottage in a place called Dunbar, made official application for British citizenship. He kept himself to himself and settled down to leading a normal life. Or at least he tried to . . .''

"It didn't work out?'' Batu was interested.

"For a while. But then he married a girl of old Russian stock. She was a psychic medium—the real thing—and naturally her talent was like a magnet to him. Perhaps he tried to resist her, but to no avail. He married her, and he killed her. At least that's how Gregor Borowitz sees it. After that—nothing.''

"He got away with it?''

"The verdict was accidental death. Drowning. Borowitz knows more about it than I do. Anyway, it's incidental. But Shukshin inherited his wife's money and house. He lives there still . . .''

"And now we are on our way to kill him . . .'' Batu mused. "Can you tell me why?''

Dragosani nodded. "If he had simply continued to keep a low profile and stay out of our hair, that would have been okay. Oh, Borowitz would catch up with him eventually, but not immediately. But Shukshin's fortunes have changed, Max. He's short of cash, generally down at heel. It's been the downfall of many another before him. So now, after all these years, finally he's turned blackmailer. He threatens Borowitz, E-Branch, the entire set-up.''

"One man poses so great a threat?'' Batu raised his eyebrows.

Again Dragosani's nod. "The British equivalent of our branch is now an effective force. How effective we're not sure, but they may even be better than we are. We know very little about them, which in itself is a bad sign. It could well be that they are clever enough to cover themselves entirely, give themselves one hundred per cent ESP security. And if they're that clever—''

"Then how much do they know about us, eh?''

"That's right,'' Dragosani looked at his companion with a little more respect. "They might even know that we two are aboard this plane right now, *and* our mission! God forbid!''

Batu smiled his moonish, ivory smile. "I don't believe in any god,'' he said. "Only in the devil. So the Comrade General fears that if Shukshin isn't silenced he might after all talk to the British?''

"That's what Shukshin has threatened him with, yes. He wants money or he'll tell British E-Branch all he knows. Mind you, that won't amount to much after all this time, but even a little knowledge about our E-Branch is far too much for Gregor Borowitz's liking!''

Max Batu was thoughtful for a moment. "But if Shukshin did talk, surely he would be giving himself away, too? Wouldn't he be admitting that he came to England in the first place as an ESP-agent of the USSR?''

Dragosani shook his head. "He doesn't have to give himself away. A letter is perfectly anonymous, Max. Even

351

a telephone call. And even though twenty years have gone by, still there are things he knows which Borowitz wants kept secret. Two things in particular, which might prove valuable beyond measure to the British ESPers. One: the location of the Château Bronnitsy. Two: the fact that Comrade General Gregor Borowitz himself is head of Russian ESPionage. That is the threat which Shukshin poses, and that is why he'll die.''

"And yet his death is not our prime objective.''

Dragosani was silent for a moment, then said: "No, our prime objective is the death of someone else, someone far more important. He is Sir Keenan Gormley, head of their ESPers. His death . . . and his knowledge—all of it—that is our prime objective. Borowitz wants both of them dead and stripped of their secrets. You will kill Gormley—in your own special way—and I shall examine him in mine. Before that we shall already have killed Viktor Shukshin, who also shall have been examined. Actually, he should not present too much of a problem: his place is lonely, out of the way. We'll do it there.''

"And you can really empty them of secrets? After they are dead, I mean?'' Batu seemed to have doubts.

"Yes, I really can. More surely than any torturer could when they were alive. I shall steal their innermost thoughts right out of their blood, their marrow, their cold and lonely bones.''

A dumpy stewardess appeared at the cabin end of the central aisle. "Fasten your seatbelts,'' she intoned like a robot; and the passengers, equally robotic, complied.

"What are your limitations?'' Batu asked. "Strictly out of morbid curiosity, of course.''

"Limitations? How do you mean?''

"What if a man has been dead for a week, for example?'' Dragosani shrugged. "It makes no difference.''

"What if he has been dead for a hundred years?''

"A dried-up mummy, you mean? Borowitz wondered the same thing. We experimented. It was all the same to me. The dead cannot keep their secrets from a necromancer."

"But a corpse, rotting," Batu pressed. "Say someone dead for a month or two. That must be quite awful . . ."

"It is," said the other. "But I'm used to it. The mess doesn't bother me so much as the risk. The dead teem with disease, you know? I have to be very careful. It's not a healthy business."

"*Ugh!*" said Batu, and Dragosani actually saw him give a small shudder.

London's lights were gleaming in the dark distance on the curve of night's horizon. The city was a hazy glow beyond the small, circular windows. "And you?" said Dragosani. "Does your talent have its 'limitations,' Max?"

The Mongol gave a shrug. "It, too, has its dangers. It requires much energy; it saps my strength; it is debilitating. And as you know, it is only effective against the weak and infirm. There is supposed to be one other small handicap, too, but that is a matter of legend and I do not intend to put it to the test."

"Oh?"

"Yes. There is a story told in my country of a man with the evil eye. It's an old story, going back a thousand years. This man was *very* evil and used his power to terrorize the land. He would ride with his bandits into villages and rape and plunder, then ride out again unscathed. And no one dared hold up a hand against him. But in one viliage there lived an old man who said he knew how to deal with him. When the robber band was seen riding that way, the villagers took all their corpses and gave them spears and propped them on the walls. The robbers came and in the dusk their leader saw that the village was protected. He cast his evil eye upon the watchers at the walls. But of course, the dead cannot die twice.

The spell rebounded and struck him down. He was shrivelled up no larger than a roasted piglet!''

Dragosani liked the story. ''And the moral?'' he asked.

Batu grunted and shrugged again. ''Doesn't it speak for itself? One must never curse the dead, I suppose, for they have nothing to lose. In any argument, they must always win in the end . . .''

Dragosani thought of Thibor Ferenczy. *And what of the undead?* he wondered. *Do they, too, always win? If so, then it's about time someone changed the rules . . .*

They were met and whisked through Customs by ''a man from the embassy,'' their baggage delivered as if by magic to a black Mercedes bearing diplomatic plates. As well as their cold-eyed escort there was also a silent, uniformed driver. On their way to the embassy their escort sat in the front passenger's seat, his body half-turned towards them, his arm draped casually along the back of the driver's seat. He made small-talk in a frigid, mechanical fashion, trying to assume an air of friendly interest. He didn't fool Dragosani for a minute.

''Your first time in London, Comrades? You'll find it an interesting city, I'm sure. Decadent, of course, and full of fools, but interesting for all that. I, er, didn't have time to check on your business here. How long do you plan to stay?''

''Until we go back,'' said Dragosani.

''Ah!'' the other smiled, thinly, patiently. ''Very good! You must excuse me, Comrade, but for some of us curiosity is—shall we say—a way of life? You understand?''

Dragosani nodded. ''Yes, I understand. You're KGB.''

The man's thin face went icy in a moment. ''We don't use that term much outside the embassy.''

''What term do you use?'' smiled Max Batu, his voice a deceptive whisper. ''Shitheads?''

"What?" the escort's face slowly turned white.

"My friend and I are here on business which is no concern of you or yours," said Dragosani in a level tone. "We have the very highest authority. Let me make that clear: the Very Highest Authority. Any interference will be very bad for you. If we need your help we will ask for it. Apart from that you'll leave us alone and not bother us."

The escort pursed his lips, drew one long, slow breath. "People don't usually talk to me like that," he said, his words very precise.

"Of course if you persist in obstructing us," Dragosani continued, without changing his tone of voice, "I can always break your arm. That should keep you out of the way for two or three weeks at least."

The other gasped. "You threaten me?"

"No, I make you a promise." But Dragosani knew he wasn't getting anywhere. This was a typical KGB automaton. The necromancer sighed, said: "Look, if you have been tasked to us I'm sorry for you. Your job is impossible. Moreover it's dangerous. This much I'll tell you, and this much only. We're here to test a secret weapon. Now, ask no more questions."

"A secret weapon?" said the other, his eyes widening. "Ah!" He looked from Dragosani to Batu and back again. "What weapon?"

Dragosani smiled grimly. Well, he had warned the fool. "Max," he said, carefully turning his face away. "A small demonstration, perhaps . . . ?"

Shortly after that they arrived at the embassy. In the grounds of the place Dragosani and Batu stepped down from the car and took their luggage from the boot. They looked after their own cases.

The driver attended to their escort. The last they saw of him was as he staggered away, leaning on the driver's arm. He looked back at them only once—stared round-eyed and fearfully at Max Batu—before stumblingly disappearing inside the gloomily imposing building. And that was the last they saw of him.

After that no one bothered them again.

The second Wednesday after New Year, 1977. Viktor Shukshin had known this feeling of encroaching doom for well over a fortnight now, a leaden psychic depression which had lifted only marginally upon the arrival of Gregor Borowitz's fourth monthly registered letter containing one thousand pounds in large denomination notes. In fact it worried Shukshin that Borowitz had surrendered so readily, that he had made no counter threats of his own.

Today had been especially bad: the skies were overcast and heavy with snow; the river was frozen over with thick grey ice; the big house was cold and seemed invaded by icy draughts that followed Shukshin everywhere. And for the first time in as long as he could remember—or at least the first time that he had noticed it—there was a strange and ominous quiet about everything, so that sounds seemed muffled as if by deep snow, though little had fallen as yet. The ticking of an old grandfather clock sounded heavy, dull—even the warped floorboards seemed to creak a little less volubly—and all in all it had put Shukshin's nerves in a very bad way. It was as if the house held its breath and waited for something.

That "something" came at 2:30 P.M., just as Shukshin poured himself a glass of iced vodka and sat down in his study before an electric fire, looking gloomily out through neglected, fly-specked windows on a garden frozen into white crystal. It came with the nerve-jangling clamour of his telephone.

Heart hammering, he put down the drink he'd almost spilled, snatched up the handset and said, "Shukshin."

"Stepfather?" Harry Keogh's voice seemed very close.

"It's Harry here. I'm in Edinburgh staying with friends. How've you been keeping?"

Shukshin choked back the anger which came on the instant, boiling to the surface. So that was it; this damned spawn of an ESPer was here, close at hand, sending out his psychic aura to crush Shukshin's sensitive spirits! He bared his teeth, glared at the telephone in his hand, fought down the urge to curse and rage. "Harry! Is that you? In Edinburgh, you say? How thoughtful of you to call me." *You bastard! Your mutant aura is* hurting *me!*

"But you sound so well!" the other sounded surprised. "When I saw you last you seemed so—"

"Yes, I know," Shukshin tried not to snarl. "I hadn't been too well, Harry, but I'm fine now. Was there something you wanted?" *I could eat your heart, you unnatural little swine!*

"Why, yes, I wondered if perhaps I might come to see you. Maybe we could talk a little about my mother. Also, I've got my skates with me. If the river's frozen I could do some skating. I'm only up here for a few days more, you see, and I—"

"No!" Shukshin snapped, and at once checked himself. Why not get it over with? Why not get this shadow from the past out of the way once and for always? Whatever it was that Keogh knew or suspected—however he had come by Shukshin's ring, which the Russian had believed lost in the river, and whatever the psychic link between this youth and his mother, which apparently bound them still—why not bring it to an end right here and now? Commonsense stood no chance against the bloodlust which surged in Shukshin now.

"Stepfather?"

"I meant only—Harry, my nerves still aren't up to much, I'm afraid. Living here all alone—you know, I'm not used to company. Of *course* I'd like to see you, and the river is perfect just now for skating, but I really couldn't do with a houseful of young people, Harry.''

"Oh, no, Stepfather, I didn't intend bringing anyone with me. I wouldn't think of imposing on you to that extent. Why, my friends don't even know I have a relative up here! No, chiefly I'd just like to visit the house again and go on the river. I'd like to skate where my mother used to skate, that's all.''

That again! The bastard *did* know something—or at least suspected something—definitely! So he wanted to skate, did he? On the river, where his mother skated. Shukshin's face twisted into a leer. "Well in that case . . . when can I expect you?''

"In about, oh, two hours?" came Harry's answer.

"Very well," said Shukshin. "About 4:30 to 5:00 P.M., then. I shall look forward to it, Harry.''

And he put the phone down before an utterly animal growl of hatred could burst from his writhing mouth and betray his true feelings: *Oh, how I shall look—forward —to—it!*

Harry Keogh wasn't nearly so far away as Edinburgh. In fact he was in the foyer of the hotel where he'd been staying the past few nights in Bonnyrigg itself. After speaking to Shukshin on the phone he shrugged into his overcoat and went out to his car, a battered old Morris he'd bought on the cheap especially for this trip. He had passed his driving test the first time around—or at least an ex-driving instructor in the cemetery in Seaton Carew had passed it for him.

Now he drove on icy roads to the top of a hill some quarter of a mile from the old house and overlooking it, where he parked and got out of the car. There was no one about; the scene was bleak and bitter; shivering, Harry carried binoculars to a stand of trees rising starkly naked against the sky. From behind the bole of one of them, he trained the glasses on the house and waited—for no more than a minute or two.

Shukshin came out through the study's patio doors and hurried through his courtyard garden, finally emerging from a door in the wall facing the river. In his hand he carried a pickaxe . . .

Harry drew breath sharply, let it out slowly to plume in the frosty air. Shukshin scrambled through brittle shrubbery and brambles down to the river's rim. He let himself down carefully on to the ice, tested it, sprang up and down at its very edge. Then he turned and looked all about. The place was quite deserted.

He walked to the centre of the grey-shining expanse of ice and bounded again, and once more seemed satisfied. And now Harry's eyes were riveted to the scene, that monochrome tableau which he almost felt he'd watched before, and the act which he was absolutely certain Shukshin had performed before.

For the figure trapped and enlarged in the lenses of his binoculars now crouched down, took his pickaxe and swung it in a wide circle, scoring a boundary, a demarcation, in the crusty surface of the ice. And all around that etched circle he strode, hacking periodically with all the strength and passion of a madman, until spouts of water jetted up each time the point of the pick struck home; so that in a matter of minutes a great disc of ice nine or ten feet across floated free in a pool of its own. Then the final touch:

Once more pausing to peer all about, finally Shukshin walked the perimeter of the circle, using his feet to brush icy debris from his assault back into the gap. The water would freeze over again, of course, but it would not be safe for hours yet, certainly not before tomorrow morning. Shukshin had set his trap—but he didn't know that the intended victim had watched him do it!

Harry could scarce control his shivering now, the trembling in all his limbs which had little or nothing to do with the actual temperature. No, it had more to do with the mental *condition* of that hunched figure down there on the ice. The binoculars were not powerful enough to bring the figure really close, but still Harry was sure that he'd seen its face working hideously through all the hacking. The face of a lunatic, who for some reason lusted after Harry's life as once he had lusted after—and taken—his mother's.

Harry wanted to know why, would not rest until he had the answer. And there was only one way to get it.

Feeling physically and mentally weary, and yet knowing that his work wasn't over yet, Viktor Shukshin returned to the house. Inside the walled courtyard, he dragged his pickaxe behind him across frosted flags, letting its haft fall clattering from his fingers before he stepped through the open patio doors and into his study. Head down and arms dangling at his sides, he took two more paces into the room—and froze!

What? Was Keogh here already? The entire house felt filled with strange forces. It reeked of ESP-aura, its very atmosphere seeming to vibrate with alien energies.

Instantly inflamed, now Shukshin sensed movement: the patio doors clicking shut behind him! He whirled, saw, and his jaw fell open. "Who . . .? What . . ." he choked.

Two men faced him, stood there in his own study where they had waited for him, and one of them held a gun pointed straight at Shukshin's heart. He recognized the weapon as Russian service issue, recognized the coldly emotionless looks of the two men, and felt Doom closing its fist on him. But in a way it was not entirely unexpected. He had thought there might be some sort of visit one day. But that it should be *now*, of all ill-omened moments.

"Sit down—Comrade," said the tall one, his voice harsh as a file on Shukshin's ragged nerves.

Max Batu pushed a chair forward and Shukshin very nearly collapsed into it. Batu moved to stand behind him where he sat facing Dragosani. The ESP-aura washed all about Shukshin now, as if his mind swam in bile. Oh, yes, they were from the Château Bronnitsy, these two!

The blackmailer's face was ravaged, eyes sunken deep in black sockets. Looking over his head at Dragosani, finally Batu's round face cracked into a grin. "Comrade Dragosani," he said, "I had always thought *you* looked ill—until now!"

"ESPers!" Shukshin spat the word out. "Borowitz's men! What do you want of me?"

"He has every reason to look ill, Max." Dragosani's voice was deep as a pit. "A traitor, a blackmailer, probably a murderer . . ."

Shukshin looked as if he might spring to his feet. Batu placed heavy, stubby hands on his shoulders. "I asked," Shukshin grated, "what you want of me?"

"Your life," said Dragosani. He took a silencer from his pocket, screwed it tightly to the muzzle of his weapon, stepped forward and placed it against Shukshin's forehead. "Only your life."

Shukshin felt Max Batu step carefully to one side behind him. And he knew they were going to kill him.

"Wait!" he croaked. "You're making a mistake. Borowitz won't thank you for it. I know a lot—about the British side. I've been giving it to Borowitz bit by bit. But there's a lot he doesn't know yet. Also, I'm still working for you—in my way. Why, I'm on a job now! Yes, right now."

"What job?" said Dragosani. It had not been his intention to shoot Shukshin, merely to frighten him. Max's getting out of the line of fire had only been a natural reaction. Shooting was messy and made for bad necromancy. The way Dragosani had planned Shukshin's death was much more interesting:

When he had obtained all he could get this way, by simple questioning, then they would take Shukshin to the bathroom and bind him. They would put him in a bath half full of cold water and Dragosani would use one of his surgical sickles to slit his wrists. As he lay there in water rapidly turning red as his life leaked out, then Dragosani would re-question him. The promise would be that if Shukshin told all, his wounds would be bound and he'd be released. Dragosani would show him bandages, surgical tape. But of course, Shukshin would only have so much time to respond. All the time the water was darkening with his blood, until he lay in a cold, crimson soup. It would have been a warning, a promise that if Shukshin continued to give them trouble, then Dragosani and Batu—or others like them—would be back to finish the job. That is what they would tell Shukshin, but of course the job would be finished right there and then.

Even so, still Shukshin might hold something back. Something, perhaps, which he did not consider important, something forgotten—maybe something too damning to tell. Maybe, for instance, he was already working for the British . . .

But whatever he said it would make no difference. When he was dead they would flush his drained corpse with fresh water, take him out of the bath, and *then* . . . then Dragosani would continue to question.

Now Dragosani took the gun away from Shukshin's forehead, sat down facing him. "I'm waiting," he said. "What job?"

Shukshin gulped, tried to force his fear of these men—and his hatred of their weird ESP talents—to the back of his mind. It was there, it wouldn't go away, but for now he must try to ignore it. His life hung by a thread and he knew it. He must get his thoughts in order, lie as he'd never lied before. Some of it would be the truth anyway, and of that much at least he could speak with absolute conviction:

"You know I'm a spotter?"

"Of course, it's why Borowitz sent you here: to find them and kill them. You haven't been too successful, apparently." Dragosani's sarcasm was acid.

Shukshin ignored that, too. "When I came in here a moment ago—the moment I stepped into this room—I knew you were here. I could almost taste your presence. You're powerful ESPers, both of you. Especially you," he glared at Dragosani. "There's a terrific, a monstrous talent in you. It . . . it *hurts* me!"

"Yes, Borowitz told me that," Dragosani answered drily. "But we know about spotters, Shukshin, so stop stalling and get on with it."

"I wasn't stalling. I was trying to explain about the man I'm going to kill—today!"

Dragosani and Batu exchanged glances. Batu looked down on the top of Shukshin's head and said: "You were going to kill a British ESPer? Why? And who is he?"

"It was my way of getting back into Borowitz's good books," Shukshin lied. "The man's name is Harry Keogh. He is my stepson. He got his talent—whatever it is—from his mother. Sixteen years ago I killed her, too . . ." Shukshin continued to glare at Dragosani. "She fascinated me—and she infuriated me! Is she the one you meant when you said I was 'probably' a murderer? No 'probably' about it. Oh, I killed her all right. Like all ESPers, she hurt me. Her talent drove me mad!"

"Never mind her," snapped Dragosani. "What about this Keogh?"

"That's what I was trying to tell you. With you two,

powerful as you are, still I had to actually enter the house to know you were here. But with Harry Keogh—''

"Yes?"

Shukshin shook his head. "He's different. His talent is . . . vast! I *know* it is. You see, the bigger it is, the more it hurts. So I'm not only killing him for Borowitz but also for myself."

Dragosani was interested. He could always finish this thing with Shukshin later; but if Harry Keogh was *that* powerful, he would like to know more about him. And in any case, if he was a member of the British E-Branch it would be like killing two birds with one stone. As his interest expanded he forgot to ask Shukshin the important question: *was* Keogh a member of the British E-Branch? And that was something the other wasn't going to volunteer.

"I think we might be able to accommodate you," Dragosani finally said. "It's always good when you can reach an understanding with old friends." He put away his gun. "When, exactly, were you going to kill this man, and how?"

And Shukshin told him.

After Shukshin had gone back to the house, Harry returned to his car and drove it to the foot of the hill in the direction of Bonnyrigg. Down there he parked again, off the road, then made his way on foot across a field to the river. Frozen over, the area was unfamiliar and made more so by the first feathers of snow where they drifted down from the leaden skies. Everything began to take on the soft, misty aspect of a winter painting.

Harry began to make his way upriver. His mother's resting place was up there somewhere, he couldn't say where exactly. That was one of the reasons he'd come again to this place: to make sure he knew exactly where she was, that he could find her under any and all circumstances. Walking on the frozen water, he reached out his mind:

"Ma, can you hear me?"

She was there immediately. "Harry, is that you? So close!" And at once her apprehension, her agony of fear for him: "*Harry!* Is it . . . now?"

"It's now, Ma. But don't give me any more problems than I have already. I need your help, not arguments. I don't need anything to trouble my mind."

"Oh, Harry, Harry! What can I say to you? How am I supposed to stop worrying about you? I'm your mother . . ."

"Then help me. Don't say anything, just be still. I want to see if I can find you, blind."

"Blind? I don't—"

"Ma, please!"

She was silent, but her worry gnawed at him, in his head, like the pacing of a troubled loved one in a small room. He kept walking, closed his eyes and went to her. A hundred yards, maybe a little more, and he knew he was there. He stopped walking, opened his eyes. He stood in the curve of the overhanging bank, on the thick white ice which formed his mother's headstone. Her marker, and his marker, too. Now he knew he could always find her.

"I'm here, Ma." He crouched down on the ice, scuffed away a thin layer of snow, looked at the heavy jack-handle in his gloved hand. That was the second reason he had come.

As he began to batter at the ice, she said: "I see it all now, Harry. You've been lying to me, deceiving me," she reproached him. "You think there will be problems after all."

"No I don't, Ma. I'm much stronger now, in many ways. But if there is a problem . . . well, I'd be a fool not to cover all the possibilities."

Here, close to the bank, the ice was a little thicker.

Brian Lumley

Harry began to perspire, but soon he'd made a hole almost three feet across. He cleared as much as he could of the broken ice fragments from the hole and straightened up. Down there, the water swirled blackly. And under the water, under the cold silt and mud . . .

All done, now Harry must go, and quickly. No good to let his sweat grow cold on him. Also, it was beginning to snow a little heavier. It began to get dark as the early winter dusk came with the snow. He had time now for a brandy at the hotel, and then, then it would be time for his showdown with Viktor Shukshin.

"Harry," his mother called after him one last time as he hurried back across the field to his car. "Harry, I love you! Good luck, son . . ."

One hour later Dragosani and Batu stood behind a clump of young conifers on the river bank twenty-five or thirty yards upstream of Shukshin's house. They had been there for a little less than half an hour but already were beginning to feel the cold biting through their clothing. Batu had commenced a rhythmic swinging of his arms across his chest and Dragosani had just lit a cigarette when at last the yellow light above the door to Shukshin's courtyard snapped into life—his signal to them that the scene was now set for murder—and two figures came out into the evening.

In real time it was not yet night, but the winter darkness was almost that of night and but for the stars and a rising moon, visibility would be poor. The clouds, so dense only an hour ago, had now drifted away and no more snow had fallen; but to the east the sky was black with a heavy burden and what little wind there was came from that direction. It would yet snow tonight, and heavily. But for the moment the stars lit the scene with their cold, soft light and the rising moon made a silver ribbon of the winding river of ice.

As the figures from the house picked their way down to the river Dragosani took a last drag on his cigarette behind cupped hands, threw it down and ground it out beneath his heel; Batu stopped swinging his arms; they both stood like stone and watched the play unfold.

At the river's rim the two figures shrugged out of their overcoats and placed them on the bank, then adopted kneeling positions as they put on their skates. There was a little conversation, but it was low and the wind was in the wrong direction. Only snatches of talk drifted back to the hidden watchers. Shukshin's voice, dark and very deep, sounded openly aggressive to Dragosani and wolfish—like the growling of a great dog—and he wondered why Keogh didn't take fright or at least show something of suspicion; but no, the younger man's voice was flat and even, almost carefree, as the two glided out on to the ice and began to skate.

At first they went to and fro, almost side by side, but then the slighter figure took the lead. And moving with some skill he rapidly picked up speed to come skimming upriver towards the spot where the watchers were hiding. Dragosani and Batu crouched down a little then, but at the last moment before he drew level with them Keogh turned in a wide loop which took in the entire breadth of the river and headed back the other way.

Behind him, Shukshin had almost slowed to a halt as Keogh made his run. The older man was far less certain on the ice, seemed awkward and even clumsy by comparison; but as Keogh sped back towards him he now turned to skate in the same direction, but in such a way as to impede the faster man. Keogh leaned over in a slalom at such an angle that his skates threw up a sheet of snow and ice as he missed the other by inches, then threw himself over the other way at a similar angle to bring himself back on course. And a scant twelve inches away, his skates carved ice on the very rim of the sabotaged circle where fresh-formed ice barely held the central disc in place.

And Shukshin was so close on his heels that he, too, must swerve wildly, his arms windmilling, to avoid his own trap! "Careful, Stepfather!" Keogh called back over his shoulder as he sped away. "I almost collided with you then."

Dragosani and Batu heard. Batu said: "A fortunate young man, this one—so far."

"Oh?" Dragosani wasn't so sure fortune had anything to do with it. Shukshin had been unable to specify Keogh's talent: what if he was a telepath? He would have the power to pluck his stepfather's treacherous thoughts right out of his head. "Myself, I think our blackmailer will find this more difficult than he thought."

Shukshin had come to a halt now, standing still on the ice in a peculiar hunched stance and watching Keogh intently where he continued to skate. The Russian's shoulders and chest rose and fell spasmodically and his body visibly shook, as if he were in pain or suffering from great emotional stress. "This way, Harry," he called harshly. "This way! You're too good for me, I'm afraid. Why, you could skate circles around me!"

Keogh came back, circled the other's hunched figure, and again. And with each sweep his skates went inches closer to disaster. Shukshin held out his arms and Keogh took his hands, spinning round the older man and turning him on his own axis.

"And now," Max Batu whispered to Dragosani where they looked on, "The *coupe de glâce!*"

Suddenly Shukshin stopped turning and appeared to stumble into Keogh. Keogh twisted his body to avoid him. Their hands were still locked. One of Keogh's skates dug in where it cut through a skim of powdery snow and into the groove of the channel hacked by Shukshin. He was jerked to a halt and only Shukshin's grip on his wrists kept him from falling onto the infirm disc of ice.

Shukshin laughed then, a crazed, baying laugh, and thrust Keogh away from him—thrust him towards death!

But Keogh held tight to the sleeves of Shukshin's coat and as he was pushed so he pulled. Caught off balance Shukshin jerked forward; Keogh bent to one side and threw him over his hip—but when he released Shukshin, still the Russian held fast to him! With a cry of outrage the older man fell inside his own circle, dragging Keogh after him.

Both of them crashed down in a tangle on ice which at once shifted beneath them. The circle made cracking sounds at its rim, like small gunshots; water spouted up in black jets as the disc tilted and broke in two halves; Shukshin gave a cry of horror—a strange, mad cry like a wounded beast—as the semicircle of ice supporting him and Keogh stood on end and tipped them into the freezing, gurgling water.

"Quick, Max!" Dragosani snapped. "We can't afford to lose both of them." He charged from behind the cover of the conifers with Batu close on his heels.

"Who would you prefer to save?" the Mongol rasped as they jumped down onto the ice.

"Keogh," he answered at once, "if it's possible. He'll know more about the British organization than Shukshin. And he has this talent of his—whatever it is."

Even as he spoke those words a fantastic idea had come to Dragosani, one he had never even considered before. If he could "learn" necromancy from an undead Thing and with it steal the thoughts and secrets of the dead, mightn't he also steal their talents? At the Château Bronnitsy the agents were all allies, working on the same side, towards the same end. But here in England the ESPers were ene-

mies! Why not steal Keogh's as yet unknown talent itself—
and use it to his own ends?

From the hole in the river where cakes of ice churned in
dark, frenzied water, a great grunting and gasping sounded
as Batu and Dragosani drew closer; but as they more
cautiously approached the rim itself all sounds ceased and
they were greeted only by the gurgle and slap of water
moving under and against the ice. For a moment a clutching hand shot dripping into view and clawed at the rim,
but before they could make a move to grab it the hand was
gone, sucked under.

"This way!" Dragosani gasped. "Follow the course of
the river."

"You think there's a chance?" Batu obviously thought
not.

"A very slim one," said Dragosani.

They ran on the ice as best they could under a silent
moon.

Beneath the ice, tumbled and turned by the current,
Harry Keogh somehow got his jacket off and let it go.
Under his shirt he wore a rubber wet-suit vest, but still the
cold was terrific. It must surely finish Shukshin, who was
completely unprotected.

Harry started to swim, kept his head turned sideways
with his face against the ice, actually found places where
cold air was trapped in shallow pockets. He swam towards
his mother, following her stream of troubled thoughts just
as he had followed them unerringly two hours ago with his
eyes closed. Except then there had been plenty of air to
breathe and he had been warm.

Panic gripped him momentarily but he put it out of his
mind. His Ma was over there—that way! He began to
swim more strongly—and something grasped at his feet,
his legs. Something fastened its grasp on him and clung to
his trousers. Shukshin! The river was bobbing them along

in tandem, like matches down a drain, gluing them together through gravitational attraction.

Harry swam more desperately yet, with his arms, with one leg. He swam as never before, his lungs bursting, his heart a great gong clanging away in his chest. And Shukshin clawing his way up his body, his hands like the pincers of some great crab, snatching at Harry as if to pull him to pieces.

This was it; he could swim no more; the water was the black blood of some giant alien into whose veins Harry had been injected, where Shukshin was an alien antibody bent on his destruction.

"Ma! Ma! *Help me!*" Harry cried out with his mind as at last he was forced to draw breath, but drew only icy water which gushed into his straining jaws and nostrils.

"Harry!" she answered at once, loudly, close at hand, her own voice frantic in his head. "Harry, you're here!"

He kicked backwards, lashed out with both feet at Shukshin, and thrust upward with his back and head, crashing himself against the ice cover—which immediately, mercifully, shattered into thin shards as his head and shoulders emerged into air!

And suddenly the water was still and his feet touched a muddy bottom five feet down, and even before his eyes had focused and his battered senses stopped spinning, Harry knew he had made it. Now he summoned his last reserves, threw out his hands and grasped at tough roots where they projected from the overhanging bank. And slowly he began to draw himself up and out.

Beside him the water swirled and gurgled as from some hidden commotion. Harry half-turned and terror drew his lips back from his teeth—as Shukshin's mad face came surging up alongside him, choking and gagging! The madman saw him, spewed water and a babbling scream of rage into his face, clutched at his throat with hands like steel grapples.

Harry brought his knee up into the maniac's groin. Bones broke but still Shukshin hung on. He dragged Harry inexorably back, slavered into his face. For a long moment Harry thought he meant to bite him, savage him like a rabid dog! He fought Shukshin, slammed his clenched fists again and again into his ghastly face, to no avail. The madman would win. Harry was about to go under . . .

He reached out again for the tough roots in the river bank, but Shukshin's hands at his throat were shutting off the air, shutting off life itself.

"Ma!" Harry silently cried. "You were right, Ma. I should have listened. I'm sorry."

"No!" came her denial of defeat. *"No!"* Shukshin had killed her, but he must not be allowed to kill her son.

And again the bitter water gurgled and churned—but more blackly yet!

Dragosani skidded to a halt not fifteen feet away, grabbed at Batu and drew him also to a standstill. Panting, their breath forming fragile feathers of snow in the air, they looked—they saw—and their jaws fell open. Two men had gone down under the ice back there, had been washed downstream to this hole, and until a moment ago two figures had fought and torn at each other here in the still water beneath the river bank. But now there were *three* figures there in the water, and the third one was as terrible a thing as ever Dragosani had heard of or imagined or seen in his blackest nightmares!

It was . . . not alive, and yet it had the mobility of life, the authority of life. And it had purpose. It clung to Shukshin, wrapped itself about him, put its mud-and-bones arms around him and its algae and plastered-hair skull against his. Of eyes there were none, but a putrid glow shone out from empty sockets with a semblance of sight.

And where before Shukshin had only howled and gibbered and laughed like a madman, now he quite literally went mad.

Shriek after shriek pealed out from him as he fought with the awful thing, the shrillest lunatic screeching that Dragosani and Batu had ever thought to hear; and at the very end, just before the horror dragged him under, words which at last the petrified watchers could understand:

"Not you!" Shukshin babbled. "Oh God, oh no, *not you!*"

Then he was gone, and the thing of bones and mud and weeds and death with him . . .

And Harry Keogh was left to scramble out on to the river bank.

Batu might perhaps have gone blindly, numbly after him but Dragosani still clutched at his arm. He clutched it, almost for support. Batu began to adopt his killing crouch but Dragosani stopped that, too. "No, Max," he hoarsely whispered, "we don't dare. We've seen something of what he can do, but what other talents does he possess?"

Batu understood, relaxed, drew himself upright. On the bank above them Harry Keogh became aware of their presence for the first time. He turned his face towards them, found them, stared at them. His eyes focused on them at last and he looked as though he might speak, but he said nothing. For long moments they simply stared at each other, all three, and then Keogh glanced back at the jagged patch of black water. "Thanks, Ma," he said, simply.

Dragosani and Batu watched as he turned, staggered, stumbled and then began to run weavingly back towards Shukshin's house. They watched him go, and made no attempt to follow. Not yet. When he was out of sight Batu hissed:

"But that thing, Comrade Dragosani? It wasn't—couldn't be—human. So what was it?"

Dragosani shook his head. He believed he knew the answer but wouldn't commit himself now. "I'm not sure," he said. "It had been human once, though. One thing is certain: when Keogh needed help it came to him. That's his talent, Max: the dead answer his call." And he turned to the other, his eyes darker still in sunken orbits.

"They answer his call, Max. And there are a lot more of the dead than there are of the living."

Chapter Thirteen

ON THURSDAY MORNING HARRY WENT BACK TO THE RIVER, back to the place where his mother lay once more locked in mud and weed. Except that there were two of them there now, and he had not gone to talk to her but to Viktor Shukshin. He took a cushion from the car and carried it down to the river bank, putting it down in snow six inches deep before seating himself and hugging his knees. Below where he sat the ice had crusted over again and snow had settled on the place where he'd cut his escape hole, so that only an outline showed through.

After sitting in silence for a while, he said: "Stepfather, can you hear me?"

". . .Yes," came the answer in a little while. "Yes, I can hear you, Harry Keogh. I hear you and I *feel* your presence! Why don't you go away and leave me in peace?"

"Be careful, Stepfather. Mine might be the last voice you ever hear. If I 'go away and leave you in peace,' who'll speak to you then?"

"So that's your talent, is it, Harry? You speak to the dead. You're a corpse rabble-rouser! Well, I want you to know that it hurts me, like all ESP hurts me. But last night, for the first time in many long years, I lay here in my freezing bed and slept soundly, and there was no pain. Who'll speak to me? I don't want *anyone* to speak to me! I want peace."

"What do you mean, it hurts you?" Harry pressed. "How can my just being here hurt anything?"

Shukshin told him.

"And that's why you killed my mother?"

"Yes, and it's why I tried to kill you. But in your case, it might also have served to save my own life." And now he told Harry about the men Borowitz had sent to kill him, Dragosani and Batu.

Harry wasn't satisfied. He wanted to know it all, from the beginning right to the present. "Tell me about it," he said, "all of it, and I swear I won't bother you again."

And so Shukshin told him.

About Borowitz and the Château Bronnitsy. About the Russian ESPers where they worked for world conquest through ESP in their secret den in the heart of the USSR. He told of how Borowitz had sent him out of Russia to England to find and kill British ESPers, and how he had broken away and become a British citizen. And he told him again about the curse that dogged him: how ESP-talented people rubbed his nerves raw and brought on the madness in him. And at last Harry understood and might almost have pitied Shukshin—were it not for his mother.

And as Shukshin talked so Harry thought of Sir Keenan Gormley and the British E-Branch, and he remembered his promise to go and see Gormley and perhaps join his group when all of this had been sorted out. Well, now it was sorted out. And now Harry knew that he *must* go and see Gormley. For Victor Shukshin wasn't the only guilty one.

There were others far worse than he could ever be. The one who had sent him out on his murderous mission in the first place, for instance. For if Shukshin had never come here, Harry's mother would still be alive.

And at last Harry was satisfied. Until now his life had seemed greatly aimless, unfulfilled—his one ambition had been to kill Shukshin—but now he knew that it was bigger than that, and suddenly he felt small in view of the task which still awaited him.

"All right, Stepfather," he finally said, "I'll leave you now and let you rest. But it's a peace you don't deserve. I can't and won't forgive you."

"I don't want your forgiveness, Harry Keogh, just your promise that you'll leave me alone here." Shukshin told him. "And you've given me that. So now go and get yourself killed and let me be . . ."

Harry climbed stiffly to his feet. Every bone in his body ached—his head, too—and he felt completely sapped of strength. It was partly physical, but mostly emotional. It was the calm which follows the storm, and, although he couldn't yet know it, it was also the lull before the greater storm still to come.

But now he shrugged himself upright, left the cushion lying there forgotten in the snow, headed back towards his car. Behind him and yet with him a voice said in his mind: "Goodbye, Harry." But it wasn't Shukshin's voice.

"Goodbye, Ma," he answered. "And thanks. I'll always love you."

"And I'll always love you, Harry."

"What?" now came Shukshin's horrified mental gasp. "*What!* Keogh, what's this? I saw you raise her up, but—?"

Harry didn't answer. He let Mary Keogh do it for him:

"Hello, Viktor. No, you're wrong. Harry didn't raise me up. I raised myself up. For the sake of love, which is something you can't understand. But that's over now and I'll not do it again. My Harry has others to look after him now; so I'll just lie here, lonely in the mud. Except maybe it won't be so lonely now . . ."

"Keogh!" Shukshin frantically called out after Harry again. "Keogh, you promised me—you said you were the only one who could talk to me. But now she is talking to me—*and she hurts me most of all!*"

Harry kept on walking.

"Now, now, Viktor," he heard his mother's answer, as if she spoke to a small child. "That will get you nowhere. Did you say you want peace and quiet? Oh, but you'll soon get bored with peace and quiet, Viktor."

"Keogh!" Shukshin's voice was a diminishing mental shriek now. "Keogh, you have to get me out of this. Dig me up—tell them where to find my body—*only don't leave me here with her!*"

"Actually, Viktor," Mary Keogh remorselessly continued, "I think I'll rather enjoy talking to you. You're so close to me here that it's no effort at all!"

"Keogh, you bastard! Come back! Oh . . . *please* . . . come . . . back!"

But Harry kept on walking.

By 1:30 P.M. Harry was back in Hartlepool. The roads were nightmarish, layered with compacted snow for more than half the journey, so that in the main he was driving on his nerves. This only served to drain more of his strength, and when at last he got home it was as much as he could do to drag himself upstairs.

Brenda, his wife of eight weeks, was bright and chirpy about the flat, which had undergone some fantastic and inexplicable metamorphosis since she had moved in after their registry office wedding. She was less than three months pregnant but already blooming. Harry, too, had been in fine fettle when last she had seen him; but now, in complete contrast—

He barely managed the effort of kissing her on the cheek, was asleep almost before his head hit the pillows.

He had been away for three days, doing "research," she knew, for a new book he was planning—what and where exactly he'd never bothered to say. Well, that was Harry and she should be used to it by now—but she was not used to him turning up looking like he'd spent three days in a concentration camp!

After he had slept right through the afternoon and seemed to have developed a fever, she called the doctor who visited at about 8:00 P.M. Harry didn't bother to wake up for his visit; the doctor thought it might be pneumonia, though the symptoms weren't quite right; he left pills, instructions and his telephone number. If Harry got worse during the night, especially if his breathing became irregular or he started coughing, or if his temperature went up appreciably, Brenda was to call him at once.

But Harry got no worse through the night, and in the morning he was able to have a bite of breakfast, following which he engaged Brenda in a peculiar, guarded conversation which she was dismayed to find as depressing and morbid as any talk she'd ever had with him during his gloomy or morose periods of previous, less happy times. After listening to him for a little while, when he began to talk about making a will leaving everything to her, or to their child in the event she was unable to make use of it, then she rounded on him and laughed out loud.

"Harry," she said, taking his hands where he sat on the edge of the bed with his shoulders slumped, "what *is* this all about? I know you've had a bug of some sort or other and that you're still feeling low, and I know that when you're a bit down in the mouth it really seems like the end of the world to you, but here we are married for just eight weeks and you sound as if you expect to be dead by the spring! Yes, and me shortly after! I've never heard anything so silly! Just a week ago you were swimming, fighting, skating, full of life—so what is it that's suddenly bothering you?''

At that he decided he really couldn't hedge any longer. Anyway she was his wife now and it was only right that she should know. And so he sat her down and told her everything, with the exception of his dream of the tombstones, and of course excluding the death of Viktor Shukshin. He passed off his aggressive "exercising" of the past few months as simply a means of ensuring his fitness for work still to come, work which could well prove dangerous; which in turn led him to speak of the British ESP organization, but not in any depth. It was sufficient she should know that he wasn't the only strangely talented person— that in fact there were many more—and that there were foreign powers ranged against the free world who were not above using such talents to its detriment. Part of Harry's work with the organization would be to ensure that these alien powers failed in their objectives; his talent as a necroscope would be used as a weapon against them; the future therefore seemed at best . . . uncertain. His talk of wills and such had been simply an expression of this uncertainty: he thought it was best to be prepared for any eventuality.

Even telling her all of this—and while not being too specific on any point—still he wondered if perhaps he was making a mistake, if it would have been better to keep her entirely in the dark. And he wondered at his own motives: was he really confiding in her in order to prepare her for . . . for whatever? Or was it that she was right, that he was feeling at a low ebb and so needed someone to share the load?

Or there again, was it guilt? He had a course to run now

and must pursue it; the chase was not at an end; Shukshin had merely been a faltering step in the right direction. Did he feel that *because* he chose to go in that direction Brenda was at risk? The dream epitaph—his mother's warning—had said nothing about Brenda dying as a result of anything Harry was yet to do. He *had* impregnated her, yes, which would result in a birth; but how could any course he took now influence the physical event of the birth itself? And yet a nagging voice in the back of his mind told him that indeed it could.

And so it seemed to him that his motive for telling her was chiefly one of guilt, and also because he *needed* to tell someone—needed to tell a friend. The trouble was that he seemed to be leaning on the very one he endangered, which aggravated and magnified the guilt aspect out of all proportion!

It was all very confusing and abstruse, and trying to muddle through it made him more tired than ever, so that when he was done talking he was glad to sit back and let her think it over.

Strangely, she accepted everything he said almost as a matter of course—indeed with visible relief—and at once set about to explain why:

"Harry, I know I'm not as clever as you, but I'm not stupid either. I've known there was something in the air ever since you told me that story of yours—about the necroscope. I sort of sensed that you hadn't finished it, that you wanted to say more but you were scared to. Also, there've been times up in Harden when Mr. Hannant has stopped me and asked after you. The way he talked, I knew he thought there was something strange about you, too . . ."

"Hannant?" he frowned suspiciously. "What did he—?"

"Oh, nothing to be concerned about. In fact I think he's more than a little frightened of you. Harry, I've listened to

381

you talking to your poor dead Ma in your sleep, and I knew you were holding *real* conversations! And there were so many other things. Your writing, for instance. I mean, how come you were suddenly a brilliant author? I've read your stories, Harry, and they're not you. Oh, they're wonderful stories, all right, but *you* just aren't that wonderful! Not the real you. The real you is ordinary, Harry. Oh, I love you—of course I do—but I'm nobody's fool. And your swimming, your skating, your Judo? Did you think I'd believe you were a superman? I promise you it's easier to believe you're a necroscope! It's a relief to know the truth, Harry. I'm glad you've finally told me . . ."

Harry shook his head in open astonishment. Talk about level-headed . . . !

Finally he said: "But I haven't told you everything, love."

"Oh, I know that," she answered. "Of course you haven't! If you're to be working for your country, why obviously there'll be things you need to keep secret—even from me. I understand that, Harry."

It was as if someone had lifted a great weight off his chest. He breathed deeply, lay back again, let his head sink into his pillows. "Brenda, I'm still very tired," he yawned. "Just let me sleep now, there's a love. Tomorrow I'm to go down to London."

"All right, my love," she leaned over him to kiss his forehead. "And don't worry, I won't ask you to tell me a thing about it."

Harry slept right through until evening, then got up and ate a meal. They went out about 8:00 P.M. just to walk for an hour in the crisp night air, until Brenda started to feel the cold. Then they hurried home, took hot showers, and made love, and afterwards both of them slept right through the night.

It was the least Harry had done in any single day in his life.

Later he would have reason to recall it as the most wasteful day in his life.

Sir Keenan Gormley was thoughtful as he left ESP HQ, took the lift down to the tiny lobby and went out into the cold London night. Several things had given him cause for concern just recently, not the least of them being Harry Keogh. For Keogh had not yet contacted him, and with each day that passed Gormley felt the time weighing on him like lumps of lead. It was just after nine o'clock as Gormley walked the streets heading for Westminster tube station, and two hundred and twenty-five miles away Harry Keogh himself was just making love to his wife before settling to a night's sleep.

As for Gormley's other causes of concern: there were two of them. One was the way his second in command kept enquiring after his health, which might seem silly if his second in command weren't Alec Kyle, and if Alec Kyle wasn't a very talented seer, a man whose by no means negligible talent lay in foretelling the future! Kyle's concern for his boss over the last week or ten days had been pretty obvious, no matter how carefully he'd tried to hide it. If there was anything specific, Gormley knew that Kyle would tell him. That was why he hadn't pressed him about it, but it was worrying anyway.

And finally there was the other thing, the big thing. Over the period of that last six or seven weeks there had been at least a dozen different occasions when Gormley had known that there were ESPers about, when he'd "spotted" them in his mind. He had never come face to face with one, had never been able to pin one down, but he'd known they were there anyway. At least two of them.

It had got so he could recognize them almost as easily as

he recognized his own men, but these were not his men. Their auras were strange. And always they watched him from the safety of crowds, in the busy places, never where he could tie a face to a feeling. He wondered how long they would go on watching, and if that was all they would do. And as he reached the underground and went down to the trains he patted the bulge of his 9 mm Browning through his overcoat and jacket. At least that was a comfort. There wasn't an ESPer in the world who could think himself out of the way of a bullet—not that Gormley knew of, anyway . . .

There were only a few people on the platform and fewer in the compartment where Gormley picked up a discarded copy of the *Daily Mail* to keep him company during the journey. He found it mildly alarming that the headlines seemed completely alien to him. Was he really that much out of touch? Yes, he probably was! His work had been putting a lot of strain on him and taking up far too much of his time; this was the third night in a row he'd worked late; he couldn't remember the last time he'd really read a book right through or entertained friends. Maybe Kyle was right to be concerned about him—and on a purely personal level at that—not from the point of view of an ESPer. Maybe it was time he took a break and left his second in command to mind the shop. God only knew he would have to sooner or later. And he made himself a promise that he *would* take a break . . . just as soon as he'd initiated young Harry Keogh into the fold.

Keogh . . .

Gormley had given a lot of thought to Keogh, had considered some of the ways his talent might be put to use. Fantastic ways. All in the mind for now, but fascinating anyway. He would have started to go over them again, but just as it crossed his mind to do so the train pulled into St. James's and Gormley found himself distracted by an incredibly pretty pair of legs in a tiny skirt that passed directly in front of his eyes and out of the twin doors. It was a wonder the lovely creature didn't freeze to death, he thought—and wouldn't *that* be a loss!

Gormley grinned at his own thoughts. His wife, God bless her, was always complaining he had an eye for the girls. Well, his heart might be tricky but the rest of him seemed to be in working order. An eye wouldn't be all he had for that young lady, if he were thirty years younger!

He coughed loudly, returned to his newspaper and tried to get himself reacquainted with the world. A brave effort but he lost interest half-way down the second column. It was pretty mundane stuff, after all, compared with his world. A world of fortune-tellers, telepaths, and now a necroscope.

Harry Keogh again.

There was a game Gormley played with Kyle. It was a word-association game. Sometimes it startled Kyle's future-oriented mind into action, opening a window for him. A window on tomorrow. Normally Kyle's talent worked independent of conscious thought; he usually "dreamed" his predictions; if he consciously tried for results they wouldn't come. But if you could catch him unawares . . .

They had played their game just a few days ago. Gormley had had Keogh on his mind and had wandered into Kyle's office. And seeing the ESPer sitting there he'd smiled and said: "Game?"

Kyle had understood. "Go right ahead."

"It's a name," Gormley had warned, to which Kyle had nodded his head.

"I'm ready," he said, sitting up and putting down whatever he was working on.

Gormley paced a while, then turned quickly and faced the other where he sat at his desk. "Harry Keogh!" he had snapped then.

"Möbius!" answered Kyle at once.

"Maths?" Gormley frowned.

"Space-time!" Now Kyle went white, scared-looking, and Gormley had known they'd got something. He gave it one last shot:

"Necroscope!"

"Necromancer!" the other shot back at once.

"What? Necromancer?" Gormley had repeated. But Kyle was still working.

"Vampire!" he'd shouted then, starting to his feet. Then he was swaying, trembling, shaking his head, saying, "That . . . that's enough, sir. Whatever it was, it . . . it's gone now."

And that had been that . . .

Gormley came back to the present.

He looked up and found they'd passed through Victoria and that the train was almost empty. Already they were mid-way to Sloane Square. And that was when he began to feel a strange depression settling over him.

He felt that there was something wrong but he couldn't just put his finger on it. It might simply be the train's emptiness (which even at this hour was a rare enough occurrence in itself) and that he missed the bustle of life and contact with other human beings, but he didn't think so. Then, as the train pulled into the station he knew what it was: it was his talent working.

The doors sighed open and a middle-aged couple got out, leaving Gormley quite alone, but just before the doors hissed shut again two men got in—and their ESP-aura washed over him like a wave of icy water! Yes, and now he could put faces to feelings.

Dragosani and Batu sat directly opposite their quarry, stared straight at him with cold, expressionless faces. They made a strange pair, he thought, not designed with any degree of compatibility. Not outwardly, anyway. The taller

one leaned forward, his sunken eyes reminding Gormley
yet again of Harry Keogh. Yes, they were like Keogh's
eyes in a way, probably in their colour and intelligence.
And that was especially strange, for set in this face one got
the impression that by rights they should be feral or even
red, and that the intelligence behind them was barely
human at all but that of a beast.

"You know what we are, Sir Keenan," the stranger
said in a voice deep as it was dark, whose Russian accent
he made no attempt to disguise, "if not who we are. And
we know who and what you are. Therefore it would be
childish simply to sit here and pretend that we were ignorant of each other. Don't you agree?"

"Your logic leaves little room for argument," Gormley
nodded, imagining that his blood was already beginning to
cool in his veins.

"Then let us continue to be logical," said Dragosani.
"If we wanted you dead, you would be dead. We have not
lacked the opportunity, as I'm sure you know. And so,
when we leave the train at South Kensington, you will not
attempt to run or make a fuss, or bring unnecessary attention to yourself or to us. If you do, then we will be forced
to kill you and that would be unfortunate, of benefit to no
one. Is this understood and agreed?"

Gormley forced himself to remain calm, raised an eyebrow and said: "You're very sure of yourself, Mr. er—?"

"Dragosani," said the other at once. "Boris Dragosani.
Yes, I am very sure of myself. As is my friend here, Max
Batu."

"—For a stranger in this country, I was about to say,"
Gormley continued. "It seems to me that I'm about to be
kidnapped. But are you sure you know all you need to
know about my habits? Mightn't there be something you've
overlooked? Something your logic hasn't taken into account?" He quickly, nervously took out a cigarette lighter

from his right-hand overcoat pocket and placed it in his lap, patted his pockets as if he searched for a packet of cigarettes, finally started to reach inside his overcoat.

"No!" said Dragosani warningly. As if from nowhere he produced his own weapon and held it before him at arm's length, pointing it directly into Gormley's face, so that the older man looked straight down the rifled barrel of the stubby black silencer. "No, nothing has been over-looked. Max, could you see to that, please?"

Batu got up, eased himself on to the seat next to Gormley, drew the other's hand slowly back into the open and took the Browning from Gormley's trembling fingers. The safety catch was still on. Batu released the magazine and pock-eted it, gave the automatic back to Gormley.

"Nothing at all," Dragosani continued. "Unfortunately, however, that was the last wrong move you'll be allowed to make." He put away his gun, folded his slim fingers into his lap. His posture was unnatural, Gormley decided: very sinuous, almost feline, very nearly female. He didn't know what to make of Dragosani at all.

"Any more heroics," Dragosani continued, "will result in your death—immediately!" And Gormley knew he wasn't bluffing.

Carefully, he pushed the useless automatic back into its holster, said: "What is it you want with me?"

"We want to talk to you," said Dragosani. "I wish to . . . to put some questions to you."

"I've had questions put to me before," Gormley an-swered, forcing a tight smile. "I imagine they'll be very searching questions, eh?"

"Ah!" said Dragosani. Now *he* smiled, and it was ghastly. Gormley felt physically repulsed. The man's mouth gaped like a panting dog's, where elongated teeth gleamed sharply white. "Ah, no. There'll be no bright lights in your eyes, Sir Keenan, if that's what you mean," said

Dragosani. "No drugs. No pincers. No hose to fill your belly with water. Oh, no, nothing like that. But you will tell me everything I want to know, of that I can assure you . . ."

The train was slowing as it pulled into South Kensington. Gormley's heart gave a little lurch in his chest. So close to home, and yet so far. Dragosani had a light overcoat folded over his arm. He showed Gormley the silencer of his weapon, let it peep out of the folds of the overcoat for a moment, and reminded him: "No heroics."

There was a handful of people on the platform: young people mainly, and a pair of down-and-outs with a bottle in a paper bag between them. Even if Gormley looked for help, he couldn't find much here. "Just leave the station by the same route you take every night," said Dragosani at Gormley's shoulder.

Gormley's heart was hammering now. He knew full well that if he went with these men it was all up with him. He was an older hand at this game than the two foreign agents. When Dragosani had told him his and his squat little companion's names, that had been as good as saying: "But it won't do you any good, for you won't be around to tell anyone!" And so he must escape from them—but how?

They left the underground onto Pelham Street, walked down the Brompton Road to Queen's Gate. "I cross here, at the lights," Gormley said. But as they reached the parking lanes straddling the central reservation Dragosani's grip tightened on his arm.

"We have a car here," he said, drawing Gormley to the right and along the line of parked vehicles towards an anonymous-looking Ford. Dragosani had bought the car second-hand (tenth-hand, he suspected) and cash down, no questions asked. It would last only as long as his and Max Batu's visit. Then it would be found burned-out in some suburban lane. But it was then, as they approached the car, that Gormley saw his chance.

Not twenty-five yards away a police patrol car pulled into an empty space and a uniformed constable got out and began checking the doors of the parked cars. A routine check, Gormley guessed. Or more properly, where he was concerned, a miracle!

Dragosani felt the sudden tension in Gormley, sensed his move before he could begin to make it. Batu had just opened the nearside front and rear doors of the Ford, was turning back towards Dragosani and Gormley, when his partner hissed: ''Now, Max!''

Unprepared, still Batu instantly adopted his killing crouch, his moon face undergoing his monstrous metamorphosis. Dragosani maintained his grip on Gormley, looked away at the last moment. Gormley had opened his mouth to yell for help, but all that came out was a croak. He saw Batu's face silhouetted against the night, and one eye which was a yellow slit while the other was round and green and throbbing as if filled with sentient pus! Something passed from that face to Gormley as fast as the thrust of a mental knife; its razor edge located his spirit, his very soul, and opened them up! Except for what little traffic passed in the street, all was quiet, and yet Gormley heard the cacophonic gonging of some great cracked bell from deep inside himself, and knew it was his heart.

With that it should have been finished, but not quite. Thrown backward by the shock of Batu's awful power, Gormley slammed loudly against the wing of a car parked behind the Ford. Along the street the constable's face turned enquiringly in their direction as a second policeman got out of the patrol car. Worse, another vehicle, a blue Porsche, pulled in with a screech of brakes, its headlights dazzling where they picked the three figures out and pinned them against the darkness. In another moment the Porsche seemed to eject a tall young man into the street, his face concerned as he grabbed hold of Gormley to steady him.

"Uncle?" he said, staring into the other's bulging eyes, his blue face. "My God! It must be his heart!" The two policemen were already hurrying to see what was happening.

Dragosani found himself almost paralysed by the changing situation. Everything was going wrong. He made an effort to regain control, whispered to Max Batu: "Get into the car!" Then he turned to the stranger. By now the policemen were on hand, offering assistance.

"What happened here?" one of them asked.

Dragosani thought fast. "We saw him stumble," he said. "I thought maybe he was drunk. Anyway, I went to help, asked if there was anything I could do. He said something about his heart . . .? I was about to take him to a hospital but then this gentleman arrived and—"

"I'm Arthur Banks," said the man in question. "This is Sir Keenan Gormley, my uncle. I was on my way to meet him at the station when I saw him with these two. But look, this isn't the time or place for explanations. He has a bad heart. We have to get him to a hospital. And I mean right now!"

The policemen were galvanized into action. One of them said to Dragosani: "Perhaps you'll give us a ring later, sir? Just so we can get a few more details? Thanks." He helped Banks get his uncle into the Porsche while his driver ran back to the patrol car and got the blue light going. Then, as Banks pulled away from the kerb and swung the Porsche around in a screeching half circle, the constable yelled: "Just follow us, sir. We'll have him under care in two shakes!"

A moment later and he had joined his colleague in the patrol vehicle, by which time the siren was blaring its *dee-dah, dee-dah* warning to traffic. In a sort of numb disbelief Dragosani watched as the two cars moved off in tandem. He watched them out of sight, then slowly, unsteadily got into the Ford and sat there beside Batu trembling with rage. The door was still open. Finally Dragosani grabbed its handle and slammed it shut, slamming it so hard that it almost sprang from its fixings.

"Damn!" he snarled. "Damn the British, Sir Keenan Gormley, his nephew, their bloody oh-so-civilized police—everything!"

"Things are not going well," Max Batu agreed.

"And damn you, too!" said Dragosani. "You and your bloody evil eye! You didn't kill him!"

"Allow me to know my business," Batu quietly answered. "I killed him all right. I felt it. It was like crushing a bug."

Dragosani started the engine, pulled away. "I saw him looking at me, I tell you! He'll talk . . . ."

"No," Batu shook his head. "He won't have strength for talking. He's a dead man, Comrade, take my word for it. At this very moment, a dead man."

And in the Porsche, suddenly Gormley choked out a single word— "Dragosani!" which meant nothing at all to his horrified nephew—and slumped down in his seat with spittle dribbling from the corner of his mouth.

Max Batu was right: he was dead on arrival.

Harry Keogh arrived at Gormley's house in South Kensington at about 3:00 P.M. the following day. Meanwhile Arthur Banks had been a very busy man. It seemed a year but in fact it was only yesterday when he'd driven up from Chichester with his wife, Gormley's daughter, on a flying visit. Then there had been his uncle's heart attack, since when the entire world seemed to have gone stark, staring mad! And horribly so.

First there had been the awful business of phoning his aunt, Jacqueline Gormley, from the hospital and telling her what had happened; then her breakdown when she arrived at the hospital; and her daughter consoling her all through the long night, when she had broken her heart as she wandered to and fro through the house looking for her husband. This morning she'd stayed at the house until they brought Sir Keenan from the hospital morgue. The mortician there had done a pretty good job with him, but still the old man's face had been twisted in a dreadful rictus. Funeral arrangements were swift—that was the way Gormley had always said he would want it: a cremation tomorrow—until when he would lie in state at his home. Jackie couldn't stay there, however, not with him looking like that. Why, it didn't look like him at all! So she had to be taken to her brother's place on the other side of London. That, too, had been Banks' job; and finally he had driven his wife to Waterloo so that she could go back to Chichester to the children. She'd be back for the funeral. Until then he was stuck at the house on his own, or rather in the company of his dead uncle. Aunt Jackie had made him promise he wouldn't leave Sir Keenan on his own, and of course he hadn't refused her that.

But when he got back to the house after putting his wife on the Chichester train—

That had been the worst of all. It had been—mindless! Ghoulish! Unbelievable! And for all that it had been fifteen minutes ago, he was still reeling, still sick, numb to his brain with shock and horror, when Harry Keogh's ring at the doorbell took him staggering to the front door.

"I'm Harry Keogh," said the young man on the doorstep. "Sir Keenan Gormley asked me to come and see—"

"H—*help!*" Banks whispered, choking the word out as if there was no wind in him, as if all the spit had dried up in him. "God, Jesus Christ!—whoever you are—h-help me!"

Harry looked at him in amazement, grabbed him in

order to hold him up. "What is it? What's happened? This is Sir Keenan Gormley's house, isn't it?"

The other nodded. He was slowly turning green, about to throw up—again—at any moment. "C-come in. He's in . . . in there. In the living-room, of all bloody places—but don't go in there. I have to . . . have to call the police. Somebody has to, anyway!" His legs began to buckle and Harry thought he would fall. Before that could happen he pushed him backwards and down into a chair in the lobby. Then he crouched down beside him and shook him.

"Is it Sir Keenan? What's happened to him?"

Even before the answer came, Harry knew.

Soon to die in agony. First and foremost a patriot.

Banks looked up, stared at Harry from a green-tinged face. "Did you . . . did you work for him?"

"I was going to."

Banks bulked, burst to his feet, staggered to a tiny room to one side of the lobby. "He died last night," he managed to gulp the words out. "A heart attack. He was to be cremated tomorrow. But now—" He yanked open the door and the odour of fresh vomit welled out. The room was a toilet and it was obvious that he'd already used it.

Harry turned his face away, grabbed a mouthful of fresh air from the open front door before quietly closing it. Then he left Banks retching and walked through into the living-room—and saw for himself what was wrong with Banks.

And what was wrong with Sir Keenan Gormley.

A heart attack, Banks had said. One look at the room told Harry there'd been an attack, all right, but what sort didn't bear thinking about. He fought down the bile which at once rose up and threatened to swamp him, went back to Banks where he crouched weakly at the bowl of the toilet in the small room. "Call the police when you can," he said. "Sir Keenan's office, too, if anyone's on duty there. I'm sure he would want them to know about . . . this. I'll stay here with you—with him—for a little while."

"Th-thanks," said Banks, without looking up. "I'm sorry I can't be more help right now. But when I came in and found him like that . . ."

"I understand," said Harry.

"I'll be OK in a minute. I'm working on it."

"Of course."

Harry went back to the other room. He saw everything, began to catalogue the horror, then stopped. What stopped him was this: a Queen Anne chair with claw feet lay on its side on the floor. One of its wooden legs was broken off just below the platform of the seat. Embedded in the club-like foot was a tooth; other teeth, wrenched out, lay scattered on the floor; the mouth of the corpse had been forced open and now gaped like a black shaft in the wildly distorted, frozen grimace of the face!

Harry gropingly found himself a seat—another chair, but one free of *debris*—and collapsed into it. He closed his eyes, pictured the room as it must have looked before this. Sir Keenan in his coffin on an oak table draped in black, rose-scented candles burning at head and feet. And then, as he lay here alone, the . . . intrusion.

But why?

"Why, Keenan?" he asked.

"Noooo! No, keep off!" came the answer at once, causing Harry to rock back in his chair with its force, its fear, its freezing terror. "Dragosani, you monster! No more—for God's sake have pity, man!"

"Dragosani?" Harry reached out soothing mental fingers. "This isn't Dragosani, Keenan. It's me, Harry Keogh."

"What?" the single word was a gasp in his mind. "Keogh? Harry?" Then a sigh, a sob of relief. *"Thank God!* Thank God it's you, Harry, and not . . . not him!"

"Was this Dragosani?" Harry gritted his teeth. "But why? Is he insane? He would have to be totally—"

"No," Gormley's vigorous denial cut him off. "Oh, he is crazy, of course he is—but crazy like a fox! And his talent is . . . hideous!"

Suddenly the answer—or what he thought was the answer—came to Keogh in a flash. He felt the blood draining from him. "He came to you after you died!" he gasped. "He's like me, a necroscope."

"No, absolutely not!" again Gormley's denial. "Not like you at all, Harry. I'm talking to you because I want to. All of . . . of us, talk to you. You're the bringer of warmth, of peace. You're contact with the dream that went before and which now has faded. You're a chance—the one last chance—that something worthwhile might linger over, might even be passed on. A light in the darkness, Harry, that's what you are. But Dragosani—"

"What is his talent?"

"He's a necromancer—and that's a different thing entirely!"

Harry opened his eyes a crack and glanced once more at the state of the room. But as the horror welled up again he closed his eyes and said: "But this it the work of a ghoul!"

"That and worse," Gormley shuddered, and Harry felt it—felt the dead man's shudder of absolute terror shaking his spirit. "He . . . he doesn't just *talk*, Harry, he doesn't ask. Doesn't even try. He just reaches in and takes, steals. You can't hide anything from him. He finds his answers in your blood, your guts, in the marrow of your very bones. The dead can't feel pain, Harry, or they shouldn't. But that's part of his talent, too. When Boris Dragosani works, he makes us feel it. I *felt* his knives, his hands, his tearing nails. I knew everything he did, and all of it was hell! After one minute I would have told him everything, but that's not his way, it's not his art. How could he be sure I told the truth? But his way he *knows* it's the truth! It's written in skin and muscle, in ligaments and tendons and corpuscles. He can read it in brain fluid, in the mucus of the eye and ear, in the texture of the dead tissue itself!''

Harry kept his eyes closed, shook his head, felt sick and dizzy and totally disoriented, as if this were all happening to someone else. At last he said: "This can't—mustn't happen again. He has to be stopped. I have to stop him. But I can't do it alone.''

"Oh, yes, he *has* to be stopped, Harry. Especially now. You see, he took everything. He knows it all. He knows our strengths, our weaknesses, and all of it is knowledge he can use. Him and his master, Gregor Borowitz. And you may well be the only one who can stop him.''

With another part of his awareness, Harry heard Banks on the telephone in the lobby. Time was now short, and there was so much Gormley must tell him. "Listen, Keenan. We have to hurry now. I'll stay with you a little while longer, and then I'll find a hotel in the city. But if I stay here now the police will want to talk to me. Anyway, I'll find a place and from now until—'' he realized what he had almost said and bit the words off unspoken, but not unvisioned.

"—Until I'm cremated, yes," said Gormley, and Harry could picture him nodding understandingly. "It was to have been soon, but now it will probably be delayed.''

"I'll stay in touch," Harry said. "There's still a lot I don't know. About our organization, theirs, how to go about tracking them down. Many things.''

"Do you know about Batu?" again Gormley's fear was apparent. "The little Mongol, Harry—do you know about him?''

"I know he's one of them, but—''

"He has the evil eye—he can kill with a glance! My

397

heart attack—he brought it on. He killed me, Harry, Max Batu. That face of his, that evil eye, it generates mental poison! His power bites like acid, melts the brain, the heart. He killed me . . .''

"Then he's another I have to settle with," Harry answered, cold determination stiffening his resolve.

"But be careful, Harry."

"I will."

"I think the answers are in you, my boy, and God only knows how much I pray you can find them. Just let me give you this warning: when Dragosani was . . . with me, I sensed something else in him. It wasn't just his necromancy. Harry, there's an evil in that man that's older than time! With him loose in the world nothing, no one is safe. Not even the people who think they control him."

Harry nodded. "I'll be watching out for him," he said. "And I'll find the answers, Keenan, all of them. With your help. For as long as you can give me that help, anyway."

"I've thought about that, Harry," said the other. "And you know, I don't think it'll be the end. I mean, this isn't me. What you see here used to be me, it *was* me—but so was a baby born in South Africa, and so was a young man who joined the British Army when he was seventeen, and so was the head of E-Branch for thirteen years. They've all gone now, and after my funeral pyre this part will also be gone. But *me*, I'll still be here. Somewhere."

"I hope so," said Harry, opening his eyes and standing up, and avoiding looking at the room.

"Find yourself a hotel, then," said Gormley, "and get back to me when you can. The sooner we get started the better. And afterwards—I mean when all of this is over and done, if it ever is—"

"Yes?"

"Well, it would be nice if you could look me up some

time. You see, unless I'm mistaken, you're the only one who'll ever be able to. And you know you'll always be welcome.''

An hour later Harry locked himself in his cheap hotel room and got in touch with Gormley again. As always, having already been in contact with him, it came very easy. The ex-boss of E-Branch was waiting for him, had been considering what to tell him and gave the information in order of priority. They started with E-Branch itself—a deeper view of the branch and the people who worked in it—and went on to the reasons why at this stage Harry should not approach Gormley's second in command or in any way attempt entry into the organization.

"It would be too time-consuming," Gormley explained. "Oh, there would be benefits, of course. For one thing you'd be funded—any necessary expenses would be covered—but at the same time they'd want to give you a good close going-over. And naturally they'd be eager to test your talent. Especially now that I'm gone, and when it come out what someone has done to my corpse . . ."

"You think I'd be suspect?"

"What, a necroscope? Of course you'd be suspect! I do have a file on you, true, but it's pretty sketchy and obviously incomplete—and actually I'm the only one who could have vouched for you! So you see, by the time our side had cleared you the other side would have raced ahead. Time is of the essence, Harry, and not to be wasted. So what I propose is this: you won't attempt to join E-Branch right now but work on your own. After all, the only ones who know anything at all about you at this time are Dragosani and Batu. The trouble with that, of course, is that Dragosani knows *everything* about you, for he stole it directly from me! What we must ask ourselves is this: why did Borowitz send these two here? Why now?

What's brewing? Or is he just stretching his tentacles a bit? Oh, he's had agents here before, certainly, but they were only intelligence gatherers. They were enemy, and they sought information—but they weren't killers! So what has happened that Borowitz has decided to turn a cold ESP war into a hot one?''

Harry told him about Shukshin, gave him a brief overview of things as he saw and understood them.

Gormley's thoughts were wry indeed when he answered: "So you've been working for us for some time, it appears! What a pity I didn't know all of this that time I came to see you. We could have done the job that much more quickly. Shukshin might have been important to you, Harry, but in reality he was very small fry. We might even have been able to use him.''

"I wanted him for myself," said Harry viciously. "I wanted him used up! Anyway, I didn't know there was any connection. I only found that out after I killed him. But that's done with and now we have to get on. So . . . you want me to work on my own. But there's the rub: see, I don't have the foggiest idea of how to be an agent! I know what I want to do: I have to kill Dragosani, Batu, Borowitz. That is my priority—but I can't even begin to *think* how to go about it.''

Gormley seemed to understand his problem. "That's the difference between espionage and ESPionage, Harry. We all understand the first. All the cloak-and-daggery, the thud-and-blundering, the DTB—or Dirty Tricks Brigade—it's all old hat. But none of us really knows a lot about the second. You do what your talent tells you to do. You find the best possible ways to use it. That's all any of us can do. For some of us it's easy: we don't have sufficient talent to worry about, we can't expand it. Myself, for example. I can spot another ESPer a mile away; but that's it, end of story. In your case, however—''

Harry began to grow frustrated. His task seemed huge, impossible. He was one man, one mind, one barely mature talent. What *could* he do?

Gormley picked him up on that: "You weren't listening, Harry. I said you have to find the best way to use your talent. Until now you haven't been doing that. Let's face it, what have you achieved?"

"I've talked to the dead!" Harry snapped. "That's it, it's what I do. I'm a necroscope."

Gormley was patient. "You've scratched the surface, Harry, that's all. Look, you've written the stories a dead man couldn't finish. You've used formulae that a mathematician never had time to develop in life. Dead men have taught you how to drive, how to speak Russian and German. They've improved your swimming and your fighting and one or two other things. But what do you personally reckon all of this amounts to?"

"Nothing!" Harry answered, after only a moment's thought.

"Right, nothing. Because you've been talking to the wrong people. You've been letting your talent guide you, instead of you guiding your talent. Now I know these are probably bad examples, but you're like a hypnotist who can only hypnotize himself, or a clairvoyant who forecasts his own death—for tomorrow! You have a ground-breaking talent, but you're not breaking any ground. The problem is that you're entirely self-taught. So in a way you're ignorant: like a heathen at a banquet, stuffing yourself full of everything and savouring none of it. And not recognizing the good stuff because of the way it's dressed up. But if I'm right you had the answer at your fingertips way back when you were a kid. Except your kid's mind failed to see the possibilities. But you're a man now and the possibilities should be starting to make themselves obvious. Not obvious to me but to you! After all, it's your talent. You have to learn how best to use it, that's all . . ."

What Gormley said made sense and Harry knew it. "But where do I start?" He was desperate.

"I have what might be just a clue for you," Gormley was careful not to be too optimistic. "The result of an ESP game I used to play with Alec Kyle, my second in command. I didn't mention it before because there might not be anything in it, but if we have to have a starting point—"

"Go on," said Harry.

And with his mind, Gormley drew him this mental picture:

"What the hell's that?" Harry was nonplussed.

"It's a Möbius strip," said Gormley. "Named after its inventor, August Ferdinand Möbius, a German mathematician. Just take a thin strip of paper, give it a half-twist and join up the ends. It reduces a two-dimensional surface to only one. It has many implications, I'm told, but I wouldn't know for I'm not a mathematician."

Harry was still baffled, not by the principle but by its application. "And this is supposed to have something to do with me?"

"With your future—your immediate future—possibly," Gormley was deliberately vague. "I told you there mightn't be anything in it. Anyway, let me tell you what happened." He told Harry about his and Kyle's word-association game. "So I started with your name, Harry Keogh, and Kyle came back with 'Möbius.' I said, 'Maths?'—and he answered, 'Space-time'!"

"Space-time?" Harry was at once interested. "Now that might well fit in with this Möbius strip thing. It seems to me that the strip is only a diagram of warped space, and space and time are inextricably linked."

"Oh?" said Gormley, and Harry pictured his surprised expression. "And is that an original thought, Harry, or do you have . . . outside help?"

This gave Harry an idea. "Wait," he said, "I don't know your Möbius, but I do know someone else." He got in touch with James Gordon Hannant in the cemetery in Harden, showed him the strip.

"Sorry, can't help you, Harry," said Hannant, his thoughts clipped and precise as ever. "I've gone in an entirely different direction. I was never into curves anyway. By that I mean that *my* maths was—is—all very practical. Different but practical. But of course you know that. If it can be done on paper, I can probably do it; I'm more visual, if you like, than Möbius. A lot of his stuff was in the mind, abstract, theoretical. Now if only he and Einstein could have got together, then we really might have seen something!"

"But I have to know about this!" Harry was desperate. "Can't you suggest anything?"

Hannant sensed Harry's urgency, raised a mental eyebrow. In that emotionless, calculating fashion of his, he said: "But isn't the answer obvious, Harry? Why don't you ask him, Möbius himself? After all, you're the only one who can . . ."

Suddenly excited, Harry crossed back to Gormley. "Well," he told him, "at least I have a place to start now. What else came out of this game of yours with Alec Kyle?"

"After he came up with 'Space-time' I tried him with 'necroscope,' " said Gormley. "He immediately came back with 'necromancer.' "

Harry was silent for a moment, then said: "So it looks like he was reading your future as well as mine . . ."

"I suppose so," Gormley answered. "But then he said something that's got me stumped even now. I mean—even assuming that all we've just mentioned is somehow connected—what on earth am I supposed to make of 'vampire,' eh?"

Cold fingers crept up Harry's spine. What indeed? Finally he said:

"Keenan, can we stop there? I'll get back to you as soon as possible, but right now there are one or two things I have to do. I want to give my wife a call, find a reference library, check some things out. And I want to go and see Möbius, so I'll probably be booking a flight to Germany. Also, I'm hungry! And . . . I want to think about things. Alone, I mean."

"I understand, Harry, and I'll be ready when you want to start again. But by all means see to your own needs first. Let's face it, they have to be greater than mine. So go ahead, son. You see to the living. The dead have plenty of time."

"Also," Harry told him, "there's someone else I want to speak to—but that's my secret for now."

Gormley was suddenly worried for him. "Don't do anything rash, Harry. I mean—"

"You said I should go it alone, do it my way," Harry reminded him.

He sensed Gormley's nod of acquiescence. "That's right, son. Let's just hope you do it right, that's all."

Which was one sentiment Harry could only agree with.

Late that same evening, at the Russian Embassy Dragosani

and Batu had finished their packing and were looking forward to their morning flight out. Dragosani had not yet started to commit his knowledge to paper; this was the last place for that sort of undertaking. One might as well write a letter direct to Yuri Andropov himself!

The two Russian agents had rooms with a linking door and only one telephone, which was situated in Batu's apartment. The necromancer had just stretched himself out on his bed, lost in his own strange, dark thoughts, when he heard the phone ring in Batu's room. A moment later and the squat little Mongol knocked on the joining door. "It's for you," his muffled voice came through the stained, dingy oak panels. "The switchboard. Something about a call from outside."

Dragosani got up, went through into Batu's room. Sitting on the bed, Batu grinned at him. "Ho, Comrade! And do you have friends here in London? Someone seems to know you."

Dragosani scowled at him, snatched up the telephone. "Switchboard? This is Dragosani. What's all this about?"

"A call for you from outside, Comrade," came the answer in a cold, nasal, female voice.

"I doubt it. You've made a mistake. I'm not known here."

"He says you'll want to speak to him," said the operator. "His name is Harry Keogh."

"Keogh?" Dragosani looked at Batu, raised an eyebrow. "Ah, yes! Yes, I do know of him. Put him through."

"Very well. Remember, Comrade: speech is insecure." There came a click and a buzzing, then:

"Dragosani, is that you?" The voice was young but strangely hard. It didn't quite fit the gaunt, almost vacant face that Dragosani had seen staring at him from the frozen river bank in Scotland.

"This is Dragosani, yes. What do you want, Harry Keogh?"

"I want you, necromancer," said the cold, hard voice. "I want you, and I'm going to get you."

Dragosani's lips drew back from his needle teeth in a silent snarl. This one was clever, daring, brash—dangerous! "I don't know who you are," he hissed, "but you're obviously a madman! Explain yourself or get off the phone."

"The explanation's simple, 'Comrade,' " the voice had grown harder still. "I know what you did to Sir Keenan Gormley. He was my friend. An eye for an eye, Dragosani, and a tooth for a tooth. That's my way, as you've already seen. You're a dead man."

"Oh?" Dragosani laughed sardonically. "I'm a dead man, am I? And you, too, have ways with the dead, don't you, Harry?"

"What you saw at Shukshin's was nothing, 'Comrade,' " said the icy voice. "You don't know all of it. Not even Gormley knew all of it."

"Bluff, Harry!" said Dragosani. "I've seen what you can do and it doesn't frighten me. Death is my friend. He tells me everything."

"That's good," said the voice, "for you'll be speaking to him again soon—but face to face. So you know what I can do, do you? Well think about this: next time I'll be doing it to you!"

"A challenge, Harry?" Dragosani's voice was dangerously low, full of menace.

"A challenge," the other agreed, "and the winner takes all."

Dragosani's Wallach blood was up; he was eager now: "But where? I'm already beyond your reach. And tomorrow there'll be half a world between."

"Oh, I know you're running now," said the other contemptuously. "But I'll find you, and soon. You, and Batu, and Borowitz . . ."

Again Dragosani's lips drew back in a hiss. "Perhaps we should meet, Harry—but where, how?"

"You'll know when it's time," said the voice. "And know this, too: it will be worse for you than it was for Gormley."

Suddenly the ice in Keogh's voice seemed to fill Dragosani's veins. He shook himself, pulled himself together, said: "Very well, Harry Keogh. Whenever and wherever, I'll be waiting for you."

"And the winner takes all," said the voice a second time. There came a faint click and the dead line began its intermittent, staccato purring.

For long moments Dragosani stared at the receiver in his hand, then hurled it down into its cradle. "Oh, I surely *will!*" he rasped then. "Be sure I'll take everything, Harry Keogh!"

Chapter Fourteen

BACK AT THE CHÂTEAU BRONNITSY IN THE MIDDLE OF THE following afternoon, Dragosani found Borowitz absent. His secretary told him that Natasha Borowitz had died just two days ago; Gregor Borowitz was in mourning at their dacha, keeping her company for a day or two; he did not wish to be disturbed. Dragosani phoned him anyway.

"Ah, Boris," the old man's voice was soft for once, empty. "So you're back."

"Gregor, I'm sorry," said Dragosani, observing a ritual he didn't really understand. "But I thought you'd like to know I got what you wanted. More than you wanted. Shukshin is dead. Gormley too. And I know everything."

"Good," said the other without emotion. "But don't talk to me now of death, Boris. Not now. I shall be here for another week. After that . . . it will be a while before I'm up to much. I loved this argumentative, tough old bitch. She had a tumour, they say, in her head. Suddenly it grew too big. Very peaceful at the end. I miss her a lot. She never knew what a secret was! That was nice.''

"I'm sorry," Dragosani said again.

At that Borowitz seemed to snap out of it. "So take a break," he said. "Get it all down on paper. Report to me in a week, ten days. And well done.''

Dragosani's hand tightened on the telephone. "A break would be very welcome," he said. "I may use it to look up an old friend of mine. Gregor, can I take Max Batu with me? He, too, has done his work well.''

"Yes, yes—only don't bother me any more now. Good-bye, Dragosani.''

And that was that.

Dragosani didn't like Batu, but he did have plans for him. Anyway, the man made a decent travelling companion: he said very little, kept himself more or less to himself, and his needs were few. He did have a passion for slivovitz, but that didn't present a problem. The little Mongol could drink the stuff until it came out of his ears, and still he would appear sober. Appearance was all that mattered.

It was the middle of the Russian winter and so they went by train, a much interrupted journey which didn't see them into Galatz until a day and a half later. There Dragosani hired a car with snow chains, which gave him back something of the independence he so relished. Eventually, on the evening of that second day, in the rooms which Dragosani found for them in a tiny village near Valeni, finally the necromancer grew bored with Batu's silence and asked him: "Max, don't you wonder what we're doing here? Aren't you interested to find out why I brought you along?''

"No, not really," answered the moon-faced Mongol. "I'll find out when you're ready, I suppose. Actually, it makes no difference. I think I quite like travelling. Perhaps the Comrade General will find more work for me in strange parts.''

Dragosani thought: *No, Max, there'll be no more work for you—except through me*. But out loud he said only, "Perhaps.''

Night had fallen by the time they had eaten, and that was when Dragosani gave Batu the first hint of what was to come. "It's a fine night tonight, Max,'' he said. "Bright starlight and not a cloud in sight. That's good, for we're going for a drive. There's someone I want to talk to.''

On their way to the cruciform hills they passed a field where sheep huddled together in a corner where straw had been put out for them. There was a thin layer of snow but the temperature was at a reasonable level. Dragosani stopped the car. "My friend will be thirsty,'' he explained, "but he's not much on slivovitz. Still, I think it's only fair we should take him something to drink.''

They got out of the car and Dragosani went into the field, scattering the sheep. "That one, Max,'' he said, as one of the animals strayed close to the Mongol where he leaned on the fence. "Don't kill it. Merely stun it, if you can.''

Max could. He crouched, his face contorting where he directed his gaze through the bars of the fence. Dragosani averted his face as the sheep, a fine ewe, gave a shrill cry of terror. He looked back in time to see the animal bound as if shot, and collapse in a shuddering heap of dense wool.

Together they bundled the animal into the boot and went on their way. After a little while Batu said: "Your friend must have the strangest appetite, Comrade.''

"He does, Max, he does.'' And then Dragosani told the other something of what he could expect.

Batu thought about it for some minutes before he spoke

again. "Comrade Dragosani, I know you are a strange man—indeed we are both strange men—but now I am tempted to believe you must be mad!"

Dragosani bayed like a hound, finally brought his booming laughter under control. "You mean you don't believe in vampires, Max?"

"Oh, indeed I do!" said the other. "If you say so. I don't mean that you're mad to believe—but you are certainly mad to want to dig the thing up!"

"We shall see what we shall see," Dragosani growled, more soberly now. "There's just one thing, Max. Whatever you hear or see—no matter what may happen—you are not to interfere. I don't want him to know you're even here. Not yet, anyway. Do you understand what I'm saying? You're to stay out of it. You're to be so still and quiet that even I forget you're there!"

"As you will," the other shrugged. "But you say he reads your mind? Perhaps he already knows I'm with you."

"No," said Dragosani, "for I can sense when he's trying to get at me and I know how to shut him out. Anyway, he'll be very weak by now and not up to fighting with me, not even mentally. No, Thibor Ferenczy has no idea that I'm here, Max, and he'll be so delighted when I speak to him that he won't think to look for treachery."

"If you say so," and Batu shrugged again.

"Now," said Dragosani, "you have said I must be mad. Far from it, Max. But you see this vampire has secrets that only the undead know. They are secrets I want. And one way or the other I intend to get them. Especially now that there's this Harry Keogh to deal with. So far Thibor has frustrated me, but not this time. And if I have to raise him up to get at these secrets . . . then so be it!"

"And do you know how?—to raise him up, I mean?"

"Not yet, no. But he'll tell me, Max. Be sure of that . . ."

They were there. Dragosani parked the car off the road under the cover of overhanging trees, and in the cold bright light of the stars they trudged slowly up the overgrown fire break together, sharing the burden of the twitching sheep between them.

Approaching the secret glade, Dragosani took the animal on his shoulder and whispered: "Now, Max, you're to stay here. You may follow a little closer if you wish, and watch by all means—but remember, keep out of it!"

The other nodded, came a few paces closer, huddled down and wrapped his overcoat tightly about himself. And alone Dragosani went on under the trees and up to the tomb of the Thing in the ground.

He paused at the rim of the circle, but farther out than when last he'd visited. "How now, old dragon?" he softly said, letting the trembling, half-dead ewe thump to the hard ground at his feet. "How now, Thibor Ferenczy, you who have made a vampire of me!" He spoke softly so that Max Batu could not hear, for as always he found it easier to speak out loud than merely think his conversation at the vampire.

Ahhhh! came the mental hiss, drawn out and sighing, like the waking breath of one roused from deepest dreams. *And is it you, Dragosani? Ho!—and so you've guessed, have you?*

"It didn't take much guesswork, Thibor. It has been only a matter of months, but I'm a changed man. Indeed, not entirely a man."

But no rage, Dragosani? No fury? Why, it seems to me that this time you come almost humbly! Why is that? I wonder.

"Oh, you know why, old dragon. I want rid of this thing."

Ah, no (a mental shake of some monstrous head), *unfortunately not. That is quite impossible. You and he are one now, Dragosani. And did I not call you my son, right from the very beginning? It is only fitting, I think, that my real son now grows within you.* And he laughed in Dragosani's mind.

Dragosani couldn't afford the luxury of anger. Not yet. "Son?" he pressed. "This thing you put in me? Son? Another lie, old devil? Who was it told me that your sort have no sex?"

I think you never listen, Dragosani, the vampire sighed. *You, his host, have determined his sex! As he grows and becomes more properly part of you, so you become more like him. In the end it is one creature, one being.*

"But with his mind?"

With your mind—but subtly altered. Your mind and your body too, but both changed a little. Your appetites will be . . . sharper? Your needs . . . different. Listen: as a man your lusts, passions and rages were limited by a man's strength, a man's capabilities. But as one of the Wamphyri . . . What end would it serve to have that great engine in you with nothing to drive but a bundle of soft flesh and brittle bones? What—a tiger with the heart of a mouse?

Which was more or less what Dragosani had expected from the monster. But before coming to a final, perhaps irrevocable decision, he tried one last time, made one last threat. "Then I shall go away and give myself into the hands of physicians. They're a different breed to the doctors you knew in your day, Thibor. And I shall tell them a vampire is in me. They'll examine, discover, cut the thing out. They have tools you wouldn't dream of. When they have it they'll cut it open, study it, discover its nature. And they'll want to know how and why. I shall tell them. About the Wamphyri. Oh, they'll laugh, measure me up for a strait-jacket—but they won't be able to explain it

413

away. And so I shall bring them here, show them you. It will be the end. Of you, of your 'son,' of an entire legend. And wherever the Wamphyri are, men will seek them out and destroy them . . .''

Well said, Dragosani! Thibor was drily sardonic. *Bravo!*

Dragosani waited, and after a moment: "Is that all you have to say?"

It is. I don't converse with fools.

"Explain yourself."

Now the voice in his mind grew extremely cold and angry, a controlled anger now, but real and frightening for all that. *You are a vain and egotistical and stupid man, Boris Dragosani,* said Thibor Ferenczy. *Always it is "tell me this" and "show me that" and "explain"! I was a power in the land for centuries before you were even spawned, and even that would not have happened but for me! And here I must lie and let myself be used. Well, all that is at an end. Very well, I will "explain myself" as you demand, but for the very last time. For after that . . . then it will be time for proper discussion and proper bargaining. I'm tired of lying here, inert, Dragosani, as you well know, and you have the power to get me up out of here. That is the only reason I've been patient with you at all! But now my patience is no more. First let us deal with your assessment of your situation.*

You say that you will give yourself into the hands of physicians. Well, by now certainly the vampire will be discernible in you. It is there, physically and tangibly, a real organism existing with you in a sort of symbiosis—a word you taught me, Dragosani. But cut it out? Exorcize it? Skilled your doctors may well be, but not that skilled! Can they cut it from the individual whorls of your brain? From the fluids of your spine? From your tripes, your heart itself? Can they wrest it from your very blood? Even if you were fool enough to let them try, the vampire would

414

kill you first. It would eat through your spine, leak poison into your brain. Surely by now you have come to understand something of our tenacity? Or did you perhaps think that survival was a purely human trait? Survival—hah! —you do not know the meaning of the word!

Dragosani was silent.

We made promises, you and I, the Thing in the ground finally continued. I have kept my part of the bargain. Now then, what of yours? Is it not time I was paid, Dragosani?

"Bargain?" Dragosani was taken aback. "Are you joking? What bargain?"

Have you forgotten? You wanted the secrets of the Wamphyri. Very well, they are yours. For now you are Wamphyri! As he grows within you, so the knowledge will come. He has arts which you will learn together.

"What?" Dragosani was outraged. "My impregnation by a vampire, with a vampire, was your part of the bargain? What the hell was that for a bargain? I wanted knowledge, wanted it now, Thibor! For myself—not as the black, rotten fruit of some unnatural, unwanted liaison with a damned parasite thing!"

You dare spurn my egg? For each Wamphyri life there is but one spawning, one new life to move on down through the centuries. And I gave mine to you . . .

"Don't act the proud father with me, Thibor Ferenczy!" Dragosani raged. "Don't even try and make out I've hurt your pride. I want rid of this bastard thing in me. Do you tell me you care for it? But I know you vampires hate one another even worse than men hate you!"

The Thing in the ground knew that Dragosani had seen through him. Proper discussion, proper bargaining, he said, coldly.

"The hell with bargaining—I want rid of it!" Dragosani snarled. "Tell me how . . . and then I'll raise you up."

For long moments there was silence. Then—

You cannot do it. Your doctors cannot do it. Only I can abort what I put there.

"Then do it."

What? While I lie here, in the ground? Impossible! Raise me up . . . and it shall be done.

Now it was Dragosani's turn to ponder the vampire's proposition—or at least to pretend to ponder it. And finally: "Very well. How do I go about it?"

Thibor was eager now: *First, do you do this of your own free will?*

"You know I do not!" Dragosani was scornful. "I do it to be free of the hag in me."

But of your own free will? Thibor insisted.

"Yes, damn you!"

Good. First there are chains here, in the earth. They were used to bind me but have long since worked loose of wasted tissues. You see, Dragosani, there are chemical ingredients which the Wamphyri find intolerable. Silver and iron in the correct proportions paralyse us. Even though much of the iron has rusted away, its essence remains in the ground. And the silver is here, too. First, then, you must dig out these silver chains.

"But I haven't the tools!"

You have your hands.

"You wish me to grub in the dirt with my hands? How deep?"

Not deep at all but shallow. Through all the long centuries I've worked these silver chains to the surface, hoping someone would find them and take them for treasure. Is silver precious still, Dragosani?

"More than ever."

Then take it with my blessing. Come, dig.

"But—" (Dragosani did not want to appear to be stalling, but on the other hand there were certain arrangements still to be made.) "—how long will it take? The entire process, I mean? And what does it involve?"

We start it tonight, said the vampire, *and tomorrow we finish it.*

"I can't actually bring you up out of the ground until tomorrow?" Dragosani tried not to show too much relief.

Not until then, no. I am too weak, Dragosani. But I note you've brought me a gift. That is very good. I shall derive a little strength from your offering . . . and after you have taken away the chains—

"Very well," said the necromancer. "Where do I dig?"

Come closer, my son. Come to the very centre of this place. There—there! Now you can dig . . .

The flesh crept on Dragosani's back as he got down on hands and knees and tore at the dirt and leaf-mould with his fingers. Cold sweat started to his brow—but not from his effort—as he remembered the last time he was here, and what had happened then. The vampire sensed his apprehension and chuckled darkly in his mind:

Oh, and do you fear me, Dragosani? For all your bluff and bluster? What? A brave young blood like you, and old Thibor Ferenczy just a poor undead Thing in the ground? Bah! Shame on you, my son!

Dragosani had scraped most of the surface soil and debris to one side and was now five or six inches deep. He had reached the harder, more solidly frozen earth of the grave itself. But as he drove his fingers yet again into that strangely fertile soil, so they contacted something hard, something that clinked dully. He worked harder then, and the first links he uncovered were of solid silver—and massive! The links were at least two inches long and forged of silver rods at least half an inch thick!

"How . . . how much of this stuff is there?" he gasped.

Enough to keep me down, Dragosani, came the answer. *Until now.*

The vampire's words, simple and spontaneous as they were, nevertheless contained a menacing something which set the short hairs at the back of Dragosani's neck standing erect in a moment. Thibor's mental voice had bubbled like boiling glue, filled with all the evil of the pit itself. Dragosani was a necromancer—he knew himself for a monster—but next to the old devil in the ground he felt innocent as a babe!

He caught hold of a great rope of silver links, stood up, used a strength which astonished even him to rip up the chains from the earth. They came up, cracking open the ground, erupting in scabs of clotted soil and crusts of dusty, smoking leaf-mould; even shaking the roots of the trees which had grown up through all the long years to cover this place and keep it secret. And dragging the treasure in three trips to the outer rim of the circle of roots and shattered flags and torn earth, Dragosani calculated that there must be at least five or six hundred pounds of the stuff! In the Western World he would be a rich man. But in Moscow . . . to even try to profit from it would be worth ten years in the Siberian salt mines at least. No such thing as treasure trove in the USSR—only theft!

On the other hand, what good was treasure to him? No good at all, except as a means to an end. He couldn't enjoy the fruits of his labours like other men. But one day soon he would be able to enjoy, when other men—*all* other men—crawled to his feet, and world leaders came to do obeisance in the courts of the Great Wallachian Hyper-State. These were thoughts Dragosani kept hidden as he hauled the last of the chains aside and stood panting, staring in darkness at the scarred, riven earth of this secret place.

And he gave a wry snort of self-derision as he remembered a time when it would have been hard to see anything at all in this dark place, even with his cat's eyes. But now:

why, it was like daylight! Yet another proof that a vampire
lived in him, battening on his body as it would one day
attempt to batten on his mind. And as for Thibor's promise
to abort the thing: Dragosani knew that wasn't worth a
handful of tomb-dirt! Well, if he must live with the leech
so be it; but *he* would be master and not the beast within.
Somehow, somewhere, he would find a way.

And these thoughts, too, he kept to himself . . .

At last he was done and the silver chains lay in a great
circle all about the torn-up area. "There," he told the
Thing in the ground. "All finished. Nothing to keep you
down now, Thibor Ferenczy."

*You've done well, Dragosani. I'm well pleased. But
now I must feed and then I must rest. It is no easy thing to
return from the grave. So now your offering, if you please,
which I trust you'll leave me in peace to enjoy. I shall
require the same again tomorrow night, before I can stand
with you under the stars. Then, and only then, will you too
be free . . .*

Dragosani kicked the ewe which at once started to life.
He trapped the shivering animal between his legs as it
lurched to its feet, yanked back its head. The glittering
blade he wielded passed through the front part of its neck
effortlessly, coming away clean before the first spurt of
blood gushed out on to the dark, unhallowed ground. Then
he picked the shuddering animal up—as a man might pick
up a cat, by scruff of neck and rump—and spun with it,
tossing it centrally into the circle. It thudded down, and
again came to its feet—and only then seemed to realize
that it was hurt and that this was the end. Awash in blood
the beast fell on its side, kicking spastically in its own reek
as the rest of its life pumped out of it.

Dragosani stepped back then, and farther yet, and in his
mind he heard the vampire's great deep sigh of pleasure,
of monstrous craving.

*Ahhhh! Not greatly to my taste, Dragosani, but satisfy-
ing beyond a doubt. I owe you thanks, my son, but they
can wait until tomorrow. Now begone, for I'm tired and
hungry, and loneliness is a drug whose addiction I've not
yet broken . . .*

Dragosani needed no second bidding. He backed away
from the broken tomb, from the twitching, huddled shape
at the centre of the circle. But even as he went his eyes
were on the alert for some sign of the vampire's new
freedom, its mobility. Oh, yes!— for Thibor Ferenczy was
mobile now—the necromancer could feel him underfoot,
could sense him stretching himself, could almost hear the
creak of leathery muscles and the groan of old bones as
they soaked in blood and something of their brittleness
went out of them.

Then—

The ewe's carcass sagged, slumped lower, closer to the
blood-soaked earth. It was as if some seismic suction had
pulled at the animal, as if the earth itself were a mouth
that sucked. Something moved beneath the slaughtered
beast, but Dragosani could make out nothing for certain.
He backed away, backed up against a tree and quickly
groped his way around it, putting the rough bole between
himself and what was happening. But still he kept his eyes
riveted on the ewe's carcass.

The animal was large and heavy with wool, but even as
Dragosani watched so it seemed its bulk shrank down a
little, caved in upon itself—diminished! The necromancer
sent out a mental probe towards the Thing in the ground,
but such was the lusting bestiality it was met with that he
at once withdrew it. And still the ewe continued to shrink,
shrivel, dwindle away.

And as the ewe was devoured, so the cold ground about
began to smoke, a stinking mist rising and rapidly thickening, obscuring the rest of the act. It was as if the earth

sweated—or as if something down there breathed, which had not breathed for a long, long time.

That was enough. Dragosani turned away and quickly joined Max Batu. With a finger to his lips he beckoned the other to follow, and quickly they descended the fire-break together and made their way back to the car.

Earlier that same day and some seven hundred miles away, Harry Keogh decided, standing at the grave of August Ferdinand Möbius, (born 1790, died 26th September 1868) that it had been a very bad day for the science of numbers, a very bad day indeed. Or more specifically, a bad day for topology, and not forgetting astronomy. The day in question was the date of Möbius' death, of course.

There had been students here earlier—East German, mainly, but much like students anywhere else in the world—long-haired and tattily attired; but properly respectful, Harry had thought. And so they should be. He, too, felt respectful; even awed that he stood in the presence of such a man. In any case, not wanting to appear too strange, Harry had waited until he was alone. Also, he had needed to think how best to approach Möbius. This was no ordinary figure lying here but a thinker who'd helped guide science along many of the right paths.

Finally Harry had settled for a direct approach; seating himself, he let his thoughts reach out and touch those of the dead man. A calm came over Harry then; his eyes took on their strange, glassy look; for all that it was bitterly cold, a fine patina of sweat gleamed on his brow. And slowly he grew aware that indeed Möbius—or what remained of him—was here. And active!

Formulae, tables of figures, astronomical distances and non-Euclidean, Riemannian configurations beat against Harry's awareness like the pulses of mighty, living computers. But . . . all of this in one mind? A mind which processed all of these thoughts very nearly simultaneously? And then it dawned on Harry that Möbius was working on something, flipping through the pages of memory and learning as he sought to tie together the elements of a puzzle too complex for Harry's—or for any merely living man's— comprehension. All very well, but it might go on for days. And Harry simply didn't have the time.

"Sir? Excuse me, sir? My name is Harry Keogh. I've come a long way to see you."

The phantasmal flow of figures and formulae stopped at once, like a computer switched off. "Eh? What? Who?"

"Harry Keogh, sir. I'm an Englishman."

There was a slight pause before the other snapped: "English? I don't care if you're an Arab! I'll tell you what you are: you're a nuisance! Now what is this, eh? What's it all about? I'm quite unused to this sort of thing."

"I'm a necroscope," Harry explained as best he could. "I can talk to the dead."

"Dead? Talk to the dead? Hmm! I considered that, yes, and long ago came to the conclusion that I was. So obviously you can. Well, it comes to us all—death, I mean. Indeed it has its advantages. Privacy, for one—or so I thought until now! A necroscope, you say? A new science?"

Harry had to smile. "I suppose you could call it that. Except I seem to be its one practitioner. Spiritualists aren't quite the same thing."

"I'll say they're not! Fraudulent bunch at best. Well then, how can I help you, Harry Keogh? I mean, I suppose you've a reason for disturbing me? A *good* reason, that is?"

"The best in the world," said Harry. "The fact is I'm tracking down a fiend, a murderer. I know who he is but I don't know how to bring him to justice. All I have is a clue as to how I might set about it, and that's where you come in."

"Tracking down a murderer? A talent like yours and you use it to track down murderers? Boy, you should be out talking to Euclid, Aristotle, Pythagoras! No, cancel that last. You'd get nothing from him. Him and his damned secretive Pythagorean Brotherhood! It's a wonder he even passed on his Theorem! Anyway, what is this clue of yours?"

Harry showed him a mental projection of the Möbius strip. "It's this," he said. "It's what ties the futures of my quarry and myself together."

Now the other was interested. "Topology in the time dimension? That leads to all sorts of interesting questions. Are you talking about your probable futures or your actual futures? Have you spoken to Gauss? He's the one for probability—*and* topology, for that matter. Gauss was a master when I was a mere student—albeit a brilliant student!"

"Actual," said Harry. "Our actual futures."

"But that is to presuppose that you know something of the future in the first place. And is precognition another talent of yours, Harry?" (A little sarcasm.)

"Not mine, no, but I do have friends who occasionally catch glimpses of the future, just as surely as I—"

"Twaddle!" Möbius cut him off. "Zöllnerists all!"

"—talk to the dead." Harry finished it anyway.

The other was silent for a moment or two. Then: "I'm probably a fool . . . but I think I believe you. At least I believe *you* believe, and that you have been misled. But for the life of me I can't see how my believing in you will help you in your quest."

"Neither can I," said Harry dejectedly. "Except . . . what about the Möbius strip? I mean, it's all I have to go on. Can't you at least explain it to me? After all, who would know more about it than you? You invented it!"

"No," (a mental shake of the head,) "they merely

stamped my name on it. Invented it? Ridiculous! I *noticed* it, that's all. As for explaining it: once there was a time when that would be the very simplest thing. Now, however—''

Harry waited.

"What year is this?"

The abrupt change of subject bewildered Harry. "Nineteen seventy-seven," he answered.

"Really?" (Astonishment.) "As long as that? Well, well! And so you see for yourself, Harry, that I've been lying here for more than a hundred years. But do you think I've been idle? Not a bit of it! Numbers, my boy, the ultimate answer to all the riddles of the universe. Space and its curvature and qualities and properties—properties still largely unimagined, I imagine, in the world of the living. Except I don't have to imagine, for I *know!* But explain it? Are you a mathematician, Harry?"

"I know a little."

"Astronomy?"

Reluctantly, Harry shook his head.

"What is your understanding of science—of SCIENCE, that is. Your understanding of the physical, the material, and the conjectural universe?"

Again Harry shook his head.

"Can you understand any of . . . this—" and a stream of symbols and equations and calculi flashed up on the screen of Harry's mind, each item in its turn more complex than the last. Some of it he recognized from talks with James Gordon Hannant, some he knew through intuition, but most of it was completely alien.

"It's all . . . pretty difficult," he finally said.

"Hmm!" (The slow nod of a phantom head.) "But on the other hand . . . you do have intuition. Yes, and I believe it's strong in you! I suppose I could always teach you, Harry."

"Teach me? Mathematics? Something you worked on all your life and for a hundred years since that life ended? Now who's talking twaddle? It would take me at least as long as it has taken you! Incidentally, what's a Zöllnerist?"

"J. K. F. Zöllner was a mathematician and astronomer—God help us!—who outlived me. He was also a crank and a spiritualist. To him numbers were 'magickal'! Did I call you a Zöllnerist? Unpardonable! You must forgive me. Actually, he wasn't far wrong. His topology was wrong, that's all. He tried to impose the *un*physical—or mental universe—on the physical one. And that doesn't work. Space-time is a constant, fixed and immutable as pi."

"That doesn't leave much room for metaphysics," said Harry, certain by now that he'd come to the wrong place.

"No room at all," Möbius agreed.

"Telepathy?"

"Twaddle!"

"What's this, then? What am I doing right now?"

Möbius was a little taken aback. But then: "Necroscopy, or so I'm given to believe."

"That's picking nits," said Harry. "What about clairvoyancy, or far-sightedness; the ability to view events at a great distance through the medium of the mind alone?"

"In the physical world, impossible. You would perpetuate Zöllner's errors."

"But I *know* these things can be done," Harry contradicted. "I know where there are people who do them. Not all the time, never easily or with any great accuracy, but occasionally. It *is* a new science, and it requires intuition."

After another pause Möbius said, "Again I'm tempted to believe you. What point would there be in your lying to me? Man's knowledge—of all things—increases all the time. And after all, *I* can do it! But then, I'm not of the physical world. Not any longer . . ."

Harry's head whirled. "*You* can do it? Are you telling me that you can scry out distant events?"

"I see them, yes," said Möbius, "but not through any crystal ball. Nor are they strictly distant. Distance is relative. I *go* there. I go where the events I wish to watch are scheduled to occur."

"But . . . *where* do you go? How?"

" 'How' is the difficult bit," said Möbius. "Where is far easier. Harry, in life I wasn't only a mathematician but also an astronomer. After I died, naturally I was restricted to maths. But astronomy was in me; it was part of me; it would not let me be. And everything comes to those who wait. As time passed I began to feel the stars shining down on me, through the day as well as the night. I became aware of their weight—their mass, if you like—their great distance, the distances between them. Soon I knew far more about them than ever I had known in life, and then I determined to go and see them for myself. When you came to me I was calculating the magnitude of a nova soon to occur in Andromeda, and I shall be there to see it happen! Why not? I am unbodied. The laws of the physical universe no longer apply."

"But you've just denied the metaphysical," Harry protested. "And now you're saying you can teleport to the stars!"

"Teleportation? No, for nothing physical is moved. As I keep telling you, Harry, I am not a physical thing. There may well be a so-called 'metaphysical' universe, but neither the real nor the unreal may impose itself upon the other."

"Or so you believed until you met me!" said Harry, his strange eyes opening wider, his voice full of a new awe. For suddenly a bright star was shining in Harry's mind, but shining brighter than any nova in the mind of Möbius.

"What? What's that?"

"Are you saying," Harry became relentless, "that there is no meeting point between the physical and the metaphysical? Is that your argument?"

"Exactly!"

"And yet I am physical, and you are purely mental—*and we have met!*"

He sensed the other's gape. "Astonishing! It seems I've overlooked the obvious."

Harry pressed his advantage: "You use the strip, don't you, to go out amongst the stars?"

"The strip? I use a variant of it, yes, but—"

"And you called me a Zöllnerist?"

For a moment Möbius was speechless. Then: "It seems my arguments . . . no longer apply!"

"You *do* teleport!" said Harry. "You teleport pure mind. You're a scryer. That's your talent, sir! In a way it always was. Even in life you could see things that others were blind to. The strip is a perfect example. Well, scrying in itself would be a marvellous weapon, but I want to take it a step farther. I want to impose—I mean rigidly *impose*—the physical me on the metaphysical universe."

"Please, Harry, not so fast!" Möbius protested. "I need to—"

"Sir, you offered to teach me," Harry couldn't be restrained. "Well, I accept. But only teach me what's absolutely necessary. Let my instinct, my intuition do the rest. My mind's a blackboard, and you've got the chalk right there in your hand. So go ahead teach me . . .

"Teach me how to ride your Möbius strip!"

It was night again and Dragosani had climbed back into the cruciform hills. Across his back he carried a second ewe, this one stunned with a large stone. The day had been a busy one, but its proceeds must surely show a profit; Max Batu had had the chance to display yet again the

morbid power of his evil eye, this time to one Ladislau
Giresci; eventually the old man would be found in his
lonely house, "victim of a heart attack," of course.

But Max's work had not stopped there, for only an hour
or so ago Dragosani had sent the Mongolian out upon
another crucial mission; which meant that the necromancer
was now alone—or to all intents and purposes alone—as
he approached the tomb of the vampire and sent his words
and thoughts before him to penetrate the cold gloom beneath dark and stirless trees.

"Thibor, are you sleeping? I'm here as directed. The
stars are bright and the night chill, and the moon is creeping on the hills. This is the hour, Thibor—for both of us."

And after a moment: *Ahhhh! . . . Dragosaaaniiii? Sleeping? I suppose I was. But I have slept a grand sleep,
Dragosani. The sleep of the undead. And I dreamed a
grand dream—of conquest and of empire! And for once my
hard bed was soft as the breasts of a lover, and these old,
old bones were not weighed down but buoyant as the step
of a lad when he meets his lass. A grand dream, aye, but
. . . alas, only a dream for all that.*

Dragosani sensed . . . despondency? Alarmed for his
plan, he asked? "Is anything wrong?"

*On the contrary. All goes well, my son—except I fear it
may take a little longer than I thought. I took strength
from your offering of yestereve, indeed I did!—and I fancy
I've even put on a little flesh. But still the ground is hard
and these old sinews of mine stiff from the salts of the
earth . . .*

And then, more eagerly: *But did you remember, Dragosani,
and bring me another small tribute? Not too small, I
hope? Something, perhaps to compare with my last repast?*

For answer the necromancer came to a halt on the rim of
the circle, tossed down from his shoulder to the ground at
his feet the inert mass of the ewe in a grunting heap. "I

didn't forget," he said. "But come on, old dragon, tell me what you want. Why will it take longer than you thought?" Dragosani's disappointment was real; his plan depended upon raising the vampire up tonight.

Have you no understanding, Dragosani? came Thibor's answer. *Among the men who followed me when I was a warrior, many were so injured in battle that they were carried to their beds. Some would recover. But after months of lying still, often they were wasted and full of aches and torments. Picture me, then, after five hundred years! But . . . we shall see what we shall see. Even as we talk I grow more eager to be risen up—and so perhaps, after a little more refreshment—?*

Dragosani wryly nodded his understanding, drew out a small glinting sickle of honed brightness from its sheath in his pocket, and stooped towards the ewe.

Hold! said the vampire. *As you surmise, Dragosani, this may well be the hour—for both of us. An hour of great moment! For both of us. For my own part, I think we should treat it with the respect it warrants.*

The necromancer frowned, cocked his head on one side. "How do you mean?"

So far, my son, I think you would agree that I have not stood on ceremony. For all that I have had my food hurled at me, as if I were some rooting pig, I have not complained. But I would have you know, Dragosani, that I too have supped at table. Indeed, I've dined in the courts of princes! —aye, and will again, with you perhaps seated upon my right hand. May I not, therefore, expect treatment more nearly gracious? Or must I always remember you as a man who poured my food over me like slops into a pigsty?

"A bit late for niceties, isn't it, Thibor?" Dragosani wondered what the vampire was up to. "What exactly do you want?"

Thibor was quick to note his apprehension. *What? And do you still distrust me? Well, and I suppose you have your reasons. Survival was mine. But come, have we not agreed that when I'm up and about, then I'll drive out the seed of my own flesh from your body? And in that moment, will you not be entirely in my hands? It seems a foolish thing, Dragosani, that you would put your faith in me walking abroad but not in my grave! Surely if I were so inclined, I'd be capable of more harm to you up than down? Also, if it were my plan to harm you, who then would be my guide in this new world I'm about to enter? You shall instruct me, Dragosani, and I you.*

"You still haven't said what you want."

The vampire sighed. *Dragosani, I am forced to admit a small personal flaw. I have in the past accused you of a certain vanity, yet now I tell you that I, too, am vain. Aye, and I would celebrate my rebirth in a manner more fitting. Therefore, bring unto me the ewe, my son, and lay it down before me. This one last time, let it be by way of a genuine tribute—even as a ritual sacrifice to one who is mighty— and not merely swill and roughage for the fattening of swine. Let me eat as from a platter, Dragosani, and not out of a trough!*

"Old bastard!" thought Dragosani, while continuing to keep his thoughts secret. So he was to be the vampire's serf, was he? Just another poor gipsy dolt to be cuffed about and follow at heel like a whining dog? "Ah, but I've news for you, my old, my *too* old friend!" and Dragosani hugged his secret thoughts tightly to himself. "Enjoy this, Thibor Ferenczy, for it's the very last time a man will fetch and carry for the likes of you!" And out loud he said:

"You want me to bring you the beast, as if it were an offering?"

Is it too much to ask?

The necromancer shrugged. Right now, nothing was too much to ask. He would be doing a little ''asking'' himself, shortly. He put away his razor-edged knife and took up the sheep. He carried it to the centre of the circle, crouched down and placed it where last night's offering had lain. Then again he took out his sickle blade.

Until now the glade had been quiet, still as the tomb it was, but now Dragosani sensed a gathering. It was as if muscles were suddenly bunched, the silent creep of a cat's paws as it closes on a mouse, the forming of saliva on a chameleon's tongue before it strikes. Quickly, thrilling with horror of the unknown—even a monster such as Dragosani, filled with horror—he drew back the stunned beast's head and made its throat taut. And—

No need for that, my son, said Thibor Ferenczy.

Dragosani would have leapt away, for in that selfsame moment he knew—but knew too late—that the Thing in the ground had had its fill of piglets and sheep! Not one eighth of an inch had he straightened from his crouch before that phallic tentacle burst from the ground beneath him, shearing through his clothing like a knife and up, *into* him. And how he would have leapt then, to be free of it, even if the tearing should kill him; he *would* have leapt—but he couldn't. Growing barbs within him, the pseudopod stretched itself through all the lower conduits of his body and filled him, and drew him down like a fish yanked from water on a hook!

Dragosani's feet flew out from beneath him as he was slammed down against the dark and seething earth; and after that there was no longer room even for the thought of flight. For that was when the pain, the torment, the ultimate agony commenced . . .

His bowels were melting, his entrails were on fire, he was seated upright on a fountain of acid! And through all the incredible pain Thibor Ferenczy howled his triumph and taunted Dragosani with the truth—the *real* truth—the one final question whose answer had eluded the necromancer through all these years:

Why did they hate me, my son? My own kith and kin, as it were? Why do all vampires hate other vampires? Why, the answer to that is the very simplest thing! The blood is the life, Dragosani! Oh, the blood of swine will suffice if there's nought better to sup, and the blood of fowls and sheep. Better far, however, the blood of men, as you'll very soon be obliged to discover for yourself. But over and above all other vessels, the true nectar of life may only be sipped from the veins of another vampire!

Dragosani burned in a double hell; he felt torn apart inside; his parasite twin within clove to him in *its* agony as Thibor's nightmare appendage fastened upon it and leeched its essence. And yet that terrible tentacle did no real harm, no damage. Protoplasmic, it moulded itself to organs without crushing them, penetrated without puncturing. Even its barbs caused no injury, for they were fashioned to hold without tearing. The agony lay in its being there, in its contact with raw nerves and muscles and organs, in its advance through all the tracts of Dragosani's raped physical body. It could not hurt more if some insane doctor had dripped an acid solution into an open vein—but it would not kill. It *could* kill, certainly, but not now, not this time.

In his torment Dragosani could not know that. And through his torment he cried: "Get . . . it . . . done with, damn you! Damn your . . . black heart, liar of liars! Kill . . . me, Thibor! Do it now. Put an end to it, I . . . I beg you!"

He sat there in the darkness under the trees amidst the shattered flags and the crumbling ruins of the ancient tomb, and horror ate at his mind like a rat set loose in his brain and left to eat its way out. Someone had set a meat mincer in motion inside him and it was reducing his guts to squirming red worms. He jerked and threshed, fell to one side. The agony drove him upright again, only to fall the other way. And so he twitched and jerked and lolled and screamed, and still Thibor Ferenczy fed.

Strength you gave me, Dragosani. aye. Strength and bulk in the blood of beasts. But the true life is the blood of a fellow creature—even the thin, immature blood of that child of mine who now gibbers inside you as he grows weak from his loss even as you grow weak from pain. But kill him! Kill you! Nay, nay! What? And rob myself of a thousand feasts to come? We go together into the world, Dragosani, and you in thrall to me until that time when you shall flee. By which time you'll not need to ask but know why all the Wamphyri share a mutual bond of hate!

The vampire was sated. The tentacle slid out of Dragosani and down into the earth out of sight. Its going was, if anything, even worse than its coming: a white hot sword drawn out of him by a careless hand.

He cried out, a shriek that echoed like the cry of a wild thing through the cold, cruel cruciform hills, and toppled over on his side. But hadn't Thibor told him that they named the Vlad "the Impaler" after him? He had, and now Dragosani could more fully understand just why!

The necromancer tried to stand and could not. His legs were jelly, his brain a seething acid soup in its skull bowl. He rolled, cleared the tainted circle, again tried to rise. Impossible. Will was not enough. He lay still, sobbing in the night, gathering wits and strength both. The vampire had spoken of hate, and he had been right. It was hate that kept Dragosani conscious now. Hate and only hate. His and that of the creature within him. Both of them had been ravaged.

Finally he propped himself up on his side, glared his hate at the black earth which now steamed and smoked as the vapours of hell rose up from it. Cracks appeared in the sub-soil which Dragosani had cleared. The earth bulged upward, began to break open. *Something* thrust up from below. Then—

That same *something* sat up—and it was something unbelievable!

Dragosani's lips drew back from his teeth in an involuntary snarl of loathing, and in terror! For this was the Thing in the ground. This was what he had talked to, argued with, cursed and profaned time and time again. This was Thibor Ferenczy, the undead embodiment of his own bat-devil-dragon banner. But worse, it was what Dragosani had doomed himself one day to become!

The thick ears of the Thing grew close to its head but were pointed and projected slightly higher than the elongated skull, giving the appearance of horns. Its nose was wrinkled and convoluted, like that of a great bat, and squat to its face. Its skin was of scale and its eyes were scarlet, like a dragon's. And it was . . . big! The hands where they now appeared and clawed at the soil at its waist were huge, with nails projecting all of an inch beyond the fingers.

Dragosani finally fought back his terror and forced himself to his feet—just as the vampire turned its strangely wolfish head to fix him with a monstrous, almost startled stare. And its eyes opened wide as their scarlet light fell on him where he tottered. "I . . . I CAN SEE . . . YOU!" said Thibor then, his risen voice as evil and alien as any of his mental sendings from the tomb. But the statement seemed in no way threatening; it was more as if the fact of sight—and in particular of seeing Dragosani—in some way brought to the creature a mixed measure of relief and disbelief. Whichever, the necromancer cringed back and down; but in that same moment:

"Ho, Thing from the earth!" said Max Batu, stepping out from cover.

Thibor Ferenczy's head shot round on his neck in the direction of the Mongol's voice. Seeing Batu where he stood, his great dog's jaws fell open and he hissed from between teeth like blades of bone which dripped slime. And without pause Batu took one look at that face, then aimed and fired Ladislau Giresci's crossbow.

The lignumvitae bolt was five-eighths of an inch thick and steel-tipped. It sprang from the weapon and plunged at almost point-blank range into and through the vampire's heaving chest, transfixing him.

Thibor gave a hissing shriek and tried to draw himself back down into the steaming earth, but the bolt jammed in the sides of the hole and prevented him, tearing his grey flesh. He gave a second shriek then—a soul-wrenching thing to hear—and tossed himself to and fro with the bolt still in him, cursing and spewing out slime from his chomping, grimacing mouth.

Batu loped quickly to Dragosani's side, supported him, handed him a full-sized sickle whose edge gleamed silver from a recent sharpening. The necromancer took it, shook Batu off, staggeringly advanced upon the struggling monster trapped half-in, half-out of its grave.

"The last time they buried you," he gasped, "they made one big mistake, Thibor Ferenczy." And the muscles of his neck and arm bunched as he drew back the sickle. "They left your fucking head on!"

The monster tugged at the shaft in its chest, stared at Dragosani with a look beyond his comprehension. There was something of fear in it, yes, but more than this there was that baffled astonishment, as if the beast could not take in or understand this sudden reversal.

"WAIT!" it croaked as he drew close, the cracked bass sound of its voice like so many saplings snapping in an avalanche. "CAN'T YOU SEE? IT'S *ME!!!*"

But Dragosani didn't wait. He knew who and what the

monster was, knew also that the only real way he could inherit its knowledge, its powers, was this way: as a necromancer. Yes, and such a wonderful irony in it, for Thibor himself had given him the gift! "Die, you bastard Thing!" he snarled, and the sickle became a blur of steel as it sheared the monster's head from its trunk.

The awful head sprang aloft, fell, bounced. And even rolling it cried, "FOOL! DAMNED FOOL!" before lying still. Then the scarlet eyes closed. The mouth opened one last time and a gob of red-tinged filth shot out—and a final word, the merest whisper: *"Fool!"*

Dragosani's answer was to swing the sickle a second time, splitting the head in two parts like some great grey overripe melon. Inside the skull, the brain was a mush with a writhing core: in effect two brains, one human and shrivelled and the other—alien! The brain of the vampire. Without pause, without fear, knowing for once *exactly* what he did, Dragosani stuck his hands deep into the two halves of the skull cavity and let his trembling fingers feel the reeking fluids and pulp. All the secrets and the lore of the Wamphyri were here, *here*, just waiting for him to search them out.

Yes! Yes!

Even now the brains were rotting, falling into the natural decay and corruption of centuries . . . but Dragosani's necromantic talent was already tracking the undead (now utterly dead) monster's secrets through the very juices of its crumbling brain. Grey as stone, his eyes standing out obscenely in his head, he lifted up the mess to his face—but too late!

Before his frantic eyes everything rotted away, boiled into smoke, trickled in streams of dust through his twitching fingers. Even the misshapen skull, dust in his hands.

With a cry almost of anguish, wildly swinging his arms like a windmill run amok, Dragosani spun and made a headlong dive for the vampire's headless body where it still sat upright in its grave. The severed neck was beginning to steam away, settling into the scaled chest which itself slumped down into the unseen trunk below. And even as the necromancer plunged his hand and arm down into that hole, into the rot and the stench, so the earth belched up a great mushrooming cloud of poisonous vapour and collapsed in upon the now almost liquid corpse.

Dragosani howled like a banshee and drew out his arm from the quag, then crawled away from the shuddering, belching hole as the ground quickly settled into quiescence. At the edge of the circle he paused, head hanging limply, shoulders slumped, and sobbed his frustration long and rackingly.

Breathless, shaken to his roots by all he had seen, Max Batu watched the necromancer a little while longer then slowly came forward. He got down on one knee beside Dragosani and gripped his shoulder. "Comrade Dragosani," Batu's voice was hushed, little more than a dry, croaking whisper. "Is it over?"

Dragosani stopped sobbing. He let his head continue to hang down while he considered Batu's question: was it all over? It was all over for Thibor Ferenczy, yes, but only just beginning for the new vampire, the as yet immature creature which even now shared Dragosani's body with him. They would supply each other's needs, (however grudgingly,) learn from each other, become as one being. The question still remained as to whose will would eventually achieve dominance.

Against any ordinary man the vampire must, of course, be the winner. Every time. But Dragosani was not ordinary. He had the power in him to accumulate his own lore, his own talents. And why not? Perhaps somewhere in his learning, in his gathering of secrets and strange new powers, he might yet find a way to be rid of the parasite. But until then . . .

"No, Max Batu," he said, "it's not over yet. Not for a while yet."

"Then what must I do now?" the squat little Mongol was anxious to be of assistance. "How can I help? What are your needs?"

Dragosani continued to stare at the dark earth. How could Batu help? What were the necromancer's needs? Interesting questions.

Pain and frustration died in Dragosani. There was much to do and time was wasting. He had come here to gather new powers to himself in the face of whatever threat was posed by Harry Keogh and the British E-Branch, and that was a job he still must do. Thibor's secrets were beyond him now, dead and gone forever like the vampire himself, but that must not be the end of the matter. However weak and battered he felt right now, still he knew that he had not been permanently damaged. The pain may well have scarred his mind and soul (if he still had a soul), but those were scars which would heal. No, he had suffered no real or lasting injury. He had merely been—depleted.

Depleted, yes. The thing inside him needed, and Dragosani knew what it needed. He felt Batu's hand on his shoulder and could almost hear the blood surging in the other's veins. Then Dragosani saw the sharp, curved surgical tool with which he would have slit the ewe's throat. It lay there close to his hand, silver against the black earth. Ah, well, he had intended this eventually. It would be so much sooner, that was all.

"Two things I need from you, Max," Dragosani said, and looked up.

Max Batu gasped aloud and his jaw fell open. The necromancer's eyes were scarlet as those of the fiend he had just killed! The Mongol saw them—saw something else that glittered silver in the night—and saw . . . nothing else.

Ever . . .

Interval Two:

"I have to stop," Alec Kyle told his weird visitor. He put down his pencil, massaged his cramped wrist. The desk was littered with the curled shavings of five pencils, all of them whittled away to nothing. This was Kyle's sixth and his arm felt mangled from frantic scribbling.

A thin sheaf of papers was stacked in front of Kyle, with pencilled notes and jottings covering each sheet top to bottom and margin to margin. When he had started to write all of this down (how long ago? Four and a half, five hours?) the notes had been fairly detailed. Within an hour they'd become jottings, barely legible scrawl. Now even Kyle himself could scarcely read them, and they were reduced to a listing of dates alongside brief headlines.

Now, for a moment resting his wrist and mind both,

Kyle glanced at the dates again and shook his head. He still believed—instinctively knew—that all of this was the absolute truth, but there was one massively glaring anomaly here. An ambiguity he couldn't ignore. Kyle frowned, looked up at the apparition where it floated upright on the other side of the desk, blinked his eyes at this shimmering spectre of a man and said: "There's something I don't quite understand." Then he laughed, and not a little hysterically. "I mean, there are a good many things here which I don't understand—but until now I've at least believed them. This is harder to believe."

"Oh?" said the apparition.

Kyle nodded. "Today's Monday," he said. "Sir Keenan is to be cremated tomorrow. The police have discovered nothing as yet and it seems almost blasphemous to keep his body, well, lying about in that condition."

"Yes," the other nodded his agreement.

"Well," Kyle continued, "the point is I know a lot of what you've told me to be the truth, and I suspect that the rest of it is too. You've told me things no one else outside myself and Sir Keenan should ever have known. But—"

"But?"

"But your story," Kyle suddenly blurted, "has already outstripped us! I've been keeping a record of your timescale and you've just been telling me about the coming Wednesday, two days from now. According to you, Thibor Ferenczy isn't yet dead, won't be until Wednesday night!"

After a moment the other said, "I can see how that must appear strange to you, yes. Time is relative, Alec, the same as space. Indeed the two go hand in hand. I'll go further than that: *everything* is relative. There is a Grand Scheme to things . . ."

Some of that escaped Kyle. For the moment he saw only what he wanted to see. "You can read the future? *That* well?" His face was a mask of awe. "And I thought *I* had a talent! But to be able to see the future so clearly is almost unbe—'' and he stopped short and gasped. As if things weren't incredible enough, a new, even more incredible thought had crossed his mind.

Perhaps his visitor saw it written in his face. At any rate he smiled a smile transparent as smoke from a cigarette, a smile that reflected not at all the light from the window but allowed it to pass right through. "Is there something, Alec?'' he asked.

"Where . . . where are you?'' Kyle asked. "I mean, where are *you* . . . the real, physical you—right now? Where are you speaking from? Or rather, *when* are you speaking from?''

"Time is relative,'' the spectre said again, still smiling.

"You're speaking to me from the future, aren't you?'' Kyle breathed. It was the only answer. It was the only way the spectre could know all of this, the only way he could do all of this.

"You'll be very useful to me,'' said the other, slowly nodding. "It seems you have a sharp intuitive ability to match your precognition, Alec Kyle. Or maybe it's all part of the same talent. But now, shall we continue?''

Still gaping, Kyle again took up the pencil. "I think you better had continue,'' he whispered. "You'd better tell me all of it, right to the end . . .''

Chapter Fifteen

Moscow, Friday evening, Dragosani's flat
on the Pushkin Road.

IT WAS GROWING DARK BY THE TIME DRAGOSANI GRATEFULLY
let himself into his flat and poured himself a drink. The
trains had been maddeningly slow on the journey from
Romania, and Max Batu's absence had made the return
trip seem that much longer. Batu's absence, yes, and
Dragosani's growing feeling of urgency, this sensation of
being rushed towards some colossal confrontation. Time
was quickly passing and still there remained so much for
him to do. Achingly tired, still he couldn't rest. Some
instinct urged him onward, warned him against pausing in
his set course.

With a second drink inside him and beginning to feel a
little better, he telephoned the Château Bronnitsy and
checked that Borowitz was still in mourning at his dacha at

Zhukovka. Then he asked to speak to Igor Vlady but Vlady had alread left for home. Dragosani phoned him there, asked if he could come round. The other agreed at once.

Vlady lived in his own state flatlet not too far away but Dragosani took his car anyway; in less than ten minutes he was seated in Vlady's tiny living-room, toying with a welcoming glass of vodka.

"Well, Comrade?" Vlady finally asked when they'd done with the usual formalities and preliminaries. "What can I do for you?" He peered curiously, almost speculatively at Dragosani's dark glasses and gaunt grey features.

Dragosani nodded, as if he silently confirmed something or other, and said: "I can see you've been expecting me."

"Yes, I thought I might be seeing you," Vlady carefully answered.

Dragosani decided against beating about the bush. If Vlady failed to produce the right answers he would simply kill him. He probably would anyway, eventually. "Very well, I'm here," he said. "Now tell me: how's it going to be?"

Vlady was a small dark man and normally open as a book. That was the impression he achieved, anyway. Now he raised an eyebrow, put on an expression of mild surprise. "How's what going to be?" he asked, innocently.

"Look, let's not fool around," said Dragosani. "You probably already know exactly why I've come here. That's what you're paid for: your ability to see things in advance. So I'll ask you again: how is it going to be?"

Vlady drew back, scowled. "With Borowitz, you mean?"

"For starters, yes."

Vlady's face grew strangely impassive, almost cold. "He'll die," he said, without emotion. "Tomorrow, at midday or thereabouts. A heart attack. Except—" and he paused and frowned.

"Except?"

Vlady shrugged. "A heart attack," he repeated.

Dragosani nodded, sighed, relaxed a little. "Yes," he said, "that's how it will be. And what about me—and you?"

"I don't do readings for myself," said Vlady. "It's tempting, of course, but far too frustrating. To know the future and not be able to change it. Also, it's frightening. As for you . . . that's a bit odd."

Dragosani didn't like the sound of that. He put down his drink and leaned forward. "What's odd?" he asked. This might be very important to him.

Vlady took up both of their glasses and poured more vodka. "First let's get something straight, you and I," he said. "Comrade, I'm not your rival. I have no ambitions in respect of E-Branch. None at all. I know Borowitz had me in mind for the job—along with yourself—but I'm just not interested. I think you should know that."

"You mean you'll step aside for me?"

"I'm not stepping aside for anyone," the other shook his head. "I just don't want the job, that's all. I don't envy any man that job. Yuri Andropov won't rest until he's crushed the lot of us—even if it takes the rest of his lifetime! Frankly, I wish to hell I was out of it altogether. Did you know I was a trained architect, Dragosani? Well, I am. Read the future? I'd far prefer to read the plans of great buildings any day."

"Why do you tell me this?" Dragosani was curious. "It has nothing to do with anything."

"Yes it has. It has something to do with living. And I want to live. You see, Dragosani, I know that you will have something to do with Borowitz's death. With his "heart attack." And if you can tackle him and win, which you will, then what chance would I have? I'm not brave, Dragosani, and I'm not stupid. E-Branch is all yours . . ."

Again Dragosani leaned forward. His eyes were pricks of red light gleaming through the dark lenses of his spectacles. "But your job is to tell Borowitz this sort of thing, Igor," he rasped. "Especially *this* sort of thing. Are you saying you haven't told him? Or does he in fact already know that I'll be . . . involved?"

Vlady shook himself, sat up straighter. For a moment he'd felt almost hypnotized by Dragosani. The man's gaze was like that of a snake. A wolf? Something not quite human, anyway. "I really don't know why I've told you any of this," he finally said. "I mean, for all I know the old warhorse might even have sent you here!"

"But wouldn't you know it if he had?" said Dragosani. "Isn't that something your talent would have foreseen?"

"I can't see everything!" Vlady snapped.

Dragosani nodded. "Hmm! Well, he didn't send me. Now tell me truthfully: does he know he's going to die tomorrow? And if so, does he know that I'll be involved? Well, I'm waiting . . ."

Vlady bit his lip, shook his head. "He doesn't know," he mumbled.

"Why haven't you told him?"

"Two reasons. First, it wouldn't change anything even if he did know. Second, I hate the old bastard! I have a fiancée and want to be married. I've wanted it for ten years. But Borowitz says no. He needs me to keep my wits sharp. He doesn't want my talent dulled. Too much sex might ruin me, he says! Damn the old bastard—he rations me with my own fiancée!"

Dragosani sat back and laughed out loud. Vlady saw the gape of his mouth and the length of his teeth and once more felt that he talked with some strange animal rather than a man. "Oh, I can believe that!" Dragosani's laughter finally rumbled into silence. "Yes, that's just typical of him. Well, Igor," he nodded knowingly. "I think you can now safely go ahead with your wedding arrangements. Yes, just as soon as you like.''

"But you'll want to keep me in the branch, eh?" Vlady's tone remained sour.

"Of course I will," Dragosani nodded. "You're much too valuable to be a simple architect, Igor Vlady—and far too talented! But the branch? That is merely a beginning. There's more to life than that. After this is over I'm going on and up. And you can come with me.''

Vlady's response to that was a blank stare. Suddenly Dragosani was sure he was hiding something. "You were going to tell me what you've read in my future," he reminded. "Now that we've dealt with Borowitz, I think that would be a good idea. I think you said there was something . . . odd?''

"Odd, yes," Vlady agreed. "But of course I could be wrong. Anyway, you'll know all about it—tomorrow." And he gave a nervous twitch at Dragosani's startled expression.

"What? What's that about tomorrow?" the necromancer came slowly to his feet, uncoiling from his chair. "Have you been wasting my time and confusing me with trivialities when all the time you knew there was something in store for me tomorrow? When, tomorrow? And where?''

"Tomorrow night—at the Château," said Vlady. "Something big, but I don't know what it will be.''

Dragosani began to pace the floor, searched his own mind for clues, "KBG? Is it likely they'll find Borowitz's body that fast? I doubt it. Even if they did, why should they suspect the branch? Or me? After all, it will only have been a 'heart attack.' That could happen to anyone. Or is it someone inside the branch itself? Maybe you, Igor, having second thoughts about your loyalties?" (Vlady hastily shook his head in denial.) "Will it be sabotage?" Dragosani continued to pace. "And if so what form of sabotage?'' He angrily shook his head. "No, no, I can't see that! Damn it, come on, Igor you know more than you're saying! What is it, *exactly*, that you've seen?''

"You don't seem to understand!" Vlady shouted. "Man, I'm not superhuman. I can't *be* exact all the time!" It was true and Dragosani knew it; Vlady's voice betrayed his own exasperation; he, too, wished he had an answer. "Sometimes, things are very vague—like that time when Andrei Ustinov got his. I knew there would be a ruckus that night and warned Borowitz about it, but I couldn't for the life of me say who or what would be involved! It's the same this time, too. There'll be big trouble tomorrow and you'll be right in the middle of it. It will come from outside and it will be . . . *big* trouble! Of that much I'm certain, but that's all.''

"Not quite all," said Dragosani, ominously. "I still don't know what you meant by 'odd.' Why do you avoid the issue? Will I be in any danger?''

"Yes," said Vlady, "a great deal of danger. And not just you but everyone at the Château.''

"Damn it, man!" Dragosani slammed his fist down on the table. "You make it sound like we'll all be dead men!''

Vlady's face slowly lost some of its dark colour. He half turned his face away but Dragosani leaned over him, clasped his cheeks in the fingers of one great hand, drew his averted face and the O-shape of his quivering mouth back towards him. He looked deep into the other's frightened eyes. "Are you quite sure you've told me everything?" he asked, forming his words slowly and very carefully. "Can you not at least try to explain what you meant by your use of the word 'odd'? Is there a chance, perhaps, that you've also foreseen my death for tomorrow?''

Vlady jerked his face free and pushed back in his chair away from Dragosani. The white pressure marks of the other's fingers faded on his cheeks, were replaced by a dark pink flush. Dragosani was capable of murder beyond a doubt. Vlady must at least try to satisfy his demands. "Listen," he said, "and I'll explain as best I can. After that . . . you must make what you will of it.

"When I look at a man—when I try to see into his future—I normally detect a straight blue line extending forward. Like a line drawn down a sheet of paper from top to bottom. Call it his line of life, if you wish. From the length of this line I can work out the length of the man's life. From kinks and deviations which occur in it, I can determine something of future occurrences and how they will affect him. Borowitz's line ends tomorrow. At the end there is a kink which indicates a physical malfunction: his heart attack. As to how I know you will be involved: it is simply that at the end *your* life-line crosses his—and goes on alone!"

"But for how long?" Dragosani demanded to know. "What about tomorrow night, Igor? Is that where my line ends?"

Vlady shivered. "Your line is entirely different," he finally answered. "I hardly know how to read it at all. Some six months ago Borowitz demanded that I prepare weekly readings on you for his eyes only. I tried but . . . it was impossible. There were so many deviations in your line that I couldn't read it with any degree of accuracy at all! Kinks and wriggles I'd never come across before. Also, as the months passed, what had started out as one line began to divide, to split into two parallel lines. The new one wasn't blue but red, which was something else I had never seen before. As for the old, original line: it too slowly turned red. You are like . . . like twins, Dragosani. I know no other way to put it. And tomorrow—"

"Yes?"

"Tomorrow night one of your lines terminates . . ."

Half of me will die! thought Dragosani. *But which half?* Out loud he asked, "The red or the blue?"

"The red line terminates," said Vlady.

The vampire—dead! Dragosani's spirits soared but he controlled the laughter he felt welling inside. "What of the other line?"

Vlady shook his head, patently at a loss for any reasonable explanation. Finally he said, "That is the oddest thing of all. It's something I simply cannot explain. The other line loses its red tinge and forms a loop, bends back on itself, rejoins the other where the division first occurred!"

Dragosani sat down again and took up his drink. What Vlady had given him wasn't satisfactory but it was better than nothing. "I've been hard on you, Igor," he said, "and I'm sorry for that. I can see you've tried to do your best for me and I thank you. But you've said that this thing tomorrow will be big, which tells me that you've probably done readings for the others who'll be at the Château. So now I want to know just how big it will be?"

Vlady bit his lip. "You won't like the answer, Comrade," he warned at last.

"Tell me anyway."

"It will be very nearly total! A force—a *power*—will visit itself upon the Château Bronnitsy, and it will bring devastation."

Keogh! It could only be Harry Keogh! No other threat existed . . . Dragosani stood up, grabbed his coat, headed for the door. "I have to go now, Igor," he said. "But again I thank you. I won't forget what you've done for me tonight, believe me. And if you should see anything new, I'd be obliged if—"

"Of course," said Vlady, breathing a sigh of relief, following him to the door; and, as Dragosani went out into the night: "Comrade . . . what happened to Max Batu?" It was a dangerous question, but he must ask it.

Dragosani paused just beyond the threshold, glanced back. "Max? Ah, you know about him, do you? Well, it was an accident."

"Oh," said Vlady with a nod. "Of course . . ."

When he was alone again, Vlady finished off the vodka and then sat deep into the night, wrapped in his own thoughts. But as a clock tolled midnight somewhere out in the cold city he started up and shivered, and finally decided to break his own rule. Quickly he cast his mind into the future, followed his own life-line to its inevitable end. Which came in just three days' time, and with a violent, wrenching terminal squiggle!

Automatically, then, Vlady began to pack a few things and prepare to flee. And uppermost in his mind was the thought that with Borowitz gone Dragosani would be the head of E-Branch, or head of what survived. Whatever else Gregor Borowitz was, at least he was human! But Dragosani . . . ? Vlady knew he could never serve under him. Oh, it could well be that Dragosani would die tomorrow night—but what if he didn't? His line was so very confusing, so very alien. No, there was only one course for Vlady now. He must try—at least try—to avoid the unavoidable.

And almost a thousand miles away, where a dark watch-tower overlooked the wall in East Berlin, a Kalashnikov machine-gun waited for Igor Vlady. He didn't know it, but even now his and the weapon's futures were bending towards each other. They would meet at exactly 10:32 P.M.—in just three days' time.

Dragosani drove straight back to his flat. From there he phoned the Château and got hold of the Duty Officer. He passed on Harry Keogh's name and description for immediate transmission to border crossing points and incoming airports within the USSR, along with the information that

Keogh was a spy for the West who should be arrested on sight or, if that should prove difficult, shot dead without delay. The KGB would get to know about it, of course, but Dragosani didn't mind. If they took Keogh alive they wouldn't know what to do with him, and one way or the other Dragosani would get his hands on him. And if they killed him . . . that would be the end of that.

As for Vlady's predictions: Dragosani had some faith in them but it was by no means total. Vlady insisted that the future could not be changed. Dragosani thought differently. One of them must be right but they must wait until tomorrow night to find out which one. In any case, the promised "trouble" at the Château Bronnitsy might well turn out to be nothing to do with Harry Keogh after all; and so, until then at least, things must continue according to plan.

After passing on his information to the Château, Dragosani had another drink—a stiff one, which was not his normal habit—and at last fell into his bed. Exhausted, he slept right through until mid-morning . . .

At 11:40 A.M. he parked his old Volga in a copse off the main road half a mile from the closest dacha, turned up the collar of his overcoat and walked the rest of the way into Zhukovka precinct. Just before noon he turned off a track inches deep in snow and walked through a strip of woodland lying parallel to the river, until he came to Borowitz's dacha. Smiling grimly, he went quickly along the paved path to the door and knocked gently on the rustic oak panels. While he waited, he sniffed at wood smoke where it hung in the bitter cold air. The fine hairs inside his nostrils crackled, but melting icicles where they hung from Borowitz's roof told him that already the temperature was rising. Soon the snow would melt and Dragosani's footprints would disappear; there would be nothing to connect him with this place.

451

There came slow footsteps from within and the door cracked open. Pale, shaggy and red-eyed, Gregor Borowitz peered out, blinked in the grey light of day. "Dragosani?" he frowned darkly. "But I said I wasn't to be disturbed. I—"

"Comrade General," Dragosani cut in, "if it wasn't a matter of the utmost urgency . . ."

Borowitz stepped aside, opened the door wider. "Come in, come in," he grumbled, but without his accustomed fire. He had been alone here for a week; he no longer seemed robust; his grief was very real and had left him old and tired. All of which suited Dragosani very well indeed.

He entered, followed the other down a short corridor and through hanging curtains into the small, pine-panelled room where Natasha Borowitz lay silently in her shroud. The woman had been a peasant, pleasant enough in life but plain and dowdy in death. Like a stout, badly fashioned candle she lay there, the wax of her face wrinkled, the wick of her hair coarse and sparse. Borowitz patted her cold face and bowed his head as he turned away. But he could not hide a very real tear glittering in the corner of his eye.

Now he led Dragosani through into the more familiar living-cum-dining room and offered him a seat close to a window. The rest of the dacha's windows were shuttered but this one's shutters stood open, letting in the light. With a silent shake of his head, Dragosani declined to sit, watched Borowitz flop heavily down on to a padded couch. "I prefer to stand," the necromancer said. "This won't take long."

"A flying visit?" Borowitz grunted, scarcely interested. "You might have waited, Dragosani. Tomorrow they take my Natasha away from me, and then I return to Moscow and the Château Bronnitsy. What is it that brings you here so urgently anyway? You told me that your trip to England was successful.''

"So it was,'' said Dragosani, ''but something has come up since then.''

"Well?''

"Comrade General,'' said Dragosani, ''Gregor, I want you to ask no questions just yet but simply tell me something. Do you remember a conversation we once had, you and I, about the future of E-Branch? You said that one day you would decide who would take over from you when you . . . retired. Also, you said the decision would lie between myself and Igor Vlady.''

Borowitz drew his brows together, stared at Dragosani disbelievingly. "So that's why you're here!'' he growled. "A matter of the utmost urgency, eh? You think I'm ready to step down, do you? Or maybe you think it's *time* I stepped down! Now that Natasha's gone, maybe I'll think of retiring, eh?'' He sat up straighter, his eyes flashed something of the fire Dragosani was used to seeing in them. Except that the necromancer no longer stood in awe of this man.

"I said you should ask no questions,'' he reminded, a low, dark rumble in his voice. "I am the one who seeks answers, Gregor. Now tell me: who did you decide would be your replacement? Indeed, have you yet decided? And if so, have you made a record of your decision?''

Borowitz was astonished, outraged. "You dare . . . ?'' he scowled, his eyes bulging. "You *dare* . . . ? You forget yourself, Dragosani. You forget who I am and where you are. And apparently you forget—or choose to ignore the fact—that I am recently bereaved! Well, *damn* you, Dragosani! But in answer to your questions: no, I have committed nothing to paper—there's nothing to commit for I'll be going on as the head of E-branch for a long time yet, I assure you. Moreover, even if I had chosen a successor, as of this moment you could erase from your mind any thoughts of yourself in that position!'' He stood up, shaking with rage. ''Now get your damned arse out of here! Get out before I—''

Dragosani took off his dark, wide-rimmed spectacles.

Borowitz looked at Dragosani's face and was suddenly staggered by the massive metamorphosis taken place in him. Why, it hardly seemed like Dragosani at all standing there but someone else entirely. And those *eyes*—those incredible scarlet eyes!

''I am retiring you, Gregor,'' Dragosani rumbled. ''But you don't go empty-handed. Not after so many years of faithful service.'' He crouched down into himself, his shoulders and back seeming to bunch up with a grotesque life of their own.

''Retiring me?'' Borowitz tried to back away from Dragosani but the couch was right behind him. ''You, retiring me?''

Dragosani nodded, opened his long jaws and smiled, displayed fangs like scythes. ''We have a small retirement gift for you, Gregor.''

''We?'' Borowitz croaked.

''Me and Max Batu,'' said Dragosani. And in the next moment Borowitz looked into the face of hell itself.

Then—it was as if a mule had kicked him in the chest. He flew backward, his arms thrown wide, crashed into the wall and bounded off. Small shelves and pictures were brought crashing down. Borowitz fell, half-sprawling on the couch. He clutched at his chest, fought to take control of his rubber limbs and climb to his feet, gulped air to his straining lungs. His heart felt crushed—and if he didn't know how, at least he knew what Dragosani had done to him.

Finally he struggled upright. ''Dragosani!'' he held out

wildly fluttering, pudgy hands towards the necromancer. "Drago—"

Again Dragosani hurled his psychic bolt, and again.

Borowitz was swatted like a fly by the first blast, knocked over backwards on to the couch. He actually managed to sit up, to finish the last word he would ever speak, before the second blast hit him: *"-sani!"*

Then it was done. The ex-boss of E-Branch sat there, upright, dead as a doornail, showing all the signs of a heart attack.

"Classic!" Dragosani grunted his approval.

He glanced about the room. The door of a corner cupboard stood open, displaying a battered old typewriter on a shelf with papers, envelopes and other items of stationery. He quickly carried the machine to a table, inserted a blank sheet of paper, began to type laboriously:

I feel unwell. I think it is my heart. Natasha's death has affected me badly. I think I am finished. Since I have not yet nominated another to carry on my work, I do so now. The only man who can be trusted to carry on where I leave off is Boris Dragosani. He is completely faithful to the USSR, and especially to the aims and welfare of the Party Leader.

Also, if as I fear the end is coming, I want my body put in Dragosani's care. He knows my wishes in this respect . . .

Dragosani grinned as he rolled the typewritten sheet up a space or two. He read over the note, took up a pen and scrawled "G.B." as nearly as possible in the style of Borowitz at the end of the last line, then dusted the keys with his handkerchief where he'd touched them and carried the machine to the couch. Sitting down beside the dead man, he took his hands and laid his fingers briefly on the keys. And all the time Borowitz watching him through sightless, popping eyes.

"All done, Gregor," said Dragosani as he took the typewriter back to the table. "I'm going now, but I'll not say goodbye just yet. After they find you we'll be meeting again, eh, at the Château Bronnitsy? And what price your innermost secrets than, Gregor Borowitz?"

It was 12:25 P.M. when he let himself out of the silent cabin in the trees and backtracked to his car.

Since it was a Saturday there were fewer people about than one would usually find at the Château Bronnitsy, but as the guards on the outer wall checked Dragosani through, so they sent word of his arrival ahead of him. At the central cluster of buildings the Duty Officer was waiting for him. Wearing the Château's uniform of grey overalls with a single diagonal yellow stripe across the heart, he came breathlessly forward to greet Dragosani where he parked his Volga in its designated space.

"Good news, Comrade!" he declared, walking with Dragosani through the complex and holding a door open for him. "We have word of this British agent, this Harry Keogh, for you."

Dragosani at once grabbed him by the shoulder, his grip like a vice. The other carefully disengaged himself, stared curiously at Dragosani. "Is anything wrong, Comrade?"

"Not if we've got Keogh," Dragosani growled. "No, nothing at all. But you're not the man I spoke to last night?"

"No, Comrade. He has gone off duty. I read his log, that's all. And of course I was here this morning when word of Keogh came in."

Dragosani looked more closely at the speaker. He saw him remotely. Thin and slope-shouldered, a typical nothing to look at—and yet puffed up with his own importance.

Not an ESPer, the Duty Officer was simply Senior Ground Staff. A good clerk, mainly, and efficient, but a bit too pompous—too smug and self-satisfied—for Dragosani's liking.

"Come with me," he said coldly. "You can tell me about Keogh as we go."

With the DO at his heels, Dragosani loped easily through the Château's corridors and began climbing stairs towards Borowitz's private office complex. Finding it hard to keep up, the man said, "Slow down a little, Comrade, or I'll not have breath to tell you anything!"

Dragosani kept going. "About Keogh," he snapped over his shoulder. "Where is he? Who has him? Are they bringing him here?"

"No one 'has' him, Comrade," the other puffed. "We merely know where he is, that's all. He's in East Germany, Leipzig. He got in through Checkpoint Charlie in Berlin—as a tourist! And no attempt to hide his identity, apparently. Very strange. He's been in Leipzig for three or four days now. Seems to have spent most of his time there in a graveyard! Obviously he's waiting for a contact."

"Oh?" Dragosani came to a brief halt, glared at the other, sneered at him. "Obvious, did you say? Let me tell you, Comrade, that nothing is obvious about that one! Now, quickly, come into my office and I'll give you some instructions."

A moment later and the DO followed Dragosani into the antechamber of Borowitz's suite. "Your office?" he gaped.

Behind his desk, Borowitz's secretary, a young man with thick-lensed spectacles, thin eyebrows and a prematurely receding hairline looked up, startled. Dragosani jerked his thumb towards the open door. "You, out! Wait outside. I'll call when I want you."

"What?" bewildered, the man stood up. "Comrade Dragosani, I must protest! I—"

Dragosani reached across the desk, grabbed the man by the left cheek of his face and dragged him bodily across the desk top, scattering pens and pencils everywhere. Amidst a squall of muted, pained squawkings, he whirled him towards the open door and aimed a kick at his backside as he released him. "Protest to Gregor Borowitz next time you see him," he snapped. "Until then obey my orders or I'll have you shot!"

He continued through into Borowitz's old office, the DO trembling as he followed on behind. Without pause Dragosani lowered himself into Borowitz's chair behind his desk, continued to glare at the DO. "Now, who's watching Keogh?"

Completely overawed, the DO stuttered a little before settling down. "I . . . I . . . we . . . the GREPO," he finally got it out. "The Grenzpolizei, the East German Border Police."

"Yes, yes—I know who the GREPO are," Dragosani scowled. Then he nodded. "Good! They're very efficient, I'm told. Right, these are my orders—on behalf of Gregor Borowitz. Keogh is to be taken, alive if possible. That was what I ordered last night, and I hate to repeat myself!"

"But they had no holding charge, Comrade Dragosani," the DO explained. "He is not listed, this Keogh, and so far he has done nothing wrong."

"The charge is . . . murder," said Dragosani. "He murdered one of our agents, a sleeper, in England. Anyway, he *will* be taken. If that proves difficult, the orders are to shoot him! I ordered that, too, last night."

The DO felt that he, personally, was being accused. He felt he had to make excuses: "But these are Germans, Comrade," he said. "Some of them like to believe that they still govern themselves, if you see what I mean."

"No," said Dragosani, "I don't. Use the telephone next

door. Get me the headquarters of the Grenzpolizei in Berlin. I'll speak to them.''

The DO stood gaping at him.

"Now!" Dragosani snapped. And as the man scurried out he called after him: ''And send in that dolt from outside.''

When Borowitz's secretary entered Dragosani said, ''Sit. And listen. Until the Comrade General returns I'll be in charge. What do you know about the working of this place?''

''Almost everything, Comrade Dragosani,'' answered the other, still pale and frightened and holding his face. ''The Comrade General left many things to me.''

''Manpower?''

''What about it, Comrade Drag—''

''Cut that out!'' Dragosani snapped. ''No more 'Comrade,' it wastes time. Simply call me Dragosani.''

''Yes, Dragosani.''

''Manpower,'' Dragosani said again. ''What do we have here right now?''

''Here at the Château? Right now? A skeleton staff of ESPers, and maybe a dozen security men.''

''Call-in system?''

''Oh, yes, Dragosani.''

''Good! I'll want at least enough men to make our numbers up to thirty. And I'll want them by 5:00 P.M.—at the very latest. I want our best telepaths and forecasters, including Igor Vlady, to be among them. Can that be done? Can we muster these men by 5:00 P.M.?''

The other immediately nodded. ''In more than three hours? Oh, yes, Dragosani. Definitely.''

''Then get on with it.''

When he was alone Dragosani settled back in his chair and put his feet up on the desk. He thought about what he was doing. If the East Germans took Keogh, especially if they killed him (in which case Dragosani must make sure that he, personally, got hold of the body) that must surely cancel out the possibility of Keogh's being part of tonight's disturbance. Mustn't it? In any case it was difficult to see how Keogh could possibly make it here, from Leipzig, in just a few hours. So perhaps Dragosani should be concentrating on some other eventuality—but what? Sabotage? Was the cold ESP war finally starting to heat up? Had his murdering Sir Keenan Gormley lit some sort of slow fuse, laid perhaps a long time ago? But what could possibly harm the Château? The place was impregnable as a castle. Fifty Keoghs wouldn't even make it over the outer wall!

Angry with himself, with the gradual build-up of tension inside him, Dragosani forced Keogh out of his mind. No, the threat must come from somewhere else. He gave a little more thought to the Château's fortifications.

Dragosani had never fully understood the need to fortify the Château, but now he was glad indeed for its defences. Of course, old Borowitz had been a soldier long before he had started E-Branch; he was an expert strategist, and doubtless he'd had his reasons for insisting on this degree of security. But here, right next door to Moscow itself? What had he feared? Insurgency? Trouble from the KGB, perhaps? Or was it just one of the old man's hangups from his political or military feuding days?

Not that this was the only fortified place in the USSR, far from it. The space centres, nuclear and plasma research stations, and the chemical and biological warfare labs at Berezov were all security hotspots, tight as proverbial drums.

Dragosani scowled. How he wished he had Borowitz here now, downstairs in his operating theatre, stretched out on a steel table with his guts hanging open and all the secrets of his soul laid bare. Ah, well, and that too would come to pass—when they finally found the old bastard's body!

"Comrade Dragosani!" the DO's voice calling from next door shattered his thoughts to shards. "I have GREPO HQ in Berlin for you. I'm putting them through now."

"Good," he called back. "And while I'm speaking to them there's something else you can do. I want the Château searched top to bottom. Especially the cellars. To my knowledge there are rooms down there no one ever went into. I want the place turned inside out. Look for bombs, incendiary devices, for anything at all that looks suspicious. I want as many men on it as possible—particularly the ESPers. Understood?"

"Yes, Comrade, of course."

"Very well, now let me speak to these damned Germans."

It was 3:15 P.M. and Arctic cold in the city cemetery in Leipzig.

Harry Keogh, his overcoat turned up around his ears and a flask of coffee (long empty) in his lap, sat frozen at the foot of August Ferdinand Möbius' grave and despaired. He had sought to apply his ESPer's mind—his "metaphysical" talent—to the equally conjectural properties of altered space-time and four-dimensional topology and failed. Intuition told him it was possible, that he could in fact take a Möbius trip sideways in time, but the mechanics of the thing were mountain-sized stumbling blocks that he just couldn't climb. His instinctive or intuitive grasp of maths and non-Euclidean geometry was not enough. He felt like a man given the equation $E = mc^2$ and then asked to prove it by producing an atomic explosion—but with his mind alone! How do you go about turning unbodied numbers, pure maths into physical facts? It's not enough to know that there are ten thousand bricks in a house; you can't build the house of numbers, you need the bricks! It was one thing for Möbius to send his unbodied mind out beyond the farthest stars, but Harry Keogh was a physical three-dimensional man of living flesh and blood. And just suppose he succeeded and actually discovered how to teleport himself from "A" to some hypothetical "B" without physically covering the space between. What then? Where would he teleport himself to—and how would he know when he was there? It could prove as dangerous as stepping off a cliff to prove the law of gravity!

For days now he'd occupied his mind with the problem to the exclusion of almost everything else. He had taken food and drink and sleep, yes, attending to all of Nature's needs, but to nothing else. And still the problem remained unsolved, space-time refused to warp for him, the equations remained dark unfathomed squiggles on the now grubby, well-thumbed pages of his mind. A wonderful ambition, certainly—to impose himself physically within a metaphysical frame—but how to go about it?

"You need a spur, Harry," said Möbius, wearily breaking in on his thoughts for what must be the fiftieth time in the last day or so. "Personally, I think that's all that remains. After all, necessity is the mother of invention, you know. So far you know *what* you want to do—and I for one believe you have the knack, the intuitive ability, even though you haven't found it yet—but you haven't a good enough *reason* for doing it! That's all you need now, the right spur. The prod that will make you take the final step."

Harry gave a mental nod of acknowledgement. "You're probably right," he said. "I know I *will* do it; it's just that I . . . haven't tried yet? It's something like giving up smoking: you can but can't. You probably will when it's too late, when you're dying of cancer. Except I don't want to wait that long! I mean, I have all the maths, all the theory—I have all the ego, really, the intuition—but I

462

haven't the need, not yet. Or the spur, if you like. Let me tell you what it feels like:

"I'm sitting in a well-lighted room with a window and a door. I look out the window and it's dark out there. It always will be. Not night but a stronger darkness that will last for ever. It's the darkness of the spaces *between* the spaces. I know there are other rooms out there somewhere. My problem is that I don't have any directions. If I go out that door I'll be part of the darkness, surrounded by it. I might not to able to come in again, here or anywhere else. It's not so much that I can't go out but more that I don't want to think about what it's like out there. Actually, to know it's there is to know I can go out into it. I feel that the going will just be an extension of the other things I can do, but an untried extension. I'm a chicken in a shell, and I won't break out until I have to!"

"Who are you talking to, Mr. Harry Keogh?" asked a voice that wasn't Möbius', a flat, cold voice, as curious as it was emotionless.

"What?" Startled, Harry looked up.

There were two of them, and it was obvious who or what they were. Even knowing nothing about spying or East-West politics, he would have recognized these two on sight. They chilled him more than the thin wind which now began to keen through the empty cemetery, blowing dead leaves and scraps of paper along the aisles between the tombs.

One was very tall, the other short, but their dark-grey overcoats, their hats pulled down at the front and their narrow-rimmed spectacles were so uniform in themselves as to make them appear twins. Certainly twins in their natures, in their thoughts and their petty ambitions. As plain-clothes men—policemen, probably political—they were quite unmistakable.

"What?" Harry said again, coming stiffly to his feet.

"Was I talking to myself again? I'm sorry about that, I do it all the time. It's just a habit of mine."

"Talking to yourself?" the tall one repeated him, and shook his head. "No, I don't think so." His accent was thick, his lips thin as his mirthless smile. "I think you were talking to someone else—probably to another spy, Harry Keogh!"

Harry backed away from them a pace or two. "I really don't know what—" he began.

"Where is your radio, Mr. Keogh?" said the short one. He came forward, kicked at the dirt of the grave where Harry had been sitting. "Is it here, buried in the soil, perhaps? Day after day, sitting here, talking to yourself? You must think we're all fools!"

"Listen," Harry croaked, still backing away. "You must have the wrong man. Spy? That's crazy. I'm a tourist, that's all."

"Oh?" said the tall one. "A tourist? In the middle of winter? A tourist who comes and sits in the same grave-yard day after day, to talk to himself? You can do better than that, Mr. Keogh. And so can we. We have it on good authority that you are a British agent, also that you're a murderer. So now, please, you will come with us."

"Don't go with them, Harry!" it was Keenan Gormley's voice, coming from nowhere, unbidden to Harry's mind. *"Run, man, run!"*

"What?" Harry gasped. "Keenan? But how . . . ?"

"Oh, Harry! My Harry!" cried his mother. *"Please be careful!"*

"What?" he said again, shaking his head, still backing away from the two men.

The small one produced handcuffs, said, "I must warn you, Mr. Keogh, against resistance. We are counterespionage officials of the Grenzpolizei, and—"

"Hit him, Harry!" urged Graham "Sergeant" Lane in

464

Harry's innermost ear. *"You have the measure of both these lads. You know the way. Do it to them before they do it to you. But watch it—they're armed!"*

As the short one took three quick paces forward, holding out the handcuffs, Harry adopted a defensive stance. Also closing in, the tall one yelled: "What's this? You threaten violence? You should know, Harry Keogh, that our orders are to take you dead or alive!"

The short one made to snap the cuffs on Harry's wrists. At the last moment Harry slapped them aside, half-turned, lashed out with his heel at the end of a leg stiffened into a bar of solid bone. The blow took the short one in the chest, snapped ribs, drove him backwards into his tall colleague. Screaming his agony, he slipped to the ground.

"You can't win, Harry!" Gormley insisted. *"Not like this."*

"He's right," said James Gordon Hannant. *"This is your last chance, Harry, and you have to take it. Even if you stop these two there'll be others. This isn't the way. You have to use your talent, Harry. Your talent is bigger than you suspect. I didn't teach you anything about maths—I only showed you how to use what was in you. But your full potential remains untapped. Man, you have formulae I haven't even dreamed of! You yourself once said something like that to my son, remember?"*

Harry remembered.

Strange equations suddenly flashed on the screen of his mind. Doors opened where no doors should be. His metaphysical mind reached out and grasped the physical world, eager to bend it to his will. He could hear the felled plain-clothes man screaming his rage and pain, could see the taller one reaching into his overcoat and drawing out an ugly, short-barrelled weapon. But printed over this picture of the real world, the doors in the Möbius space-time dimension were there within reach, their dark thresholds seeming to beckon.

"That's it, Harry!" cried Möbius himself. *"Any one of them will do!"*

"I don't know where they go!" he yelled out loud.

"Good luck, Harry!" shouted Gormley, Hannant and Lane, almost in unison.

The gun in the tall agent's hand spouted fire and lead. Harry twisted, felt a hot breath against his neck as something snatched angrily at the collar of his coat. He whirled, leaped, drop-kicked the tall man and felt deep satisfaction as his feet crashed into face and shoulder. The man went down, his weapon clattering to the hard ground. Cursing and spitting blood and teeth, he scrambled after it, grasped it in two hands, came up into a stumbling crouch.

Out of the corner of his eye, Harry spied a door in the Möbius strip. It was so close that if he reached out his hand he could touch it. The tall agent snarled something incomprehensible, swung his gun in Harry's direction. Harry knocked it aside, grabbed the man's sleeve, tugged him off balance and swung him—

—Through the open door.

The German agent was . . . no longer there! From nowhere, an awful, lingering, slowly fading scream came echoing back. It was the cry of the damned, of a soul lost for ever in ultimate darkness.

Harry listened to that cry and shuddered—but only for a moment. Over and above it as it dwindled, he heard shouted instructions, the crunch of running feet on gravel. Men were coming, dodging between the tombstones, converging on him. He knew that if he was going to use the doors, it had to be now. The injured agent on the ground was holding a gun in hands that trembled like jelly. His eyes were impossibly round for he had seen . . . *something!*

He was no longer sure if he dared pull the trigger and shoot at this man.

Harry didn't give him time to think it over. Kicking his gun away, he paused for one last split-second and let the screens in his mind display once more their fantastic formulae. The running men were closer; a bullet whined where it struck sparks from marble.

Printed over Möbius' headstone, a door floated out of nowhere. That was appropriate, Harry thought—and he made a headlong dive.

On the cold earth, the crippled East German agent watched him go, disappearing *into* the stone!

Panting men came together in a knot, skidding to a halt. All held guns extended forward, ready. They stared about, searched with keen, cold eyes. The crippled agent pointed. He lay there with his broken ribs and drained white face and pointed a trembling finger at Möbius' headstone. But for the moment, stunned to his roots, he said nothing at all.

The keening wind continued to blow.

By 4:45 P.M. Dragosani knew the worst of it. Harry Keogh was alive; he had not been taken but had somehow contrived to make his escape; what means he had employed in that escape were unknown, or at best the accounts were garbled and not to be trusted. But one agent was missing believed dead and another seriously injured, and now the East Germans were making angry noises and demanding to know just who or what they were dealing with. Well, let them demand what they would—Dragosani only wished he knew what *he* was dealing with!

Anyway, the problem was his now and time was pressing. For there could no longer be any doubt but that Keogh was coming here, and coming tonight? How? Who could say? When, exactly? That, too, remained impossible to gauge. But of one thing Dragosani was absolutely certain: come he would. One man, hurling himself against a small army! His task was impossible, of course—but Dragosani knew of the existence of many things which ordinary men considered impossible . . .

Meanwhile, the Château's emergency call-in system had worked well. Dragosani had all the men he had asked for and half-a-dozen more. They manned machine-gun posts on the outer walls, similar batteries in the outbuildings, also the fortified pill-boxes built into the buttresses of the Château itself. ESPers "worked" down below in the laboratories, in surroundings best suited to their various abilities and talents, and Dragosani had turned Borowitz's offices into his tactical HQ.

The Château had been searched, as per his orders, top to bottom; but as soon as he had learned of Keogh's escape he had called a halt to that; he had known where the trouble must originate. By then the lower vaults of the place had been explored to the full, floorboards and centuried flagstones had been ripped up in the older buildings, the foundations of the place had been laid bare almost down to the earth itself. Three dozen men can do a lot of damage in three hours, particularly when they've been told that their lives may well depend upon it.

But what enraged Dragosani most of all was the thought that all of this was on account of just one man, Harry Keogh, and that utter chaos had been forecast in his name. Which meant quite simply that Keogh wielded an awesome power of destruction. But what was it? Dragosani knew he was a necroscope—so what? Also, he had seen a dead thing rise up from a river and come to his aid. But that had been his mother and the location had been Scotland, thousands of miles away. There was no one here to fight Keogh's battles for him.

Of course, if Dragosani was so worried by all of this he

could always flee the place (the trouble was scheduled for the Château Bronnitsy and nowhere else), but that just wouldn't be in his own interest. Not only would it smack of utter cowardice, it wouldn't fulfill Igor Vlady's prediction —his prediction that the vampire in Dragosani would die this night. And that was one prediction Boris Dragosani desired fulfilled above all others. Indeed it was his ambition, while his mind was still his own to crave for it!

As for Vlady himself—the call-in squad had found a note at his place which explained his absence, a note intended for his fiancée. Vlady would call for her soon, the note said, from the West. Dragosani had been delighted to put out the traitor's description to all relevant points of egress. Nor had he given him any quarter: he was to be shot on sight, in the name of the security of the mighty USSR.

So much for Vlady, and yet . . . would he have fared any better here? Dragosani wondered about that. Had he, Dragosani, terrified Vlady that much, or had it been something else he'd fled from?

Something he'd seen approaching, perhaps, out of the very near future.

Chapter Sixteen

IT WAS AS HARRY HAD SUSPECTED IT WOULD BE: BEYOND
the Möbius doors he discovered the Primal Darkness itself,
that darkness which existed before the universe began.

It was not only the absence of light but the absence of
everything. He might be at the core of a black hole, except
a black hole has enormous gravity and this place had none.
In one sense it was a metaphysical plane of existence, but
in another it was not—because nothing existed here. It was
simply a "place," but a place in which no God as yet had
uttered those wonderful words of evocation, "Let there be
light!"

It was nowhere, and it was everywhere; it was both
central and external. From here one might *go* anywhere, or
go nowhere forever And it *would be* for ever, for in this
timeless environment nothing ever aged or changed, except by force of will. Harry Keogh was therefore a foreign
body, an unwanted mote in the eye of the Möbius continuum, and it must try to reject him. He felt matterless

forces working on him even now, pushing at him and attempting to dislodge him from the unreal back into the real. Except he must not let himself be pushed.

There were doors he could conjure, certainly, a million million doors leading to all places and all times, but he knew that most of these places and times would be totally lethal to him. No use, like Möbius, to emerge in some distant galaxy in deep space. Harry was not merely a creature of mind but also of matter. He had no desire to freeze, or fry, or melt, or explode.

The problem, then, was this: which door?

Harry's dive through Möbius' tombstone might have carried him a yard or a light-year, he might have been here for a minute or a month, when he felt the first tentative tug of a force other than the rejection forces of this hyperspace-time dimension. Not even a tug, as such, it was more a gentle pressure that seemed to want to guide him. He'd known something like it before, when he'd tracked his mother under the ice and come up in her pool beneath the overhanging bank. There seemed nothing of a threat in it, anyway.

Harry went with it, following it and feeling it intensify, homing in on it as a blind man homes in on a friendly voice. Or a moth on the bright flame of a candle? No, for his intuition told him that whatever it was there was no harm in it. Stronger still the force bobbed him along this parallel space-time stream, and like seeing a light at the end of a tunnel, so he sensed the way ahead and began to will himself in that direction.

"Good!" said a distant voice in Harry's head. "Very good. Come to me, Harry Keogh, come to me . . ."

It was a female voice, but there was little of warmth in it. Thin, it keened like the wind in the Leipzig graveyard, and like the wind it was old as the ages.

"Who are you?" Harry asked.

"A friend," came the answer, stronger now.

Harry continued to will himself towards the mental voice. He willed himself . . . *that* way. And there before him, a Möbius door. He reached for it, paused. "How do I know you're a friend? How do I know I can trust you?"

"I asked that same question once," said the voice, almost in his ear. "For I too had no way of knowing. But I trusted."

Harry willed the door open and passed through.

Stretched out in his original dive, he found himself suspended maybe three inches above the ground, and fell— then clung to the earth and hugged himself to it. The voice in his head chuckled. "There," it said. "You see? A friend . . ."

Dizzy and feeling sick, Harry gradually withdrew his fingers from loose, dry soil. He lifted his head a fraction, stared all about. Light and colour struck almost physical blows on his reeling vision. Light and warmth. That was the first impression to really get through to him: how warm it was. The soil was warm under his prone body, the sun unseasonally warm where it shone on his neck and his hands. Where on God's earth was he? Was he on Earth at all?

Slowly, still dizzy, he sat up. And gradually, as he felt gravity working on him, so things stopped revolving and he uttered a loud "Phew!" of relief.

Harry wasn't much travelled or he'd have recognized the terrain at once as being Mediterranean. The soil was a yellowy-brown and streaked with sand, the plants were those of scrubland, the sun's warmth in January told of his proximity to the equator. Certainly he was thousands of miles closer to it here than he'd been in Leipzig. In the distance a mountain range threw up low peaks; closer there were ruins, crumbling white walls and mounds of rubble; and overhead—

A pair of jet fighter planes, like speeding silver darts against the pure blue of the sky, left vapour trails as they hastened towards the horizon. Their thunder rolled down over him, muted by distance.

Harry breathed easier, looked again towards the ruins. Middle-Eastern? Probably. Just some ancient village fallen victim to Nature's grand reclamation scheme. And again he wondered where he was.

"Endor," said the voice in his head. "That was its name when it had a name. It was my home."

Endor? That rang a bell. The biblical Endor? The place where Saul went on the night before his death on the slopes of Gilboa? Where he went to seek out—a witch?

"That is what they called me, aye," she chuckled drily in his mind. "The Witch of Endor. But that was long and long ago, and there have been witches and witches. Mine was a great talent, but now a greater one is come into the world. In my long sleep I heard of him, this mighty wizard, and such were the rumours that they awakened me. The dead call him their friend and there are those among the living who fear him greatly. Aye, and I desired to speak with this one, who is already a legend among the tomb-legions. And lo!—I called and he came to me. And his name is Harry Keogh . . ."

Harry stared at the earth where he sat, put down his hands and pressed upon it. His hands came away dusty and dry. "You're . . . here?" he said.

"I am one with the dust of the world," she answered. "My dust is here."

Harry nodded. Two thousand years is a long time. "Why did you help me?" he asked.

"Would you have me damned for ever by all the teeming dead?" she answered at once. "Why did I help you? Because they asked it of me! All of them! Your fame precedes you, Harry. 'Save this one!' they begged me, 'for he is beloved of us.' "

Again Harry nodded. "My mother," he said.

"Your mother is but one," answered the witch. "She is your chief advocate, certainly, but the dead are many. She pleaded with you, aye, and many a thousand with her."

Harry was astonished. "I don't know thousands," he said. "I know a dozen, two dozen at most."

Again her chuckle, long, dry and mirthless. "But they know you! And how may I ignore my brothers and sisters in the earth?"

"You wish to help me?"

"Yes."

"Do you know what I have to do?"

"Others have informed me, aye."

"Then give me whatever aid you can—*if* you can. Frankly, and while I don't wish to seem ungrateful, I don't see how there's a lot you can do."

"Oh? But I controlled some of these same powers you control two thousands years ago. And are my arts forgotten? A king came to me for help, Harry Keogh!"

"Saul? Little good it did him," said Harry, but not unkindly.

"He asked me to show him his future," she answered defensively, "and I showed him."

"And you can show me mine?"

"Your future?" She was silent for a moment. Then: "I have already looked upon your future, Harry, but of that ask me not."

"That bad, eh?"

"There are deeds to be performed," she answered, "and wrongs to be righted. If I were to show you what will be, it would not make you strong for the task ahead. Like Saul, perhaps you too would faint away upon the earth."

"I'm going to lose?" Harry's heart sank.

"Something of you shall be lost."

Harry shook his head. "I don't like the sound of that. Can't you say more?"

"I will not say more."

"Then perhaps you'll help me with the Möbius dimension. I mean, how may I find my way about in it? I don't know what I'd have done if you hadn't guided me out of there."

"But I know nothing of this thing," she answered, obviously puzzled. "I called to you and you heard me. Why not let them also guide you who love you?"

Was that possible? Harry thought it probably was. "At least that's something," he said. "I can give it a try. Now, how else can you help me?"

"For Saul the king," she answered, "I called up Samuel. Now there are also some who would speak to you. Let me be the medium of their messages."

"But it's self-evident I can speak to the dead for myself!" he said.

"But not to these three," she answered, "for you know them not."

"Very well, let me speak to them."

"Harry Keogh," a new voice now whispered in his head, a soft voice that belied the once-cruelty of its master. "I saw you one time and you saw me. My name is Max Batu."

Harry gasped, spat his disgust on to the sand. "Max Batu? You're no friend of mine," he scowled "You killed Keenan Gormley!" Then he thought about who he was speaking to. "But you? Dead? I don't understand."

"Dragosani killed me," the other told him. "He did it to steal my talent with his necromancy. He slit my throat and gutted me, and left my body to rot. Now he has the evil eye. I make no pretence of being your friend, Harry Keogh, but I'm much less a friend of his. I tell you this because it might help you to kill him—before he kills you. It is my revenge!"

And as Max Batu's voice faded, another took its place:
"I was Thibor Ferenczy," it said, its timbre sad and soulful. "I could have lived for ever. I was a vampire, Harry Keogh, but Dragosani destroyed me. I was undead; now I am merely dead."

A vampire! Just such a creature had cropped up in Gormley's and Kyle's word-association game. Kyle had seen a vampire in Harry's future. But: "I can hardly condemn Dragosani for killing a vampire!" he said.

"I don't want you to condemn him," the voice grew harsh in a moment, shedding its sorrow like a worn-out snakeskin. "I want you to kill him! I want the lying, cheating, illegitimate necromantic dog dead, dead, dead! —like me! And I know he *will* be dead—I know you *will* kill him—but only with my help. Only if you'll . . . bargain with me?"

"Do not, Harry!" the Witch of Endor warned him. "Satan himself is no match for a vampire where lies and deceit are concerned."

"No bargains," Harry took her point.

"But it is *such* a small thing I want!" Thibor protested, his mental voice growing into a whine.

"How small?"

"Only promise me that now and then—once in a while, be it ever so long—when you have the time, then that you'll speak to me. For there are none so lonely as I am now, Harry Keogh."

"Very well, I promise."

The ex-vampire sighed his relief. "Good! And now I know why the dead love you. Now know this, Harry: Dragosani has a vampire in him! The creature is still immature, but it grows fast and learns even faster. And do you know how to kill a vampire?"

"A wooden stake?"

"That is only to pin him down. But then you must behead him!"

476

"I'll remember that," Harry nodded, nervously licking dry lips.

"And remember too your promise," said Thibor, his voice fading into nothing. For a moment then it was silent and Harry was left to think about the awesome *nature* of this composite creature he'd pitted himself against; but then, out of the silence, he heard the voice of the third and last informer:

"Harry Keogh," growled this final visitation, "you don't know me, but Sir Keenan Gormley may have told you something of me. I was Gregor Borowitz. Now I am no more. Dragosani killed me with Max Batu's evil eye. I am dead in my prime, by treachery!"

"So you too seek revenge," said Harry. "Had he no friends, this Dragosani? Not even one?"

"Yes, he had me. I had plans for Dragosani, great plans. Ah, but the bastard had plans of his own! And I wasn't part of them. He killed me for my knowledge of E-Branch, so that he can control what I created. But it goes farther than that. I think he wants—everything! I mean literally everything under the sun. And if he lives he might very well get everything, eventually."

"Eventually?"

There came a great mental shudder from Borowitz. "You see, he's not finished with me yet. My body lies in my dacha where he left it, but sooner or later it will be delivered into his hands, and then he'll deal with me as he dealt with Max Batu. I don't want that, Harry. I don't want that scum wading through *my* guts in search of my secrets!"

Something of his horror transmitted itself to Harry, but still the necroscope could feel no pity for him. "I understand your motivation," he said, "but if he hadn't killed you I would have. If I could. For my mother, for Keenan Gormley, for everyone you've hurt or would hurt."

"Yes, yes, of course you would," said Borowitz without enmity, "if you could. I was a soldier before I was a schemer, Harry Keogh. I understand honour even if Dragosani doesn't. It's because of all these things that I want to help you."

"I accept your reasons," said Harry. "How can you help me?"

"First I can tell you all I know about the Château Bronnitsy: its design and layout, the people who work there. Here, take it all," and he quickly imparted to Harry all knowledge of the place and of the ESPers who worked there. "And then I can tell you something else, something which you, with your special talent, can use to good advantage. I've said I was first a soldier. So I was, and my knowledge of warfare was second to none. I had studied the entire history of warfare from Man's beginnings. I had traced his wars right across the face of the planet, and knew all the old battlefields intimately. You ask how I can help you? Well listen and I'll tell you."

Harry listened, and slowly his strange eyes opened wider and a grim smile spread itself across his face. He had been weary until now, burdened. But now a massive weight was lifted from his shoulders. He did have a chance, after all. Finally Borowitz was finished.

"Well, we were enemies," said Harry then, "even though we never met in the flesh. But I thank you anyway. You know of course that I intend to destroy your organization as well as Dragosani?"

"No more than he'd destroy it," the other growled. "Anyway, I have to go now. There's someone else I want to find, if I can . . ." And his voice, too, faded into silence.

Harry looked at the rugged terrain all around and saw how the sun dipped lower in the sky. Dust devils raced along a ridge. Kites wheeled in the sky as the day turned towards evening. And for a long while, as the shadows lengthened, he sat there on the sand and pebbles with his chin in his hands, just thinking.

At last he said, "They all want to help me."

"Because you bring them hope," the Witch of Endor told him. "For centuries, indeed since time itself began, the dead have lain still in their graves and that was that. But now they stir, they seek each other out, they talk to each other in a manner you have taught them. They have found a champion. Only ask of them, Harry Keogh, and they will obey . . ."

Harry stood up, gazed all around, felt the chill of evening beginning to creep. "I see no reason to stay here any longer," he said. "As for you, old lady: I don't know how to thank you."

"I have all the thanks I want," she answered. "The teeming dead thank me."

He nodded. "Yes, and there are some of them I want to speak to—first."

"Go then," she answered. "The future waits for you as it waits for all men."

Harry said no more but conjured the Möbius doors, chose one and walked through it.

He went first to his mother, finding his way to her without difficulty; then to "Sergeant" Graham Lane at Harden, including a quick jump of only fifty yards or so to the grave of James Gordon Hannant; then to a Garden of Repose in Kensington, where Keenan Gormley's ashes had been scattered, but where Gormley himself remained; and finally to Gregor Borowitz's dacha in Zhukovka. He spent perhaps ten to fifteen minutes in each location with the exception of the last. It was one thing to talk to dead men in their graves but quite another to talk to one who sat there and looked at you with glassy, pus-dripping eyes.

In any case, by the time Harry was through he was satisfied that he knew his business, that he could now safely negotiate the intricacies of the Möbius continuum; and by then there was only one place left to go. But first he took down a double-barrelled shotgun from the wall and filled his pockets with cartridges from a drawer.

It was just 6:30 P.M. East European time when he started to ride the Möbius strip from Zhukovka to the Château Bronnitsy. Along the way he became aware that someone rode the strip with him, knew he wasn't alone in the Möbius continuum. "Who's there?" he called out with his mind in the ultimate darkness of the journey.

"Just another dead man," came the answer, but in a voice wry and humourless. "In my life I read the future, but I had to die to understand and finally realize the full extent of my talent. Strangely, in your 'now' I am still alive, but I shall be dead shortly."

"I don't understand," said Harry.

"I didn't expect you to understand immediately. I'm here to explain. My name is Igor Vlady. I worked for Borowitz. I made the mistake of reading my own future, my own death. That will happen two days from your 'now,' as a result of Boris Dragosani's ordering it. But after death I will go on to explore my own potential. What I did in life I will do even better in death. If I wanted to I could see backward to the beginning of time, or go forward to its end—if time had a beginning and an end. But of course it has not; it is all a part of the Möbius continuum, an endlessly twisting loop containing all space and time. Let me show you:"

And he showed Harry the doors into the future and the past, and Harry stood on their thresholds and viewed time that had been and time still to come; except that he could not understand what he saw. For beyond the future-time door all was a chaos of millions of lines of blue light, and one of these streamed from his own being out through the door and into the future—*his* future. Likewise beyond the past-time door: the same blue light pouring out of him and fading into the past—*his* past—along with the light of countless millions of others. And such was the dazzling blue brilliance of all those life-threads that he was almost blinded by it.

"But no light shines from you," he said to Igor Vlady. "Why is that?"

"Because my light has been extinguished. Now I am like Möbius: pure mind. And where space holds no secrets for him, time holds none for me."

Harry thought about it, said: "I want to see my life-thread again." And again he stood on the threshold of the door to the future. He looked into the bright blue furnace of the future and saw his life-thread shimmering into it like a neon ribbon, and he could see it clearly where it curved away into future time. But even as he watched, so the end of his thread of life came into view; and then it seemed to him that the blue life-light of his body was not flowing out of him but flowing in! The thread was being eaten up by him as he approached his own end! And now that end was plainly visible, speeding towards him like a meteor out of the future!

Quickly, in terror of the Unknown, he stepped back from the door and once more into darkness. "Am I going to die?" he asked then. "Is that what you're telling me, showing me?"

"Yes—" said the time-travelling mind of Igor Vlady "—and no."

Again Harry failed to understand. "I'm about to pass through a Möbius door to the Château Bronnitsy," he said. "If I'm going to die there I'd like to know it. The Witch of Endor told me that I would lose 'something' of myself. Now I've seen the end of my life-thread." He

481

gave a nervous mental shrug. "It seems I'm coming to the end of my tether . . ."

In answer he sensed a nod. "But if you were to use the future-time door," said Vlady, "you could go on *beyond* the end of your thread—to where it begins again!"

"Begins again?" Harry was baffled. "Are you saying I'm to live again?"

"There's a second thread which is also you, Harry. It lives even now. All it lacks is mind." And Vlady explained his meaning; he read Harry's future for him, just as he once read Boris Dragosani's. Except that where Harry had a future, Dragosani had only a past. And now, at last, Harry had all the answers.

"I owe you my thanks," he told Vlady then.

"You owe me nothing," said Vlady.

"But you came to me just in time," Harry insisted, little realizing the significance of his words.

"Time is relative," the other shrugged and chuckled. "What will be, has been!"

"Thanks, anyway," said Harry, and passed through the door to the Château Bronnitsy.

At 6:31 P.M. exactly, Dragosani's telephone came janglingly alive, causing him to start.

Outside it was dark now, made darker by snow falling heavily from a black sky. Searchlights in the Château's outer walls and towers swept the ground between the complex itself and the perimeter wall, as they had swept it since the fall of dark, but now their beams were reduced to mere swaths of grey light whose poor penetration was of little or no consequence.

Dragosani found it annoying that vision should be so reduced, but the Château's defences had more going for them than human eyesight alone; there were sensitive tripwires out there, the latest electronic detection devices, even a belt of anti-personnel mines in a circle just beyond the outbuilding pill-boxes.

None of which gave Dragosani any real sensation of security; Igor Vlady's predictions had ignored all such protections. In any case, the call did not come from the pill-boxes or the fortified perimeter: the men in their defensive positions were all equipped with hand radios. This call was either external or it came from a department within the Château itself.

Dragosani snatched the handset from its cradle, snapped, "Yes, what is it?"

"Felix Krakovitch," a trembling voice answered. "I'm down in my lab. Comrade Dragosani, there's . . . something!" Dragosani knew the man: a seer, a minor prognosticator. His talent wasn't up to Vlady's standard by a long shot, but neither was it to be ignored—not on this of all nights.

"Something?" Dragosani's nostrils flared. The man had put an eerie emphasis on the word. "Make sense, Krakovitch! What's wrong?"

"I don't know, Comrade. It's just that . . . something's coming. Something terrible. No, it's here. It's here now!"

"What's 'here'?" Dragosani snarled into the phone. "Where, 'here'?"

"Out there, in the snow. Belov feels it, too."

"Belov?" Karl Belov was a telepath, and a good one over short distances. Borowitz had often used him at foreign embassy parties, picking up what he could from the minds of his hosts. "Is Belov there with you now? Put him on."

Belov was asthmatic. His voice was always soft and gasping, his sentences invariably short. Right now they were even more so: "He's right, Comrade," he gasped. "There's a mind out there—a powerful mind!"

Keogh! It had to be him. "Just one?" Dragosani's

once-sensitive lips curled back from a mouthful of white daggers. His red eyes seemed to light from within. How Keogh had come here he couldn't say, but if he was alone he was a dead man—and to hell with that traitor Vlady's predictions!

On the other end of the line, Belov fought for air, struggled to find a means of expression.

"Well?" Dragosani hastened him.

"I . . . I'm, not sure," said Belov. "I thought there was only one, but now—"

"Yes?" Dragosani almost shouted. "Damn it all!—am I surrounded by idiots? What *is* it, Belov? What's out there?"

Belov panted into the phone at his end, gasped. "He's . . . calling. He's some sort of telepath himself, and he's calling."

"To you?" Dragosani's brows knitted in baffled frustration. His great nostrils sniffed suspiciously, anxiously, as if to draw the answer from the air itself.

"No, not to me. He's calling to . . . to others. Oh, God—*and they're beginning to answer him!*"

"Who is answering him?" Dragosani barked. "What's wrong with you, Belov? Are there traitors? Here in the Château."

There came a clattering from the other end—a low moan and a thudding sound—then Krakovitch again: "He has fainted, Comrade!"

"What?" Dragosani couldn't believe his ears. "Belov, fainted? What the hell—?"

Lights were beginning to flicker on the call-sign panel of the radio Dragosani had had moved in here from the DO's control cell. A number of men with handsets were trying to contact him from their defensive positions. Next door Borowitz's secretary, Yul Galenski, sat nervously behind his desk, twitching as he listened to Dragosani's raging. And now the necromancer started bellowing for him:

"Galenski, are you deaf? Get in here. I need assistance!"

At that moment the DO burst in from the landing in the central stairwell. He carried weapons: stubby machine-pistols. As Galenski started to his feet he said: "You sit there, I'll go in."

Without pause for knocking he almost ran into the other room, pulled up short, gasping, as he saw Dragosani crouched over the radio's panel of blinking lights. Dragosani had taken his glasses off. Snarling soundlessly at the radio, he seemed more like some hunched, half-crazy beast than a man.

Still staring in astonishment at the necromancer's face, his awful eyes, the DO dumped an armful of weapons onto a chair; as he did so, Dragosani said: "Stop gawping!" He reached out a great hand and grabbed the DO's shoulder, dragged him effortlessly towards the radio. "Do you know how to operate this damned thing?"

"Yes, Dragosani," the DO gulped, finding his voice. "They are trying to speak to you."

"I can see that, fool!" Dragosani snapped. "Well then, speak to them. Find out what they want."

The DO perched himself on the edge of a steel chair in front of the radio. He took up the handset, flipped switches, said: "This is Zero. All call-signs acknowledge, over."

The replies came in sharp, numerical succession: "Call-sign One, OK, over."

"Two, OK, over."

"Three, OK, over." And so on rapidly through fifteen call-signs. The voices were tinny and there was some static, but over and above that they all seemed a little too shrill, all contained a ragged edge of barely controlled panic.

"Zero for call-sign One, send your message, over," said the DO.

"One: there are *things* out in the snow!" the answer came back at once, One's voice crackling with static and mounting excitement. "They're closing on my position! Request permission to open fire, over."

"Zero for One: wait, out!" snapped the DO. He looked at Dragosani. The necromancer's red eyes were open wide, like clots of blood frozen in his inhuman face.

"No!" he snarled. "First I want to know what we're dealing with. Tell him to hold his fire and give me a running commentary."

White-faced, the DO nodded, passed on Dragosani's order, was glad that he wasn't stuck out there in a pillbox in the snow—but on the other hand, could that be any worse than being stuck in here with the madman Dragosani?

"Zero, this is One!" One's voice crackled out of the radio, almost hysterical with excitement now. "They're coming in a semicircle out of the snow. In a minute they'll hit the mines. But they move so . . . so slowly! *There!* One of them stepped on a mine! It blew him to bits—but the others keep coming! They're thin, ragged—they don't make any noise. Some of them have—swords?"

"Zero for One: you keep calling them 'things.' Aren't they men?"

One's radio procedure went out the window. "Men?" His voice was completely hysterical. "Maybe they are men, or were—once. I think I'm insane! This is unbelievable!" He tried to get a grip on himself. "Zero, we're alone here and there are . . . many of them. I request permission to open fire. I *beg* you! I must protect myself . . ."

A white foam began to gather at the corners of Dragosani's gaping mouth as he stared at a wall-chart, checking One's location. It was an outbuilding pill-box directly below the command tower but fifty yards out from the Château itself. Occasionally as the snow swirled he could see its low, squat dark outline through the bullet-proof bay windows, but as yet no sign of the unknown invaders. He stared out into the snow again, and at that precise moment saw a blaze of orange fire erupt to throw the outbuilding into brief silhouette—and this time there came a low *crump* of an explosion as another mine was tripped.

The DO looked to him for instructions.

"Tell him to describe these . . . things!" Dragosani snapped.

Before the DO could obey, another call-sign came up unbidden: "Zero, this is Eleven. Fuck One! These bastards are all over the place! If we don't open fire now they'll be crawling all over us. You want to know what they are? I'll tell you: *they're dead men!*"

That was it. It was what Dragosani had feared. Keogh *was* here, definitely, and he was calling up the dead! But where from?

"Tell them to fire at will," he coughed the words out in a spray of froth. "Tell them to cut the bastards down—whatever they are!"

The DO passed on his orders. But already, from every quarter, dull explosions were beginning to pound all around the Château; the harsh clatter of machine-gun fire, too. The defenders had finally used their own initiative, had commenced firing almost point-blank on a zombie army that came marching inexorably through the snow.

Gregor Borowitz had not lied. He had indeed known his History of Warfare, and especially in his native land. In 1579 Moscow had been sacked by Tartars from the Crimea; there had been arguments about the division of the loot from the city; a would-be Khan had challenged the authority of his superiors; he and his splinter-group of three hundred horsemen had then been stripped of loot, rank, most of their weapons, and whipped out of the city. Disgraced and scavenging where they could, they had ridden south. It had rained heavily and they had bogged down in a marshy triangle of forest where rivers overflowed their banks. There a five-hundred-strong Russian force riding to the relief of the beleaguered city had come across them in the mist and rain and cut them down to a man. Their bodies had gone down in mud and mire. never to be seen again—until now.

Nor had they needed much persuasion from Harry; indeed they'd seemed merely to be waiting for him, ready at a moment's notice to fight their way free of the bitter earth where they had lain for four hundred years. Bone by bone, tatter by leathery tatter they had come up, some of them still bearing the rusted arms of yesteryear, and at Harry's command they'd moved on the Château Bronnitsy.

Harry had stepped out of the Möbius continuum inside the perimeter walls; the defenders of those walls, gazing outward, hadn't even seen him or the agonizing emergence of his long-dead army. Moreover, the machine-gun emplacements on the outer walls were pointing the wrong way; which all combined with the night and the snow to give him excellent cover.

But then there had been the tripwires and other intruder detection devices, and now there was the minefield and the inner ring of disguised pill-boxes.

For Harry none of these obstacles was any great problem: they weren't even obstacles when at will he could simply step out of this universe and back into it a moment later in any room in the Château where he chose to reappear. But first he wanted to see how his back-up force was making out: he wanted the Château's defenders fully engaged in the business of protecting their own lives, not the life of Boris Dragosani.

At the moment he was down on his belly in a shallow depression, huddled behind a headless bone-and-leather thing which a moment ago had marched ahead of him towards the pill-box outbuilding where call-sign One and his machine-gunner second in command sat and gibbered through their viewing slits, firing long bursts into the wall of death which slowly bore down on them. A large percentage of Harry's army—about half of his three hundred—had emerged from the earth in this sector, and the mines were quickly taking an unfair toll of them. Even now the pill-box and its chattering gun were dealing Harry's army terrific blows.

He decided to take out the pill-box, broke open Gregor Borowitz's shotgun and slipped cartridges into the double breach.

"Take me with you," begged the Tartar who shielded him. "I helped sack a city once, and this is but a palace." His skull head had been taken off by shrapnel from a landmine, but that hadn't seemed to matter much. He still held up a massive, battered iron and bronze shield, its rim dug into the cold earth, upright in the snow, using his own bones and the shield to give Harry as much cover as possible.

"No," said Harry, shaking his head. "There won't be much room in there and I'll need to get in and get it over with. But I'd be obliged for the use of your shield."

"Take it," said the corpse, releasing the heavy plate from fingers of crusted bone. "I hope it serves you well."

A mine went off somewhere to the right, its flash turning the falling snow orange for a moment and its thunder shaking the earth. In the momentary burst of light, Harry had seen an arc of skeletal figures stumbling ever closer to the dark huddled shape of the pill-box; so had the men inside. Armour-piercing machine-gun bullets screamed in the air, blowing apart Tartar remains and coming dangerously close. For all that Harry's ancient shield was heavy, still it was rotten with rust and decay; he knew it wouldn't stop a direct hit.

"Go now!" urged the dead thing where it struggled to its bony feet and lurched forward headlessly. "Kill some of them for me."

Harry narrowed his eyes one last time through flurries of snow and fixed the location of the fire-spewing outbuilding in his mind, then rolled sideways through a Möbius door—and into the pill-box.

No time for thinkng in there, and little or no room for movement. What had looked from outside like an old cowshed was in fact a cramped nest of steel plates and concrete blocks, slate-grey gunmetal and shining ammunition-belts. Grey light fought its way in through arc-of-fire and viewing slits, turning the cordite and sweat-smelling interior to a drifting smog in which call-sign One and his second in command coughed and spluttered where they worked furiously and feverishly.

Harry emerged in the tight space behind them, dropping his shield to the concrete floor as he swung up the loaded shotgun.

Hearing the clatter as the shield fell, both Russians turned in their steel-backed swivel chairs. They saw a white-faced youth in an overcoat cradling a shotgun, his eyes bright points of light above pinched nostrils and the grim, tight line of his mouth.

"Who—?" gasped One. He looked like some strange, startled, waspish alien in his Château uniform, with his headset for antennae above goggling eyes.

"How—?" said his second in command, his fingers automatically completing the task of fitting a new belt to the machine-gun.

Then call-sign One was scrabbling to snatch a pistol from his holster, and his second in command was coming to his feet, cursing.

Harry felt no pity for them. It was them or him. And there were plenty of others just like them to welcome them where they were going. He pulled the triggers: one for One, two for his second in command, and blew them screaming into the arms of death. The stench of hot blood quickly mingled with acrid cordite and the reek of sweat and fear, causing Harry's eyes to water. He blinked them furiously, broke open the shotgun and reloaded, found another Möbius door.

The next pill-box was the same, and the one after that. Six of them in all, they were all the same. Harry took them out in less than two minutes.

In the last one, when it was done he found the chaotic mind of one of the fresh dead defenders and calmed him. "It's over for you now," he said, "but the one who brought all this about is still alive. You'd be home with your family tonight if not for him. And so would I. Now, where's Dragosani?"

"In Borowitz's office, in the tower," said the other. "He's turned it into the control room. There'll be others with him."

"I expect there will," said Harry, staring into the Russian's shattered, smoking, unrecognizable face. "Thanks."

And then there was only one thing left to do, but Harry fancied he'd need a little help to do it.

He snapped open the clamps that held the machine-gun in place on its swivelling base, took up the heavy gun and hurled it down to the hard floor, then lifted it and threw it down again. After being dashed to the concrete three or four times the hard wooden stock splintered lengthwise, allowing Harry to break off a jagged stake with a flat base and a sharp, hardwood point.

He reached for his cartridges and found only one left, gritted his teeth and loaded the single cartridge into his shotgun. It would have to be enough. Then he pulled open the pill-box door and stepped out into the swirling snow.

In the near distance, softened by night and the fast-falling snow, the Château blazed with light, its searchlight beams cutting to and fro as they searched for targets. Most of Harry's army—what remained of it—was already at the walls of the Château itself, however, from which the staccato yammering of machine-guns now sounded unceasingly. The remaining defenders were trying to kill dead men, and they were finding it hard.

Harry looked about, saw a group of latecomers leaning into the snow as they plodded towards the beleaguered building. Eerie figures they were, gaunt scarecrow men, creaking past him in monstrous animation. But death held no fears for Harry Keogh. He stopped two of them, a pair of mummied cadavers a little less ravaged than the rest, and offered one the hardwood stake. "For Dragosani," he said.

The other Tartar carried a great curving sword all scabbed with rust; Harry reckoned he'd used it in his day to devastating effect. Well, and now—with any justice—he'd use it again. He pointed to the sword, nodded, said. "That, too, is for Dragosani—for the vampire in him."

Then he opened a Möbius door, and guiding his two sere companions stepped through it.

Inside the Château Bronnitsy it had been all hell let loose almost from the beginning. The place had been built two hundred and thirty years ago on an ancient battlefield; the building itself was a mausoleum for a dozen of the fiercest of all the Tartar warriors. And its protection had kept the peaty ground pliant, so that the bodies which had lain there were more truly mummies than fleshless corpses.

Also, Dragosani had ordered the great stone flags in the cellars lifted and floorboards ripped out in his search for signs of sabotage; and so, at Harry Keogh's first call, there had been little to deter these re-animated Tartars as they'd struggled up from their centuried graves to answer his command and prowl the Château's corridors, laboratories and conservatories. And wherever they found ESPers or defenders, they had simply put them down out of hand.

Now all that remained were the fortified machine-gun positions in the Château's own walls, which allowed the men within them no egress, no means of escape. The machine-gun posts could only be entered from within the Château; there were no exterior doors, no way out. The voice of one such call-sign trapped in his fortified position told Dragosani the entire story in every gory detail where he raged and frothed in his tower control room:

"Comrade, this is madness, madness!" the voice moaned over Dragosani's control radio, blocking all other traffic—if any remained to be blocked! "They are . . . zombies, dead men! And how may we kill dead men? They come—and my gunner cuts them down and shoots them to pieces—and then the *pieces* come! Outside, a pile of pieces wriggles and kicks and builds itself into a wall against the wall of the Château. Trunks, legs, arms, hands—even the smaller pieces and the naked bones themselves! Soon they will pour in through the gun slits, and what then?"

Dragosani snarled, more animal now than ever, and shook his fists at the night and the drifting snow beyond the tower's windows. "Keogh!" he raged. "I know you're there, Keogh. So come if you're coming and let's be done with it."

"They're inside the Château, too!" the voice on the radio sobbed. "We're trapped in here. My gunner is a madman now. He raves even as he works his gun. I've jammed the steel door shut but something continues to batter at it, trying to get in. I know what it is, for I saw it; it stuck a leathery claw inside before I could slam the door on its wrist; now the hand—oh God, the hand!—claws at my legs and tries to climb. I kick it away but it always returns. See, see? Again! Again!" And his voice tapered off into static and a crackling peal of laughter.

Simultaneous with the idiot sounds from the radio, suddenly Yul Galenski cried out in terror from his anteroom office. "The stairs! They're coming up the stairs!" His voice was shrill as a girl's; he had no experience of fighting; he was a clerk, a secretary. And in any case, who had experience of such as this?

The DO had been standing at the window, white-faced, trembling; but now he snatched up a machine-pistol and rushed through to Galenski where he backed away from the outer door to the landing. On his way he grabbed blast grenades from Dragosani's desk. *At least he is a man!* thought Dragosani, grudgingly.

Then came the DO's yelp of horror, his cursing, the chatter of his machine-pistol, finally the tearing explosion of grenades where he armed them and dropped them down the stairwell. And coming immediately after the thunder of the explosives, the last message from the unknown call-sign:

"No! No! Mother in heaven! My gunner has shot himself and now they're coming through the gun slits! Hands without arms! Heads without bodies! I think I shall have to follow my gunner, for he is out of all this now. But these . . . *remains!* They crawl among the grenades! No—stop that!" There came the distinct *ch-ching* of a grenade armed, more screaming and gibbering and sounds of chaos, and finally a massive burst of static following which—nothing.

The radio sat and hissed background static at itself. And suddenly the Château Bronnitsy seemed very quiet . . .

It was a quiet which couldn't last. As the DO backed into Galenski's office from the landing, where smoke and cordite stench curled up acridly from below, so Harry Keogh and his Tartar companions emerged from the Möbius continuum. They were there, in the anteroom, as if someone had suddenly switched them on.

The DO heard Galenski's wail of abject terror and disbelief, whirled in a half-circle—and saw what Galenski had seen: a grim, smoke-grimed young man flanked by menacing mummy-things of black leather and gleaming white bone. The sight of them alone—right here, in this room with him—was almost sufficient to freeze him, unman him. But not quite. Life was dear.

Lips drawn back in a rictus of desperation and fear, the DO gurgled something meaningless and swung up his machine-pistol . . only to be lifted off his feet and thrown back out onto the landing, his face turning to raw pulp as Harry discharged his last cartridge at point-blank range.

In another moment Harry's companions had turned their attention to Galenski where he gibbered and grovelled in a corner behind his desk, and Harry had stepped through into what was once Gregor Borowitz's inner sanctum. Dragosani, in the act of hurling the extinct radio from its table, turned and saw him. His great jaws gaped his surprise; pointing an unsteady hand, he hissed like a snake, his red eyes blazing. And for the merest moment the two faced each other.

There had been dramatic changes in both men, but in Dragosani the differences could only be likened to a complete metamorphosis. Harry recognized him, yes, but in any other situation he could hardly have known him. As for Harry himself: little of his former personality or identity remained. He had inherited a great sum of talents and now surely transcended Homo sapiens. Indeed, both men were alien beings, and in that frozen moment as they stared at each other they knew it. Then—

Dragosani saw the shotgun in Harry's hands but couldn't know it was useless. Hissing his hatred and expecting at any moment to hear the weapon's roar, he bounded to Borowitz's great oak desk and fumbled for a machine-pistol. Harry reversed the shotgun, stepped forward and dealt the necromancer a crashing blow to the head and neck where he scrabbled at the desk. Dragosani was knocked flying, the machine-pistol thudding to the carpeted floor. He collided with a wall and for a moment stood there spread-eagled, then went into a crouch. And now he saw that the shotgun in Harry's hands was broken where the stock joined the barrels, saw Harry's eyes frantically searching the room for another weapon, saw that he had the advantage and needed no weapon made by men to finish this thing.

Galenski's bubbling screams from the anteroom were suddenly cut off. Harry backed towards the half-open door. Dragosani wasn't about to let him go. He leaped forward, grabbed him by the shoulder and held him effortlessly with one hand at arm's length.

Hypnotized by the sheer horror of the man's face, Harry found it impossible to look away. He panted for air, felt himself squeezed dry by the awesome power of this creature.

"Aye, pant," growled Dragosani. "Pant like a dog, Harry Keogh—and die like a dog!" And he bayed a laugh like nothing Harry had ever heard before.

Still holding his victim, now the necromancer crouched down into himself and his jaws opened wide. Needle teeth dripped slime and something moved in his gaping mouth which wasn't quite a tongue. His nose seemed to flatten to his face and grew ridged, like the convoluted snout of a bat, and one scarlet eye bulged hideously while the other narrowed to a mere slit. Harry stared directly into hell and couldn't look away.

And knowing he'd won, finally Dragosani hurled his bolt of mental horror—at which precise moment the door behind Harry crashed open and threw him from the necromancer's grasp. The door gave him cover where he fell to the floor, while at the same time another stepped creakingly into the room to take the full force of Dragosani's blast. And seeing what had entered, too late Dragosani remembered Max Batu's warning: how one must never curse the dead, for the dead can't die twice!

The bolt was deflected, *re*flected, turned upon Dragosani himself. In Batu's story a man had been shrivelled by just such a blast, but in Dragosani's case it wasn't as bad as that—or perhaps it was worse.

He seemed picked up in some giant's fist and hurled across the room. Bones snapped in his legs where they hit the desk, and he was set spinning by his own momentum. The wall brought him up short again, but this time he crumpled to the floor. And clawing himself up into a seated position, he screamed continuously in a voice like a giant's chalk on slate. His broken legs flopped on the floor as if they were made of rubber, and he flailed his arms spastically, blindly in the air before his face.

Blindly, yes, for that was where his own mind-blast had struck home: his eyes!

Coming from behind the shielding door Harry saw the necromancer sitting there and gasped. It was as if Dragosani's eyes had exploded from within. Their centres were craters in his face, with threads of crimson gristle hanging down on to his hollow cheeks. Harry knew it was over then and the shock of it all caught up with him. Sickened, he turned away from Dragosani, saw his henchmen waiting.

"Finish it," he told them. And they creakingly advanced on the stricken monster.

Dragosani was quite blind now, and so too the vampire within him, which had seen with his eyes. But immature though the creature was, still its alien senses were sufficiently developed to recognize the inexorable approach of black, permanent oblivion. It sensed the stake held in the mummied claw, knew that a rusted sword was even now raised high. Ruined shell that he was, Dragosani was no use to the vampire now. And evil spirit that *it* was, it came out of him as if exorcized!

He stopped screaming, choked, clawed at his throat. Froth and blood flew as his jaws opened impossibly wide and he began to shake his monstrous head frantically to and fro. His entire body was going into convulsions, beginning to vibrate as the pain within grew greater than that of ruptured eyes and broken bones. Any other must surely have died there and then, but Dragosani was no other.

His neck grew fat and his grey face turned crimson, then blue. The vampire withdrew itself from his brain, uncoiled from his inner organs, tore itself loose from nerves and spinal cord. It formed barbs, used them to drag itself head-first up the column of his throat and out of him. Slopping blood and mucus, he coughed the thing endlessly on to his chest. And there it coiled, a great leech, its flat head swaying like that of a cobra, scarlet with the blood of its host.

And there the stake pinned it, passed through the vampire's pulsating body and into Dragosani, driven home by hands that shed small bones even as they secured the horror in its place. And a single stroke from the second Tartar's whistling sword completed the job, striking its flat, loathsome head free from its madly whipping body.

Emptied, tortured, very nearly mindless, Dragosani lay there, his arms flopping. And as Harry Keogh said: "And now finish him," so the necromancer's twitching hand found the machine-pistol where it had fallen to the carpeted floor. Somewhere in his burning brain he had recognized Keogh's voice, and even knowing he was dying, still his evil and vengeful nature surfaced one last time. Yes, he was going—but he would not go alone. The weapon in his crab-like hands coughed once, stuttered briefly, then chattered a continuous stream of mechanical obscenities until its vocabulary and magazine were empty—which was perhaps half a second after an ancient Tartar sword had split Dragosani's monstrous skull open from ear to ear.

Pain! Searing pain. And death. For both of them.

Almost cut in half, Harry found a Möbius door and

toppled through it. But pointless to take his shattered body with him. That was finished now. Mind was all. And as he entered the Möbius continuum, so he reached out and guided, dragged the necromancer's mind with him. Now the pain was finished, for both of them, and Dragosani's first thought was: "Where am I?"

"Where I want you," Harry told him. He found the door to past-time and opened it. From Dragosani's mind a thin red light streamed out amidst the blue brilliance. It was the trail of his vampire-ridden past. "Follow that," said Harry, expelling Dragosani through the door. Falling into the past, Dragosani clung to his past-life thread and was drawn back, back. And he couldn't leave that scarlet thread even if he wanted to, for it was him.

Harry watched the scarlet thread winding back on itself, taking Dragosani with it, then searched out and found the door to the future. Somewhere out there his broken life-thread continued, began again. All he had to do was find it.

And so he hurled himself into the blue infinity of tomorrow . . .

Final Interval:

Alec Kyle glanced at his watch. It was 4:15 P.M. and he was already fifteen minutes late for his all-important governmental board. But time, however relative, had flown and Kyle felt desiccated; the papers in front of him had grown to a thick sheaf; his whole body was cramped and the muscles in his right hand, wrist and arm felt tied in knots. He couldn't write another word.

"I've missed the board," he said, and hardly recognized his own voice. The words came out in a dry croak. He tried to laugh and managed a cough. "Also, I think I'm missing a couple of pounds! I haven't moved from this chair in over seven hours, but it's been the best day's exercise I've had in years. My suit feels loose on me. And dirty!"

The spectre nodded. "I know," he said, "and I'm sorry. I've taxed your mind and body both. But don't you think it was worth it?"

"Worth it?" Kyle laughed again, and this time made it. "The Soviet E-Branch is destroyed—"

"Will be," the other corrected him, "a week from now."

"—and you ask if it's been worth it? Oh, yes!" Then his face fell. "But I've missed the board. That was important."

"Not really," the spectre told him. "Anyway, you didn't miss it. Or rather, you did but I didn't."

Kyle frowned, shook his head. "I don't understand."

"Time—" the other began.

"—Is relative!" Kyle finished it for him in a gasp.

The spectre smiled. "There's a door to all times out there on the Möbius strip. I am here—but I'm also there. They might have given you a hard time, but not me. Gormley's work—your work, and mine—goes on. You'll get all the help you need and no hassle."

Kyle slowly closed his mouth, let his brain reel for a moment until it steadied itself. He felt weary now, worn out. "I expect you'll want to be going now," he said, "but there are still a couple of things I'd like to ask you. I mean, I know who you are, for you couldn't be anyone else, but—"

"Yes?"

"Well, where are you *now*? I mean, your now? What's your base? *Where* is it? Are you speaking to me from the Möbius continuum, or through it? Harry, *where are you?*"

Again the spectre's patient smile. "Ask instead, 'who are you?' " he said. And answered: "I'm still Harry Keogh. Harry Keogh Junior."

Kyle's mouth once more fell open. It was all there in his notes but it hadn't jelled, until now. Now the pieces fell into place. "But Brenda—I mean, your wife—was due to die. Her death has been foretold. And how can anyone change or avoid the future? You yourself have shown how that's impossible."

Harry nodded. "She will die," he said. "Briefly, in childbirth, she'll die—but the dead won't accept her."

"The dead won't—?" Kyle was lost.

"Death is a place beyond the body," said Harry. "The dead have their own existence. Some of them knew it but most didn't. Now they do. It will change nothing in the world of the living, but it means a lot to the dead. Also, they understand that life is precious. They know because they've lost it. If Brenda dies, my life, too, will be in jeopardy. That's something they can't allow. They owe me, you see?"

"They won't accept her? You mean they'll give her life back to her?"

"In a nutshell, yes. There are brilliant talents there in the netherworld, Alec, a billion of them. There's not much they can't do if they really want to. As for my own epitaph: that was just my mother being over-protective—and pessimistic!" His outline began to shimmer and the light from the windows seemed to glance more readily through him. "And now I think it's time I—"

"Wait!" said Kyle, starting to his feet. "Wait, please. Just one more thing."

Harry raised ghostly eyebrows. "But I thought I'd explained it all. And even if I haven't, I'm sure you'll work it out."

Kyle quickly nodded his agreement. "I'm sure I will—I think. All except why. Why did you bother to come back and tell me?"

"Simple," said Harry. "My son will be me. But he will have his own personality, he will be his own being. I don't know how much of the real me will get through to him, that's all. There might be times when he, we, need reminding. One thing's certain, though: he'll be a very talented boy!"

And at last Kyle understood. "You want me—us, the branch—to sort of look after him, is that it?"

"That's it," said Harry Keogh, beginning to fade away,

shimmering now with a strange blue light, as though composed of a million fibre-thin neons. "You'll look after him—until he's ready to start looking after you. All of you. Do you think you can do that?"

Kyle stumbled out from behind his desk, held out his arms to the shimmering, rapidly diminishing spectral thing. "Oh, yes! Yes, we can do that!"

"That's all I ask," said Harry. "And also that you look after his mother."

The blue shimmer became a haze, snapped into a single vertical line or tube of electric blue light, shortened to a single point of blinding blue fire at eye-level—and blinked out. And Kyle knew that Keogh had gone to be born.

"We'll do it, Harry!" he shouted hoarsely, feeling tears hot on his cheeks and not knowing why he cried. "We'll do it . . . Harry?"

Epilogue

DRAGOSANI FELL INTO HIS OWN PAST ALONG THE VAMPIRE life-thread, but not very far. For all that it was short, it was a journey which left him dazed and frightened; but at its end he once again found himself clothed in flesh. And clothed in more than flesh. A body surrounded him, yes, and also a mind other than his own. He was part of someone else, and the other was also blind—*or buried!*

For even now his unknown host struggled to rise up from a shallow grave, from the blackness of a night centuries long, from the bitter imprisonment of the soil.

There was no time to consider the implications, no time even to declare his presence to the other. Dragosani felt stifled, smothered, yet again on the brink of oblivion. He had known enough of pain and wanted no more of it. He added his own will to that of his host and strove for the surface. And above him, suddenly the earth cracked open and host and Dragosani both sat up.

Scabs of earth fell from them as they turned their head

to gaze all about. It was night but overhead, viewed through the black twining branches of trees, stars gleamed bright in a cold sky. Dragosani could see!

But . . . didn't he know this place?

Someone stood there in the darkness, staring at him where he sat half-in, half-out of the earth. Dragosani's vision cleared along with that of his host—and the shock he felt then was like a sledge-hammer blow to his still teetering mind "I . . . I CAN SEE . . . YOU!" he rumbled.

He saw—he *knew*—and terror gibbered again in the night of the cruciform hills!

Then there was a second figure in the darkness, a squat figure whose voice was soft when he said: "Ho, Thing from the earth!" And in another moment the sighing thud of his lignumvitae bolt where it crashed through the host body and was wedged there. Then Dragosani added his voice to that of his awful host in a hissing shriek and tried to draw down again into the earth. But there was no escape, and he *knew* there was no escape.

He couldn't believe it. It couldn't end like this!

"WAIT!" he croaked with his host's voice as the first figure staggered closer, holding something that gleamed bright in starlight. "CAN'T YOU SEE? *IT'S ME!!*"

But the other Dragosani didn't know, couldn't understand, wouldn't wait. And the sickle he carried became a blur of steel as it struck home with an irresistible force.

"FOOL! DAMNED FOOL!" Ferenczy/Dragosani howled from a head already flying free. And he knew that this was only one of many agonies, many deaths, in the unending scarlet loop of his Möbius existence. It had happened before, was happening now, would happen again . . . and again . . . and again . . .

And, "*Fool!*" his bubbling, bloody lips whispered his final comment, his final word—only this time he spoke to himself . . .

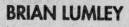

BRIAN LUMLEY

☐
☐ 50832-7   THE HOUSE OF DOORS $4.95

☐
☐ 51684-2   NECROSCOPE $4.95

☐
☐ 52126-9   VAMPHYRI! $4.95
              Necroscope II

☐
☐ 52127-7   THE SOURCE $4.95
              Necroscope III

☐
☐ 50833-5   DEADSPEAK $4.95
              Necroscope IV $5.95

☐
☐ 50835-1   DEADSPAWN $4.95
              Necroscope V - forthcoming October 1991

Buy them at your local bookstore or use this handy coupon:
Clip and mail this page with your order.

Publishers Book and Audio Mailing Service
P.O. Box 120159, Staten Island, NY 10312-0004

Please send me the book(s) I have checked above. I am enclosing $ _____
(Please add $1.50 for the first book, and $.50 for each additional book to cover postage and
handling. Send check or money order only— no CODs.)

Name _____
Address _____
City _____ State / Zip _____
Please allow six weeks for delivery. Prices subject to change without notice.